£1.50

TO THE BITTER END

Marcus Palliser gave up a career in corporate PR to work as a freelance writer and sail. He recently spent three years living aboard a small yacht, sailing in the Mediterranean and crossing the Atlantic single-handed. He now lives in Truro, Cornwall, near some of the most dramatic sea coasts in the world.

He is the author of two previous novels, *Matthew's Prize* and *Devil of a Fix*.

Also by Marcus Palliser

Matthew's Prize
Devil of a Fix

To the Bitter End

Marcus Palliser

ARROW

Published by Arrow Books in 2002

1 3 5 7 9 10 8 6 4 2

Copyright © Marcus Palliser 2001

The right of Marcus Palliser to be identified as the author of this work has
been asserted by him in accordance with the Copyright,
Designs and Patents Act, 1988

First published in the United Kingdom in 2001 by William Heinemann

Arrow Books
The Random House Group Limited
20 Vauxhall Bridge Road, London SW1V 2SA

Random House Australia (Pty) Limited
20 Alfred Street, Milsons Point, Sydney,
New South Wales 2061, Australia

Random House New Zealand Limited
18 Poland Road, Glenfield,
Auckland 10, New Zealand

Random House (Pty) Limited
Endulini, 5a Jubilee Road, Parktown 2193, South Africa

The Random House Group Limited Reg. No. 954009

www.randomhouse.co.uk

A CIP catalogue record for this book is available from the British Library

Papers used by Random House are natural, recyclable products made from
wood grown in sustainable forests. The manufacturing processes conform to
the environmental regulations of the country of origin

ISBN 0 09 928186 4

Typeset by Palimpsest Book Production Limited,
Polmont, Stirlingshire

Printed and bound in Denmark by
Nørhaven Paperback A/S, Viborg

To my grandfather, Lewis Robinson,
a soldier all his life

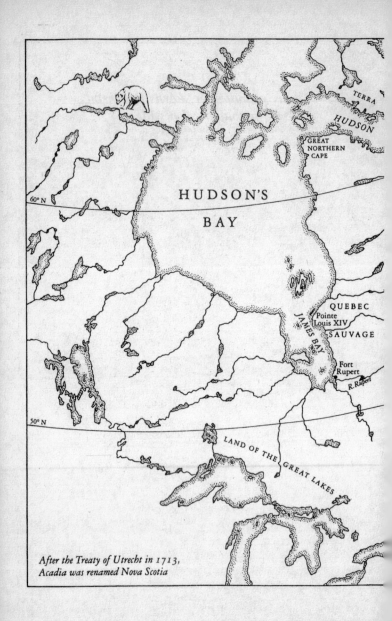

HUDSON'S

BAY

60° N

50° N

TERRA

HUDSON

GREAT
NORTHERN
CAPE

QUEBEC

Pointe
Louis XIV

JAMES BAY

SAUVAGE

Fort
Rupert

R. Rupert

LAND OF THE GREAT LAKES

*After the Treaty of Utrecht in 1713,
Acadia was renamed Nova Scotia*

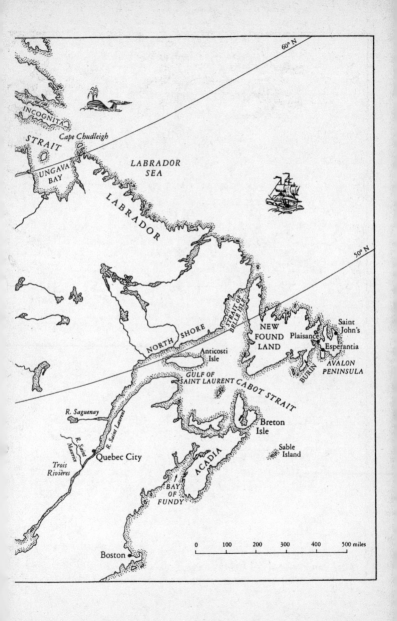

60° N

INCOGNITA

STRAIT

Cape Chudleigh

UNGAVA
BAY

LABRADOR
SEA

LABRADOR

50° N

NORTH SHORE

STRAIT OF BELLE ISLE

NEW
FOUND
LAND

Plaisance

Saint
John's

Esperantia

AVALON
PENINSULA

Anticosti
Isle

GULF OF
SAINT LAURENT

BURIN

CABOT STRAIT

R. Saguenay

R. Saint
Maurice

R. Saint Laurent

Breton
Isle

Sable
Island

Trois
Rivières

Quebec City

ACADIA

BAY
OF
FUNDY

Boston

0   100   200   300   400   500 miles

1

View from the Hill

Newfoundland, July 1708: the Free Settlement at Esperantia

With her yards braced on a reach, her topsails, courses and jibsails set and drawing, my tough little ten-gun trading bark sped along under every square inch of canvas she could muster. The *Pursuant* was making for harbour, her home port, but this looked to be no ordinary homecoming. She was running for her life.

We were only half a league from Esperantia Bay, but the rising bluffs of Barrier Heights hid the entrance from my seamen's eager eyes. I was as keen as anyone to get in. Everything I hoped for was at Esperantia, even though it was an outlying settlement of import only to fishermen and traders. But all that I owned was under my feet – the bark herself and the valuable furskins packed in her hold. Now we were being chased down. Come on old girl, I urged, see us safe into harbour.

Two hours earlier we had spied, low on the sea horizon, the topsails of three barks. They flew no English traders' pennants. Neither could they be the Royal Navy, too busy with the European war to patrol these waters. But nor were they the French, who disputed Queen Anne's claims on Newfoundland. No, these vessels were working up from the Burin Peninsula twenty leagues to the southwest. It was home to the Brothers Gillycuddy, leaders of a wild Irish clan who coveted Esperantia for themselves – the well-protected bay, the harbour and wharf, and most of all the beach, a perfect natural place for drying fish, the big lazy cod, readily hauled up in great numbers, a source of wealth surpassing even the lucrative fur trade.

The winter ice was melting, freeing up the bays, and they thought Esperantia was there for the taking. But perhaps the Gillycuddys had not reckoned on the *Pursuant*'s early return. If I had any say in the matter, we would sorely spoil their plans.

A host of excited cries rose up from the seamen gathered in the eyes of the ship.

'Entrance spied, captain,' the sailing master reported.

With a suddenness that always surprised, a cleft appeared in the seemingly impenetrable cliff walls and opened into a half-mile wide stretch of flat water spreading between lofty hills. Scattered lumps of broken sea-ice lay on either rocky shore, but the water was open to the far end. The dominating hills funnelled the breeze and forced us to beat into the bay.

'Come close-hauled,' I ordered.

My sailing master responded instantly. A Dutchman, Gaspar Rittel's only flaw at twenty years was knowing he was good enough to be captain. When he sang out his orders from the break, the weather-deck came alive with seamen running to the belays.

'Helmsman, four points to steerboard,' I said, and the wheel whirled.

Her bows swung and the wind came forward of the beam. With braces creaking and the sheets coming home bar-taut, the *Pursuant* heeled, settled into her groove and forged ahead. We were nearly home safe.

'Aloft there!' I called. 'Lookout's report.'

Perched high at the main-topmast, the seaman cupped his hands and cried, 'Deck there! Three sail, hull down to sou'west. Still bearing for Esperantia.'

The *Pursuant*, a Whitby collier built for strength and packed to the gunnels with seal and caribou skins, was not a speedy vessel, so I had run her close inshore along the Avalon coast to catch a late afternoon breeze off the land. Sure enough, bringing the wind on our beam gained us an extra knot. We had beaten the attackers in, but only just.

'Signals spied, captain,' said Gaspar, pointing.

Aiming my spy-glass up towards Beacon Top on the northern heights, I read the recognition flags hoisted to answer our own. The signallers had seen the *Pursuant*, but had they spied the distant barks? We had heard no warning rounds to rouse up the defences. The gun emplacement at Beacon Top was a pair of twelve-pounders, but there was no telling how ready the gunners might be. I swung the spy-glass southwards to Vantage Rise, commanding the bay's opposite side. Up there was a single fifteen-pounder, an ancient piece well past its prime. Mishandled, it was a greater danger to its own crew than an enemy.

As we beat in, the high ground loomed to enfold

3

the bark. At the head of the long, narrow inlet lay Stack Beach, a greystone mound of gale-thrust shingle curving across the bay's full width. Wellspring of the settlement's prosperity, this was the finest cod-drying beach in all Newfoundland. Behind it stood a nest of low buildings that constituted the village. In the cool, slackening air of day's end, curls of smoke rose languidly from chimneys and drifted across the freshwater pool of Lake Implacable, stretching crystal clear for two miles, fingering deep into wooded slopes behind, blue and dusky now in the evening light. It was a forbidding landscape, hostile to man.

Only the coastal fringes of Newfoundland offered shelter, sustenance and a working livelihood. Esperantia was a mere scrap of a settlement perched on the edge of a vast and inhospitable interior inhabited solely by shy and rarely seen natives. In truth, Queen Anne's hold on Newfoundland amounted to no more than a handful of shoreside fishing communities such as this. And here on the Avalon Peninsula, the Crown's writ ran all too tenuously. The more remote bays and offshore islands were occupied by French settlers. To the south across the Breton Channel lay the French stronghold of Acadia, guarding the entrance to the Saint Laurent Gulf and the rich Quebec farmlands of New France. Esperantia stood exposed amidst these Bourbon-claimed lands, and during six years of war the enemy had threatened more than once to seize it.

Today the threat in the offing was not French. It was Irish.

Raking the spy-glass along Stack Beach, I saw

4

dozens of fishing shallops anchored off the steep-to shore. With summer barely begun, the foreshore was already crowded with incoming fishermen and their little vessels. Each brief season, the teeming cod shoals drew as many as fifty boats and three hundred fisherfolk across the Atlantick Ocean from Brittany and the Westcountry. For a few weeks, Esperantia's single street would be busy with the to-and-fro of daily life, the beach assailed by a hubbub of foreign tongues, the inn crowded and noisy.

The *Pursuant* had been away all winter, trading in the north. She was a stout hundred footer, a three-masted single-decker of ten guns – five in the broadside – with one forward swivel and a brass stern chase, two pounders both. Hardly a new ship, she was certainly the sturdiest of vessels, double-framed all round with a false bow, heavy stringers and a keelson twice the scantling of any other boat her length. She was Whitby-built, her keel laid in the yards where my father's old collier-bark, long since gone, had risen from amongst the muddy keelways and sawing-pits. Like the colliers, she carried well, holding a hefty burthen for her size. Even better, she could shoulder her way through the loose ice and floes of spring and autumn. She could break pack ice a foot thick by running onto it and crushing it with the sheer force of her weight – and not many captains could risk their barks doing that.

At summer's end, the *Pursuant* left last of all to head north for the seal trade, and returned earliest in spring before any other dared. For six seasons running, she had been first to reach the natives and win the pick of their furskins. Six spring thaws in a row, she had beaten every bark back to market, to pluck the first silver marks and guilders from the merchants' bulging pockets.

Thinking of warm smokey rooms, hot roasted meat, a clean dry bed, and half-forgotten longings of other comforts and desires, I directed the spying tube to a point halfway up the southern hillside. A squat stone building, imposing but ugly, stood cradled in a hollow, with a prospect over the whole Roads. No doubt the Dowager Lady Trepanney was at her bay window in Providence House, watching my arrival. Her wise and dutiful daughter-in-law would surely be at her side.

I longed to jump ashore and go up to tell them of my latest trading venture. Though the Dowager might rule Esperantia with steely resolve, it was the young widow, Grace Trepanney, whose attention I sought. Until two years ago, the *Pursuant* had roamed the French Gulf and English Labrador as a private ship, free to trade furs with native tribes from the Iroquois of the southern Kanada Lands to the Esquimaux of the far north. At last it seemed I had found a place to settle, a base for my trading. Esperantia had won my heart and the *Pursuant*'s vagabond days were behind her.

But the Gillycuddys were coming, and seeing Grace must wait.

'Signalsman,' I called, still squinting through the spy-glass, 'sound for that towing launch.'

Nothing came – no blast, no blare. I lowered the tube to see my sixteen-year-old signalsman Sam Lightfoot standing by the rail, gazing open-mouthed at the village.

'Mister Lightfoot, the signal,' I repeated.

He gave a start, fumbling for his sounding horn. 'Beg pardon, captain. I was hoping Lizzie Penn'd come out to wave.'

His face was sculpted by wind and weather and tanned the colour of buckskin. After the winter months away, he was as eager for his girl as I was.

'You can see her later,' I said, hiding my smile. 'Now, give four good breaths on that instrument.'

As Sam filled his chest and the blasts echoed off the placid waters, my sailing master Mister Rittel stepped up beside me on the quarter. His every feature was a-quiver, more animated than I had seen him in weeks.

'What about the cargo, captain?' Even after six years on an English bark Gaspar's Hollandish accent remained as thick as a dyke. 'If prices are up again, we are rich men. Last season, we got two marks for every beaver pelt and four for a seal. That was double the price before.'

And double the year before that, he might have added. Rammed, jammed and packed tight into the *Pursuant*'s creaking holds were two thousand and four hundred sealskins and eight and a half thousand beaver pelts. This was the stuff with which well-born ladies from Copenhagen to Cadiz loved to trim their fancy gloves and hats. Then there were the hundred and forty bales of finest tanned caribou buckskin, a rare and expensive catch much prized for shoe leather and great-coats. The price of a cavalryman's calf-boots in Antwerp or a beaver fur hat in Amsterdam or a pair of gentlewomen's sealskin mitts in London had risen tenfold since the war began. No one was getting their hands on my cargo.

'For the Saints' sake, Mister Rittel,' I said, 'let's deal with those barks in the offing first,' I said.

'Tow coming out, captain,' said Sam Lightfoot.

A launch was being rowed out from behind the inner harbour's stone walls.

'Shall we take her in to lie alongside the wharf?' asked Gaspar.

I hesitated. The *Pursuant* would be trapped inside. Neither did I relish her standing her ground in the bay, a sitting target for three attacking vessels. There was a better way. Skull Cove lay half a league back, just beyond the bluffs, a narrow cut into seemingly solid rock. Its dog-leg channel meant that once a bark got in she was hidden inside a deep pool surrounded by sheer stone walls a hundred feet high. It got its name from hollowed sea caves and indents on the rock wall making the cliff face resemble a giant, forbidding death's head. No one would expect to find her in there.

'No, Mister Rittel,' I said. 'Make ready to take her out again.'

If he was about to question it, he thought better when he saw my face, and went off to give the orders. I called Nathaniel Gunn, a strong-built young seaman of nineteen and second mate of steerboard watch, up to the quarter-deck.

'Mister Gunn, assemble twelve fellows armed with muskets and make ready to board the harbour launch.'

When Gaspar Rittel rejoined me, his face was still a sea of unspoken questions, but I cut him off.

'There's just time to get her tucked into Skull Cove,' I told him. 'She'll be safe in there.'

'Skull Cove?' he repeated, shocked.

Even in settled weather it was a tricky berth. The bottom was too deep and smooth for anchors, so a bark had to moor by means of a web of long shore-lines. A southwesterly swell would churn the water to a luminous turquoise as it foamed against the sides until the pool became a boiling cauldron. Then any vessel, from a fishing shallop to the hundred and fifty tun, three-masted *Pursuant*, would wreck herself in minutes. But today there was no swell to speak of.

'Aye, you heard. It'll be dark in an hour. I shall slip out to you later.'

He was confused. 'Captain, you are not staying aboard?'

'I must see to the defences here.'

'O ya,' he said, still sounding doubtful.

At a shout from Nat Gunn, I moved down into the waist and readied myself to go overside into the launch. Rittel, far from issuing orders, remained standing at the break. He seemed struck rigid.

'She's all yours, sailing master,' I called up.

For sure, the entrance to the cove was daunting, but he had watched me take her in before. If I had thought it beyond him, I should never have given the bark into his command.

'Captain, should we not unload? Lighten her up, make her easier to handle?'

'There's no time,' I said. 'Get on with it, Mister Rittel.'

I descended the boarding rope and bade the oarsmen stroke over to Stack Beach. To shouts from the sailing master and chanties from the jack-tars, the *Pursuant*'s topsails and courses fell from the buntlines. She gathered way, made a stately turn and showed us her stern.

I watched her go in some trepidation. The little bark was all I had in the world.

When the launch's bow ground on the foreshore's greystones, I glanced back at the harbour heads. The sun declined behind Barrier Heights, where the *Pursuant* was slipping away. Dusk spread across the bay and soon this night would be as dark as the inside of a pitch-tub. With no moon, it made a handsome time for attack.

The hill-top beacons blazed into life. At last the lookouts had woken up. I leapt over the launch's stem and set off up the steep shingles. Nat Gunn followed close, the twelve musketmen behind, their footsteps clattering up the slope, dislodging stones. We were heading for the Salt Pillar Inn.

The village was a cluster of limestone and wood buildings, their roofs thatched over with dark moss. A melee of people ran about in every direction, alarmed. Seeing me, they came tugging at my sleeve, asking what was afoot. Was it the French from nearby Plaisance, they said, or even a new Catholick armada sent by the King of Spain? I shrugged off their questions and called on all able men to gather at the alehouse and charge up their muskets.

As my troop and I marched on towards the inn, a shawled woman well in her middle years caught us up, a basket under her arm. Lucy Skentles, the innkeeper's wife, clutched at my cuff.

'Matthew,' she puffed, for I did not alter my pace, 'we are so glad you're back.'

'Lucy,' I said, giving her elbow a kindly squeeze.

Her countenance betrayed weariness and worry from the hard work she and Malachy Skentles suffered to make Salt Pillar Inn pay. She lifted a cloth-wrapped bundle from the pile in her basket.

'Warm pork and pickle in a sourdough slice,' she said. 'I was taking it down to the wharf, expecting you to come in there.'

'The fellows first,' I said with a nod, not slackening my pace.

She handed bundles to my musketmen before coming back to me. Taking the meal gratefully, I bit into the fresh meat and new-baked bread. After the privations of a Labrador winter and a diet of seal-meat and fish, it tasted of paradise.

'Till the signals went,' she said, hurrying to keep up, 'I thought you might be off to see the Lady Trepanney.'

'She shall have to wait. It looks as if we're to be attacked. I must rally the men.'

'I don't know if anyone shall rally,' she said. 'The Factor's causing such strife.'

'He's a fair-minded man,' I said with some surprise. The Factor controlled Esperantia's markets and over the seasons had proved himself even-handed and straightforward with the *Pursuant*'s cargoes.

'O, I forgot you couldn't know,' she said. 'Old Bernard Truss is dead and gone.'

'Rest his soul,' I muttered with a frown. We were

in the village by now, not far from the inn. 'Is there a new one appointed by Lady Trepanney?'

'Yes, a Hollander,' she said. 'He's the one who's changing everything.'

The signal gun, a puny piece with a sharp report, cracked three times from the heights. If there was no answer, it meant the oncoming vessels were refusing to haul over and be identified before entering the Roads. After that it would not be many minutes before the hilltop gunners opened fire.

We approached the lighted doorlamps of the Skentles' publick house and its bright interior, fugged and warm. At our previous homecomings, it had been the scene of many a lively time of music and dance and drinking. My nostrils filled with the diverting reek of fresh-brewed small beer, ladled from clean barrels and not tasting sour. Six months on the Labrador Coast had left my appetites whetted as never before.

Lucy clutched my arm again. 'It's tearing the village apart, what the Factor's been up to. You must do something.'

'I'm only the Guardian here,' I said, thinking this was hardly the time to fret over minor quarrels. 'I don't govern Esperantia.'

Breaking off for the side passage, she cried, 'You should! How much better it would be.'

At the main door was a press of men trying to enter, pushing and shoving. With a prick of relief, I spotted two small figures waiting at the side as if afraid to enter.

'Fellows, you remember me, don't you?' I said, towering over them.

'Attacked? Who by?' came their cries. 'The French?'

'No,' I said, 'it's the Brothers Gillycuddy.'

A hush descended. The Irishmen from the lawless Burin Peninsula were feared not so much for their fighting prowess as for the marauding and plunder that followed.

'Every man with a weapon is to fight,' I told the wary, watching faces. 'You go under the command of this man here.'

I indicated Guy de Chenalles. He was the best musketeer in Avalon Peninsula, but the silence that ensued was intense. Protestant men disliked the idea of going under a Catholick.

'If you profit in Esperantia,' I said, 'you fight for Esperantia. Catholick and Protestant alike, French and English side by side. Regardless of differences.'

Heavy shots crashed out into the night, booming from the hilltops. It was the batteries opening up. So the signals had not been answered and the attack was under way. Everyone nervously looked at each other, then all began shouting at once. I gave a nod to my musketmen and they raised up their pieces with an ostentatious clatter of metal barrels.

Once again, the hubbub ceased. The look in my fellows' eyes helped. We *Pursuant* men, fresh from the rigours of the icy north, were still clad head to toe in our customary heavy fur-coats and bushy headgear, while the Esperantia fishers wore light oiled-skin jackets. They were as different from us as salmon from seals, and Labrador waters seamen like us were known throughout Newfoundland for a certain hard-headed determination.

'Pick up your weapons and fight,' I said, 'or be shot.'

There was no more argument. As the gunfire from the hilltops intensified, I ordered everyone to assemble outside in military fashion. They shuffled away and I passed the cod-dryer's confiscated weapon to my chief musketeer.

'Guy, my friend, put your musket line on the beach behind the drying and curing racks. Wait for my signal.'

He grasped my hands. 'Matthew, Esperantia is nothing without you.'

I laughed, but without humour. 'Tell that to the Dowager. I believe she thinks Queen Anne prosecutes the whole war just for her sakes.'

He shrugged. 'Ah, but she has some reason for her fears, for King Louis's ambition stretches far and he dreams of Newfoundland.'

'Let's get those musketmen in position, Guy,' I suggested with an encouraging smile. Though a Frenchman, he was as loyal to me and Esperantia as any man.

When he departed, I bent to comfort his shaking wife Catherine with a kiss on both cheeks. Then with my men behind me I followed de Chenalles down towards the seafront.

By now, the Gillycuddy barks were entering the bay.

As if designed for the purpose and constructed by a giant's hand, Stack Beach made an excellent first line of defence, a towering pile of stones stretching north and south the length of the shoreline between the rising cliffs at either side. It was broken only by the natural gap fifty paces wide at the northern end giving entrance to the sheltered wharf and, beyond it, the fathomless waters of Lake Implacable. But the beach was, too, the sole line of defence. Directly behind stood the village itself, a mix of wood-framed cottages with rough-hewn rock foundations, and crude stone-built storehouses. Bar the hilltop fortifications, Esperantia lacked any citadel or stronghold of last resort.

Guy de Chenalles was busy arranging firing positions and loading parties, detailing ammunition bearers and stretchers for the wounded. A single pistol shot crashed around the bay and a commotion emanated from near one of the anchored shallops. Some French fishers had made a dash to get their boat under way but their escape was quickly thwarted by Guy's men, who brought them miserably back to shore.

The batteries again boomed into life, firing alternately across the water, the balls dropping at the extreme of their range. At that point the bay was half a sea-mile wide, and in the darkness the attackers could dodge through under tow.

With the hilltop guns unreliable, I had long since devised a secondary means of countering a seaward assault. Now, at my behest, Guy went off to assemble a volunteer party of five strong oarsmen. Thirty or forty fishing shallops, set on bow and stern anchors, rode barely a boat's length out from the steeply sloping beach. With only a foot of tide here at springs and deep water right off the edge, even keeled boats never grounded. I chose two shallops, one English and one French, thinking that the Dowager Lady Trepanney, with her obsessive notions of equity, might acknowledge the fairness of it.

The dark expanse of the bay was lit by blinding flashes from seaward. An instant later, shots crashed into the beach stones two or three hundred paces off, throwing up showers of gritty shards that clattered back to earth like hail. A groan suggested some poor wight somewhere not far off had been struck. More flashes flamed brilliantly and this time the balls landed close by the wharf. It was clear that the attackers knew their targets, and by the looks had worked out the ranges in advance. From the position of the defending guns' flares, and knowing the heights of the hilltops, they could measure the angles by quadrant and set their levels to strike the beach or the wharf at will.

Thanking the stars for directing me to keep the *Pursuant* clear, I glanced up towards Vantage Rise where the ancient fifteen-pounder belched incandescence from its red hot snout, then below at Providence House. Dammit, it still showed a light.

Some movement in the village caught my eye. A brace of small figures scampered away from the Skentles' publick house. Why were my messenger boys, back from their first mission and supposed to await my orders, heading up to the heights? A tall, behatted figure loomed in the doorway's glow – did no one have the sense to snuff their lamps? – just long enough for me to recognise the dress of a gentleman. Who was that? And what the Devil was he doing with my messengers?

There was no time to consider it, for Guy de

Chenalles reappeared with his five volunteers. One of them was the *Pursuant*'s young signalsman, Sam Lightfoot.

'Good fellow, Sam,' I said. 'But why are you not aboard the bark?'

'Nipped away to see my Lizzie, sir.' He gave a guilty grin. 'When the harbour launch came back in.'

I could hardly chide him for it after he had volunteered for the chancy duty that now lay ahead. All five fellows declared themselves ready and willing, so we boarded a pair of skiffs, balancing as de Chenalles and a couple of others threw us two dozen hefty bags, boxes and small kegs. Guy was to hold his musket fire from the beach until I gave word. Then we tugged ourselves along the shore lines out to the chosen shallops and stepped up aboard, three to each boat. Sam was in charge of the second. These shallops were thirty foot fishing vessels, built for inshore work though seakindly enough, and ideal for our night's work. Even so, their rimey waterlines disappeared as we loaded our boxes and barrels aboard.

Cutting the cables fore and aft, we sculled unseen out into the near reaches towing the skiffs astern, for they were our escape. Sensing on my cheek the merest kiss of a breeze, not enough to shift a topsail bark but plenty for a shallop, we shipped our oars, raised sail and came closehauled.

'You understand what we're about, fellows?' I called as we fetched along side by side across the water's black and rippled surface.

'Aye, Captain Loftus,' they replied, 'we're with you.'

We sailed on in silence. Like these fellows, I was less interested in any religious quarrels or fishing rights, or indeed in the present war, than I was in saving my livelihood. The Catholick nations had been ranged against the Protestant Alliance for six years, and Newfoundland was an issue of contention. There had even been talk, at the *Pursuant*'s departure last December, of great Navies being sent out to fight over Acadia, and the Gulf, and Newfoundland itself. We preferred the armies to battle in Europe and the fleets to engage in the Caribbee Sea. No one wanted the war here.

It was the profitable fur trade that had brought me to Esperantia. It had gained me my own bark and a little wealth besides. With the priceless cargo brought in today, I had my eye on buying a second vessel up at Saint John's. Perhaps this would be enough to satisfy the Dowager. She was a formidable woman – domineering perhaps, at least of Grace – whose late husband had founded the settlement on principles of equity amongst all men, though in these days when Esperantia was awash with corrupting profits, this brotherhood of man was daily tested to its limits and beyond. Even though she had appointed me Guardian of her settlement, Lady Trepanney showed little cognisance of my worth. Only a man of substance, the old lady had sternly warned, could win her daughter-in-law's hand. But I reckoned on winning it despite the Dowager. That was what Esperantia meant to me.

Shots crashed down in the darkness, sending up columns of sea-water nearby.

'They're closing, fellows,' I said. 'Are you ready?'

'Aye, captain,' they replied.

I trusted the *Pursuant* was tucked in Skull Cove. I hoped Grace Trepanney would douse that light and keep herself safe too.

Then I steered straight towards the attacking guns' flashes.

2

Fire Power

As our two little shallops swept on, the hollow boom of the batteries thundered far above. The balls arced across the bay, whistling down to land with irregular splashes, hopelessly wide. The gunners were missing their targets.

The incoming ships closed fast, the sharp crash of their forward guns growing louder by the minute, the shots screaming low overhead to go thudding and cracking ashore. I steered for the showers of sparks falling into the sea and the dull red glow of the pieces' mouths. The battery gunners could see the flashes too but by the time they re-aimed and re-ranged those cumbersome pieces the barks had dodged away, tacking and angling all the time under the pull of their towing launches.

With a start, I realised the hilltop gunners were disobeying my orders. They were meant to keep a slow gunnery rate, for three minute intervals prevented the old pieces getting too hot. Instead, they were firing at maximum rate, about once per minute. Predictably enough, the Beacon Top battery soon faltered as one of the pair became unusable. The single cannon at Vantage Rise remained active, but already the defences were down to just two heavy guns.

In the shallops we worked fast, laying out dry

matchfuse along the gunnels, lashing it with twine high up under the rail to keep it from the slopping, fish-stinking bilges. The bags were arranged right forward under the high prow, and a sharp reek of saltpetre filled our nostrils as we lugged them into position. By the time this was done, the lit mouths of the oncoming guns, circles glowing in the dark, showed the attackers no more than two hundred paces off. In the pitch of night, I hoped we remained unseen.

'Choose a bark that side,' I called to our companion shallop, and at once they diverged their course southwards.

The enemy barks were so close we heard the grunted efforts of their oarsmen in the towing launches. Voices rang out across the intervening gap, command and acknowledgement followed by the busy sounds of reloading, then the single word 'Fire!' given in steady tones. The accents were unmistakeable. As I had surmised, it was the Brothers Gillycuddy. In the past we had beaten them off, for they had never mustered more than one or two poorly armed barks. Now they had three, fully armed, in good trim and putting up a mighty assault.

The hilltop firing grew ragged, then ceased altogether. With the heated barrels reddening ominously, the gunners would step back, holding their shotbags away in fear of an explosion. There was no dousing them either – those tired metals would crack if anything more than a wet sponge were applied. With no barrage, Esperantia's fate lay with our two little shallops alone.

The Gillycuddys had strung out their ships in

line abreast. I bade my two fellows get in the skiff towing astern and wait for me. Solo, I steered for the northernmost invader. In the other shallop Sam Lightfoot aimed his course for the middle bark. My target vessel stood close to the shore, so I let her pass ahead until the tows cleared, then bore onward to within thirty fathoms of her. Close enough, I thought, tying off the tiller-bar. I bent forward to spark off the fuse, then scrambled aft over the stern to join the oarsmen in the rocking skiff. They cut the line and pulled lustily away. The shallop ticked along on her own at two knots, fuses lit and running, heading dead for her mark.

Suddenly there were shouts. Sam Lightfoot's boat had been spied. A hail of musket balls struck his shallop with shattering force. A second later, it exploded. My eyeballs seared with heat and I twisted away. Pressure blasted in my ears. A scorchingly hot wind enveloped everything, sucking my breath away and consuming the air itself. Our skiff all but overturned as the three of us dived under its low gunnels, going flat down, gasping, our throats on fire, every inch of exposed skin burning. When the blast diminished, I raised my head to look. Where Sam's shallop had been, the whole sea was ablaze. Only his skiff remained afloat, with its brace of fellows still alive. Poor Sam, I thought, only a lad. And poor Lizzie Penn too.

Not far off, voices were raised in alarm. The ship by the northern shore had spotted us. Calls went up for muskets and there came a clatter of arms.

'Row!' I gasped.

Then I realised one of my fellows was lying quite

still. I groped for his oar and we managed a dozen strokes before the muskets barked again, but the shooters aimed wildly. I caught a glimpse of my shallop's lateen sail going alongside the attacker, just before the fuses reached the barrels. The second eruption was even greater than the first. Again the searing blast, the scorching of flesh, the sense of being flayed skinless as heat and light passed over in wave after shocking wave.

The little fishing boat, weighted to the gunnels with powder, was entirely gone. But it had done its work. Where it struck alongside, the target's hull was blown open at the waterline. Vivid flames rose into the night, shot through with fans of sparks and golden droplets hissing into the water. The Gillycuddy bark lurched, rocking back and forth on her keel. Men and guns and rigging, burning and crackling, tumbled overside. Along the ratlines, tongues of fire leapt upwards. The loose-bunted courses were set ablaze. The topsails would go next. Her towing launch dropped its line and headed for the larboard side, intent now on saving the ship.

Frantically, we stroked away until a safe distance had opened and I leaned down to tend our wounded man. He had been on the side of the blast. Moist and sticky like the skin of spit-roasting pork, his flesh was still hot enough to char my own fingers. He was inert, as dead as the morning's embers. Two men gone, and both engaged on my desperate, perilous defence. Lord above, I muttered under my breath, what a terrible cost.

Minor explosions ripped through the stricken bark, now a cable distant, as horns and shotbags went up where they were stacked ready behind the deck-pieces. Futile musket shots were loosed off, but mostly her crew were too busy dousing the great fire belching from her insides. It looked stronger than any pumps or buckets might douse. In its luminous glare, I saw canvas descending deckwards and men thrown from the tops. The bark slowed and another blast erupted on the quarter-deck, which must have wreaked a deadly toll on her commanders. There were frightened shouts and the towing launches pulled round to ply back the way they had come. Suddenly I saw the bows of the third bark swing round likewise.

They were withdrawing. Cowardly at heart, the Gillycuddys had had enough and were towing back to sea. The assault was over.

I looked down at the corpse at my feet. He at least could have a burial. But of Sam Lightfoot there was nothing to put in the grave. Someone would have to go and tell Lizzie Penn and her little brother Caswell.

That, I supposed, was yet another burden for the Guardian.

The beach resembled a scene from Hell. Several anchored shallops had been hit during the bombardment and lay burning, half sunk at the water's edge, their masts tilted crazily. Behind, one or two village houses flamed like bonfires. Belatedly, a gun at Beacon Top flared briefly into life, rained down two or three balls in quick succession, then fell silent again. Its faltering effort served to emphasise that Esperantia could not rely on those batteries. The Burin attack had very nearly paid off.

Heavy-hearted, regretting that the *Pursuant*'s home-coming should have turned into such a bloody affair, I glanced up towards Providence House. A single light still burned at the window, but all appeared well. I sent the skiff's bow crunching onto the grey pebbles. We lugged our dead fellow ashore and ran up the shingle-stones.

'Guy!' I shouted. 'Give fire!'

From behind the berms and ditches, fifty musket shots crashed out, the balls singing away into the night. Out in the bay, the crippled Gillycuddy bark had taken on a fatal list, with eruptions flaming from her hull. Her companion vessels were already fleeing the bay, towing out with all their might, but Guy de Chenalles' hail of musketry served to encourage them on their way. After some minutes, when the attackers had disappeared beyond range, I ordered the firing halted and went off to find the harbour towing launch.

With six fellows pulling on the sweeps, we stroked back out into the bay past the doomed Gillycuddy vessel lying careened and blazing on the shore. Shallops and skiffs were closing on it in numbers, bent on grabbing the spoil, if anything were left.

'Out towards the heads, fellows,' I ordered and we sped past.

There was no sign of the Irish ships flying away, lights doused. In half a glass we came upon the nigh invisible entrance of Skull Cove. We passed inside, where the oarlocks' regular clacking echoed off the wet walls of rock. Otherwise all was calm and deadly silent. There was still no swell. Rounding the dog-leg, we came upon the *Pursuant*. Her mooring lines were stretched ashore in every direction, three each from bows and stern, four from amidships either side, yet she lay easy.

As we came under her sternparts, I called up to Gaspar, 'Cast off, Mister Rittel. The launch'll tow us out.'

I scrambled aboard and found the sailing master standing at the break.

'You did well to get her in,' I told him.

'I wanted to do a battle,' he complained.

I took one step forward and grabbed his blouse. He yelped in surprise.

'There are two brave men dead out there,' I rasped. 'A fellow was burnt to a biscuit in front of my eyes. Another was blown to Kingdom Come, and that was Sam Lightfoot.'

Gaspar's mouth hung open, a look of remorse across his face.

'Poor Sammy,' he muttered.

I let go of his shirt. 'We're going after those damm'd Gillycuddy barks. When we clear the gap, come closehauled and cast off the tow. Are the deck-pieces made ready?'

He nodded dumbly.

'Then go to it, man!' I shouted.

He hopped off like a startled deer, running about in a demented fashion, seeing to the guns, giving a hand at the belays, desperate to redeem himself. Lusty chanties rang out from forward as the jack-tars went about their practised duties, shaking out topsails and courses and hoisting a pair of jibsails. When we pulled into open water, the towline fell off and the sheets came home. The *Pursuant* heeled a little and took off to give chase.

Each man aboard was tensed like cloth stretched between tenterhooks. Every pair of eyes keenly scanned the blackness ahead. Even the bark, every part of her rigging and sails from truck to chainplates working hard, showed herself willing.

The escaping Irishmen had the breeze too. Once clear of the heads, they might have stood off on a hundred headings. As we breasted the swell and plunged on into the night sea, there was no sign of them.

But the *Pursuant* would not give up yet.

The sky lightened perceptibly in the eastern quarter. Soon the sun would lift over the distant land and bring morning to Avalon.

The *Pursuant* slouched disconsolately across a sea heaving with a swell newly arrived from the Atlantick. Thank the Lord it had not come last night to Skull Cove. But the Burin barks were gone and I was ready to turn for home, leagues from Esperantia and exhausted by the night-long search. Then came a shout from high aloft. The glimmering dawn had illuminated the outline of white sails – a ship hull down on the southern horizon, but working north.

'Mister Rittel, we shall bear up and close her,' I called. 'Steer north by northwest to make the intercept.'

It could not be the Gillycuddys. The newcomer's heading was not for Burin but for Plaisance. She was an altogether mightier vessel than any of the Gillycuddy barks, with tall castling at the bow and stern and fully ship-rigged. No doubt of it, she was a Frenchman. As we closed, her lines became familiar and my spy-glass showed a Bourbon standard at the truck of the mainmast. Yet this was no bark of King Louis's Navy. She was the Plaisance-based private ship *Tourmaline*.

I searched without success for a pennant showing the Petit Seigneur was aboard. Unlike most neighbouring French and English settlements, Esperantia and Plaisance avoided the skirmishes which upset trade, chiefly because I had reached a secret accord with my French counterpart. But he had left his post the previous autumn, and I hoped the *Tourmaline*'s captain might tell me about the new man.

'Run back the deck-pieces,' I ordered. 'Close up the ports and hoist friendly signals.'

The French bark braced her yards and came close-hauled, showing us her fancily decorated forecastle and the elegant curve of her beak. She got a bone in her teeth and fetched along to join us. Her ports were closed up and she had not been looking for a fight with anyone. Coming within hailing distance, she hove to and stopped. Her master stood high on the raised poop above the quarter-deck.

'Ahoy *Tourmaline*!' I cried.

He lifted an arm in languid greeting. 'Good morning, Captain Loftus.'

'Captain Beaupré, have you sighted the Burin barks?'

'Not a sign. Have they been troublesome?'

'You might say so,' I returned. 'They attacked Esperantia and ran off.'

'If they reach Burin,' said Beaupré with a tilt of

the head, 'then even with your pilot knowledge of that coast they shall be hard to find. What was their attacking force?' He might well sound concerned.

'Three barks, well-armed,' I told him. 'We crippled one, but they have two left. You might be wise to see to your defences.'

He bowed. 'Thank you for the intelligence, Captain Loftus.'

'How's trade?'

He turned down the corners of his mouth. I concluded that the market for French wet-cured cod, already in decline, had not picked up.

'When you haul into Plaisance,' I called, 'be sure to give my regards to the new Petit Seigneur.'

The former incumbent, the elegant and clever Alphonse D'Amati, never went to sea without good cause. Diplomat and Governor he might be but ill at ease on barks, and that was one reason we had never met. The other was that it was safer to conduct our exchanges strictly by trusted intermediaries, to reach the covert accommodations that allowed fishing and trading to continue unhindered, and unbeknown to higher authorities.

'There is no one yet in that office,' Beaupré called. 'We went to Port L'Esprit intending to collect him, but there is some turmoil.' He shrugged. 'What with the war . . .'

Port L'Esprit, the Acadian capital where the Grand Seigneur reigned, was the French Naval base for these northern regions. It guarded the all-important approaches to the Gulf of Saint Laurent and the rich interior lands.

'Any sign of your Navy in the Roads?' I asked.

Even over the intervening distance I heard the chuckle. 'My apologies, captain, but that is military intelligence. May I ask what news of your Navy?'

It was my turn to smile. We might be civil with each other and accommodating over fishing rights and sea routes, but neither would give away his country's affairs. It was enough that I had warned him the Brothers Gillycuddy were on the rampage.

I changed tack. 'Where is Seigneur D'Amati posted now?'

Beaupré's voice drifted across. 'The interior – Quebec Region, I believe. Covering the Upper Saint Laurent.'

'Has he been sent to safeguard the route to Cathay?'

I could not resist the jibe. The French were fiercely proud of their Kanada Lands' founding father, Samuel Champlain, who sixty years ago had established Quebec City as a toll gate for ships passing along the as-yet-undiscovered, and perhaps fanciful, Northwest Passage. Any sea route linking the Atlantick and Pacifick was worth a fortune to the discovering nation, for it obviated the hard voyage round Africka's Cape of Storms. Moreover, it cut out the merchants of the Ottoman Empire controlling the East-West overland routes. So far the passage had evaded all exploratory sallies but, as ever, Gallick dreams endured.

My friendly joshing stung the *capitain*.

'Time will tell, Loftus,' he replied defensively. 'We shall find the route in the end.'

'*Bonne chance*, Beaupré,' I shouted with a wave. 'Till we meet again!'

With a great rattle of blocks, the *Tourmaline*'s braces were brought round and the buntlines let off the courses. She sheered off, wearing ship before standing away north and west for Plaisance. The *Pursuant* likewise let go her sheets, spread her canvas before the breeze and headed for home. With the wind on our steerboard quarter, we broad-reached back into Esperantia Bay. Tired, sore and filthier than ever, I dearly hoped this time our entry would be a more peaceful affair than last night's. My crew and I needed rest.

In the daylight we found the broken and burnt Gillycuddy ship run on the steep-to northern shore under Beacon Top. She lay careened at twenty degrees, bows jammed between boulders, stern wallowing in ten or twelve feet of water, good for nothing but salvage. Shallops and launches clustered round, hounds after the fox gone to earth, busy hauling off booty, swarming aboard to find a prize worth boasting about in the Salt Pillar Inn.

If only, I thought wearily, the Dowager Lady Trepanney understood how little her high ideals counted down here in the aftermath of death and fighting, amidst this unseemly scramble for spoils. I ordered the *Pursuant* brought close, intent on restoring a semblance of order and seeing the captives treated fair.

Then I went aboard and claimed one hundred per cent salvage rights.

By the time the *Pursuant* was safe in the inner harbour, Esperantia was doing its best to return to normality. Stripped to the waist in the weak early sunshine, village men shored up damaged buildings and cleared wreckage from the beach. I spotted Guy de Chenalles and the innkeeper Malachy Skentles directing the work. Lucy had spent the night tending the wounded, though two more fellows had died on the foreshore.

Unloading the furskins would have to wait until the *Pursuant*'s exhausted crew – and their captain – had rested, but I put Gaspar and the seamen to settling the bark, folding the sails into proper harbour stows, boxing the yards, coiling down lines. Busying myself on the quarter-deck in clearing away my sea-charts and cross-staff, I was startled by a voice right nearby.

'Damm'd Protestants and blasted Catholicks,' grumbled a bent old man, lumbering up the plank.

'Eli Savary,' I greeted him, grasping his gnarled hands. 'Are you well?'

It lifted my heart to see him. Years before, when I had been swept away from my native Yorkshire to the Caribbee Sea aboard a Dutch privateer, it was Eli who had shown me what it meant to be a seaman.

'Am I well?' he grunted, spitting a prodigious gob of baccy juice on the deck-boards. 'What, with my bones as stiff as storm canvas and my hands uncalloused like some damm'd cookboy's?'

One springtime not too far off there would be no Eli, grouching or otherwise, to greet me on the quay. Till then he would see his days out in comfort, if I had any say in the matter.

'We've done well with furs this trip,' I smiled, handing him a manila line to coil down. 'When it's sold, your two per cent share should keep you in fresh Virginia baccy a-while yet.'

'I thank you as ever, captain,' he said, working the line with practised ease, 'but I can't stand being stuck ashore with these fish-gutters and their women.' Clearing his throat, he caught a frog and ejected it over the side forcefully enough for me to hear the splat of its striking the water. 'I'd sooner be at sea with a gale on the nose. And come to that, a giant squid climbing aboard at the beak.'

Poor Eli was near seventy. He knew I could no longer risk him on our habitual hard voyaging.

All at once he grinned, giving me a look of evil glee. 'By the Saints, Captain Matthew, that was a fine affair last night. Seeing off those blasted Irishmen.' Then he cocked an eyebrow. 'I suppose you know that dam' disputatious Factor's been stirring it up while you was gone?'

I had almost forgotten. The price of my cargo depended greatly on the new Factor, so I had to step carefully. But by Lucy Skentles' lights, he had exacerbated divisions in the community. And was he the behatted figure countermanding my orders to the messenger boys, causing the guns to jam?

'Dam' me if he isn't trouble,' muttered Eli. 'He's a Dutchman and a Bible-quoter. A keener bargainer than any man this side of Antwerp. And a lifelong landsman to boot.'

By Eli's measure, that meant he wore buckle shoes and a clean shirt, with a plain wig on occasions. It reminded me of my urgent wish to change my ripe sea rig for a less malodorous garb.

'Well, one Factor's much like another to me,' I said. 'And any fisherman can up his hook and seek a fair price elsewhere. Talking of which, has the Governor's packet been with news?'

The Governor of Newfoundland, Septimus Spurgeon, kept his court at the capital, Saint John's, two or three days' sailing distant.

'The packet's only called the once since you left. She carried down the new Factor before the sea froze and hasn't been back since.'

'No packet yet? Afraid their cockleshell boat might strike a bit of loose ice?' We laughed together, then I said more soberly, 'So the merchants are not arrived to trade and there's no news of prices.'

He shook his grizzled head. 'No news but fishermen's rumours about this damm'd war. They say there's a Navy fleet hauling out from Portsmouth to station at Saint John's. That might upset things.'

He shot me a meaningful look. The old salt had always fretted over my secret understanding with the Plaisance settlement, for you never could trust a Frenchy.

'Aye, we don't much want the Navy in Esperantia,' I remarked distractedly, hoping he would not press the point. A Naval presence would bode ill, and not just for my mutually agreeable arrangement with Plaisance. Under the guise of protecting colonists, the Navy was wont to harry its own citizens and sailors more than the enemy.

Eli rubbed his florid nose. 'That priest's not helping, neither.'

'Father Groyne?' I said. Esperantia's sole clerick was a Papist, for the Protestants had sent their preacher away, saying they preferred to work on a Sabbath day.

'Aye, he's up to his usual games, playing one off against the other. The curers against the salters, church against chapel, Brittany men against Devonshires. Not that they need stirring. If it isn't the fishing, it's the curing. If it isn't the curing, then it's the blasted beach.'

A figure advanced along the square-stoned walkway.

'Speak of the Devil,' said Eli out of the corner of his mouth.

I turned to look. The newcomer wore a black long-coat and wide-brimmed hat – all frowned upon in Esperantia, where such distinctions were forbidden – but the clothes did nothing to disguise the fellow's air of comfortable self-satisfaction. He halted opposite the sternparts, his eyes fixed on mine, and called up.

'Captain Loftus, the Good Lord has seen fit to bring you and your bark home safe and whole.'

Savary crabbed over to the rail and peered down at him.

'Good morning, Father Groyne,' I said quickly, shooting Eli a warning look: he was about to say the stoutness of the vessel and her hardy crew were responsible for our deliverance, not the Lord. All the *Pursuant*'s men, but most especially Eli, preferred no priestly ceremony or invocations aboard ship, whether Roman or Presbyterian or Quaker or Muslim.

The priest, smoothing his shirtfront, delicately edged in silk to denote his rank, said, 'Captain, it is necessary for you to go at once and answer to the Dowager. She desires your presence at Providence House.'

'I intend to be on my way as soon as –'

'On the instant you touched, captain, was her phrase,' he cut in. 'The Dowager, in the wisdom granted her by God, does not lightly use such terms.'

Eli issued a contemptuous grunt and baccy juice spotted the deck-boards once again. I let fall the coil of line from my hands, vaulted the rail and landed on the quayside as I was, tarry-handed and grime-faced, the salt driven into the grain of my skin, my woollen shirt and briches reeking of dried seal's blood and oily woodsmoke and months-old layers of sweat. Before he could step back, I grasped the priest's hands in mine and pulled him as close as common politeness allowed.

'I am heartily glad to be home, Father Groyne,' I breathed, sensing his blenching attempt to move away, 'and I look forward to taking wine with you.'

He looked aghast. 'What? But you are not a Roman –'

'In the alehouse, I meant, not at Communion.'

With that, I strode off along the wharf, leaving that old fiend Eli Savary alone with the upright priest.

The Dowager, in summoning me so peremptorily, was making the point that her Guardian must come when called. Nevertheless, I was more than happy to attend at Providence House. The sooner I found myself in Grace Trepanney's delicate company, the better.

3

A Defender's Faith

In the Salt Pillar Inn's warm back room adjoining the kitchen, I wallowed in a great tin tub of hot water. Despite her peremptory command, I had decided the Lady Trepanney would have to wait while I made myself a touch less unfragrant in anticipation of women's company – not so much for the old lady's sake, of course, as for her daughter-in-law's.

When I had dried off and got briches on again, Lucy Skentles entered without embarrassment to clear away my filthy garments. I crouched before a square of glass propped on a shelf, gingerly dabbing a cloth at my bloody chin after the brutal razoring off of several weeks' beard. I decided it was opportune to broach the subject nearest to my heart, and seek advice from the female sex.

'Lucy, did Grace Trepanney talk of me while I was gone?'

'O, she keeps herself so much to Providence House,' she said, fussing with my things.

'Aye, but no doubt you called in with occasional vittles, for Saint Stephen's, or for Easter Sabbath Day, perhaps?'

'Caswell Penn does most of the running up there for me, you know.'

'Aye, of course,' I said, 'but even so –'

I felt a hand rest on my arm. Lucy was smiling.

'Yes, Matthew, she spoke of you. She's longing to see you.'

I smiled back. The innkeeper's wife had been teasing, and now I was grateful for her kind encouragement. We both knew that with Grace I had to tread carefully. Two seasons back, arriving in Esperantia and knowing nothing of her circumstances, I had pressed my suit too keenly. She was newly widowed and uncertain then, but last summer we had enjoyed a deal of each other's company – and in secret too. The young widow fretted that the Dowager would refuse to countenance my attentions. I resented the old lady being happy to have me as Guardian of her darling settlement but never as her son-in-law. Conceding to Grace's fears, I had held off making a marriage proposal outright. Now it was time the matter was settled.

'You see, Lucy, I thought that that –' I faltered, glowing red, awkward with the subject.

'If you defended Esperantia you'd become worthy of the widow's hand?' She gave me a comforting smile. 'And so you are.'

I buttoned on a fresh shirt, slung my leather weskit back on and re-buckled my heavy belt. There was a brace of pistols at the waistband and a short cutlass slung on too. As Guardian, it was necessary to show arms in the village.

'I'm getting a little wealth for myself now,' I said. 'Hoping, indeed, to buy a second bark. Don't you think that might sway her? I mean, sway the Dowager? My becoming a man of substance, and –'

Still flushed at revealing so much, I trailed off.

40

Lucy took up my bundle and moved to the door. Her face showed kindness, concern for my predicament.

'Matthew, you risked your life last night. Why cannot you speak forthrightly? Just tell the widow you love her and that nothing shall stop you marrying her. That's what sways a woman.'

With a smile, I kissed Lucy lightly on the forehead and went out to find the taproom deserted save for Malachy Skentles and the French musketeer, Guy, huddled together on a settle in sombre mood.

'It was looking like touch and go,' said Guy, 'but in the end, everyone has rallied together.'

'Even under a Papish fellow like you,' added Skentles, a lean-bellied man despite his affection for a quart of strong ale, one of which stood before him on the tabletop.

'Malachy,' I said, 'tell me about the new Factor.'

'It's him that stirred it up between Catholick and Protestant, while you were gone. There never was a divide here.'

'The Factor abolishes the Brittany men's quota, that is all,' said Guy defensively. 'But you see, it is the Westcountry men who object.'

The quotas limited the cod the French fishers – any Frenchmen, not just Catholicks – could land in Newfoundland, a hangover from the old days. Elsewhere, with growing trade, tolerance was spreading, despite the war setting things back.

'Lifting the quotas is in line with the Dowager's ideals,' I remarked. 'Fairness and all that.'

'The Factor says when trade increases – from whatever quarter – he collects more duties,' said the innkeeper. 'That's what counts. On the other hand, Father Groyne says Lucy and me should serve only Protestant drinkers.' He supped his ale as though the mug were likely to be his last, careful not to spill a drop. 'But the Papists shall be in here on an auction day, when the merchants arrive to buy.'

'Ha! A common trait,' said Guy with relish. 'The Flemish and the Dutch poldermen are always casting aside religion in favour of money.'

How right he was, I thought. It was ever a contest between God and Mammon. And if this settlement fell into the divisiveness that ruined others, it might not be worth defending. Esperantia's charter and principles – equal access to the beach, equity for all – were laid down in 1671 when Lady Trepanney's late husband Sir Oliver became Intendant Proper. But the merchants only cared that allowing in Catholicks saw more fish and furs brought in, which meant a better market.

'The Governor's packet is late this season,' I said, cutting into their argument. 'So there'll be no merchants in here yet a-while.'

Governor Septimus Spurgeon understood my role at Esperantia and I was sure he suspected my arrangement with Plaisance too. But he profited grandly, for he took a percentage of both markets.

'Do you hear these rumours about the Navy?' said Guy. 'Our independence surely does not last long.'

Malachy planted his mug noisily on the table. 'A squadron in Saint John's is the last thing we want. The blasted Frenchies might attack from Port L'Esprit.' Remembering the company at his table, he added without embarrassment, 'Nothing offensive intended, Guy.'

'Aye, well. None of us wants the war here,' I said.

The dull report of pistol shots crackled around the bay. The three of us were at the door in an instant.

White balls of smoke rose from the direction of the shallops anchored off the beach. A hue of shouts went up and women and children scattered in alarm, kicking over rounded cod-stacks, dropping their salt baskets. Two shallops, one of ours and a Frenchy, had run alongside each other a hundred paces off the stoney shore and the skippers had exchanged shots. It looked like the usual quarrel over fishing rights or anchoring room.

Guy and Malachy went inside to get their long-muskets. Then, going down the sloping shingle-stones, we commandeered a fishing boat and steered for the French shallop, distinguished by the steep sheerline and lateen mainsail. As we closed, I hailed the masters.

'Put up your weapons! You are to be boarded by the Guardian of Esperantia, Captain Matthew Loftus.'

We ran level with them and barged alongside hard enough to make their gunnels creak. With my companions' muskets levelled at them, I stepped aboard the French boat, pistol in hand.

The dispute was all too familiar. The Bretons wanted to range out their brine barrels for curing, the Westcountrymen to salt their fillets and rack them out to dry in the crisp air before stacking them in their trademark roundels for transport. It never changed. The Frenchmen claimed usurpation of their long-held traditional rights, while the English said the wet-curers had had their day. No one wanted the Bretons' slimy, gut-rotting brine-cured product any more, they said, not when they could buy clean, dry-salted, palatable English cod. The French should clear off the beach altogether.

I fined the grumbling captains ten marks a-piece – a bonus for the Guardian – then confiscated their weapons and made them anchor fore-and-aft, with no swinging, in the measures assigned to their country according to Esperantia's principles of equity. Such were the rules the *Pursuant* would enforce summer long.

Back at the beach, Guy and Malachy strolled away towards the Salt Pillar Inn.

'It's a dying trade, your wet-cure,' Malachy was saying. 'The dam' stuff reeks to make your eyes water.'

'Nonsense! It is a delicacy only a Frenchman can appreciate,' came the retort. 'At least Captain Loftus plays fair, and gives us our rightful dues.'

'He's got enough on his plate dealing with the bloody Irish,' Malachy replied, 'without your Breton fellows causing strife.'

'Not to forget the new Factor,' Guy said, 'who I remind you is a Protestant.'

Leaving them wrangling all the way to the Salt Pillar Inn door, I set off for Providence House.

The stoney track steepened until I turned off the path and the old house came abruptly into view. It was a greystone building, monumental, squatting in its hollow waiting to spring upon the unwary. It saddened me to think of Grace living in such a prison-like dwelling.

I approached the porch and rapped on the door, readying my report of last night's bloody engagement and its cost in lives and limbs. I would tell, too, of my Labrador trip – of bone-snapping cold, of iced rigging and vicious storms, of leather-skinned native peoples who drank seal's blood, of fierce beasts roaming the frozen wilderness. I would describe the risky pass through the Strait of Belle Isle and then under the very eyes of the jealous French into the John Cabot Strait, which they called the Breton Channel. Above all, I would enumerate the cargo I had brought back south. Those prized skins and dearly-sought furs, tamped tight into the *Pursuant*'s holds until her timbers groaned, were my wealth and my wherewithal.

The maid Mitty opened the door with a shy smile and ushered me into the vestibule. At once, I heard the old lady's voice raised behind the door.

'Show the captain in,' she commanded.

'Mitty,' I whispered, 'where is the widow –'

The maid swung the reception room door wide and scuttled away out of sight.

I entered to a blast of heat from the logs crackling and sparking in the massively overstocked grate. The mean windows let into the stone-block walls allowed little daylight, so the Dowager always kept whale-oil lamps lit, burning hot and bright and clean.

Ah, I caught myself thinking, this is what wealth brings – endless warmth to drown in, table food whenever the whim demands, freely lit interiors to

45

read and converse by. Perhaps I soon could leave behind my Whitby orphanhood and my years as a poor sailor, and win a little comfort. At twenty eight, I expected soon to be a double shipowner. Then, no longer spending winters in the ice-bound north, I would stay behind to oversee the profit, going to sea not for work but for pleasure, like a king in his *jacht*. And I even allowed myself to dwell on thoughts of returning one day to Yorkshire, to show them what Matthew Loftus had made of himself.

The Dowager sat loftily in her high-backed chair, a knee-height fire-screen placed between her brocaded skirts and the sputtering flames.

'Captain, I see you are safe and well.' The noble head tilted back and she stretched out a bony arm. 'Where on Earth should we be without our Guardian?'

I stepped forward, dipping momentarily to one knee to take her offered hand, my lips brushing it with the lightest of half-touches.

'In the less than tender care, Lady Trepanney,' I said, 'of the Gillycuddy brothers.'

The Dowager's eyes narrowed. 'Be seated.'

Suddenly fatigued, melting in the warmth, I sank down into my usual seat. But I hated these interviews, and glanced longingly through the windowpane. Far below by Stack Beach a string of fishers' shallops rode at anchor in their ordered lines. On the northern heights of Beacon Top stood a low hut, where I imagined those indolent and disobedient gunners off-guard and gambling at backgammon, which Puritans called the Devil's play.

'We watched your action last night, Captain Loftus.'

I bowed minutely. The flat statement was as much recognition as she would give. There would be no effusion of praise, no gratitude expressed to mark the sacrifices. The Dowager, in her sixty first or second year, wore a regal demeanour that left no doubt who held Esperantia in the palm of her hand. Since Sir Oliver Trepanney's death from a green wound eight years before, she had assumed her husband's authority. Her only son, Rodney, after marrying Grace, had then widowed her in turn by dying of fever, leaving her with the two children, little Oliver and his sister Sophie. At twenty six, beautiful and sad and alone, Grace Trepanney was caught in this powerful old woman's thrall.

'I feared it must be the French,' said Lady Trepanney, 'come to make Their War upon us.'

I returned her gaze. 'Well, Dowager, this time it was the Irish. But it might equally have been our own Navy, come to seize control.'

She chose to ignore my remark. 'The new Factor is proving a most courteous and assiduous man. He took the trouble to come here at once and account for last night's action.'

The remarks did nothing for my temper. His conscientious reporting seemed to count for more than the costly battle waged on her settlement's behalf.

'Dowager, I spent the entire night searching for –'

She cut me off. 'I wish to discuss The War. In Europe, matters do not go well, and all the worse for Esperantia. Her Majesty Queen Anne's fortunes remain mixed. Her generals march across the Low

Countries, but then there follows a reversal in which the Catholick forces repulse the Allies. The wigs and tails gather in Vienna or Antwerp or Danzig to concoct their treaty arrangements, then an ailing Prince dies in Luxembourg or Aragon, or a new Pretender is born in Savoy, and The War begins anew.'

For me, diplomacy in distant gilded palaces counted for nothing. In the New World, sea power mattered more than land battles in old Europe, and an English fleet stationed in Saint John's would profoundly alter the balance. Esperantia was the least of what was at stake. If battle there was to be, then it was for control of the Gulf.

An ossified finger tapped my kneebone. 'Esperantia has become a card in the grand game played out in the salons of Government. Her Majesty has commanded her Ministers to see that the Crown holds the most possible New World territory, to resist Bourbon claims. Yet any gains are given away by bewigged fools strutting in Pall Mall, or in King Louis's overdecorated palaces. Why, even Esperantia may be bargained away.'

'Dowager, surely under the charter from King Charles your husband's Grant of Intendancy was given in perpetuity, was it not?'

'Indeed so! Yet the new Factor brought word from the Governor's House that we are much talked of at the Royal Court. Parts of Newfoundland – whether Irish, French or English – are spoken of being exchanged like so many roundels of salted codfish. We might have been passed back and forth twice since you left.'

As if Esperantia were being talked of at the

Sovereign's Court in London! But if she were even half right, it fostered doubts within me. There was little point in being Guardian of a settlement only for diplomats to give it to the enemy.

She frowned. 'Now, Captain Loftus, listen. Governor Spurgeon must be persuaded to guarantee our charter with his seal. To reiterate the Grant of Intendancy that gave the Trepanneys the rights in perpetuity. Thus it is my intention to name an envoy, someone who can go to Saint John's and speak with authority on behalf of Esperantia.'

I sat up straight. Now she had my closest attention. An envoy had to have an office, and that could only be the Intendancy. Since Sir Oliver's passing, Lady Trepanney, disbarred as a woman from holding the office herself, had refused to name an Intendant Proper – as the Intendancy holder was known – ruling instead by no authority other than her own formidable person.

The Intendant Proper's powers included oversight of tax raising and price setting as well as final dominion over the shipping and defences. But more than that, it conferred status. The holder would *ex officio* become acceptable to the Dowager as a suitor for Grace. My eye strayed to a glass box on the mantelshelf. It held the Intendant's official seal, a weighty gold ring with an image embossed on its face – a rendering in precious metal of Stack Beach.

The old lady bent near, tapping my knee. 'There are few men – few men, mark you – to whom I would trust this position, even amongst my own flesh and blood.'

I flushed. Frankly my fidelity to her ran shallower than my desire to own barks and trade furs. And though the Intendancy was an enviable prize, for me it was more a stepping stone to Grace.

'The best hope for Esperantia's independence,' I said, assuming a purposeful air, 'is to increase trade, the furskins and fishery alike. Trade can pay for better batteries, beach defences and soldiery, giving us a stronger say in our own affairs. I propose improving the defences with four new ten-pounders either side covering the Roads. An impost could be levied to pay for it, on the pattern at Plaisance.'

'Do not speak of that settlement,' she commanded, her hand raised. 'Plaisance is an unhappy venture without prospects, beyond, that is, mere Commerce.'

She uttered the last word as if it were an unmentionable crime. Her obstinate refusal to understand plain matters was tiresome, and when something caught my eye through the window, I was glad of a chance to break off. Flags flew again at Beacon Top. I got up and went to Sir Oliver's magnificent focusing spy-glass, standing near the window, mounted on its tripod.

'With your permission, Lady Trepanney?' I said, and trained it on the harbour heads.

The Dowager made plain her irritation. 'Captain Loftus, come away from that window. What I have to say is of great import.'

The tube showed a small sloop in the offing, rounding the heads and making up into the bay. She was a lightly-built vessel of about forty five feet and easily recognised.

'It's the Saint John's packet,' I said. 'She'll be tied alongside in half a glass.'

'Fresh news at last!' she cried. 'Now, captain, come and listen.'

Obediently, I moved back to my seat.

'Someone must go to the capital,' she said, 'and speak with authority on behalf of Esperantia. Thus I have decided to appoint a Deputy Intendant.'

'Such a post,' I said, perplexed, 'has not been mentioned before.'

'It is in the charter and there is a seal of office. It has merely been in abeyance.'

'But why not appoint an Intendant Proper?'

'Being Deputy gives the holder a chance to show his mettle first.'

Very well, I thought, and waited for the declaration that her loyal Guardian would assume the post. She enjoyed keeping me on tenterhooks.

'As of yesterday, Captain Loftus,' she said, 'the Factor is Deputy Intendant.'

The room became hot and stuffy. Lady Trepanney's voice receded as she went on to speak of the Intendancy and questions of judicial rectitude that had so troubled her late husband. I paid no heed to any of it. Dammit, I had been usurped. Where was my reward for protecting the place? All the sacrifices made – not least poor Sam Lightfoot's – counted for nothing in her twisted priorities.

When she stopped prating, I said, 'So you have already made this appointment?'

She nodded. It seemed to be final.

'I see. Then if that is all, Dowager, I beg to take my leave.'

Abruptly, I rose, my short cutlass clanking against the chair's arm, and moved for the door, intending to find Grace without delay.

Her tone deepened. 'If you are thinking of seeing my daughter-in-law, Captain Loftus, she has gone out.'

Her countenance was dark with warning. The Dowager, divining my intentions as if from an opened book, was bent on keeping us apart. But to Hell with her attempts to separate us. I knew Grace's mind. At the *Pursuant*'s departure for Labrador last year she had given me every encouragement for hope.

'I shall take my leave, Lady Trepanney,' I said, striving to keep an even temper, and turned for the door.

Then I caught the tiny smile of triumph on her lips. It was too much, and I rounded on her.

'Dowager, four good and true Esperantia men died last night.' My throat tightened at the thought. I knew arguing did no good, but I could not stop. 'The defences here are wholly inadequate. Your neglect and parsimony costs brave fellows' lives. I don't suppose that was reported by your new Deputy Intendant, dam' his eyes.'

She looked shocked but said nothing. That silence was telling, for she had no answer. She had thrown my efforts back in my face. She cared more for espousing empty ideals than taking practickal measures for Esperantia. But a further loss of temper would bring no benefit. Instead, I left the house in quiet order, resolving to see Grace in my own good time.

Even though the Dowager would deny me, I was determined to ask Grace directly for her hand. She must be ready to emerge from her mourning and from Lady Trepanney's influence. By accepting me, she would break the spell. Perhaps then I should take Grace and the children away from Esperantia. The *Pursuant* could go to Saint John's, or to Fundy, or to Boston, and make her living there.

At the gate, I turned up the track towards Vantage Rise. I still owed Esperantia one last duty, though certainly not for the Dowager. Fishermen and musketmen and gunners had given their lives in the settlement's defence. As Guardian, I had profited here from the privileges that office brought, such as fines. Thus I would keep my promises about the defences. I would repair the tired old fifteen-pounder at Vantage Rise, put the twelves at Beacon Top in proper trim, and drill and drill the men to sharpen their gunnery.

But as soon as Grace accepted me, our new life could begin elsewhere. If she refused – and I had to entertain the prospect – then everything would be different. In that case, the *Pursuant* must leave Esperantia, once more to roam the seas without a home port.

At the Vantage Rise battery I uncovered the shockingly loose practices that had all but cost us the battle.

Gunnery drills had fallen slack or even been abandoned. Saltpetre kegs lay strewn about in poor condition, half empty and split open. Powder in the

ready-use bags was damp, as much a cause of intermittent gunnery as any overheating. Shot racks stood
loaded with immovable, rust-encrusted balls. Hand
weapons were stiff through lack of use. The ranging
equipment was out of service, with minute-glasses
broken and the sighting cross-staffs warped, their
brass scales unreadable. I set about teaching the gun
crews afresh how to weigh their powder accurately,
use only the cleanest balls, improve their accuracy
with proper sighting, and maximise the firing rate.
At Beacon Top battery, a similar disaffectedness
prevailed. All in all, Esperantia's victory had been
due solely to the lucky chance of one bomb shallop
finding its target.

Coming back down the hill, I was thinking about
the best way to approach Grace. Lucy's wisdom on
the matter might help, and I planned to go to the inn
after finding the packet's news from Saint John's.

Gaining the wharf, I was brought up short by the
sight of a dozen forlorn figures, wrists tied, chains
at their feet, slumped under the greystone wall. By
their cast they were Newfoundland natives, Beothuk
people. They sat with heads bent in submission like
the Africkan slaves so familiar from my time in the
Tropick lands. Before them strutted a stocky fellow
carrying a whip in the manner of a slave master.

Father Groyne was making his way along the
quay as if the sight were a common one unworthy
of note.

'What's afoot here?' I demanded.

He stopped. 'They are slaves, I understand.'

'There's no slavery allowed in Esperantia.'

'These are natives, Captain Loftus. Heathens from

54

the coastlands, embarking for the next leg of their journey.'

'Embarking what vessel? Bound where?'

'New England,' he replied with a dismissive air. 'To work the farms.'

'By whose authority?'

'The Governor's, I suppose,' said the priest, 'or the Good Lord's.'

Seeing us argue, one of the Beothuks made as if to rise. The whipsman stepped forward and struck his stave across the fellow's backbones. The native yelped in pain and shrank down. Just as I moved forward to challenge the overseer, a voice rang out.

'Lay off there, man!'

Striding towards the prisoners came a handsome and clear-faced figure, a man about twenty three or four, dressed like a landsman, though not an Esperantian. He wore heeled boots below tight knee-briches, with a brocaded weskit showing under his great-coat and a felt-brimmed hat a-top his unwigged head.

He snatched away the chargehand's stave.

'I'm certain you were not told to beat them in such fashion,' he said.

For a second I had thought he must be the Factor, but he spoke in strongly Scots cadences and for sure could not be a Dutchman.

'Just doin' me job as I was told,' said the surly overseer.

Catching sight of me, the Scotsman tilted, giving a pale smile. 'Good day, sir. I am Finlay McGruder, landsman shipped aboard the recent packet. I am come to arrange the deportations and the revised trading arrangements.'

'Thank the Lord,' said Father Groyne, 'the sooner the better, for Christianity's sake.'

The landsman cast a glance of distaste the priest's way.

Returning his bow, I announced myself and my bark, then said, 'Landsman McGruder, to what deportations and trading arrangements do you refer?'

'The Crown must secure as much of Newfoundland as can be got before the horse-trading begins.' His manner of speaking was entirely civil, if a touch cool. 'The diplomacy, Captain Loftus – treating with the alliance of Catholick Kings. To strengthen the Queen's territorial hold, the natives must be removed.'

'Aye, but away from their homelands, they die,' I warned, 'just like the Negroes down south whose spirits evaporate when transported from Africka.'

Finlay McGruder bowed again. 'Deportation is for the best. Newfoundland is destined to become a Protestant Christian land.'

It sounded ominous to my ears. 'What is your part in this?'

'The task fell to me of delivering the natives in good fettle, not broken-limbed and useless for work.' With a glare, he handed back the overseer's stave. For a moment his gaze flickered towards the sorry bunch of beaten men, then he flashed me a look. 'The pity is we found none of their women. I am told the young Beothuk wenches are quite comely.'

I ignored this. 'Why do you carry out this task?'

'Because I am a patriot and Protestant who obeys the

Sovereign's call. They are going to the Massachusetts Colony to work the farms. There is a bark coming down soon from Saint John's.'

'Aye well, as Guardian here, Landsman McGruder, I want them freed forthwith.'

The Scotsman shook his head regretfully. 'With respect, sir, I have my orders. Perhaps if you spoke to the Factor?'

Father Groyne made a noise like a stifled snigger, amused at my discomfort. This Factor had already usurped my authority, it seemed.

I addressed McGruder. 'Landsman, will you come aboard and tell me the news from Saint John's? I can offer you a drink of spirit.'

He accepted with a bow. Slighted, Father Groyne turned on his heel and stumped off along the wharf.

We passed up the boarding plank onto the *Pursuant*. She rode higher in the water by a foot, for the bales of furskins and buckskins were ashore, locked in a storehouse until the merchants came. The ship was quiet, the seamen resting, looking forward to a night's carousing in the Salt Pillar. The Scotsman and I settled in my dayroom, each with a slosh of Caribbee sugar-rum in a pewter.

He sniffed at his mug and said, 'I prefer a good cognac.'

'French brandy is banned from trade during wartime,' I replied. 'And is it not a Catholick concoction?'

He made no sign that he had heard. He was surveying the *Pursuant*'s design, the scantlings of her frames and deckbeams and bulkheads, almost as if he knew something about barks.

'This looks to be the sturdiest of vessels,' he remarked.

'Aye, built to take the ice and weather of the north. Pretty much the only vessel that can do so.'

'I understand you perform an important service for Her Majesty, Captain Loftus,' he said. 'Taking your ship annually along the Labrador Coast keeps alive the Sovereign's territorial claims. And the Hudson's Bay Company's too.'

'Hardly that!' I could not hold back a smile. 'The Hudson's Bay Company is defunct. I barely reach into their old territory anyway, but that far north the notion of territorial ownership is quite meaningless. As the Company discovered.'

'Meaningless?' He sounded affronted. 'No claim of Her Majesty Queen Anne's can be so described.'

Perhaps he was unaware that back in 1670, when the Company was founded, those claims were made by a brother to the second Charles.

'It was a Catholick venture in the first place,' I pointed out. 'Now, all that remains is a fort named after Prince Rupert.' I smiled. 'In truth, my pilotage works are more use than these empty claims. I survey the coastline and its waters, to enable barks to Navigate there in safety.'

'The Navy's barks, do you mean?'

I shrugged. 'Aye, if they chance it. More likely common sailors such as myself.'

On the chart table was my precious volume of surveys and sketches complete with sailing logs, weather records, depth soundings and angles on headlands, a storehouse of vital knowledge gleaned over my nearly six years' voyaging on the wild North Shore of the Gulf of Saint Laurent and the savage high latitudes of the Labrador Coast.

'Have a look at this, if you will.' I opened the heavy leather covers to display the meticulous observations inside.

'Has no one done this work before?' he asked, bending to examine the leaves. 'Not the Admiralty, for instance?'

'The Navy has no interest in this coast. They chart harbours of refuge on Newfoundland – and Acadia too, if they can sneak in without the enemy seeing. And they sound bottleneck passages such as the Belle Isle Strait. But my work is for the ordinary seafarer, not for grand politicks and war.'

I closed up the volume and laid it aside. 'What news is there from Europe?'

He sipped his rum, but not eagerly. 'The war sways back and forth.'

'Is there a Navy fleet sent out?'

'Indeed, and anchored now in Saint John's. I myself journeyed from Portsmouth aboard a warship.'

I stiffened. 'And what size and strength is the fleet?'

'Eighteen vessels in all, under an admiral – Admiral Tompion of the Newfoundland fleet.'

'What are their guns and armaments?'

He shrugged. 'I have little idea of such things, Captain Loftus, as a mere landsman.'

'Aye, but do you know the fleet's purpose?'

'I am hardly privy. However, it is connected with establishing territorial rule of all Newfoundland.'

My peaceful arrangement with Plaisance looked set to end. I changed tack and asked what he knew about the Factor.

The landsman took a deep swallow of spirit. 'Factor van Schreik? All I know is –'

'Beg pardon . . . is that the fellow's name – Van Shrike?'

He frowned. 'Yes, Josiah van Schreik. A Dutchman and a good Calvinist, if nothing else. Before coming here, he met with the Governor over the independence question.' He gave his thin smile. 'Van Schreik was a poor diplomat, I must tell you. At audience with Governor Spurgeon his manner was by turns obsequious, then resentful, then insolent. The Governor is a high-blooded gentleman, brooking no immoderateness from inferiors. I believe Septimus Spurgeon came close to revoking the charter there and then.'

The Dowager's charter revoked! It would take a powerful flota of barks to enforce a revocation against Esperantia's will, but no Guardian could prevent it now. Not with those Navy warships in Saint John's.

'It would be contrary to the law,' I said. 'King Charles's charter remains paramount.'

McGruder drained his rum and made a face. 'I think a charter given thirty years ago by a Catholick Sovereign no longer weighs. As for the Factor, revocation would reduce him to little more than a transport agent.' He smiled again, entirely without warmth. 'And collector for the extra duty on codfish exports.'

I groaned. 'There is not another impost, is there?'

He nodded. 'I have brought the papers myself.'

'How much this time?'

'Twenty per cent,' he said, as if it were nothing at all.

'Twenty per cent!' I cried. 'The Governor cannot expect to grow fatter on the Esperantian goose forever. These taxes are strangling the fishery.'

McGruder was unmoved. 'It is the admiral's impost. The duty applies only to the wet cure, thus driving off the French Bretons and letting the Westcountry saltcod industry flourish. Another enhancement to the Crown's negotiating position.'

I gave an angry shake of the head. 'It exacerbates the divisiveness. Here, Papist and Protestant, wet-curer and dry-curer, have lived and worked alongside for years.'

I heard footsteps patter up the plank and onto the deck-boards above. The ship was quiet, with the fellows sleeping after getting their vittles, but there was a watchman on the quarter.

'The religions are naturally apart,' said the landsman, 'not from ceremony or beliefs, but from the Catholick mind and blood. By nothing more than nature, they are divisive.'

There came a rap on the dayroom door.

'What is it?' I said, irritated at the interruption. McGruder's religious views were chilling and I wanted to counter them. Esperantia needed less of such bigotry, not more.

A seaman poked his head in with an enquiring look. There was a small figure by his side. I nodded and he let in Caswell Penn, who looked shyly down at his feet.

'Good day, Master Penn,' I said. 'Wait there a moment, if you will.'

I told McGruder the French were often prepared to accommodate even-handedly with their so-called sworn enemy, particularly if it promoted trade.

'In the long run,' I said, 'trade is stronger than war or religion. Trade combines, rather than divides.'

He remained unswayed. 'The nation must come first. True Protestants are unquestioning patriots to their country. To Great Britain – to the Union of Scotland and England.'

He held ardent opinions, perhaps received from others, but at any rate he was open about them. The Scotsman raised his mug and we toasted the Sovereign one last time. Then I saw him out, and the boy, waiting quietly, took a hesitant step nearer.

'I've got a message, sir. From the lady at Providence House.'

I grimaced. 'Not the Lady Trepanney again?'

'No, sir, not the Dowidge-a-lady. The other lady, the pretty one. She says will you come along to the Salt Pillar Inn and see her, please?'

I was surprised. 'What is Mistress Trepanney doing there?'

'She's waiting in the private room at the back, sir. And she said, would you do her the kindness, if you possibly could, of coming soonest?'

I was already heading for the door.

'Sir – Captain Loftus, sir,' the boy said. 'May I ask you something?'

'See Mister Rittel for a coin,' I said over my shoulder. 'You deserve it.'

'No, sir, it's not that. It's – I want to go to sea with you!'

'You're too young, lad,' I called over my shoulder.

I was away, bounding up the companionway steps and off the ship.

Pound of Flesh

Lucy Skentles greeted me at the side passage by the inn and showed me into a private room. When she closed the door behind me, I knew why Esperantia had come to matter so much.

Standing there was Grace Trepanney, as serene and tranquil as I remembered her. Dressed in the simple woollen smock and lace shawl which was uniform garb for all townswomen, she waited quietly with her hands clasped together. Over her shoulders was thrown a long black cloak pinned at the neck with a small silver brooch, the only concession to her status as the Dowager's daughter-in-law.

Even in the plainest of clothes her beauty was unmistakeable, and not merely because of her elegant bearing, the head held high, the lovely face tilted towards me. It was her eyes that held me, telling of the wise, intelligent mind, the thoughtfulness and compassion for which I loved her as much as anything. Seeing her after so long an absence, I found myself overwhelmed by a steely determination. Try as she might, I vowed, Lady Trepanney shall never come between us.

'Matthew,' she said gently, 'I am so glad you are safe.'

We gazed at each other but did not come together,

even though I yearned for her touch. Lucy Skentles had urged me to speak forthrightly of my love, but I was treading on ice so thin it might not bear the burden of too sudden a passion. Grace had withdrawn before and might do so again.

'And are you well?' I said lightly, as if nothing more were on my mind. 'How are the children?'

'They are well. Lucy is looking after them, so that we may talk. O, but you're burnt,' she murmured, reaching for my hand, turning the palm over to caress the scabbed and split flesh. 'You sent word you were unharmed, but look at you.'

I had seen myself in the shaving mirror and knew that much of my hair – grown unkempt during the winter sojourn – had gone, singed away, and my cheeks were red and high where the searing heat had stripped off a leaf of skin, even after its toughening in months of sun and salt. Remembering the mirror's image, I laughed, a sudden shock of happy relief welling up inside. I was alive. I was with Grace.

'Thank the Lord you are whole,' she said with a smile. 'The Factor described the terrible fighting.'

My levity flew away at the mention of van Schreik. 'The Factor very nearly cost us the battle,' I said. 'Since then he seems to have disappeared.'

'No, he's gone aboard the packet.'

'The packet? Why?'

She seemed uneasy. 'To depart for Saint John's. The war's changing everything. Josiah's going to –'

'Josiah? Does the old lady condone such informality?' I said a little sharply. Then I softened my tone. 'Do you know he is made Deputy Intendant?'

She looked away, eyes lowered, as though I had

been too harsh. 'The Factor has visited Providence House many times and has always shown concern for Esperantia's future. He worries that the Navy might want control of the harbour.'

'In Saint John's, they have the securest harbour in Newfoundland. Why would they want this one?'

She frowned. 'To hold as a bargaining counter, so he says.'

Perhaps it was van Schreik who had infected the Dowager's mind with those notions.

'Grace,' I said suddenly, 'I didn't come here to talk about politicks and the Factor.'

'Nor I, Matthew.' Her eyes were deep pools of resolve. 'It's the future I must think of. Especially my son's.'

From down the passage came excited shrieks and shouts. I recognised the voices of Oliver and Sophie.

'Aye, I've been thinking about that too. With this trip's furskins and now the Gillycuddy salvage too, I reckon on buying myself that second bark.'

She smiled again. 'You always wanted to become a man of substance, did you not? I'm so pleased.'

She meant much more, I could tell. To me it was like a signal flaring on the hilltop. Encouraged, I held on to her hand, thinking of what Lucy had said, that I should speak out boldly.

With her husband's death, Grace had been lost and alone. Earlier, I had been too precipitate. Her husband had been less than considerate and gentle when it came to the marriage bed, as she herself so delicately put it, and she had confessed herself unready to accept a man's embrace so soon again. Yet last December, at the *Pursuant*'s off, she had come to the wharf – against the Dowager's wishes – and seen me off with a kiss. The merest brush of our lips together, it was nevertheless the spark that lit my hopes and kept them inflamed through the dark winter months in Labrador.

A heavy tread approached along the corridor outside and there came a loud rapping on the door.

'Mistress Trepanney, the children are waiting,' called Malachy Skentles.

Instantly I heard Lucy shushing him, urging him to come away and leave us.

Grace and I shared a smile. Then I said brightly, 'May we not start afresh? Make a new beginning?'

At once she looked downcast. 'I want to, but I must think of the children's future.'

'The old lady and her settlement are not everything, you know. What does it truly matter whether Oliver inherits the Intendancy? There are other prospects than remaining here.'

She tugged gently at my hand, but I held on.

'I know,' she said. 'But Lady Trepanney determines everything. And I want my son to have his grandfather's position.'

'Grace, we can go away. I can trade in Fundy or New England. Or even New France, in the Gulf and Acadia. The war doesn't prevent private barks from trading.'

There was whispering in the passageway outside, the sounds of a suppressed argument. Then came Lucy's tentative voice.

'Mistress Trepanney? The children are restless.'

I gripped Grace's arm fiercely. 'I want to marry you. I will marry you.'

Her face crumpled. 'Please don't. You're hurting.'

Lord, it was the last thing I wanted. But I could not let her go, and pulled her close, my body hard against to hers, hugging her small frame to me.

'Marry me!'

'Matthew, I cannot.'

'Why not?' I demanded. 'You love me, don't you?'

'Don't force me to say!'

Suddenly she broke away and crossed to the door.

'Go and see her,' she said, her voice trembling. 'Go now.'

I stood there, bereft, my hands stretched out. She had snapped the bond between us.

'Who?' I said dumbly. 'Go and see who?'

'The Dowager.' She barely spoke it aloud.

'You've no need to be in thrall to her, Grace. Give me your own answer.'

'You've got your answer.' She was close to tears, her voice quiet. 'You must seek your explanation at Providence House.'

There was a knock and Malachy opened the door, looking helpless. 'Beg pardon, ma'am, but it's the children, you see.'

She drew away and went quickly out. Stupefied, I listened to Sophie and Oliver's excited chatter as she gathered them up and they left the inn.

'At once, Mitty,' I said when the maid's face appeared in the gloomy porchway. 'I demand to see her at once.'

'Show him in, if it is the captain,' cri[...]
Dowager from her grand room.

The frightened maid flung open the receiv[...]
room door and held it wide.

'Ah, Captain Loftus,' said the old lady without a[...]
hint of welcome.

'Dowager,' I said, 'I must speak about your
daughter-in-law.'

'It is I who shall speak to you, captain, and
not about the Widow Trepanney, who is no business of yours. I wish to talk about the future of
Esperantia.'

I sat down heavily in the usual chair, fatigued,
rubbing my eyes. Patience, I admonished myself,
have patience.

'The Factor is setting off for Saint John's,' she
announced. 'Such a very foresightful man. And
brave, to undertake so arduous a journey.'

So what counts in the old lady's book as courage, I thought bitterly, is the Factor's forthcoming
fairweather ride on the packet sloop to Saint John's.

'He is to demand of Governor Spurgeon,' she
went on, 'that he reiterate the Trepanney Charter,
the Grant of Intendancy.'

If McGruder was right about the Governor having
been on the point of revoking the charter altogether,
the Factor was in for an unwelcome surprise.

'Dowager, I would no more trust Josiah van
Schreik with such a mission than put a common
jack-tar to look after the ship's purse.'

She wagged a finger at me as though to a miscreant
child. 'Really, captain, that is beyond rude. The
Factor is most worthy, level and fair. And though you

nay know guns and muskets and harbour defences, he knows politicks. There is much delicacy required in diplomacy.'

I got up and went to the window to collect my senses. The packet was slipping from the wharf, with the towing launch on station nearby to take her out into the bay. There goes the Factor, I mused, likely on his way to another diplomatick disaster. And everything I had dreamed of in Esperantia seemed to be falling apart.

I turned back to face the old lady. 'Lady Trepanney, I insist on speaking about your daughter-in-law.'

She raised a claw-like hand. 'You may not see Grace as in the past. From henceforth, you may see her only in publick.'

Politeness deserted me. 'By all the fires in Hell, you cannot stop me!'

'Captain Loftus, I shall endure no disputes or arguments,' she said with finality. 'My niece must prepare herself for remarriage.'

'Remarriage?' I gasped with incomprehension. 'Remarriage to whom?'

'That,' she said flatly, 'is none of your affair.'

My thoughts whirled back to the Salt Pillar Inn. Had Grace been trying to tell me? Had I been too full of my own prospects and promises to pay proper attention? Somehow, this scheming old woman by her furnace of a fireside had outmanoeuvred me. Then, with the shock of a cannon exploding, it fell into place.

'It's that damnable van Schreik! You're forcing Grace to marry the Factor. That's why you made him Deputy Intendant.'

The Dowager blinked. 'Captain Loftus, you must

comport yourself more decorously. It is as well my daughter-in-law's behaviour with you went no further than minor indiscretion. Can you not bring yourself to consider her interest? She seeks security for my grandson, who shall in time become Intendant Proper.'

'As if your first concern were for her and her children,' I snapped. 'I shall see no such marriage take place.'

The Dowager struggled to compose herself. 'I remind you that as Guardian your sole interest is the safeguarding of Esperantia.'

'Dammit, as of now I am Guardian no longer!'

'As I thought, you care nothing for Esperantia.' she retorted, 'Perhaps we are better off without you.'

'And who shall defend your precious Esperantia then?' I muttered.

But she had recovered herself. 'Grace's wisdom and forbearance shall go a long way to securing her future. I shall let you do nothing to jeopardise it.'

By now the full import had sunk in.

'It's not her future you care about,' I said. 'You're trading her away to save your blasted Esperantia.'

'There are principles at stake, Captain Loftus,' she said, 'ideals for the betterment of men. They are emboided here in the settlement my late husband founded. I must – I *shall* – forever preserve his works and his ideals.'

I glared back. 'Take your damm'd ideals and burn in Hades,' I blazed, and stalked from the house.

* * *

I was half way down the hill before I calmed enough to wonder about Grace. Where had she been going? She had been dressed as if for walking or riding, but the only roadways led to the harbour and the village. There was no overland route out of the settlement. The tracks up to the batteries were too steep for anything save mules, and anyway the Dowager had ruled out carriage riding as a mark of inequality.

Then it struck me. She was attired for sea-going! That was why the children had been so excited. I ran over to the cliff edge. The packet sloop was clearing the harbour gap under tow. As the towline fell away, the main and jibsail were hoisted and in the afternoon's breeze she gathered way. I squinted. Was that a woman's figure standing by the taffrail, gazing astern? Dam' and blast, I cursed – dam' the Dowager, dam' the Factor. I should have taken Grace in my arms and never let her go.

In ten minutes, the packet would be beyond sight behind the bluffs and angling away southward down the Avalon coast before rounding Cape Race to turn north for the capital. On anything but a close fetch, the *Pursuant* could just about outrun such a little craft. But I had to hurry.

Then I spied a distant spread of sail far out beyond the sloop, a substantial ship making her way in towards the heads. Dam' for my spy-glass. Was it the Gillycuddy brothers returning, bent on vengeance? The *Tourmaline* coming in with news from Plaisance? O Lord, not the Navy come down from Saint John's?

As I stumbled on down the hill, a gunshot crashed out, echoing across the bay. The warning gun from

72

Beacon Top. When the noise died away, it left a pall of expectancy hanging over the harbour. Then came an answering signal from the approaching vessel to say she was not hostile. More shots crashed out, two, three, and then the replies.

Dashing headlong down the path, I rounded a bend and met a breathless boy, making his way up at speed and puffing like a furnace bellows.

'Caswell, what's the news?'

'More ships, sir, three of them,' he panted. 'One's a two-decker of thirty guns, they reckon.'

'Do the lookouts give what standard she flies?'

'The Cross of Saint George, sir. And an admiral's flag too.'

So I was right – the Navy had come.

'What signals does she show?' I said, fearing they might blockade the harbour.

'None sighted yet, sir.'

But I knew the Navy of old. I had been on the run from them for a year, back in the Caribbee Sea, falsely accused of mutiny and murder, though I won my pardon in the end. No, the Navy occupied no benign place in my mind and I guessed their intentions full well: to seize and sequester and extort, imprisoning those who stood in their way. In war, the Navy could commandeer the *Pursuant*, impress my seamen and arrest her captain. It was no longer a question of chasing down the packet sloop and snatching Grace from van Schreik. Everything was at stake now – my bark, my livelihood, my freedom.

Desperate, I squinted over the harbour. Already, the warships' looming presence seemed to fill half the Roads. With a pulse of excitement, I realised the packet was sailing straight into their arms. Surely they must haul her over and search her, so I had a chance. But to do what – slam into the packet and rescue Grace? Ridiculous. The best I could do was sail the *Pursuant* clear while their attention was diverted, and remain free to fight another day.

By the time I reached the wharfside, the Navy's heavyweight thirty gunner had entered the Roads. Her two companions were smaller, twelve or fifteen guns, but each on its own far too formidable for a one-on-one fight. A pair of longboats was down, packed with armed men, rapidly closing the shore. Madly, I stumbled up the plank, calling for the harbour towing launch, shouting at Gaspar to make ready for sea.

Amidst the confusion of hastily roused jack-tars running to obey, I snatched up my spy-glass and angled it onto the packet. She had hauled over to windward of the admiral's vessel and stopped, and was being spoken to by the Navy. Then she fell in close, put out lines and lay alongside. What a piece of luck! It might distract the Navy enough to give me a chance to slip away.

The *Pursuant* cleared the harbour gap under tow, only to be confronted with the imposing sight of the thirty gunner right close in. She seemed to be in the full expectation of a fight, with her ports open and the pieces run out. The smaller vessels had done the same. Though warships commonly ran out their guns for extra below-decks room while in harbour, this was no officers' kindness for the overcrowded seamen. Its meaning now was perfectly clear.

Still hoping against hope, I flew signals of friendship and submission, thinking that if I could not sail free then at least we might lay alongside the packet and prevent her getting away. Then a third longboat appeared from under the Navy ship's massive stern, stroked clear and put herself across my path.

'Hold off, there!' I shouted. 'I'm going alongside the packet.'

An officer stood up in the stern and waved his arms in a forbidding motion.

'Haul over or be fired upon!' came his cry.

I let the *Pursuant* run on, aware of a worried Gaspar at my side, glancing from me to the great ship's fifteen gun broadside. To approach the sloop, we must run right under the black mouths of those destructive ten-pounders. When the flagship's forward swivel let off a warning shot which hit the water a bark's length ahead of the *Pursuant*'s stem, I knew the Navy meant what they said.

'Take your bark back in the harbour,' demanded the longboat's officer.

With a despairing wave of my hand, I bade the sailing master stand down the men. To my amazement, no sooner had I given this order than the packet hauled her sheets and set off once more. They were letting van Schreik go on his way! Defeated, I sat on the quarter-deck, stunned, unable to give orders, as Gaspar silently, fearfully, took the *Pursuant* back inside the inner harbour and tied us alongside once more.

Several longboats landed on Stack Beach, where each put off twenty marines bearing muskets. They strode towards the defence positions meeting no opposition, for the fishers and settlers were no fools when it came to resisting the Crown's might. The marines took control of the village and blocked all entry to and from the wharf. I observed in severe humour as the Navy towed their thirty gun man o' war close in. She was the *Ascendant*. Not far off Stack Beach, she dropped a kedge astern, then ran on before letting go the bower. The other two barks did the same until the harbour was blocked by walls of wood and iron in line astern. A chain of signals hoisted at the flag haulyards announced that no vessel was to be allowed in or out, on pain of coming under fire.

When the warships lay back to their moorings with military precision, their guns remained ranged all over the village, the beach defences and the wharf where the *Pursuant* lay tied up. The Navy had no fear of resistance from our ancient and unreliable batteries, nor from my bark and her armament of ten puny six-pounders. As surely as if blood had been spilled by the barrel-load, Esperantia had changed hands.

And van Schreik had stolen Grace from under my very eyes.

Esperantia underwent an overnight transformation.

The *Pursuant* had a Naval Notice of Intended Impressment pinned to her mainmast. She was forbidden to move from the wharfside and her crew confined aboard, with a dozen musket-toting marines stationed on the quay.

The Navy disembarked another hundred foot-
men and billeted them in the villagers' cottages.
The Skentles' publick house was taken over as a
packed and stinking soldiers' mess. The fishermen
were corralled at one end of Stack Beach while
the Sovereign's forces commandeered the northern
end for its longboats and water barrels. Livestock
was rounded up without compensation and herded
aboard to feed the *Ascendant*'s three hundred seamen. It was their first fresh meat in the weeks since
leaving Portsmouth, Governor Spurgeon having had
the temerity to forbid such open plunder when the
warships called at Saint John's.

The settlement was in turmoil. No one knew
whether to carry on with their fishing and salting and
curing or whether they were all to be impressed or
deported. Their fears were great. Had the war spread
like a plague to Newfoundland? Would the French
confront the Navy and attack coastal settlements?
The confused and frightened Esperantians could no
longer run to their Guardian, though some gathered
disconsolately at the wharf's far end until cleared
away by marines. How much they depended on me,
I thought, with a twinge of guilt.

But I was too downcast to give much room for
their sorrows. I was deranged at the prospect of
losing my bark, for it meant my livelihood. It looked
certain my cargo of furskins stored ashore would be
seized. Most of all, I despaired at losing Grace.

The Navy's Admiral Tompion allocated himself
handsome sleeping quarters at Providence House,
where he took to entertaining the Dowager with
his skills at the spinet, singing seamen's chanties

and other story-songs set to music, though somewhat altered to suit what he presumed were her delicate sensibilites. Tompion, I learned, was bred of Lincolnshire farming stock and more at home in a country house withdrawing room than a Great Cabin. This intelligence, and much else, was brought down by the boy Caswell, running breathlessly over from the Salt Pillar Inn to nip past the cordon of bored marines and scamper up the boarding plank. His childishly retold gossip had the unimpeachable source of the Dowager's maid, on her daily visit to the village for supplies.

Bitter amusement at the admiral's antics offered scant relief. If only I had paid more attention to the war, I might have kept the *Pursuant* clear of Esperantia altogether. Or if I had acted sooner, might I have run the bark out before the Navy entered? If I had not left Grace alone so long in the proud and obsessed Dowager's orbit, what then? Might I have saved her from the obnoxious suitor chosen by Lady Trepanney?

One thing was sure. Whatever else, I must try to get the bark out somehow. I had to get up to Saint John's to prevent the marriage. But how? I went to the top of the companionway and called my sailing master.

'Mister Rittel, get Billy Jenks to bring some vittles to my dayroom. Come yourself – and bring a bottle of sugar-rum from my stores.'

A minute later, the fair-haired Dutchman appeared hesitantly at the cabin door. I had hoped to discuss some escape plan, but when he came in holding the bottle, my spirits fell further. In the days since the blockade began, his chin had grown uncharacter- istically bristly and his shirt unsavoury. He looked as if enough rum to fill a chamberpot had passed his lips.

'For Neptune's sake, pull yourself together, Gaspar,' I told him. In private we used the familiar, though never on the quarter-deck. 'Give me that bottle.'

When I splashed three fingers into a mug, he gazed longingly at it.

'You've had enough,' I said, sitting down at the rectangular table and swallowing a draught. 'Are you keeping the bark shipshape and all in trim? I want her ready to sail at a moment's notice.'

'The bark?' he mumbled. 'O, aye aye, captain.'

In truth, the *Pursuant* was spick and span enough to let a lady step aboard. He had done his work before taking to the rum.

There was a knock at the door and the bosun- cook's florid face appeared. Billy Jenks put down a platter of cold roasted deer-meat with a couple of hands of soft bread.

'Gaspar, take that dam' morose look off your face,' I said, as Jenks exited, 'and relieve the gloom in here. Sit.'

He perched edgily at the table, ignoring the meal, staring at the bottle before him as if it were a prayer book.

'This place has always been riven from truck to keel with arguments and disputes,' I said, biting into the venison. 'If it hadn't been so good for the fur trading, I'd never have come here. But we've made some money, have we not?'

The Dutchman was on a five per cent share –

generous to a fault, some might say – but all he did was shrug.

'And we've built up the fishery, expanded the fur market,' I pointed out. 'Many people have grown rich on it.'

I took an unnecessarily long swig of spirit. The plain fact was we might have gone to Plaisance or into Saint John's or even south to Boston itself and made almost as good a fist of selling our stuffs. Yet I had chosen to make Esperantia my first settled home in years. And spent two summers wasting costly shot and powder settling a hundred and one petty squabbles the Dowager never even heard about. Driving off those blasted Irishmen from Burin had cost much more than the two hundred marks' worth of munitions drawn from the *Pursuant*'s magazine to restock the batteries. Worse, it had cost lives, a terrible truth the Dowager wholly disregarded. No doubt of it, the rot had been there all along. It was only Grace I had come back for.

'You know, I shall never forget the look on Lizzie Penn's face,' I said sadly, 'when I told her young Sam was killed. They're on their own, you know, she and little Caswell.'

Gaspar said nothing – he never made much of a conversational companion – so I let my gaze wander. It passed over the furniture and fittings, the bookcases with my Navigation volumes and tomes of Natural Philosophy, the rack of instrument boxes encasing my precious cross-staff and quadrant, the writing-desk the carpenter built to my design and where I would sit on winter evenings drafting the pilot book for Newfoundland and the Labrador

Coast. One day it would be printed and published in London, and make my name.

I poured another finger of sugar-rum and helped myself to more slices of cold meat.

'Somehow, Gaspar, I've got to get us out of here.'

'I feared you had lost your spirit, captain.' His eyes focused on me with difficulty. 'You must never give up.'

'They shan't take my *Pursuant* away,' I said, 'not while there's a breath left in my body. Especially not the Navy.'

'If she were mine,' he muttered, 'no one would get her. I would see her in splinters and embers first.'

I stopped chewing. Rittel and I had been together in the Caribbee days aboard the fast Dutch privateer, the *Cornelius*. We could speak frankly.

'I don't relish hearing such talk, my friend,' I said, 'even in jest.'

'Don't let the Navy take her.' His face darkened, and he pointed at the seatback behind my head. 'You could set fuses to the magazine.'

I twisted round to follow his eye. The *Pursuant*'s builder had a penchant for intricate detail, uncommon amongst his fellow Yorkshiremen. Along the upright settles' backs were miniature carved whale's head motifs. One of these, the ugly right-whale – as common in Newfoundland waters as in the Whitby whaling fleet's Spitzbergen grounds – had a mouth that hinged open. Behind was a narrow gap between the settle-backs and the hull planking. What was my sailing master talking about?

Suddenly Gaspar was leaning half across the table, his face close to mine.

'Supposing those Gillycuddy men had got her!'

'Calm down, man,' I said, pushing him off.

He slumped opposite. 'I have followed the route, captain. A matchfuse can run all the way down to the powder room. It would be easy to rig a line of fuse –'

'What in blazes are you thinking of?' I said, throwing down the meat and bread. 'No dam' fool's going to fuse this bark!'

I had never considered there might be a lead through the ship's netherworks to the magazine. Right away, I determined to get Carpenter Sedgewick crawling into the gaps and spaces between her knees and the deckbeams to block the ways.

'It's just that I could not see her in someone else's hands,' muttered Gaspar.

It was time to lighten the mood. 'I know what you want, my Dutch friend. Just to be master of a leaky barrel, you'd let a walrus bugger you.'

He stood up, his face ablaze, and snatched up the bottle, making as if to hurl it across the cabin.

I raised a warning hand. 'Gaspar, these are trying times, but I can only make so much allowance for you having taken drink.'

He lowered the bottle, though his temper had not diminished.

'For years I follow you, captain. I wish only to work for you.' His face was suffused with righteous anger. 'But you do nothing to help yourself by coming back here. The place was never worth it. You shall lose your bark.' He wiped a dirty cuff across his mouth. 'Maybe, captain, you deserve to.'

With that, he marched from the cabin and slammed the door.

Why, dam' and blast his insolence! My temper flared like hot oil spilling from an overturned lamp. If he showed such disrespect again, I would pay him off. Then as quickly as it had flamed, my anger doused itself. My head drooped in shame. Gaspar was a good fellow and there was truth in what he said. Only Grace had pulled me back to Esperantia, and my stubbornness had brought us to the point of losing everything we had worked for.

Exhausted, distraught, I retired to my bunk. There I dreamt, tossing, of getting the *Pursuant* away, by some means, by any means. Not half a glass later, or so it seemed, someone was tapping insistently on my shoulder. The pestering continued till it brought me to wakefulness.

A voice piped, 'Captain, captain, wake up – please wake up.'

Rubbing my eyes, I found the messenger boy standing by my bunk, wide-eyed and breathless.

'Lord above, Caswell,' I said, half-sitting, 'you'll run yourself into an early grave at this rate. What's the matter?'

'There's a Navy officer outside,' he whispered.

I quickly stood up, conscious of being caught on the hop. Footsteps drummed across the deckboards and down the steps. As I opened the door, a uniformed figure entered and Caswell dashed out, squeezing past like a rabbit. The officer, a callow representative of the glory and might of Her Majesty Queen Anne's Sovereign Navy, looked me up and down. His clean dress with its shining brightwork contrasted with the fur-trimmed coat-jacket I had just thrown on, not to mention my scuffed leather weskit and well-worn canvas briches.

'Sir, do I address Captain Matthew Loftus, master of this vessel?'

'The same,' I said, tilting from the waist. Even if I was being arrested, there was no need to abandon civility.

He announced himself as Fourth Lieutenant Walston of Her Majesty's two-decker, the *Ascendant*. He would be glad if I did him the service of accompanying him aboard ship for an interview with the admiral.

Grimly, I pulled on my sea-boots and went on deck, where Rittel stood watching. Glaring at him to keep his peace, I followed the Navy man down the gangplank and along the dock to a waiting longboat.

And they sent a Fourth Lieutenant to fetch me, I muttered under my breath. A blasted Fourth Lieutenant.

5

A Stoney Heart

'It is hardly any concern of yours, Captain Loftus,' said the admiral, 'what business the Navy had with the Governor's packet.'

I was seated at the enormous polished oaken table bolted to the sole in the centre of the *Ascendant*'s Great Cabin. Directly opposite sat Sir Geoffrey Tompion, Baronet, Admiral of the Newfoundland Fleet. He was a skeletal, drawn figure and hardly the overfed porker of a common jack-tar's rum-fuelled imaginings. We were flanked either side by the flagship's officers, a post-captain and two lieutenants – barring Fourth Lieutenant Walston who, having delivered me, had retired discreetly, too junior for this Great Cabin discussion. At intervals his reedy voice could be heard issuing orders on the quarter-deck above, where the usual busyness of a Naval ship in harbour was under way.

The table was covered with rolls of parchment and opened papers. In the midst of these stood a silver coffee pot in the shape of a bull's head, from which the bitter liquid was served into the admiral's own bone china cups. The higher a Navy man's rank, it seemed, the more necessary for hot and bothered seamen to lug his trappings aboard whichever ship he chose for his pennant. The chinaware was decorated with a motif showing what I took to be the admiral's family home in Lincolnshire, with ovals depicting stud horses at stable, prize bulls in their fields, and stiff overdressed women bearing parasols, scattered here and there on sunlit parkland. All these were trophies of apparently equal value and rank in his estates.

Sir Geoffrey's countenance was as rigid as an oil painting done by a second rate dauber engaged to fix the family's faces at a job lot price. Stubbornly refusing to answer my questions about van Schreik, he was going to give nothing away. I raised my cup.

'The coffee is splendid, admiral, and Jamaickan if I am not mistaken. But is there not a charge of brandy to go with it?'

Admiral Tompion maintained his straight-backed stance. With the sternlights behind him, through which the bright late morning sun streamed into the high-ceilinged cabin, his face was obscured in the half-light but a Puritan's disapproval radiated from his every bone and sinew.

'The *Ascendant*, sir, serves no drink before ship's noontime,' he said. 'Her captain observes rules that accord with my own preferences.'

Captain James Petherwick, at the admiral's right hand, momentarily closed his eyes, at the same time inclining his head exactly two degrees in my direction.

I smiled. 'A pity. It stimulates the coffee's flavour and enhances its enjoyment. If enjoyment is allowed aboard here before ship's noontime.'

Tompion coughed, shuffled his papers and minutely consulted a document.

'Captain Loftus,' he began, 'the settlement of

Esperantia Bay is now formally brought under the Navy's direct rule. Your little trader – the *Pursuant*, I believe? – may be commissioned permanently into the service. It requires nothing more than my signature and seal upon this.' He held a document between finger and thumb, raised its edge off the table and hoisted his brows.

I inclined my head. 'As her captain and owner, I should be willing to do a service for Her Majesty. At the usual rate.'

Sir Geoffrey looked affronted. 'There is no question of payment. Nor would the Navy warrant into officer service the master of a fur trader.'

Over my dead carcass, I thought, do you take my bark away from me. Perhaps Gaspar had been right, that it was better to see her in smithereens first.

'There is a role,' continued the admiral, 'for which your vessel is well suited. A somewhat demanding role.'

'With or without her captain?'

Tompion's eyes narrowed and he studied me from behind these defences for fully half a minute. The *Ascendant* creaked on her cables and over our heads footsteps thudded across the deck-boards as jacktars went about their harbour work at the bosun's bidding.

'That depends on you, Captain Loftus,' he said, and shifted his bony limbs as if settling down to the business at hand. 'You are educated in celestial Navigation methods. I take it I am correctly informed.'

'Aye, you are. I was taught by the Navigator of the King's own bark, Jedediah Franklin.'

'King William's bark.'

'No, the restored King's – His Majesty Charles the Second. Franklin was an old man when he taught me.'

'I see. And you have over-wintered four seasons in the Labrador region.'

'No, sir, not four but these last six.'

'You are familiar with the coast as far as latitude sixty degrees north, or better.'

'Aye, that much is true,' I said.

'Or better.'

'A little, but not much,' I acknowledged.

'As far as the Frigid Zone itself.'

'Not quite.' I smiled. 'Few seamen have entered the Arctic Circle.'

'Yet you have Navigated in high latitudes. Despite the difficulties of observation and calculation.'

'Aye, so I have. And despite the Mercator's Projection charts becoming impractickal at those latitudes.'

'Is that so?' He paused. 'You have taken exceptional recordings of the unusual magnetick variation rates caused by the Polar region's influence. And made extensive surveys of the Labrador Coast.'

Suddenly I was uneasy. He seemed to know a great deal about me. Where was this leading?

'And what if I have, sir?'

'I take that as an affirmation.' The admiral sounded pleased. 'You shall publish a pilot book of this work.'

'I intend to,' I said guardedly, choosing my words, 'in the fullness of time.'

'For England's use, one is to assume – or I should

say Great Britain's. Rather than, for argument's sake, the Queen's enemies.'

I glanced sharply round the table. By the codfish's whiskers, what was all this about? Even with the admiral's face in half shadow, I caught his smile, a wholly mirthless and pinched affair.

'Captain Petherwick,' he said, 'be so kind as to outline the difficulty Her Majesty presently faces with regard to Hudson's Bay.'

Petherwick had waited for his moment. He unfolded a large chart, punctiliously spreading it on the table, smoothing the creases away with clean pink hands. It showed all the High Kanada Lands and what King Louis termed New France, from Newfoundland in the east, north up the Labrador Coast, round the capes and south again into Hudson's Bay, including all the uninhabited Quebec Regions, as well as the Gulf, the Saint Laurent River and the land of lakes beyond.

'This is James Bay,' said Petherwick, 'the southerly extension of Hudson's.'

The captain's delicate hand, not one used to turning chain-pump handles or hauling hempen sheets, pointed to where the waters of Hudson's Bay – a sea, in truth – encroached so far south they came within a hundred and fifty leagues of those largely unexplored inland waters known only as the great lakes. The map showed it to be less than five hundred miles overland from the bottom of James Bay to reach the Saint Laurent River and Quebec City, the French stronghold, yet by the circuitous northerly sea route, the distance must have been three thousand miles or more.

'Fort Rupert guards the coast where the Rupert River reaches James Bay,' the captain went on. 'It is the English – or British, as I might say now – fortification protecting fur traders' rights. These traders bargain with the savages of the region, who are supposedly first-rate trappers. Possibly you are familiar with this?'

'Aye, somewhat,' I said dubiously. The fort looked to be the remotest and most tenuous outpost of English sovereignty anywhere on Earth.

'Fort Rupert's true purpose,' put in the admiral, 'is to keep open Her Majesty's claim on the sea passage and all the territory around Hudson's Bay first given over to the Company of that name. King Louis has declared both the trade and the fort an illegal intrusion into France's sovereign territory. Preposterous.' Again came the mirthless laugh. 'You are perhaps aware that France's strategy is to control all the overland routes – what are they called, Petherwick?'

'Portages, admiral, whereby the natives and trappers carry their canoes over unnavigable ground from one river or lake to the next. The terrain is impossibly –'

'Quite so. The natives can cross the land, I am told, between James Bay and the French stations at Quebec. Their portage routes secure the fur trade, whose profits replenish the enemy's war purse.'

Sir Geoffrey paused, as if I were expected to speak.

'I know little of such politicks,' I said innocently, but with a growing suspicion of where all this might be going.

'Ah, the politicks of the thing. The French have a grand design on all Americka. Using the river system to surround our colonies.'

Such an idea seemed hardly likely, though Admiral Tompion's head tilted as if to say, contest me and you shall hear the argument in its entirety. As I had no wish to sit all day drinking bad coffee, surrounded by starched Navy shirts and shiny boots, I shirked his challenge.

'If Her Majesty's war ministers see such a grand design,' I said, maintaining politeness, 'then surely they are right. But it is sea power that matters, not inland water routes.'

He raised an eyebrow, and there was a pause during which all I heard were the footshuffles of sailors on the decks overhead and the distant shouts of the ship's masters sending seamen about their hundred and one harbour tasks.

Keen to break the awkward silence, I said with a deferential smile, 'I merely intended to suggest that your fleet must eventually meet the French Navy. Why else has it been sent across the Atlantick?'

The quiet in the cabin was as heavy as lead crystal. He would not, I thought, be the first sea commander in history to be leery about taking his fleet to sea to face the enemy.

'My fleet tactics,' snapped Tompion with sudden force, 'are no concern of yours. Moreover, there is no French Naval presence in the region, by treaty.'

'Surely in time of war,' I said, thinking of the enemy, 'treaties may be broken.'

'Treaties are never broken,' said Tompion, 'as

long as all parties consider themselves locked into the bargain.'

I refrained from pointing out that the arrival of his fleet at Saint John's demonstrated that England did not feel obliged to keep her part of a treaty which supposedly kept these waters free of either sides' Naval forces.

The admiral pressed his lips tightly together, then said, 'Continue, Petherwick.'

The captain rehearsed again the Sovereign's interest in Hudson's Bay, namely that Fort Rupert kept open Britain's claims. Yet the whole region north of the Saint Laurent River, called Quebec and the High Kanada Lands, was reckoned an inhospitable frozen wilderness. For me, it could hardly be of import for any European war.

'You know of the trading bark, the *Beaver*?' the captain asked.

I straightened at once, my curiosity whetted. She was the fur trader Governor Spurgeon sent to Hudson's Bay each summer to load skins and horn and pelts brought down from the hinterland by natives in their pack canoes. The furs were sold at Saint John's, though the cost of her voyaging was said to diminish the otherwise vast profits.

'She remains the only ship ever to complete the arduous journey more than once,' said Petherwick. 'In seven seasons, the *Beaver*'s contribution has been invaluable.'

'Incalculable, captain,' put in Admiral Tompion sombrely.

Petherwick accepted the correction with grace.

'However, the *Beaver* did not return to Saint John's last year.'

'Is she lost?' I said. 'What was her complement?'

'Her complement?' repeated the captain, as if the men aboard were of no consideration. 'O, I see. It was – ah, I think – it was fifty officers and men.'

'Fifty loyal servants of the Crown,' added the admiral.

'Fifty private seamen,' I countered. 'Captain Petherwick said she was a trading bark.'

'Those seamen were performing a service for Her Majesty as much as for their own selves,' replied Sir Geoffrey. 'Captain Loftus, we are not prepared to give her up as lost. Her presence is crucial to the Hudson's Bay Company.'

Perhaps that was why it was rumoured that Governor Spurgeon, though reluctant, was obliged to subsidise her voyages from his revenues – to keep alive the long-forgotten, unworkable Company.

'That Company is largely defunct, as I understand it,' I pointed out. 'The fort is the last remnant, is it not?'

'Perhaps, but there is a politickal dimension,' said the admiral. 'The Sovereign must show France that the route is open and that we can resupply Fort Rupert.'

'It appears you cannot,' I said, 'for this season the bark has failed again.'

There was another loaded silence.

'She may have reached the fort,' said Tompion, 'we simply do not know. She must be found, that is all. And that is why you are taking the *Pursuant* north – to find her.'

I had seen it coming, but still I shifted uncomfortably in my seat. For me, such a voyage was out of the question. The huge region was all but uncharted. The storms were unpredictable and violent. The seas were strewn with icebergs and half-sunken ice boulders large enough to stove in the stoutest bark's planking. In Hudson's Bay, the pack ice shifted on wind and current without warning, entrapping and crushing a vessel as if she were an eggshell. I was not the least surprised that the *Beaver* had failed to return.

I looked the admiral squarely in the eye. 'I am obliged to refuse, for reasons of practickal common sense. However, if you have a more attainable proposal for the *Pursuant* to give some service to Her Majesty, I shall be honoured to consider it.'

'The Navy is not asking whether you wish to undertake this trip for your own amusement. The Navy is ordering you.' Tompion glowered across the table. 'You shall take your wretched little bark to find the *Beaver*, or whatever remains of her. Do I make myself plain?'

It came to me then, with the sharp clarity of freshwater ice, that they had no one else remotely capable of the mission. And they had me boxed in at their mercy. In time of war, the Navy could do to me and my bark what they dam' well liked.

'Plain as a beacon, Sir Geoffrey,' I said. When eight bells clanged noisily on the quarter-deck above our heads, I grasped at a chance to gain time for thinking. 'Admiral, since it is noontime, might the brandy be allowed an airing?'

With an irritated sigh he nodded at a second lieutenant, who got up and called for a steward.

Moments later, I was savouring a first-class distillation captured some years before in a glorious action commanded by Tompion, so he said, in which he took a magnificent French warship for his prize. As I drank, the admiral leaned forward.

'Loftus, you are a perceptive enough fellow. You understand the consequences.' He gave out a hollow chuckle, the sound of a holystone being scraped across dry deck planks. 'Howsoever, I prefer encouragement to coercion. Petherwick, the document.'

The captain pushed across a lavishly enscribed parchment.

'Have a look, Loftus,' said Sir Geoffrey.

I put the brandy glass carefully back on the table and craned over to see.

'There is a space there for the name,' the admiral was saying. 'On your successful completion of the mission, the name entered shall be your own.'

With a flourish of penmanship, some secretary had written boldly across the top, *Appointment of an Intendant Proper at Esperantia.*

I stared from the scripted document to the admiral and back. 'Have you the power to appoint an Intendant Proper?'

Sir Geoffrey nodded confidently. 'I have taken upon myself that power.'

Suddenly I thought, to Hell with the Dowager, to Hell with the Factor. If the Navy made me Intendant Proper over their heads, Esperantia would be my reward. The villagers, the merchants, the tradesmen, the publicans, the fishers – even the priests – would answer to me. Best of all, if the Dowager were left with no more influence than a cod-dryer's wife, then Grace Trepanney could marry me without a qualm.

Admiral Tompion raised his brows enquiringly. He seemed to know so much. I wondered how far he had divined my train of thought.

Then I said, 'What conditions are there?'

He gave the thinnest of smiles. 'Very good, Loftus. The chief condition is that you must conduct an ordered and meticulous search for the *Beaver*, to the utmost of your abilities.'

'Beginning and ending where?'

'Beginning after you pass the most northerly point, the Great Northern Cape. Ending only when you find the bark, or reach south as far as Fort Rupert.'

I thought rapidly. 'There must be a time limit on the search or my bark would become entrapped.'

The admiral shook his head.

'Sir, think on this,' I said quickly. 'There are spies everywhere. When the French learnt the rescue mission was lost too, they would crow like cocks.'

Petherwick leaned across and whispered into Tompion's ear.

'I am advised,' said Sir Geoffrey, 'that given the lateness of the season a time limit may be put on the search.'

'How shall that be determined?'

They embarked on another whispered consultation.

'The *Beaver*'s logs,' said Petherwick officiously, 'were lodged annually at Saint John's by her master at the end of each voyage. They show she cleared the Great Northern Cape no later than the thirtieth of September. That shall be your time limit.'

'I must have those logs,' I said at once.

Tompion nodded. 'You shall have them all. And you shall also take aboard,' he added, 'my own place man, who shall see the search done properly.'

'Who shall that be?'

'Landsman McGruder.'

Finlay McGruder – the landsman and politickal zealot, the transporter of those miserable Beothuks. The Scotsman had professed himself no seaman, and thus would be in no position to interfere with my captaincy or running of the ship. It could have been worse.

The admiral produced another paper and pushed it at me.

'The mission's terms for you to sign,' he said. 'On a Naval commission, you must possess a recognised status. You shall be Intendant Proper on your return, but on signing this with immediate effect you are made Deputy Intendant.'

I nearly burst out laughing. 'But the Dowager has given that post to Factor van Schreik!'

Tompion's severe features remained set in stone. 'That was not ratified by me. I have assumed all charter powers here.'

'O aye, of course. So what happens to van Schreik?'

The admiral shrugged. 'He may remain as Factor, though not Deputy. I understand he has an eye for a price.'

I smiled at the thought of Josiah van Schreik, stripped of his office and forced to see me assume the Intendancy in his place.

There was a knock at the cabin door.

'Enter,' said Petherwick.

Fourth Lieutenant Walston came shyly into the room.

'Step forward, Walston,' said Sir Geoffrey, not taking his eyes off me, 'and show the good captain.'

The young lieutenant stood in the middle of the Great Cabin clutching something to his breast as if it were his mother's Bible. The buckskin cover was unmistakeable.

'Your Newfoundland and Labrador pilot book,' said Tompion. 'I understand you value it somewhat. As a further encouragement, it is confiscated till you return.'

They were holding it hostage. My pilot book had become their hostage against my return! Of course, it was little use on this voyage, as it covered waters I knew rather than the unfamiliar seas where the *Pursuant* was bound now. But the Navy had already given me every reason to complete the mission to its fullest. Without further argument, I took up the quill and scratched my name.

The admiral held out a glinting object.

'Deputy Intendant Loftus,' he said, 'your seal of office.'

I reached out and took the heavy signet ring. It was similar but smaller than the solid gold one the Dowager kept on her mantel-shelf, and made only of silver, though with a golden face set into it. Like the Intendant Proper's full-sized seal, deeply embossed upon its face was an image of Stack Beach. I slipped it onto the middle finger of my right hand, feeling its weight. Despite myself, the blood pumped a little quicker in my veins.

'The ring remained in the Dowager Lady Tre-panney's safekeeping,' explained Admiral Tompion, 'until, as she herself said, its rightful holder could be appointed.'

Perhaps not the rightful holder she expected, I thought, gazing at it. Then I took off the ring and put it carefully in my weskit pocket. No seaman could wear such a thing by habit, for fear of it snagging or cutting into his hand as he gripped a line.

Flushed, sensing that I had won a small triumph in rescuing myself from disaster, I raised my glass to the company.

'Shall we drink, gentlemen, to the *Pursuant*'s successful return from the Frigid Zone?'

Malachy Skentles, with Lucy clutching his arm, watched the *Pursuant*'s crew run up and down the doubled boarding planks across the gap between the quay wall and the bark. Sweating in the afternoon warmth, the seamen were loading the last of a great burden of stores. The innkeeper could always lay hands on the best vittles, even in times of short supply, as now. But he sorely resented the hard bargain I had driven.

'Anyone but you, Matthew,' said Malachy, 'and I'd have told him to go to Hades and rot.'

All day, since leaving the *Ascendant*, my head had swirled with a thousand thoughts of the stores and spares and supplies vital to our safe return. The plainest item forgotten now was a loss that magnified with every league we travelled further north. It was vital to load everything we needed – all the dry stores and cooking oil, spare mitts and woollen under-garments and head coverings, camomile and balm-oils for cracked skin – for there was no resupply up there.

When Skentles complained at my prices, I was in no mood for arguing. Taking out the Deputy Intendant's seal, I reminded him that supplies could be requisitioned if necessary. The Navy had shown no compunction in taking what they wanted, from the inn, from the storehouses, even seizing fresh codfish off the beach. At least I was paying something.

His face remained dark. 'This affair's all but cost me my livelihood.'

As he and Lucy stamped off along the wharf, they passed Guy de Chenalles approaching. He looked glum.

'Well?' I demanded. 'What about that boat?'

Spreading his hands wide, he said, 'I cannot see why you must take a Frenchman's shallop, that is all.'

The *Pursuant*'s own ship's boat – a stoutly-built twenty-foot harpooner of the type carried by Whitby whalers – was a first rate sea-keeper, but I wanted a lighter boat for the search, for frequent launching and recovering. And for a spare, in case mine was smashed by ice.

'Guy, I simply chose the best vessel for the purpose.'

'That is exactly what your Royal Navy is saying,' he muttered, 'when they seize six Breton shallops and no Westcountrymen's boats.'

'Aye, maybe, but will the fisherman give up his vessel or must I send my musketmen down there?'

He gave a shrug – I could almost hear him

thinking, what choice am I having? – and then made his way off back down the wharf.

All the seamen had gone aboard by now, their loading completed. They idled about in the waist, talking and smoking, so I sat down on a stone bollard, glad to be alone for a moment.

My patience was wearing thin with those good people who had suggested I was abusing my powers. If only they knew of my more radical plans for the settlement. The potential was rich, a ripe and fulsome prospect, and as Intendant Proper I would show them what Esperantia could be.

That afternoon, passing by the main storehouse, I had looked in at the storeroom to see roof-high piles of furs, pelts and buckskins. With no alternative, I had to leave my valuable cargo in the Factor's hands, to let him trade it on my behalf when he returned from Saint John's. The same went for the salvaged Gillycuddy bark, which the Navy had grudgingly let me keep. Of all people, the Factor was to be my agent. In a few days, though, the *Pursuant* would be calling in at Saint John's harbour, for our route meant sailing right by the entrance. No one could stop me going in, so at last I could confront the man. Yet in truth it was not the merchanting issue that drew me there. It was Grace Trepanney.

I surveyed my bark, resting quietly at the wharfside. Her decks were crowded with all twenty four common seamen and my five officers. They chatted and gossiped easily enough, as if to show how ready they were for this new departure into the forbidding, mysterious waters of the Frigid Zone.

My trading ventures had always rested on the sea-men's hardiness, their preparedness to over-winter on the Labrador coast, and on the *Pursuant*'s ability to force her way southwards at the first sea-ice thaw. Our mission into Hudson's Bay was more severe than any other voyage, and the distances an order of magnitude greater. Thank the Lord, then, for a crew hardened to such icy rigours, and praise be for my officers – from the expert Gaspar and the indomitable Nat Gunn right down to the bosun-cook, Billy Jenks, whose way with seal steaks and whale's blubber, his sheer vittling knowhow, was irreplaceable. A belly full of hot dinner made all the difference between tolerable survival and unendurable misery.

There was a shout on deck. The sailors were called below to mess, their last supper before the off – fresh-killed and roasted pig-meat with sourdough bread baked in the Salt Pillar Inn's ovens. Stretching my limbs, which had stiffened in the chilly evening air, I clambered up the boarding plank and almost failed to notice the hunched form of an old man, leaning alone by the wheel. He was gazing out to seaward.

'Eli,' I said in surprise, 'have you come to wish us well on our way?'

He chewed on a tobacco plug of such proportions that his cheeks bulged both sides. He opened his mouth wide and fingered out this speech-impeding object, the mere sight of which – large and moist like something a gannet spews up for its chicks – all but made me gag on the spot.

'Captain,' he mumbled, pressing the sodden baccy into his palms with a squelch, 'I'm coming with you.'

My heart lurched. Once he had been the *Pursuant*'s first mate and a better hand had never shipped aboard. Now, far from being able to pull on a brace, harden in a sheet or spring aloft in a rising wind, he struggled to haul himself up an ordinary boarding rope. In a running sea, he would likely fall down and break his neck or be blown over the side in a squall.

I gave him a kindly squeeze on the elbow. 'Eli, old friend, don't you prefer to spend your comforts ashore, to sit by a sparking fire of spruce-wood, with warmed ale in your pewter?'

He spat on the deck-boards with great vigour. 'I'd as soon peg out here in this Godforsaken pit of vipers you call Esperantia as spend a summer on a farm baling hay. I'm ever grateful for the pension, but I'd give it up if I could go back to sea. Let me come, just one more time.'

'No, Eli. It'd be the death of you.'

A smile as wide as the bay spread across his deep-lined face, bristly and tanned like beaten leather, scarred as much from fighting with men as with landing giant tunny fish.

'That's the spirit, Captain Matthew! I want to die where there's no land in sight – but don't forget to bury me ashore.' At his feet was a bundle resembling a small dead moose. 'See, I've brought my own slops and oiled-skins, biscuit and other vittles too. I'll take no beer nor pork from the cook's stores, nor get under any jack-tar's feet. I shan't be any bother, captain, no bother at all.'

I scanned the decks, minutes before aswarm with jack-tars hefting bags aboard, reeving lines through blocks, tarring the shrouds, reaming up deadeyes. Thirty seamen sailed aboard the *Pursuant* as her usual complement, and in age they ranged from a wan fourteen-year-old sea-boy already stultified by years of tweendecks life – all he knew of the sea and its ways – to bosun-cook Billy Jenks, well on towards sixty and looking at his last couple of seasons in the north. Eli Savary was ten years older even than Jenks. Yet how many times had Eli's been the guiding hand on the ship's wheel, or his the firm arm to hold on to when we went aloft in a gale? From my earliest days aboard the big ships, the old salt had shown me how to stay on a wet spar in a rolling sea, how to troll for kingfish and above all how to laugh in a tempest's face.

His eyes were large and sad. 'Take me with you, captain, for old times' sake.'

Sometimes being captain is a burden, I thought, swallowing hard.

'I'm sorry, old salt. There's no chance. Not this voyage.'

When Eli saw I would not be moved, he picked up his bag and went slope-shouldered down the gangway, jaws working like an ancient pelican. At the foot of the gangplank, he was shoved aside by some fellow boarding in a hurry. This figure was followed by a Navy seaman carrying a bulky sack.

'Captain Loftus!' said the fellow, stepping briskly up.

'Good day, Landsman McGruder,' I said, little in the mood for pleasantries. 'Have your accoutrements put in the cabin next to my dayroom.'

Eli hung back on the quayside, watching, his

seaman's bag thrown down in a heap. I got busy about the quarter-deck checking the state of the compass and my instrument cases, but after a little while I noticed a small figure sidling up beside Eli. It was Caswell, whom I had told was too young for the sea. He reached out shyly and took Savary's hand, leaning lightly against the old salt. The two disappointed sea-going hopefuls stood together, gazing my way.

As I could not bear to meet either's eye, I went below to get McGruder settled in. It was important to see him properly done by. I might not relish his presence aboard, but neither could I afford to antagonise him. After all, he was to oversee the mission's conduct, and declare the search correctly done.

At her captain's word, the *Pursuant* threw off the docklines at four in the afternoon and towed out through the harbour gap. We breached the stone walls guarding the entrance and the bay opened before us. Casting about, I took in with a single sweep the whole scene, from the profile of the big gun just visible at Vantage Rise to the Dowager's house below, then all along Stack Beach with the village behind its rocky mounds, and the usual row of tatty shallops riding on fore and aft anchors twenty fathoms off the shore. To the north, the steeply angled slopes of scattered scrub and bare turf led up to Beacon Top, where the twin pieces glinted black in the bright glare of the afternoon sun escaping away to the southwest.

When I turned to seaward, there was the mighty bulk of the *Ascendant* chafing gracelessly at her anchors in the middle of the Roads, with the two twelve gunners moored fore and aft in line astern. A brace of longboats waited under the flagship's stern quarters, ready for ferrying officers and marines on their Naval affairs to and from the harbour they now ruled so assiduously.

A long wavering blast of sound echoed across the silent bay, and for a painful moment I thought of Sam Lightfoot with his hunting horn. But the signal came from the *Ascendant*'s quarter-deck. Putting off from under her bulky topsides were the two longboats, packed to the gunnels with armed men.

They were heading straight for the *Pursuant*.

'Captain Petherwick, this was not in the agreement,' I protested.

The *Pursuant*'s weather-deck was crowded as never before. The captain's marines were shepherding my seamen, all twenty four of the foc's'le party, over to the rail where they disconsolately shouldered their bags and descended via slung-over boarding ropes into one of the waiting boats. From the other, two dozen strangers scrambled up, likewise toting sea-bags. They huddled in the waist, bemused, awaiting orders, leaning on the deck-pieces, smoking or chewing, gazing about at their new ship.

'I must go aboard the flagship to speak with the admiral,' I insisted.

Petherwick held up his hand. 'The admiral is engaged ashore. He left explicit instructions with me.'

'But this is the worst of news!' I cried. 'These men know nothing of the sea and ice in northern waters.'

He shrugged. 'You have your officers.'

I had been allowed to keep back just four fellows. Nearby on the quarter stood Gaspar Rittel. Then there were the second mates, Nathaniel Gunn and Luke Tatchell, and the bosun-cook Billy Jenks.

'There's no time to temper the new fellows,' I said. 'They know nothing of the *Pursuant* or her ways.'

The captain smiled benignly. 'Take your cue from the Navy. We commonly ship landlubbers aboard, fresh from the farms and the fields. They are knocked into shape soon enough.'

'Aye, but never a whole company at once. And the Navy's impressment always seeks out able seamen where they can, not lubbers.'

Petherwick gave a dismissive shrug. By now the longboat had left my crew standing dejectedly on the beach, stranded ashore like storm-blown sea hogs. Once again, it seemed I had no choice. Fuming, I sent Gaspar and the other officers to settle the new fellows in the foc'sle quarters.

'Make ready for sea forthwith,' ordered Petherwick. 'I shall stay aboard till you clear the heads.'

Further argument was pointless. I gave orders to tie off the longboats and tow them astern. As the bark moved off, a shout was raised up at the forepeak hatch where the newly-boarded *Ascendant* men were gathering to go below and find hammocks. Nat Gunn broke through the throng and came aft to the break. He was holding a small boy by the scruff of the neck.

'Bring him up on the quarter, second mate.' With a stern look, I squatted down. 'Well, Master Penn, where have you been hiding?'

107

'I hid in a hammock, sir,' came Caswell's high voice. He was red-cheeked from his struggles, unable to stand still, feet pawing restlessly as if he needed to relieve a pressure on his bladder. 'I want to go with you, sir. Please take me!'

I patted his arm. 'You're a good and brave lad, but you can't come.'

Tears fell down his cheeks.

'When I'm back,' I said, 'you can sail a summer season with me.'

He sniffed, wiping his eyes. 'Do you really promise, sir? Truly?'

'What's the delay, Loftus?' called Petherwick, coming over. 'I cannot walk these boards all day.'

Minutes later, the *Pursuant* had hoisted all plain sail, caught the breeze just abaft the beam and cleared the Roads. Within a turn of the hour-glass, we had dropped Captain Petherwick and his men back into the longboats. Caswell's diminutive figure was almost lost amongst the oarsmen.

'Sir, can I truly sail aboard next year?' came his piping voice. 'Do you give your word?'

I looked down over the rail at the little fellow's eager face, ten feet below.

'Aye, I do, Caswell. I give my word, man to man.'

Captain Petherwick pulled him back into his seat and cuffed his ear. The oars clacked rhythmically and the longboats drew away.

By the time the glass was next spun, Esperantia Bay had closed to our sight and the land called Avalon had receded to nothing more than a smudge on the horizon.

6

Bay of Storms

In northern waters, for a bark heading into high latitudes the scarcest commodity is time. With July turning to August, weeks of voyaging ahead of us and the short summer well under way, the *Pursuant*'s time was perilously curtailed.

Around the Gulf and western Newfoundland, the sea-ice cracks in April, loosens in May, and floats free in June. The higher latitudes of Labrador are colder and not until much later are the waters passable into sixty degrees north and beyond. Up there in October, as the days shorten and the sun's warmth fails, the sea freezes early and the capes are again seized in an icy grip. From mid-November, ice creeps southward from the Polar wastes and by year's end all Labrador lies under a frozen blanket. We had barely time to make our way past the Great Northern Cape, enter Hudson's Bay, search for the *Beaver* and slip out again before winter's onset.

Nevertheless, as we sailed northwards along the Avalon Peninsula's eastern shore, all I could think of was Saint John's. To gain the Labrador Sea, the bark had to pass within a league of the harbour entrance. I was sure that as soon as I told Grace of my imminent return as Intendant Proper, she would have the iron will to resist any marriage arrangement forced on her.

After rounding Cape Race at Avalon's southern extremity, the *Pursuant* had set her course due north. Now, in the dark minutes before dawn, as we headed stubbornly onward under the stars, the sky lightened to show the sea-horizon. Though the coast was invisible, these were familiar waters and I knew Saint John's lay not far off.

'Come two points to larboard, steersman,' I said.

The sailing master registered the change. Gaspar Rittel stood swathed from head to toe in oiled-skins with a bush of seal fur poking out at the neck and a tattered beaver pelt hat perched a-top his salty hair. He craned upwards, studying the pull and draw of the sails, the straining sheets and lifting luffs, then strode to the break and pointed up the foremast.

'You two – Higham, Tallis!' he called down into the waist. 'Aloft on the larboard side and see to those loose buntlines.'

A brace of fellows sitting under the lee rail uncrooked their limbs. My officers were keeping this untried crew under severe scrutiny until we saw their mettle.

'Lively there,' said Gaspar, as the pair moved reluctantly to the ratlines.

The Dutchman caught my eye and turned down the corners of his mouth.

Soon we approached the coast, but to my despair the infamous Newfoundland fog closed in. Heavy mists rolled down to envelop the *Pursuant* in a clammy miasma, obscuring everything – sun, sea, sky and shore. In minutes it was so thick that from the quarter-deck the anchors stowed in their catheads right forward were invisible. When men went aloft, they were lost to sight halfway up the ratlines, and worked together by shouts and chanties in the silent, damp clouds above.

There was nothing to be done but wait, so I hove the ship to, hoping the fogbanks would lift by noon. But they did not, and at nightfall we were still hemmed in, going nowhere, facing the long watches till morning. Stumping down the companionway steps, banging my palms together to bring the life back, I ducked along the passageway. In the captain's dayroom, seated by the table, was Finlay McGruder.

'A drink to cosset your insides, captain?' he said with that worryingly insincere smile, rising to go to the sideboard and fill two mugs.

He had secured a stock of French brandy for the voyage. The spirit warmed my gullet but did not humour me towards the Scotsman. He struck me as a clever sort, book-educated and always ready in argument, yet he took the difficulties of the voyage ahead all too lightly, dismissing as unimportant my misgivings about being served with a crew of pressed men.

'Captain, I am given to understand you wish to call at Saint John's,' he said. 'But am I right in thinking the fog does not prevent us continuing north, clear of the land?'

'You are,' I said, wondering what he was aiming at. His brief was to oversee the search, not direct the vessel.

'So this is an unnecessary delay, which could amount to a breach of your mission terms. You are shortening the time available for the search.'

'That's ridiculous,' I said.

He looked pensive, then sought another tack. 'Have you considered how you may be jeopardising your prospects at Esperantia?'

'With respect, neither my prospects nor the settlement's are any concern of yours.'

'Ah, but I do think Esperantia should be allowed to prosper,' he remarked smoothly.

At once suspicious, I laid aside my pewter. Making pleasant conversation for its own sake seemed unsuited to this fellow's nature.

'I did not think,' I said, 'that the place meant anything to you.'

He sat back, wiping his lips with a napkin. 'To the contrary – I see great potential. The salt-cod trade is expanding richly because the dry-cured fish travels so much better. It keeps well at sea and is quite palatable when soaked in sweet water and boiled. Even in the south of France, I am told, they no longer want the stinking brine-cured stuff produced by their own Breton fellows, despite the dry-cod commanding twice the price. There is much to be said for Esperantia's future,' he added, 'if only it is properly administered.'

He lifted the bottle and suggested we drink to the salt-cod trade.

'You might like it less,' I said, 'if you knew that the French Navy vittles their ships with English salt-cod. They furnish it aboard their men-o'-war and galliards at Toulon. So it fills Catholick bellies – the bellies of the very matelots who make war on our Navy.'

Finlay McGruder showed himself unamused, and

began to speak about the war against the Papists, but the brandy helped me ignore his opinionated rants. The Scot was praising Admiral Tompion's divisive imposts and bemoaning that the Bretons – 'and the rest of those damm'd Catholicks' – were not transported wholesale to Acadia along with their fellow Romans. His unremitting bigotry and dour humourlessness reminded me of what I had been told of the Factor.

'On my return I shall have to deal with all that,' I said, thinking aloud. 'Van Schreik, I mean. The fellow's going to answer to me when I take office.'

'Take office?' McGruder's eyes were wary.

'As Intendant Proper.'

'Ah, yes, I see. You refer to your terms from the admiral,' he said with a complacent look. His being privy to all the detail of Tompion's conditions rattled me. 'Well, captain, my terms –' he stressed the possessive '– are these. There is to be no more delay, for whatever reason. I order you to get the bark under way forthwith.'

I was outraged. 'Dammit, you have no power to give such an order. I captain this vessel.'

'Of course you do. However, you must think of my reports.'

'Dam' your reports,' I muttered, but somehow I felt control slipping away.

He wore a smug air. 'Why do you look so melancholick, Loftus? You know my reports determine whether or not you get your reward.'

'You have no powers over the ship's day-to-day affairs,' I retorted, but it had struck me with force just how far his remit might affect my actions.

113

'Perhaps, but I could declare that the mission was not properly carried out.'

He knew damm'd well I could not afford to risk that. It would allow Tompion to withhold the Intendancy. For the first time, I understood the sway McGruder had over me and the ship and the voyage, and I cursed myself for not having seen it. I stood up without a word, too angry to speak. A minute after, I was on deck ordering the sailing master to haul sheets and get the bark moving. The ship gathered way and we headed north into the blind wall of fog. All I could hope was that Grace would wait.

A day later, by which time we had gained the open reaches of the Labrador Sea, the fog cleared as if blown away by an unseen hand. But my black mood did not lift so readily. I feared the zealous young Scotsman's interference so early was an augury of things to come.

I realised he had me between finger and thumb, like a piece of sailcloth awaiting the needle's prick.

With a small gale on her larboard beam, the *Pursuant* kept the coast below the western horizon, all the while stemming the great icy current that flowed ceaselessly from the Polar icefields. The air was like a cold, damp cloth around my head, and it did nothing for my foul mood.

At dawn, high on the exposed quarter-deck, well muffled in a fur-lined oiled skin jacket, I wrestled with the cross-staff, intent on getting a latitude from the Pole-star if it fleetingly appeared between the clouds. My task was becoming ever more difficult. The further northwards a bark progresses, the more directly she comes under Polaris and the harder to read the angle. In the Tropicks, angling on the overhead sun is equally tricky but where the Equatorial Navigator is blessed with constant sunshine to warm his bones, here my freezing fingers fumbled and tripped as the cross-staff's transom slid jerkily across the sticking scale.

By the time I had got a satisfactory sighting and bent to record the numbers, the *Pursuant* was progressing into the reluctant gloom of first light, plunging gamely across the white-topped swells of the unending Labrador Sea under a vast, pallid sky. Leaving the watchmen huddled on deck sheltering from the cold, banging their hands and slapping their legs, I went below to work the sight.

'It seems to be getting rougher,' McGruder remarked, sounding queasy.

He had been unwell since the moment we cleared the Esperantia bluffs and met the first sea. After being on passage for a week, he was finding even the captain's dayroom a stuffy and dank place to be.

'You're well advised to leave that drink alone,' I told him, nodding at the brandy tumbler in his hand as he lolled by the chart table, 'and go on deck for the air. Dress warm, though.'

There were shouts and commands ringing out above, and the scrabble of footsteps on the quarterdeck as men were sent to the mizenmast ratlines. The wind was getting up and Gaspar Rittel was shortening down.

'Are we in for a storm?' he asked.

'Not yet, not with a plain grey sky and a steady westerly. But this weather might change any day. If a southerly gale blows against the Labrador current flowing from the north, it rips up the sea into awful heaps.'

I was determined to maintain common civility, despite everything. By contrast, McGruder showed no such sensibility, forever expressing thoughts better left unspoken.

With a mock-regretful air, he said, 'And not even the company of women to console me in my sickness. Shall we encounter any native females where we are going?'

'My advice to you, Landsman, is to keep away from the women, if we encounter any. The menfolk dislike it.'

'It is not my habit to let them argue,' he said.

I shot him a look. 'The men or the women?'

He laughed. 'These heathen wenches are there for the taking, are they not? God does not count them as having a soul, so why should a man credit them with bodily privacy?'

He toyed with a pair of dividers on the table, fingering them lasciviously, his eyes challenging me. There was no reward in arguing. I held out my hand for the brass tool.

'If you please, that is a valuable instrument.'

He yawned hugely, and I noticed a sheen of sweat across his brow. Both yawn and sweat were sure signs of his sea-sickness, though even that thought failed to comfort me. He tossed the dividers back.

I took out my almanacks, settling down to calculate the latitude and step off our course. Though the Navy had handed me the few chartings that existed, along with the *Beaver*'s logs, this was still a voyage of the most difficult Navigation.

To my annoyance, McGruder craned over, seemingly unaware he blocked the glow of the candle-lantern swinging from its hook on the deckbeam above.

'A poor light for close work,' he remarked. 'Such numbers and angles as I never saw at my schooling. There was little of Arithmeticks, and nothing of the Navigation.'

I leaned back and studied him. His interest seemed genuine.

'Do you know about this land, the seas where we are going?' I asked, and he shook his head.

Welcoming a safe topic and believing frankness about the voyage must help, I pointed to the chart, indicating the interminable, barren shores of the Labrador Coast. It was cut with a thousand uncharted inlets where only natives dwelt, living on fish and caribou.

'Labrador extends as far as Resolution Point,' I said. 'After that, this sea between the Kanada mainland and Greenland –' my finger swept north-west, covering a hundred leagues '– is the Hudson Strait, passing the unknown region marked Terra Incognita.' I traced north to the latitudes of Ungava Bay. 'Only Esquimaux people are said to survive here, and their diet is little more than seal meat. Finally the land terminates at the Great Northern Cape, latitude sixty three degrees, where the ice stays longest and reappears soonest. That is our gateway in and out.'

Then I drew my fingertip south from the cape into

the wide reaches of Hudson's Bay, crossing nearly another thousand sea-miles till it came to rest near a reach of water extending like a down-pointing thumb deep into the Kanada heartlands.

'And this is James Bay,' I said, 'with Fort Rupert here.'

He stretched across and examined it minutely while I listened to the sounds of a loose and ragged chanty from far aloft where the jack-tars were aloft reefing the maincourse – and by the sounds of it, taking their time. I resolved to get them working sharper.

When McGruder straightened, I said, 'Well, as for Navigation, we are still in the easy part. The compass is reliable so far, but further north the needle varies unpredictably. After Resolution Point, the waters are unknown to me. The sea-charts are very poor and even the *Beaver*'s old logs of little use. The higher the latitude, the more problematickal the Navigation and the more treacherous the weather. Then there's the ice. Not just sea ice and brash and broken floes, but the pack ice that gets into a cove and heaps up –'

The Scotsman held up his hands in a show of mock defeat. 'Captain, are you bent on frightening your landlubber out of his sea-boots?' His tone became more serious. 'Tell me, with all the difficulties, how do you rate our chances?'

I leant back from the sight workings and looked at him. Was this the first crack in McGruder's self-assurance?

'The risks of this voyage are high,' I said. 'The Admiralty must be paying you at first rate.'

'Pay is not the thing. My reward is to see the Sovereign and her beliefs carried forward. To build a great nation. I am a Scotsman first, but a Unionist to the same degree. You know about the Parliament of last year?'

I nodded. News drifted across the Atlantick in slow, partial stages, and the doings of Queen Anne's Ministers at Westminster seemed remote from daily life at Esperantia or Labrador. But I knew the union of Parliaments between England and Scotland had brought with it a conjoined coinage, free trade and the combined flag. All that remained separate were the Law and the Church – the two established Protestant Churches, that is.

'Some Scots bemoan the loss of politickal independence,' he said, 'but the Act of Union forges something strong and good. A Christian reformed Great Britain, an undivided nation under a right-minded Queen. A bulwark against the heretickal warmongerers of Catholick Europe.'

The bulwark was less a religious than a military one, I thought. Where the two Navies and militias had readily combined under the Union flag, the bishops had not.

Footsteps stumped across the deck-boards overhead. There was some commotion on deck but Rittel was capable of seeing to the work. I wanted to put the landsman straight.

'We are here to find a lost ship,' I said, 'not build a Protestant empire.'

'Do not dismiss the Catholick threat. The French are said to be on the point of despatching a Grand Fleet to the Gulf.'

I sat up. That would explain Admiral Tompion's arrival at Newfoundland.

'The enemy have broken an accord,' McGruder continued, 'the Chessapeak Bay Accord by which Naval fleets are kept to the south. The Sovereign must deal with the Catholick King's perfidy by force of arms. Teach the faithless Bourbons a lesson.' Suddenly the eyes were alight with fervour. 'They have a grand design, you know. By holding the Gulf of Saint Laurent and the great lakes to the far west, they intend to gain control of the north-south river system from Mitchiggan to Louisiana. You have heard of the Missippissi River, I presume.'

'It is said as "Mississippi",' I corrected.

'No matter what it's called! It's a great river that drains to the Louisiana Delta Territories. It gives the French a water route all the way from the Saint Laurent to the Gulf of Mexico. By connecting the Kanada lands with the Caribbee Sea, France shall control and blockade Queen Anne's farming colonies on the eastern coast. Her Majesty's colonies, prosperous to a degree unlike his own ventures, are dearly coveted by the swinish Catholick King.'

Admiral Tompion had spoken about a French grand design, and it seemed McGruder believed in it too. But I recognised that only sea power determined such overweening strategies.

'If what you say is so,' I suggested, 'then why is Tompion's main fleet staying at Saint John's? And why is he so concerned with Esperantia? He should be out in the Breton Channel, intercepting the enemy, forestalling their grand design.'

McGruder hesitated. Again I listened with some

concern to Gaspar's shouts ringing out far above. With this laggardly crew, it was taking far too long to shorten down to smaller canvas. What if we were hit by a sudden squall at night?

The Scotsman was glaring at me.

'You seem to have an answer for everything,' I said, 'save that one. But I can tell you why Tompion hides himself and his ships. The war allows Sir Geoffrey to enrich himself with easy prizes – little frigates, lone traders, fishing shallops and the like. And he'll be taking a share of the Governor's imposts too, diverting them from the Sovereign's Treasury. That's why he's unwilling to come out and fight.'

The Scotsman's face was like stone. 'As one well versed in war affairs, I disapprove of such talk. And the admiral is my cousin.'

It stopped me dead. He looked triumphant, and no wonder. He could afford to be a cocky cove with such connections.

'Well then, you should persuade your cousin to act,' I said at length. 'A decisive victory at sea would give England control of the Gulf.'

'Great Britain,' he corrected. 'Diplomacy is the key, Loftus. Take Hudson's Bay, for instance. By proving the sea route viable, we strengthen our nation's bargaining hand.'

'As you are versed in the niceties of diplomacy,' I said, 'you must know such claims are empty. It would be as well to suspend the annual fur bark altogether, in return for something of more immediate value.'

I was thinking of Plaisance and the failing wet-cure fishery. I had always suspected the French might cede it for a very little in return. A man like Alphonse D'Amati, the former Petit Seigneur, would have seen the sense of that, but he was gone elsewhere.

'Suspend the fur bark? Never!' The landsman thumped the table. 'We shall never relinquish our claims to the High Kanada Lands. They must be upheld come what may. That is our mission.'

The shouts from above magnified until I could no longer ignore them. They sounded rebellious in nature.

'Our mission,' I retorted, half rising, 'is to conduct a search for the *Beaver*. And we can only do that with a stout bark and a damm'd good crew. Thanks to your cousin, it looks like we've shipped fellows aboard who'd sooner cower by the galley hearth than go aloft in a breeze.'

Footsteps clattered down the companionway and the sailing master stuck his head through the door.

'Captain, will you come on deck?'

I was already out of my seat.

'Is there trouble?' inquired McGruder, as if he had heard nothing of the ruckus above our heads.

He might be innocent of ship's ways, but everything this well-connected young religious bigot said seemed designed to incense me. My temper snapped.

'Of course there's trouble, dammit. Admiral Tompion's selection of seamen was wilful – almost as if he wanted us to fail. Why don't you put that in your blasted reports?'

I left the dayroom and stamped up the steps to the quarter.

All twenty four seamen were assembled in the ship's

waist, restlessly shuffling their feet and mooning about like cattle by the slaughterhouse gate.

'Well, Mister Rittel,' I said, raising my voice to carry across the break, 'what's the matter here?'

'They don't like the voyage, sir,' said the sailing master.

The entire company was gathered, barring Billy Jenks who stayed at the galley-furnace, doubtless scolding his sea-boy for idling. My faithful second mates Nathaniel Gunn and Luke Tatchell stood below the break, their faces thoughtful. We nodded to each other, then I fixed the crew with my eye.

'Does any of you speak for his fellows?' When one man came out and stood in front, I demanded, 'Name yourself.'

'Michael Higham, seaman ordinary. Pressed aboard the *Ascendant*.'

'Is that your grievance, that you were pressed?'

'No sir. We was better off on the warship in a way. It wasn't so damm'd cold, for one thing.'

Another seaman piped up, 'Aye, and there was more fellows to do the work!'

He was right. Navy ships carried many extra men for gunnery than were needed merely to sail the vessel.

'And who are you?' I demanded.

'Benjie Tallis, sir.'

The man Higham chipped in again. 'There's not one of us here, sir, knows where we's supposed to be going.'

I gave a mocking smile. 'And aboard the *Ascendant*, no doubt, the captain came tweendecks every day to give you the bark's precise course and position? And you were well-fed on mutton and pork? Kept dry and cosy, and addressed politely by the mates and officers?'

One or two chuckled, but Higham scowled. 'We knowed where we stood, captain, is all.'

There was a rumble of assent from the rest.

'Very well, you shall hear where you stand now,' I said. 'You are seamen of the *Pursuant*. We are going far away from any theatre of war, and shall see no action. You are more likely to return whole in your limbs than from any Naval voyage.'

These comforting notions did not send them into unrestrained joy.

'You get your vittles and your Arctic slops paid for – that's fur hats and mitts as well as a jacket. When the air freezes and your breath is ice, there's a tot of rum twice a day, morn and eve. You get all that,' I said, 'along with your Navy pay, a shilling a day and no deductions.'

Michael Higham was about to speak out again.

I cut him off. 'And then there's the prize money.'

Higham shut his mouth. There were murmurs as if to say, you've got our ear, captain. Their attention was fixed on me like a sailor's eye on the shore beacon of his home port and they listened in silence as I told them about our search for the missing bark, and the importance to our Sovereign Queen of finding her, and the weight the Navy gave to the *Pursuant*'s mission.

'If we find the *Beaver*, there's to be a gold sovereign per seaman. And if we bring her safe home, another sovereign – all payable at Esperantia.'

It was the sort of prize division jack-tars got if the Navy took an enemy gold-ship or a three-decked man o' war.

'What do you say?' I demanded.

They chorused their ayes of approval, and Michael Higham led the cheering.

'Very well, but now you'll pull your weight like seamen,' I told them. 'Jump to it when the mates call up the watch. No man sleeps on lookout duty. No one refuses to go aloft, no matter what. Any man who falters shall be sent ashore penniless, with not a coin in his pocket.'

As it sank in, silence reigned. But their assent – if such it was – was all too muted. Either we knocked this raggle-taggle of laggards and sloths into a tight, working band of seamen or the voyage was bound for failure.

'You are private men serving on a private ship,' I reminded them. 'That means if a man imperils his crewmates or the vessel, it goes to the vote of his mates.'

That was a more terrible prospect than even the Navy's punishment roll so cherished by captains such as Petherwick. I stood at the break, my hands resting on the rail. The men looked away, casting nervously out to sea, or down at their feet. Some members of the throng turned to their spokesman, seeking a lead.

'Well, Mister Higham?' I demanded. 'You desired to know where you stood. Do you know it now?'

'Aye aye, sir,' he said with a contrite air.

I turned to his mate. 'And you, Mister Tallis, do you say it's fair?'

'Aye aye, captain,' said Benjie Tallis, 'it's fair.'

Seeing their chiefs assenting, the other seamen nodded in agreement. I pressed home the point.

'Let me hear it from every last man of you. Do you fall in with the *Pursuant*'s ways?'

'Aye, captain!' they sang as one.

'Very well then,' I said, 'jump to it like proper jack-tars.'

When the second mates told them off to work, they leapt away at once, and Gaspar Rittel shot me a relieved look. I turned for the companion only to find Finlay McGruder standing right behind. He must have been there all along.

'Captain Loftus, may I be permitted to speak with candour?'

'About what?' I snapped. His close interest in ship's affairs was more than unwelcome.

'Aboard the *Ascendant*,' he said, 'I observed these ruffians' rebellious natures. Captain Petherwick exerted an iron discipline upon them. Rabble rousers were curbed with a firm stroke and I saw several of these very fellows laid on the grate and whipped. You are too lax with them.'

'Shipboard discipline is strictly my concern.'

He pursed his lips. 'Very well, but from where arises the prize money you spoke of? Not from the Navy's coffers. Admiral Tompion did not sanction it.'

He seemed to know everything, dammit.

'My most recent Labrador venture, Landsman, promises to be highly profitable.'

'You are funding it yourself? Why, you shall be beggared.'

126

Hardly, I thought. Handsome profits from my furskins and the Gillycuddy salvage awaited me back at Esperantia. And the Intendancy, with its tax-raising powers, would far outweigh my investment here.

'Wait and see,' I told him. 'I shall turn this job lot into a proper crew before I'm done.'

'Indeed? That would confound Factor van Schreik. He seemed quite amused that they were such a mean looking lot of good-for-nothing coves.'

I frowned. When had van Schreik seen these seamen?

McGruder caught my puzzlement. 'The Factor stepped aboard as the packet was leaving harbour.'

'How so? The Navy let the sloop go on at once.'

'Indeed, but he remained on the warship. Later, he was below-decks, as you say, even while you were interviewed by Admiral Tompion. I think he did not show himself because he was afraid of confronting you.'

Suddenly I was appalled. 'Did Grace stay aboard the flagship?'

'Grace? Ah, the Widow Trepanney, you mean. No, she did not. She went on to Saint John's.' He licked his lips, cracked now in the cold, dry air. 'But I don't wonder the Factor kept out of your sight.'

'Aye, but why did he remain aboard the *Ascendant*?'

'To discuss with the admiral various matters concerning Esperantia. Including the salvage arrangements.' He studied me calmly. 'The Gillycuddy bark, as I believe it is termed. He declared it a hazard to shipping and recommended it be towed to sea and scuttled.'

'Why, dam' and blast, that was the money for –'

I stopped. The landsman was studying me with unsettling intensity.

'For paying the crew their prize reward?' he enquired.

'No,' I said quickly, 'no, it was money towards my second bark.'

'I see. Then you must be rather disappointed. And I suppose the furskins difficulty hardly helps.'

'What about the furskins?' I said, too sharply.

'Ah, more bad news, I'm afraid. The Factor predicted that following the Navy's arrival in Newfoundland, the market would be severely depressed. Down by as much as fifty per cent below last year's prices, he forecast. This was by his own account at the admiral's dinner table.'

'Ease topsail sheets!' came Gaspar's cry.

Relieved at the interruption, I stumped off to the break on the pretext of overseeing the work. Dammit, this Factor seemed bent on ruining me. Not only was he scuttling or stealing the salvage bark, but he was patently bent on cheating me over the skins. I could not drive from my head a picture of him consorting with the admiral. He must have laughed behind his hand at the loose assortment of rogues and dodgers assigned me.

The more I thought about it, the more I reckoned Josiah van Schreik had manoeuvred me out of the way. He had got me sent on this doomed mission in the certainty of its failure. He banked on us never finding the *Beaver*. He hoped the voyage would prove not just a failure but a disaster. How had I missed it? The plain truth was that he calculated on the *Pursuant* never being seen again. And that would mean Matthew Loftus out of the way for good.

A wave broke astern of the *Pursuant*'s poop and roared past, a froth of white water foaming by. Looking up, I caught sight of Finlay McGruder, gripping the rail like a man in a tumbrel. Yet as ever, he seemed to know what I was thinking.

Green-faced and queasy, he still managed a small, knowing smirk.

7

Dangerous Latitude

Four days later, the *Pursuant* was further north than ever before, in waters remote and perilous to a degree.

The charts were sketchy and unreliable. The compass could no longer be trusted. Navigation by celestial sights was ever more difficult in the high latitudes, and more often than not the sun and stars were hidden behind a pall of blank cloud. There was ice all about, half-sunken and invisible, like iron, hard enough to stove in a frailer vessel's planking – and these growlers knocked constantly at the *Pursuant*'s waterline. Legend or myth said the fragments broke from rivers of frozen snow compacted into ice over centuries, and it was unsettling – other worldly – to contemplate that they might be as ancient as the Earth itself.

In the face of these elemental forces, my worries over the Factor and the Landsman were pushed aside by the business of getting the ship through the passage at sixty three degrees north and into Hudson's Bay. We were attempting to weather Cape Chudleigh before crossing the open bight of Ungava Bay and rounding the Great Northern Cape, marking the journey's highest point of latitude. With our course angling but the wind steady from west-southwest, the bark came ever more close-hauled, her movements grew livelier and spray flew from the bows. Though to a seaman the water was hardly churned up, the motion was enough to drive Finlay McGruder back to his bunk.

The *Pursuant* ploughed north northwest under topsails and two jibsails, heeling as she smashed over the close-ranked waves. Every so often she lifted her stern to a longer ocean swell running under the keel, barrelling up from the southeast at a rate of knots and setting up a nasty cross sea that had the bark yawing about like a broken-wheeled cart. Overhead, the topmasts groaned at the trestletrees, where they were joined to the lower masts, adding the nagging worry of gear failure to my other concerns.

Any sea voyage held its terrors, but we were entering waters barely travelled by barks before us – except perhaps the *Beaver*. We all knew few seamen had chanced the passage, and many of those had never returned.

Ahead and to the north lay a vast shore marked on the sea-charts only as Terra Incognita, but whether island or continent no man knew. Somewhere to the northwest lurked the sheer black mountains of High Labrador. Between these land masses the sea narrowed into the Hudson Strait, where we lacked what was most necessary in case of a blow – sea room. With my dead reckoning likely in error by many leagues, the *Pursuant* was forced to close Cape Chudleigh in order to sight it, for without a fix of some sort we were sailing blind.

'Ease topyard braces!' cried Gaspar, lurching across to me. 'Captain, drop jibs and reef topsails?'

'Aye aye, sailing master,' I said. 'Snug her down good and tight. See the hatches battened and all loose gear stowed good and proper.'

Soon after midday the wind strengthened. The sky came down to meet the sea, the wave-tops ripped into white and frothing spume and the gale brought moans and trembles from the rigging. I reduced the lookout spells, swapping the half-frozen fore-topman about every half a glass to keep him alert not just for land but for growlers. Swirling past the *Pursuant*'s heaving hindquarters were chunks of blue-grey ice the size of a pram dinghy – broken, half-melted floes or pieces knocked from larger bergs. She shrugged these aside easily enough, though for seamen in the foc'sle the ice battering the foreparts of the hull was a constant, unwelcome tattoo destroying sleep.

The second mates, who slept in foc'sle hammocks alongside the tars, reported mutterings about flying in the face of God's will by venturing so far north. It was against Nature, claimed the jack-tars, and all too likely to goad the Fates into a fearsome retribution. Only the prospect of those two gold sovereigns a-piece steeled their resolve to go on.

Since my pay offer, the second mates had kept the jack-tars hard at work. Till now, when the bark's awkward motion prevented it, they had been busy reaming up the standing rigging, holystoning the deck-boards and scrubbing the main bower cable. All in all, a distinct air of brisk, well-disciplined determination had broken out. Though the cost looked like beggaring me, the prize money had transformed their willingness to work.

With the swells heaping up to the height of a

townhouse, the bark rolled and yawed but she rode the seas contentedly enough. Under topsails alone she handled herself well, only once or twice getting too much speed surfing down the biggest waves' backs. As with the lookouts, I halved the steersman's tricks too, but of the *Ascendant*'s so-called time-served helmsmen only one or two could keep a true course. As the weather hardened I heartily wished for the reliable *Pursuant* fellows left behind at Esperantia.

The lee shore of Cape Chudleigh weighed on my mind. The *Beaver*'s pilot chart showed a rough hand drawing of an unmistakeable promontory in the shape of an animal's head, not one known to mankind but rather a nightmarish monster from an antediluvian world. Yet all the seas and land hereabouts were unknown to me, and the cape would at least give us a new departure from which to Navigate.

The sailing master came over. 'Heave to for the night, captain, if we don't sight the land before dark?'

'Too chancy – I don't want us put down on the cape.' With nightfall at half past seven and no dawn till gone six, she might drift ten leagues in that time. 'Mister Rittel, let's keep those leery jack-tars ready for anything.'

A figure emerged from the hatchway, bundled head to toe in oiled-skins. Hunched up against the sharp wind, he staggered towards the weather rail.

'Other way, Landsman!' I shouted and dragged McGruder protesting to the lee side. He clung on and stared at the churning, surging sea eight or ten feet below. Like a cathedral gargoyle, mouth widening into a ghastly yawn, he released a stream of juices and pottages from the bottom of his guts.

'Never spew to windward,' I said, banging his back, unable to suppress a half smile.

Wiping his eyes with a dirty rag, he muttered, 'It was not as bad as this coming over from England. Where are we?'

'Coming up under Cape Chudleigh, five or six leagues ahead by my reckoning. We must clear past and run on into the Hudson Strait. This wind should swing from southwest to south and the rapidity of the veer foretells the strength of the blow to come.' To a landlubber like him, it could not have meant a damm'd thing, so I added, 'But you can be sure it'll be a hard one.'

'What about the crew?' he gasped. 'Are you more content?'

'Aye, they're in better trim.'

They were more willing, but I questioned their hearts. Not that I would let McGruder know that.

The *Pursuant* lifted high to a swell roaring in under her stern. It smashed against the rudderblade and the steersman struggled against the wheel's kick. The rollers had grown hugely, charging down upon the bark. Though it was only early afternoon, low on the southern horizon the sky was black as night.

The landsman, still queasy, said, 'Can she take a storm?'

'The *Pursuant*? No doubt of it. Stay below in your bunk with the lee cloths up to keep you in. I'll send Cookmaster Jenks down with a hand of bread and a slice or two of salted pork to see you through.

Drink plenty,' I called to his receding back, 'but only sweetwater.'

Not many minutes later, to my great surprise, he reappeared on deck, looking greener than ever.

'I told you once,' I called, 'it's dangerous up here.'

He brushed a hand across his mouth. 'What concerns me is not on deck, but below.'

'What in blazes are you talking about?'

'The matter, captain, of your stowaway.'

Grimly, I followed the Scotsman down the swaying companionway steps and into my dayroom. Standing straight-backed by the table, one gnarled hand on its polished surface to steady himself against the ship's sway and surge, was Eli Savary.

'Where the Devil were you hiding, old man?' I said, shaking my head. Lord, his stowing away was the last thing I needed.

He involuntarily barked out a hacking cough. The poor old wight was as weak as a sea-boy, thin and trembling after days in hiding.

'Beg pardon, captain. I got myself in behind the quarters. Between the panels and the knees, where that ham-fisted Wapping-rat Sedgewick pulled them away.'

After Gaspar's drunken rantings about fuseways, I had told Carpenter Sedgewick to start the panelling free of its fixings and block any channels or gaps running down to the powder store. The work had barely begun when the *Pursuant* got her new mission and I put him to more pressing tasks.

Eli jerked his head at McGruder. 'I was hard by his cabin, so he was bound to hear me.' He cackled. 'Or smell me. There's no heads in there.'

Fighting to suppress a grin, I said, 'Sit down, my old friend.'

He half fell into the seat and I reached for the brandy bottle nestling as usual in the fiddle-hole, part of the Scotsman's plentiful store. But even French cognac did nothing to allay Finlay McGruder's mood.

'This man is a stowaway,' he said, resolutely stern-faced.

'The old fellow's done no harm.' I was not about to give McGruder any satisfaction. 'In fact, he's a good hand aboard, better than any *Ascendant* skiver half his age. Soon as he's fit, I shall put him to work.'

'That's the idea, captain,' wheezed Eli, slurping back the spirit. 'And as ever, I shall do my best.' He made a sour face. 'By the Saints' relicks, what muck is this?'

McGruder was incensed. 'An admirable and spirited defence of your man, Loftus, but futile. This goes in my report. You shall both face charges.'

'Dammit, I had no idea he was aboard,' I said angrily. 'Anyhow, he's here, so what's the difference?' I managed a note of sarcasm. 'You're not going to sign an order for the bark to turn home, are you?'

He glared defiantly and held his peace.

Eli gave out another chesty bark. 'All right if I go and find myself quarters in the foc'sle, captain?'

'I shan't hear of it,' I said. 'Take the cabin next to the landsman's for a day or so.'

'Can't say I love it down here, captain,' he said. 'I prefer to be on deck for the air.'

I filled a pewter and insisted he take another shot to settle his pains. An awkward silence prevailed as he supped, glowering all the while at McGruder. When the drink had calmed his chest, I asked after his bones. Many was the time we had been forewarned of a blow by the throbbing of a bent Savary thumb or a work-hardened knee joint.

'The jaw's playing me up, captain.' He rubbed his bristly chin, by the old musketball wound from our days together aboard the fast Dutch flyer, the private ship *Cornelius*. 'Giving me an ache like a jack-tar's belly after a plate of bad mussels.'

When at last I sent the old fellow off to his cabin, the Scotsman refilled his pewter with brandy.

'You should have disciplined the man, Loftus.'

'Dam' your eyes, McGruder,' I said, hardly listening.

He and his reports could go to Hell. It was Eli's jawbone, the surest weather-cock of all, that worried me now. Its aching foretold the worst kind of storm. Going back on deck, I stood on the quarter breathing the cold sea air and surveying the seascape. The only certainty that bleak afternoon was the coming weather.

The high gale was developing into a full-blown Labrador screamer.

No matter how weather-hardened a sailor may be, the blind ruthless passion of the sea beneath a tormenting wind undermines his every resolve. As the timber frames protest and the mast-steps creak, he begins to wonder. He ponders the tree the shipwright chose for a keelson. Was it straight and true, and without a lurking flaw? He frets about the strength of the stempost, and the carpenter's scarf-joints at the deadwood. Misgivings about the knees and frames in way of the shrouds and channels chip at his confidence in the rig's integrity. Off watch, nagging doubts about the plank fixings or the scantlings of the ribs can start him wide-eyed from a sweaty bunk. A seaman might have gone through many a storm, and living gales too, yet still he wonders if the weather gods have saved just for him, just for now, the hardest tempest of all, the worst the world has ever seen – a tempest into which he is plunged, helpless as an insect in a maelstrom.

The *Pursuant* could take her punishment. She was as strong and safe as any bark ever built. Still, no matter how often I reassured myself, persistent doubts refused to quieten. This was too far north. The wind up here was denser and colder than any other. It carried more weight in it, pressed harder on canvas and spars, tore more fiercely at blocks and clews, ripped away a man's frozen hands as he scrabbled for grip on an icy yard.

Above all, what no ship can stand is the land – or rather being thrown upon it, hurled willy-nilly ashore. Where was Cape Chudleigh? The sea-scape under driven clouds was visible for at best half a league to leeward, far less when vicious squalls enveloped the bark. I cast my eye again and again off to the west and north, searching for a sight of the land. The *Beaver*'s log described the cape as a clear landmark – a massive, blackstone cliff rising sheer from sea-level for seven hundred feet or more. Yet from the foretop and maintop lookouts, no shout came. Should the bark hold her present course? Turn north by east to seek clear water? Heave to and wait?

As ever, my early apprehension became mingled with fascination at the sea's sheer magnificence when roused into tempestuousness. It was as if the bark had been picked up in a giant's hand, to be played with like a toy. From astern, the onrushing waves, their smooth faces fifteen or twenty feet high, reared up and raced down to catch the little *Pursuant*, swinging her quarters this way and that, taking each roller with an insouciant wiggle. The noise was infernal, a roar like a landslide as the top of a wave broke and a hundred tuns of sea raced towards us, a curtain of white foam running on the face, barrelling down to explode against the quarters. The steersman spun the wheel when her stern rose and yawed one way, centred it as the wave lifted higher, tried to keep her heading straight as she balanced on the crest, then twisted it back and forth as it passed and she sank into the trough behind with a welter of foam rising about her topsides. As she wallowed, all fell silent and the seamen stared fixedly forward, knowing better than to glance astern and see the next great comber bearing down.

Every eye remained ahead, all but one. One man had to anticipate the bark's heave and sway and yaw, to order the wheel spun at the first hint of movement before she drove sideways, always to be half the tick of a pendulum clock ahead of her broaching. So it was that in the pause of every trough, I twisted round and looked, judging the height, the forward speed, the steepness and the angle of each oncoming wave.

'Larboard a full turn,' I would cry, or 'Hard to steerboard and hold her!' or 'Centre up there!'

The spokes blurred and we were through. Still the greybeards came on, the next rising astern before the last one passed, coming on one after the other without relent.

After two hours, Gaspar came aft to call the wheel while I dipped below to reckon the course. With a clear sky the Navigation might give me a latitude, but for two cloud-covered days we had seen neither star nor sun. The compass needle grew ever more untrustworthy, and my deduced reckoning was stretched beyond the limits of error. The Longitude was a guess, and my sea-charts were unproven. Before nightfall, the *Pursuant* must turn on a northeasterly heading for open waters. For now, though, I gritted my teeth and held the course. I had to try and close the cape.

An hour later came a shout from far aloft, faintly reaching me in the dayroom. I flung on my oiled-skin jacket and regained the deck to find the long northern twilight already begun.

'Land sighted, captain,' called Gaspar. 'Lookouts say fine on the larboard bow, a league off.'

'How does it lie?' I said.

'High and dark, sheer cliffs and steep at the foot,' came the reply. 'Lookouts say it resembles a beast's head.'

A welter of relief flooded through me. The description tallied well enough with that in the *Beaver*'s logs.

140

'Wear ship,' I ordered. 'Bring her on to steerboard tack and steer north by east. We shall run off for sea room.'

Rittel mustered the watch and half went to stand by the sheets, half at the braces.

'Ready to go about,' I told the helm.

Facing astern, I waited to pick the right moment. A wave passed under the keel and receded with great rapidity, leaving a smooth patch. Further behind was a set of two or three swells, tossing violently on the broken seas as they bore on towards our bark, but of lesser size and weight than the run of the wavetrain.

'Come six points to steerboard,' I ordered, 'a point at a time.'

The *Pursuant* responded by swinging her head round. The mates' commands rose from the waist as the jack-tars, muffled head to toe in fur jackets and beaver pelt hats and boots, went about freeing off the leeward sheets, bringing the yards round and hardening in on the weather sheets. Some of the fellows seemed half-dazed, slowed down by the bitter cold, slipping on the icy deck-boards, caught out by rimes of ice forming on decks and handholds. When they ran to the wrong belays, the sailing master with ripe curses exhorted them to find the right one.

Yet all was not as bad as it might be. Under my eye or Rittel's, the steersman kept a steady hand on the wheel. The second mates, Gunn and Tatchell, whose strength matched their sailing experience, encouraged the more reluctant jack-tars by example and the *Ascendant*'s men had begun to look up to them. Once or twice, I spotted Michael Higham being first to reach the belays, his friend Benjie Tallis falling in just as eagerly. Then I spotted a bent figure stumbling across the waist, and felt a catch in my throat. Eli Savary was there too, showing his fellows which was a braceline and which a sheet, which the fore and which the main, or simply giving a hand to a youngster.

Between us – the quarter-deck, the mates, the tars – we were keeping the ship safe. For the first time since leaving Esperantia, the *Pursuant* had a crew combined in their work.

As time wore on towards nightfall, the swells rose higher and began to topple. The sea's surface whitened into a field of driven foam. The leaden grey skies turned black and menacing, while spats of freezing droplets peppered down in the gusts. Our field of visibility diminished, first with a misty curtain drawing in, then with squally rain in horizontal blasts hard enough to tear the wave-tops to shreds and fill the air with salt spray. When day ended, the night and the weather enfolded us, cutting us off from the world save for the little disc on which we rode, a whirling circle barely two hundred paces across. Eli's forecast blow was well and truly upon us.

Hours later, matters were worse by a degree. The bark was difficult to steer under topsails, wilful at the helm, slow to answer at the critical moment of broaching. The wind had risen to a shrieking tempest. Spray torn from the surface went hurtling downwind amidst a banshee wail of noise. We progressed through a crazily twisting and diving universe in which all that could be seen were the dark shapes of heaping seas, streaked with white, shouldering past like enraged beasts, careless of how they ill-treated the ship.

I called the sailing master over and shouted above the howl.

'She wants slowing again, Mister Rittel. Reef top-sails, main and fore. Gather the best of this laggardly bunch and send six aloft to the mainyard.'

'Ya, captain.' He was about to say more, but hesitated.

'Aye, let's see how they go,' I said. 'Give the order.'

Gaspar's premonition was right. One or two men stood in the waist holding the rail against each violent lurch, shaking their heads. They had reason enough to fear going aloft now. When Rittel came back to report, I glimpsed a figure launching himself towards the ratlines. Stiff and bent, he had difficulty making it to the top of the deck rail, let alone up the shrouds.

'Stop him!' I bellowed, but no one heard above the tempest. I threw myself down the steps and reached the ratlines in two or three paces. Flinging myself up onto the rail, I grasped his legs.

'Come down, Eli,' I shouted.

At first, he held on, then his strength gave out and we tumbled back on deck together.

'Those buggers wouldn't go up,' he mumbled.

Eli had always said he'd rather die at sea than ashore, but if I could help it the time would not be yet. He was exhausted, so I helped him to the break and ordered him taken below, giving him an encouraging bang on the shoulder. It wrenched my heart to think of the man's undying courage, and in such a storm.

Then I called the tars together. I reminded them of the penalty for disobedience and asked again for a reefing party. This time, shamed by Eli's example, their ayes rang out readily. I chose four fellows, amongst them the formerly outspoken Michael Higham and Benjie Tallis. Two went aloft under Nat Gunn, the big, hard-muscled second mate of steerboard watch, and the other pair went up with Luke Tatchell, three men each side.

They departed to the shrouds and began their climb up the foremast. Sailors stood ready to tend the lines on deck. With the steersman keeping the bark steady, Mister Rittel stayed at the taffrail calling the waves while I stood by the break to oversee the reefing.

The tars moved slowly and deliberately up the ratlines, with the unmistakeable figure of Nathaniel – only nineteen but built like a sternpost – urging them up as he climbed in the van. At length, three huddled figures shuffled out along each yardarm, larboard and steerboard, feeling for the footropes as they went. Half of me yearned to be with them, as so many times in a gale before, for the sheer exhilaration of being aloft with the bark surging and swaying fifty or sixty or seventy feet below. Up there, as the masts yawed and arced across the sky, and your hands clawed at the heavy wet canvas with freezing fingers struggling to tie off the reefing pennants while the wind whipped at the lines, a bight of loosened canvas, caught by a gust, could render a man insensible or knock him clean off the yard.

Soon, they had tamed the fore-topsail with a reef, halving the spread of canvas, and at once the bark rode easier. As the party descended from the foremast and struggled along the heaving deck to mount the mainmast and continue reefing there, a figure emerged from the stern hatchway.

'Get below!' I shouted. 'It's not safe on deck.'

Finlay McGruder did not seem to hear.

Just then Rittel shouted at the helmsman, waving his arms and pointing astern. Looming from the night and bearing down upon us at speed I saw an immense wall of water, a monumental greybeard towering above the mizentop. All at once, our stout bark seemed no more substantial than a sprat caught in the fall of a weir. There was barely time to raise a cry of warning.

'Hang on for your lives!' I bellowed to no one in particular, and flung myself at the weather rail, wrapping both arms around the stanchions. Gaspar did the same. The steersman fell on the wheel and embraced it like his dear mother. A moment of drawn-out silence ensued as the rearing wave blanketed the wind's wail. In this premonitory shelter, the air felt warmer, its chilling bite temporarily diminished as the water towered over the quarter-deck, blocking out the storm. I drew a deep breath before the wave struck.

Then I remembered Finlay McGruder. He stood dumbly by the lee rail, a landlubber wondering why the world had gone quiet. The ship began to roll and lifted her stern. He staggered. Good God alive, he wasn't even holding on.

I relinquished my grip on the stanchions and

threw myself bodily across the gap. McGruder's legs gave way and we tumbled together towards the open rail, grasping for something to fasten onto. My fingers closed around his briches belt. The struggling *Pursuant* heeled to steerboard, going further and further, tilting towards what felt like an endless slope. Groping, I tried to get a hand on the ship but found only empty air.

The wave toppled. With a roar, it fell from high above and struck hard. Tuns of freezing water washed aboard and we were sent tumbling by the torrent. My right arm closed on something solid and wooden, too big around to be a stanchion. It was the deck rail. With the bark's heel, we had been lifted up to the top. I clung to the landsman's belt, but we were half over. Empty space yawned, and below it the heaving, black sea.

Sickeningly, the bark sagged and her stern dipped under the weight of boarding water. She shuddered bodily, like a man entering a warm room from the chill outside. There came an abrupt crack, penetrating even the tempest's howl. I thought of frames breaking or rudder fixings parting. The bark fell into the chasm and laid herself down in the water, plunging the rail clean under, McGruder, myself and all. The breath was pounded from my body. My mouth filled with saltwater, forcing its way up my nose. My grip on the landsman's belt abruptly felt loose and light. There was no longer any weight on it.

I sank deeper under water as the bark rolled and rolled further, going so far it seemed she must turn right over. All I could do was cling to the rail with the grip of a madman, praying she would right herself.

The ship stopped falling. She steadied, and I knew she wanted to go no further. The keel ballast was doing its work, and she began a long slow heave to come upright. Then with sudden vigour the bark rapidly regained the vertical. The masts whooshed through the air like swept cane-sticks. The water lifted off my body, gurgling and draining away all around. There was a hissing of the great wave's back as it disappeared into the night, departing like a Satanic angel bent on vengeance somewhere downwind.

Fish-mouthed, I drew air into my tortured chest and opened my eyes, blinking away the salty water. The whole scene was nothing but a dark blur, but it was plain I had not gone overboard, for my arm was still wrapped around the rail-top. Slowly, indistinct shapes on the quarter resolved themselves into the figures of Gaspar and the steersman, tumbled together at the wheel. They were picking themselves up, dazed but safe. In my left hand, I grasped something wet and leathery and weightless. It was the end of McGruder's belt.

There was movement nearby, wriggling in the scuppers like a giant tunny fish. Finlay McGruder's face appeared. He was whimpering, stunned by the onslaught. Clambering to my knees, I saw a second fellow lying inert in the scuppers as water foamed and drained away back to sea. It was Eli Savary.

'Lord above, old salt,' I panted, 'I don't believe it.'

When I bent to him, I found his gnarled fingers gripping the top of McGruder's briches so hard they would not be prised away.

'All right, Eli, you can let go now,' I urged.

He was trying to speak, his voice all but inaudible. 'That Dutch bargehand let us be pooped.'

'Come on, old fellow,' I encouraged. 'No one could do anything about a wave like that.'

He gave a groan and lay still.

'Give a hand here!' I shouted.

A couple of seamen came over. Together, we bore him off to the hatchway to get him into a dry bunk below. When I turned back to call for a damage report, there was the Scotsman, standing upright, still barely hanging on.

'You get below too,' I rasped, 'before you cause more trouble.'

He shambled off and disappeared down the companionway. I peered into the waist where figures, white in the gloom, moved uncertainly about.

Then came more shouts of alarm. This time Gaspar was not looking astern but pointing up the mast. I followed his arm. Aloft, tattered sails streamed in the wind. Clewlines and buntlines and reefing pennants thrashed and snaked wildly, smashing blocks and clattering against the masts. Broken yards hung askew. The upper ratlines drooped slack and lifeless. The fore-topmast shrouds were frayed to thread. It looked as if half the rigging was gone.

Six men had been aloft when the wave struck. And it was me who had sent them there.

8

Backlash

Slowly down the mainmast ratlines came the three fellows off the steerboard yardarm. One was injured, and Luke Tatchell and another man helped him on his painful progress.

In trepidation, I scanned the larboard shrouds. Alone, Michael Higham descended the ratlines step by careful step. Of the two other tars with him out on that side, there was no sign. Then I saw a seaman far out on the yardarm. He clung to the main-topyard, feet flailing free of the jack-stays, too shocked or deranged to recover to the main-top. He was holding on, but only just. But the sixth man was gone.

The rigging was in poor shape. There was no sign of the fore-topsail, reefed or otherwise. It was worse than merely a sail having been carried away. The spar itself was snapped in two. The whole fore-topmast – all thirty foot of it, laden with blocks and deadeyes and other torn gear, a tun or more of wood and ropes and iron bracings – hung down at an angle to the lower mast. With the topyards buried in the sea during the broach, the force of the bark righting herself had parted the spar. The crack I heard was the mast-cap and trestletrees letting go. Hanging there by the least of threads, the weighty boom swung back and forth with every roll, smashing and tearing at anything in its way. The prospect of going aloft threw me into a pit of fear, but I could ask no one else.

'Mister Rittel, take the ship,' I said, trying to steady my voice. 'Get her to lie easy.'

My legs felt oddly shaky as I got myself down the four steps from the quarter. In the waist, men were helping Luke Tatchell and the others as they regained the weather-deck, half drowned, bruised and shocked. Everyone else hung back at the belays. There was no asking for volunteers for this.

'Give me that coil, sailor,' I said, pointing, for a man is rarely any use aboard a ship without a length of line in his hand.

The fellow handing me the rope was Michael Higham, who had volunteered for the reefing party.

'You're a good man,' I told him.

He looked dazed. 'Benjie – I saw him go. He went in the sea.'

There was no hope, no turning back, no chance of finding a man in such a maelstrom, and every one of us aboard knew it. Fleetingly, I rested a comforting hand on the fellow's arm. Then I put the coil on my shoulder and headed for the ratlines.

The bark was lying a-hull, wallowing in the troughs, being tossed on the crests, every now and then putting her leeward rail down. Going up hand over hand I made it to the futtock shrouds without pause, then swung up onto the maintop and launched myself into the ratlines stretching away above. The topmast gave a ghastly sway. The yard was swinging unrestrained.

With all my might, I bellowed down. Far below, nearly seventy feet, where miniature figures moved about the weather-deck, a white face turned my way. Luke Tatchell, bless his mother and father, saw me and sent men to the bracelines. Lines creaked in the blocks overhead and the yard jerked round, its far end coming inboard. The spar steadied, bringing the stricken jack-tar in over the ship. If he fell off now he would clatter down through the rigging, but at least he might stay on board.

Getting up to the maintopmast crosstrees, I braced myself with an arm around a shroud and bent one end of the line onto a deadeye. At this height, each time a wave passed under the keel the mast swung through an arc of sixty or seventy degrees. First it lurched one way as the face lifted her and she hung a fraction of a second. As the crest foamed by and she fell off down the roller's back, the mast scythed back again.

Timing my moves to the motion, I got out on the spar – denuded entirely of its canvas after its brush with the sea – and felt along for the footropes. With my arms circled round the bare yard, clutching the wet wood, icy cold and salt-sticky from its ducking, I flinched as broken buntlines and trailing gaskets or loose reefing lines whipped at my face. The seaman at the yard's end seemed a mile away, though in truth he was less than twenty feet off. He had fallen quite still. His legs no longer thrashed. His strength to grip the yard seemed all but gone.

'Hang on, man!' I yelled into the wind.

'Leave me be, captain,' he said. 'Don't come out any further.'

It was Nathaniel Gunn. Reaching the outboard end, I ran the line under his arms and tied a bowline so that at worst his fall was limited to the yard's length. Then I bent double to get his feet on the footrope. All the while, the bark seemed wilfully intent on throwing us off, but somehow I got us moving along the spar. Regaining the crosstrees, I took a breath and looked around.

The broken fore-topmast swung violently, crashing about just a few feet away. Worse, the very spar now supporting Nat and myself was insecure. From level with the cap of the lower mainmast, a split ran up the topmast for a good ten or twelve feet. One shroud on the larboard side had parted, and the remaining two groaned evilly under the extra load.

Nat Gunn, drenched and half drowned when the topyard had doused him in the sea, shivered with cold and fatigue, the freezing wind sapping his strength by the minute. I manhandled him into the ratlines and he half scrambled, half fell as far as the maintop while I paid out the rope. Somehow we got all the way back down without injury. But not until the weather-deck boards were firmly beneath my feet did I breathe easy.

'Take this fellow to the foc'sle,' I told the nearest jack-tar. 'Swaddle him in dry furskins and put him by the galley furnace. Tell Billy Jenks to keep a blaze fired up no matter what.'

Now we needed to deal with the rigging, to save us from the disaster of losing an entire mast. Luke Tatchell had recovered and already had the weather-deck in some semblance of order, seeing to the belays and clearing away wrecked or loose gear.

'The fore-topmast's broken,' I shouted in his ear. 'It'll have to come down.'

'I'll go up, captain, with an axe.'

'Good man,' I said, and turned to Gaspar. 'Mister Rittel, the main-topmast's split and a shroud's gone. We'll need a manila line long enough to reeve up a makeshift shroud.'

Tatchell was already half way aloft at the fore-mast, axe in hand. A minute later, the Dutchman and I were likewise hauling ourselves up the rat-lines, over the maintop and all the way to the topmast crosstrees. With a two hundred foot length of half inch manila on my shoulder, it was a hard climb. We worked quickly with our knives, cutting off the broken middle shroud at the eyes, then roughly winding the new rope round the spar above the two remaining shroud fixings. Rittel climbed back down to the maintop while I payed out the manila to him, then followed it down. We had no choice but to belay the line to the topmast deadeyes even though, without taking it to the deck, there was no way we could sweat the shroud full-hauled, for that was the work of six men. Nevertheless, between us we reamed it up just hard enough to suffice.

We worked on, lost amongst the crosstrees and swaying spars and wind-thrumming shrouds and stays. Meanwhile, Luke hacked away the broken fore-topmast and let the debris fall overside, for the *Pursuant* would carry no fore-topsails for now. But we had kept the main-topmast in place.

Back on the quarter-deck, the steersman had the helm right down, keeping the bark steady.

'Mister Rittel, let's get her moving again,' I called. 'Set a close-reefed storm course on the lower main.

Try a mizen topsail too. See how she goes on larboard tack.'

He grimaced. 'She'll steer poorly, captain.'

'Aye, it's bad enough. Let's hope that spar holds. Keep her heading north by east.'

'Aye aye,' he said, and went off.

Soon the *Pursuant* got steerage way again, enough to keep safe from all but another freak wave. That monster had exacted a high price, with one man lost overboard, Nat Gunn laid low, and Eli Savary in even poorer shape. Worse, it had left the bark crippled.

The storm continued unabated as the bark wallowed along, handling like an overweight porker. After a while the mizen topsail was all we could safely leave aloft, as even the smallest storm course became too much. Grossly undercanvassed without her two forward topsails, barely under steerage, she was sorely exposed to another broach. I stepped below intent on reckoning where the Devil along this desolate and unknown land there might be any such thing as a safe anchorage, a sanctuary of the least kind, somewhere to attempt repairs. The *Pursuant* could not sail on without her topmasts, no matter what her mission. I was filled with grim premonitions.

McGruder sat in the dayroom, wrapped in blankets, shivering violently.

'You should not have gone into the rigging,' he said. 'Losing our captain would have compromised the voyage.'

'If you want to stay alive,' I retorted, 'you had better listen to orders and keep below when I tell you.'

He was impossible – stubborn, ignorant of the sea, yet all too willing to advise or interfere. With a shake of my head, I bent to concentrate on the Navigation.

The sea-charts were cursory at best. They lacked any latitude markings, and the *Beaver*'s pilot notes were based on little or no survey work. Even so, it was clear this awful coast offered few places of sanctuary. Did McGruder appreciate this? Was he too dazed to understand how nearly he had become another meal for the fishes? He gave no sign of gratitude for his narrow release. When I glanced up from my work, his questioning gaze was still fixed on me.

Through chattering teeth, he said, 'Is the damage serious?'

'Aye, blast it – can't you see? The fore-topmast is gone altogether and the main-topmast is hanging on by a few jury stays. We must haul in somewhere safe, and damm'd soon. Though in these parts, only the Lord knows where that might be.'

He did not seem to register the jeopardy.

'We cannot afford any delay to the mission,' he replied.

I threw down my dividers. 'Do you still not understand? If we cannot get in and make good, the mission is finished.'

His voice was flat, expressionless. 'There can be no question of turning back.'

'Dammit,' I exploded, 'the captain decides if the bark is fit to continue – not you!'

I glared. The look in his eyes was disturbing, distant and unworldly, lacking entirely in human warmth. No emotion tempered his tones when he spoke.

'We shall never abandon the mission,' he said. 'Not while there's breath in my body.'

Two days later, McGruder and I stood together on the quarter-deck watching the repair work.

'It is a question of discipline,' said the Scotsman.

I could hardly credit it. We were at sixty degrees north, with a broken rig, a crewman lost, two injured and the rest little better than fourth rate. The *Pursuant* sheltered perilously in the most tenuous of refuges with her mission, like her rig, hanging by a thread. But Finlay McGruder's only concern was to see Eli Savary in the dock.

'The stowaway must face the consequences,' he repeated.

'For Saint Peter's sake, McGruder, he saved your life. Have you forgotten?'

In sheer frustration, I raised my eyes heavenward. High overhead, the foremast stood bare and topmastless, festooned in loose shrouds hanging forlornly deckwards, a stark reminder of our predicament.

Once the tempest subsided, the *Pursuant* had made her way tentatively towards the coast. Since that brief sighting of Cape Chudleigh, we might have been blown tens of leagues off course. The compass was dangerously erratic, making my dead reckoning worse than suspect – even after snatching a first fleeting sight of the sun for days. Still, by some miracle we had gained a lee on the eastern side of Ungava Bay, where we hauled in to recover.

We were as far from aid or human settlement as anywhere on the Earth. Under the shadow of bare black mountains, we had found an indent – it could hardly be called an anchorage – from which the loose ice had been driven away by the southerly gale. The rocky steep-to coast was approachable only with the highest degree of circumspection and a deal of hard work with the longest leadline in the locker. Feeling her way along, seeking a bottom, the ship came within her own length from the shore before sounding at a hundred fathoms. It was impossible to lay out an anchor in such deep water, so I sent down the ship's main boat – the Whitby harpooner – as well as the commandeered shallop, and ran out lines on four sides. The men found little purchase for stakes. No soft ground, nor clean sand, nor even a pebbled beach, only minute cracks in the great smooth boulders thrown carelessly down from high above. Nevertheless, they drove their irons into these crevices and the lines held fast. The *Pursuant* lay in a hempen web just as she had done in Skull Cove.

With the bark in flat water, repairs could begin. The weather-deck came alive with bustle. For a replacement fore-topmast, we prepared our spare yard to be sent aloft and fixed at the re-carpentered trestletrees. The split main-topmast was stripped of its yard and rigging before being sent down and laid out lengthwise on deck while Billy Jenks got busy at the galley furnace smithing up four iron bands. Beaten and folded time and again to make well-tempered metal, these bands were heated red hot and slipped one by one around the broken spar, evenly spaced to strengthen the split wood. There would be no need to douse the bands in cold water to seize them around, for the icy air alone was enough.

Of all the men aboard, Finlay McGruder had the least conception of the difficulty in carrying out full shipyard work in the frozen conditions. Exasperated, I went to the rail and scanned the seascape. The damaging tempest had blown itself out. Far off to the north a band of sunlight broke through a gap in the clouds and shone on the silver-hued sheet of the sea, adding a tinge of blue to the still-tossing wavetops. Then, as suddenly as it came, the sun was gone and once more the monotony of grey held sway. The scene looked innocuous compared to the storm, but the wind had veered sharply to a light northwesterly. It was now an onshore breeze, and broken lumps of green and bluish ice crept in from seaward, some floes riding well out of the water, others half-submerged and visible only from aloft. Within an hour, large pieces were bumping and jostling around the bark's waterline, then going on their way to pile up against the shore. Silently, wind-borne and with deadly stealth, the ice was building.

'McGruder, shipboard discipline is the least of my concerns,' I said, rounding on him. 'And let me make plain that the question is no concern of yours. You oversee the search and make your reports, but that is all.'

He was intransigent. 'There has already occurred what amounted to an insurrection. You should have made exemplary punishments of –' he consulted a paper in his hand '– Michael Higham and Benjamin Tallis, whom I take to be the ringleaders.'

'Tallis is dead,' I snapped. 'He was the one washed overboard.'

'And Higham?'

This was driving me to distraction. 'Michael Higham has redeemed himself! He volunteered to go aloft.'

He crossed something off his list. 'Very well, Benjamin Tallis might be before his God, but Higham shall answer to the secular authorities. He is a Navy seaman, after all.'

'By the Lord's own blood, I don't doubt you'd have flogged Tallis's corpse if we'd dragged it back aboard.'

'If it had the desired effect on discipline, then yes indeed.'

If he was bent on stirring me into outrage, he succeeded.

'Landsman McGruder, I believe you might be deranged,' I snapped.

Suddenly I realised we were arguing in open view of the seamen. They shot glances up at the quarter-deck even as they went about their tasks. I took the Scotsman firmly by the arm and bore him off to the hatchway, down to my dayroom.

'Henceforth, you remain below and out of sight,' I told him. 'And if you attempt again to interfere with the running of the ship, I shall call the voyage off.'

He sat down at the chart table before the brandy bottle in its nesting place and glared at me with undisguised rancour. But at least he did not argue.

'And talking of the voyage's end,' I said, 'you had better know about the way I intend to conduct the search once we reach Hudson's Bay –

assuming we do so. I want no further arguments between us.'

He remained motionless and silent.

'Look McGruder, either we agree on the next stage of the voyage, or I call it off. And take any consequences you may try and throw at me.'

He gave a grudging, sullen nod. I sat down and collected myself, determined that he should understand the position.

The *Beaver*'s captain, I reminded McGruder, had lodged with the Admiralty the logs of her voyages as proof of the route. From these I knew she habitually sailed direct through the thawing ice of early summer, completed a resupply of Fort Rupert and turned for home, working along the eastern shore of James Bay, meeting natives and traders of a people called the Missacaibi and buying furskins. As the return leg always took longer, there was more chance she had been on the way home, laden with cargo. Thus, Admiral Tompion had ordered the search begun at the Great Northern Cape and continued south along the coast until either the missing bark was found or time ran out. And when that time came was for me to decide, not McGruder.

'So I intend to hug the coast, hunting in and out of the inlets,' I explained, tracing the coastal outline. 'It's nearly three hundred leagues sailing direct to Fort Rupert, but searching this way we shall likely cover four hundred. Do you understand?'

He nodded.

'And does the method meet with your approval?'

He nodded again, leaning forward. 'You cannot object if I inquire about the time allocated. Having

160

come all this distance, it would be absurd to end the search too soon.'

'Aye, but it would be lunacy to carry it on too long,' I rejoined. 'The ice will re-form early at the Great Northern Cape. The admiral agreed that the *Pursuant* is to turn back to clear the cape by the last day of September. With luck, that gives us thirty days for the search.'

He sat back. 'Ah, but is it long enough to find the *Beaver*?'

'It's long enough to conduct a thorough search. And fulfil the terms of my mission. Agreed?'

He acceded reluctantly. 'Very well.'

I heaved a sigh. At least I had gained his unequivocal assent. I collected up all the charts, folding them away and replacing the logs in the drawer.

'I have noticed,' said the Scotsman, his eye on the logs, 'that you are seldom away from your instruments and calculations. Is it so necessary?'

I stopped, unsure what he was driving at. There could be no harm in him knowing my purpose, though. And if I was frank with him it might serve to rebuild what little trust had existed before. Reaching for a secure locker above the settle-back, I threw open the lid and drew out another sheaf of papers. For extra protection against dampness and salty air, these precious items were kept in a costly buckskin cover.

McGruder's eyes widened. He had not known about this.

'This is the reason for my diligence,' I said. 'These observations shall be added to my pilot book, when the admiral returns it. In here is recorded every detail of our voyage, culled from my own observations and the mates' sailing logs. There are compass courses, distances covered, wind strength and direction, the weather and its changes. Latitudes morning, noon and evening – if the sky is ever clear – from shooting either the sun or the planets and stars. I enter the deduced reckonings, estimates of the Longitudes, and notes on the compass's variations from True North.' I patted the cover. 'The *Beaver*'s captain kept no such details, only the barest sailing logs. Sailors after us shall reckon these efforts well worth the ink and paper. All this learning is precious – angles on headlands and promontories, sketches of islands and bays, frequent soundings to record the depths. Besides the Navigator,' I added, 'the leadline parties are going to be the hardest worked men aboard.' I put the bundle away. 'Admiral Tompion knows its value. He kept my earlier work back against my return – all my pilots and charts and logs of the Labrador Coast, the Gulf North Shore, and parts of Newfoundland never before surveyed.'

His eyes narrowed. 'The Admiralty shall mightily appreciate your efforts.'

'Perhaps, if they buy a copy of the works.'

He started in surprise. 'Surely they are the Crown's property?'

'No, the *Pursuant* is a private bark.'

'But so was the *Beaver*, and her logs were deposited for Admiralty use.'

'Admiral Tompion demanded only that I hand over the sailing logs, which I shall. These other works are mine. I shall publish them for the benefit of not just the Navy but all English sailors.'

'British sailors,' he corrected.

I smiled thinly, and carefully slid the papers back in the buckskin cover. Then I locked it inside the drawer and exited the dayroom.

Back on deck, I found that the mates reckoned the iron-banding of the main-topmast a success. Going aloft to see for myself, I found both it and the repaired fore-topmast, while far from perfect, secure enough to carry reefed topsails. We could go on.

The sailing master went ashore to retrieve the stakes and mooring lines, and the bark put to sea without delay. As she got under way, amongst the former *Ascendant* men there were murmured conversations, sly glances and signs of their former shiftiness. My crew of resentful, unwilling pressed men had once been progressing towards a semblance of seamanship, but now I sensed a change in the ship's spirits. They had seen their captain arguing on the quarter-deck. I blamed myself for allowing it. But much more, I damm'd Finlay McGruder for causing it.

Towards morning, at the change of the watch, passing preoccupied along the passage heading for the companionway, I heard a croaking voice issue from the sleeping cabin where Eli lay.

'Captain Matthew – a word, if you will.'

I poked my head into the below-decks gloom and saw him lying all but buried under a tottering pile of sealskins and woollen blankets. The old fellow's recovery had stalled, and he wheezed like a sawyer cutting dry wood.

'Captain, I trust that Scots fellow like I'd trust the galley-cook with the compass course. Disturbs me, it does, his creeping about all hours, fussing and muttering. Maybe I should have let him go overside.'

I had not even told the old man about McGruder's threat to arraign him. After all, it looked as if he might not survive the journey home.

'I'm keeping a close eye on him, old salt.'

'Aye, but Captain Matthew, if you won't keep him locked up, let me shoot him for you.'

'No need for that,' I said with a half-hearted chuckle. 'He's learnt his lesson.'

That night as the *Pursuant* tilted along at five and six knots across an easy sea and under a frosty, crystal sky, I stayed up topside until the dawn watch, observing the canopy studded with a million stars. Despite all my misgivings, the seamen were still working as a band. My officers were in good fettle and fully in charge of the ship. The jury fore-topmast and repaired main-topmast held together well. For once, we were untroubled by bad weather. There was hope for the mission.

Three days later, benefiting from the continuing light northerly breeze, we rounded the Great Northern Cape and at last entered the vast and little known waters of Hudson's Bay.

Our quest had begun in earnest.

9

Beaver's Trap

I kept my promise to Finlay McGruder. As we progressed warily ever deeper into the unexplored reaches of Hudson's Bay, league by league and hour by hour I conducted the search for the *Beaver* to the utmost of my ability.

The *Pursuant* was now heading south from the Great Northern Cape, into Hudson's Bay and back down the latitudes she had won with such difficulty passing up the Labrador Coast. With each minute of southing, we diligently scoured every indent and cove and islet along the coastline. At nightfall, the bark would anchor if we could find a bottom. Otherwise, she hove to and forereached slowly until the first glimmers of pre-dawn light, when the vigil resumed. By this means, we covered vast distances of this trackless region with all speed yet with the best hope of spying a wreck.

Many days had passed since we departed Ungava Bay, but on my orders McGruder remained confined below. We could not risk being seen arguing again, giving malcontent elements in the crew an opportunity for disruptive whisperings. Nevertheless, mindful of the Scotsman's forthcoming reports, I encouraged him to examine the daily logs when I brought them to the dayroom.

He seemed to appreciate the immensity of the task and my thoroughness in executing it. One day, as the search was nearing the end of its allotted time, we sat at my table with dozens of charts spread out.

I looked up and said, 'I'm breaking your confinement, McGruder. Come on deck and see for yourself how it's done.'

It was late afternoon. The sun, pale yellow and half-hearted, shone low in the southwestern sky as the *Pursuant* rustled along under all plain sail in a moderate westerly, reaching across a three-foot swell. On the larboard side a league distant lay the low and uninviting land, a featureless strip of dark brown humps undulating across the horizon, treeless, barren and lifeless. Now, in late September, the ice had melted enough to reveal the ground, but I knew it would soon lie again under several feet of snow.

Aloft at both the fore- and maintops stood a brace of fellows, each with a spy-glass, an extra gold coin awaiting the first man to hail out a mast spied or a broken hull descried.

McGruder looked round in some wonder.

'What a bare place,' he remarked, scanning the landscape of bleak tundra. 'And surely bereft of any presence of mankind. Are there animals to shoot at with a musket, or to trap and snare?'

'Nothing except these damm'd gnats,' I said, slapping at the myriad tiny black flies drifting from the shore and biting our arms, bared to the weak late-summer sunshine. 'And the great white bear, so fierce no one dares find out if he makes good eating.'

McGruder made a noise that I took to be amusement. Thinking the quarter-deck's fresh air had lifted his black mood, I seized my chance.

'Landsman, you understand,' I said, 'that tomorrow the *Pursuant* must turn for home.'

He studied me with a peculiar look, a mixture of suspicion and contempt. I had sorely misread his temper.

'You mean, Loftus,' he said icily, 'the search is to be curtailed.'

'Not curtailed. I told you we must clear the Great Northern Cape by the last of September. We have just time to get back there.'

He stood clenching and unclenching his fists like a frustrated boy. 'And so you are calling it off? Even though the *Beaver* is not found?'

He knew that dam' well. It had been agreed. Why was he arguing now?

'We cannot risk being trapped,' I said, glancing sideways at Gaspar Rittel, standing nearby minutely examining his topsail luffs. I hoped he would not overhear.

Too late. The simmering resentment in the landsman's eyes suddenly took fire.

'To Hell with you, Loftus – you shan't stop me!'

Next second he was upon me like a madman, his flailing fists sending blow after blow against my body, his bunched hands slamming against my chest.

He was not a strongly-built fellow, nor tall. His punches carried no weight. With one hand I pushed him away, glimpsing his reddened face and distorted mouth uttering the foulest curses. Bent on dealing with him swiftly, I struck a single blow to his chin, whereupon he crumpled like an empty sack. I bore him to the companionway under the sailing master's astonished gaze.

But the bored lookouts had observed it all. As I locked the stunned Finlay McGruder in his sleeping cabin, I knew that once again the forepeak would hear of divisiveness on the quarter-deck.

In the morning, disturbed and sleepless after a troubled night, I lay on my bunk listening for seven bells of the early watch. Soon, it would be time to rise up, assemble the men and announce that the search was over. The Scotsman had no conceivable grounds for objection. We had scoured several hundred leagues of unknown coastline and recorded every detail as incontestable proof of our thoroughness. He would be obliged to write in his reports that the rescue attempt, carried out under Captain Loftus' scrupulous oversight, had nevertheless failed. I knew we had done more than enough to satisfy the admiral, McGruder or no McGruder. The mission had been done as requested, and we were going home. Before the ice blocked the route, the *Pursuant* would sail between the bergs, past Ungava Bay and down the Labrador Coast with the pack ice closing rapidly astern. In a fortnight or three weeks, my stout little bark would sight the shores of Newfoundland.

Stretching and yawning, loth to leave the warmth under my skins and pelts and sacking, I allowed for the first time that a favourable outcome might yet be looming. The *Pursuant* would return safe and I would become Intendant Proper of Esperantia. Drifting luxuriously in a sleepy reverie in which a vision of Grace Trepanney floated before me like a benign wraith, I was slow in becoming aware of the chorus of excited shouts from aloft. The thump and thud of feet on the companion steps brought me fuzzily awake, half sitting up. The cabin door burst open without a knock and an excited face appeared.

'The lookouts, captain,' cried a breathless Gaspar. 'Not half a league off – masts spied ashore!'

Dreams of Esperantia dissolved into the air as if they were no more than steam rising from the galley boiling pans.

When I gave the order to take the *Pursuant* shore-wards, a thrill of excitement gripped the bark.

Under topsails only, with the utmost caution and sounding all the way, she ghosted along until the breeze that half a league off the coast had sent us ahead at three knots flickered and died. Down went the launch and the shallop to give tow. Low humps of islands dotted the inshore waters, some no more than rocks awash or just below the surface, others rising ten and twenty feet and extending a quarter of a land mile. The tows sought a deep water channel and steadily we approached the scene.

The two masts stood out like flagstaffs, though the rest of the bark was hidden by islands and rock outcrops. From the quarter my spy-glass showed the spars not only tilted crazily but lying at angles to each other. Likely, the vessel's back was broken.

Shouts went up from the seamen as we saw a column of blue smoke rising into the crisp northern air, slanting away in the remnant breeze aloft. Could there still be men alive?

Choosing a deep pool sheltered by two smooth-backed islands – the weather might break with sudden violence in these waters – I ordered the bark's bower and kedge anchors laid out fore and aft. The excitement and the ship's movements filtered below to Finlay McGruder. He began calling for his release but despite his most vehement protestations, I left him locked below. There was too much at stake to risk his interference. I sensed the prize within my grasp, and nothing was going to stop me, least of all him.

Taking Gaspar Rittel and Nathaniel Gunn, armed with cutlasses and pistols, I stepped into the launch and bade the six oarsmen stroke us in. As the oars clunked in their locks and we approached the dismal shore, I held my breath. This voyage had tested the crew to the very ends of their endurance, and tried my captaincy to its limits too. This might be its culmination.

Rounding an island, of a sudden we came upon the bark – or what remained of her. Once, she had been a vessel of the *Pursuant*'s size and burthen, about two hundred tuns and a hundred foot in length, single-decked and with four guns in each broadside. No other sailing ship – no vessel of any kind, as far as God knew – ever visited these remote and terrifying lands. She could only be the *Beaver*.

Her mizenmast was gone altogether, broken off at deck level. Of the two remaining, the fore-topmast had split and hung crookedly by a few shrouds, though the mainmast still stood. Everywhere the rigging was in tatters, the stays and ratlines nothing but shreds of twine. The fore and mainyards had been sent down, doubtless to reduce windage before she was driven ashore. No sails were left aloft, either manhandled off the yards or stripped away in the Polar wind. Her hull lay angled along the beach, resting half on and half off a narrow stony strand, the bows driven ashore. The stern was sunk in the water, with the rudder gone and the sternlights smashed open, presenting a blank-faced, abandoned aspect. She was far down enough for the sea to wash not just into the exposed stern quarters but as far as her midships. The sheerline was out of true. She had been crushed by the inexorable pressure of the pack ice and reduced to scrapwood.

'Stroke in to the strand, fellows,' I told the oarsmen.

When the launch grazed the beach, I leapt out and gave a shout for men to show themselves. There was only silence. Nat, Gaspar and I cocked our pistols and approached the wreck. She was a sorry sight for any seaman, broken-backed, stripped bare of all her fittings, a ship who had found her end before her time. The sea lapped at her sunken parts, and long fronds of green weed hung in curtains ten feet above where the waterline once was. Her hull was stove in all round. The ice must have enclosed her, pushed her up the shore, then heaped and pressed relentlessly until it broke her where she lay. Barely one plank rested next to its mate, for every seam had been struck out of true so that in parts she had the appearance of a clinker-built boat, board overlapping board. Crunching up the pebbled slope of her ghostly graveyard, I rounded the bows to find her larboard hull even worse dismembered and gaping open. Then, beyond the corpse of the ship, I saw them.

A hundred paces off, half a dozen figures stood or sat or lay about by the fire's remains, the source of the column of smoke. They seemed struck insensible by our presence. I could not tell if they were white or black, or what race they were, or what origins their dress might have. They appeared only as human silhouettes, primitive and mistrustful, standing out against the grey stones and desolate ice fields.

'Ahoy, there,' I hailed.

No one moved.

'Are you the *Beaver*'s men?'

No answer. With sidelong glances at each other, the mates and I hefted up our pistols and approached. The site resembled a village midden, with discards and rubbish blackening the strand, dark rags lying about in piles, the shreds of makeshift shelters of ship's canvas hanging between boulders, the remains of earlier abandoned hearths.

'Ahoy, crew of the *Beaver*,' I repeated, taking a few tentative paces forward.

One fellow struggled to rouse himself into life. He walked towards us shambling and stumbling. Shrouded in rags and tatters of furs, hooded with torn pelts and cloths, he appeared monk-like, a spectral figure alien not just to this landscape but to the world itself. The sun-browned skin was deep-lined and desiccated, yet now I saw the two eyes, protuberant, staring, burning icily as the skeletal shape advanced. The cheekbones stuck out below them, the spike of his nose was prominent, the mouth drooped half open in a gap-toothed grimace. He carried nothing, bore no arms, and seemed struck in sheer awe of us.

'Halt there,' I commanded, and he stopped in his tracks. Awkwardly, embarrassed at his ceaseless gaping and strange reluctance to speak, I said, 'Identify yourself.'

'Hanson,' he gasped.

A hand came up and wiped a trickle of saliva from the corner of his cracked mouth, but the eyes never left mine.

'Captain . . . Edward Hanson,' he croaked haltingly, 'master . . . of the . . . the *Beaver*.'

He fell to his knees, the rounded beach stones clinking as he dropped, and clasped his hands together in prayer, his beseeching, disbelieving eyes fixed upward.

'Are we saved?' he said. 'Can I believe . . . you have come at last?'

With that he prostrated himself, sobbing, his hands reaching out to clutch at my feet. By instinct I withdrew, half afraid, half disgusted. An intolerable stench arose from the fellow, rank and penetrating, as if he had been thrown in a cesspit and steeped there for a month.

I had given little thought to what shape this encounter might take. In truth, as we journeyed further south by each day and each week, its prospect receded to remoteness. When my imagination did run ahead, I pictured us finding a few timbers or spars, a board with a carved name faintly visible on it, or the shell of a bark, lifeless and derelict. Otherwise the *Beaver* must be lost at sea and no single trace of her would ever be discovered, afloat or ashore. Instead, we had found not just the bark, but survivors too.

The other figures gathered themselves to rise up, each one as emaciated and stupefied as their captain. I realised with a shock there were only six men in all.

'Captain Hanson, I would be obliged if you could stand,' I said. Overcoming my natural resistance, I put away my pistol and bent to help him up. I told him who we were and that our ship lay just offshore, hidden from sight the other side of the near islands.

Without warning, he threw his head back and shouted into the air, 'O praise be to the Lord! We are saved – saved!'

By now the others were either hanging back sobbing, or coming forward to clutch at our clothes. One or two tried to bend and kiss our hands. Despite their awful appearance and the appalling odours from their bodies, I found myself gripping these poor men as if they were long forgotten friends, squeezing their hands in return, clasping their arms and muttering comforting phrases. I told them that they were saved, that we would return them to their wives and their homes, that there was food and warmth and shelter aboard our ship. For some minutes, I refused to catch Gaspar's or Nathaniel's eye, for a drop of water flowed down my cheek, cooling to salty ice at the corners of my mouth.

Who can say what it is to be greeted as saviours? For our part, we felt we had done nothing but sail our bark here and only by sheer fortune come upon these hapless and forsaken men. They were seamen like us. It crossed our minds to wonder how we might act if ever we were left in despair on a desert shore a thousand miles from the nearest human presence.

To give them time to compose themselves, I encouraged them back to their half-dead fire. We stoked it into life and took more fuel from their precious supplies – broken timbers and barrels and boxes from the wreck – and got from the launch some biscuit and broth we had brought, which they fell upon with wonder and gratitude. After clearing the launch of all vittles, I sent Gaspar away to the *Pursuant* to bring the shallop back with more food and hot beverage, thinking to ease the survivors' transition back to human company. And sure enough, as we sat by the flames, the *Beaver*'s men by degrees returned to the world.

Swallowing the broth and chewing hard biscuit – a painful act, for his gums were shrunken, the teeth loosened – Captain Hanson told me how his vessel had been struck by a northwesterly, in August of last year, while coasting along the Hudson's Bay shore.

'Such a storm,' he said, champing greedily, his voice strengthening, 'can strike any summer month hereabouts. I had never seen one like it before. After two days and nights fighting to keep her offshore – everything down aloft – we could not stop her. She struck and was holed – there at the larboard bow.' He pointed to cracked frames poking out from the empty shell. 'We tried to pull her off, but both boats were smashed to pieces.' He paused, resting. Then, 'I let her drive onto this beach, hard as she'd go. Lord, that tempest . . . to live through it.' He halted again, chewing slowly and gazing around, as if unable to take in his sudden salvation. 'We lost most of her supplies in the wrecking. We have languished here more than a twelvemonth.'

'What happened to the rest of your men?'

His hollow eyes turned on me. 'A dozen drowned in the boats, frozen in the sea. Others . . . lost heart, died quickly, two and three a day sometimes. Lord knows why a few of us remain. Perhaps we are spared for some purpose.' His voice was a whisper. 'Just we six are left – all that live of fifty two souls.'

'Captain Hanson,' I said, patting his arm, 'that you have saved even one man is close to a miracle.'

Soon, they had revived enough to be put in the boats and taken out to the *Pursuant*. While this was done, I cast about, searching for anything worth salvaging, and spied some muskets lying nearby.

'Second Mate Gunn, take these aboard,' I said.

Nat followed the others to the boats and I moved off to look around for other items of use. Even a hundred paces distant from the fire, the midden-like stench was little reduced. Finding dark bundles in rows, I pushed at one with my foot. It was lighter than a board of wood and rustled dryly like a husk. When I rolled it over, it lay there, silent and staring, showing a row of grinning teeth. Above its hollow eye sockets, the whitened bones of the skull's dome shone palely in the northern sun.

Moving slowly along the rows, I turned over body after body, my heart dinning at the thought of these poor fellows dying one by one, shivering and frost-bitten, chilled to the marrow, starving and without hope. And how much the worse for those left behind, with these gruesome reminders of their mates lying a bare few feet from where they lived.

At the end of the line was a more disturbing sight yet. The last bodies were not so old, not desiccated and bared to the bone like the rest. One or two still had dark red flesh attached to the bones, rotting now in the warm summer sun, although mostly it had been stripped away.

With a cloth covering my mouth, I examined the remains, wondering if the wind blew here fiercely enough to rip still-moist flesh from its bony attachments. Perhaps there were hungry birds like the great sea eagles and ospreys that soared in high circles above the forested valleys cutting across the plains of Labrador. Brown bears and wolves might venture this far north, though the land here was dry open tundra rather than the tree cover those beasts preferred. The white bear was said to roam the ice and floes, yet we had seen none along the shore.

I walked pensively back to the midden on the strand and watched the survivors being handed unsteadily into the boats. When they were aboard, I stepped in the launch and sat alongside Captain Hanson. Though he remained the cadaverous, distant apparition we had first encountered, his face was animated with new life and hope.

But his eyes showed the human spirit broken.

* * *

The *Pursuant* was at sea, her courses and topsails set, beam reaching at a brisk canter for the Great Northern Cape, intent on beating the ice.

Five of the surviving *Beaver* men, sick and weak, were being cosseted and fed and brought back to vibrant life under the care of Billy Jenks and his cookboy. The sixth, Captain Edward Hanson, sat droop-shouldered at my cabin table facing McGruder. He was confused and distraught, shaking his head as if he could barely remember his own name.

The Scotsman, stoney-faced, was demanding answers in a brutal inquisition that had begun the moment the captain was brought aboard. McGruder wanted to hear nothing of the accident that had driven the fur bark ashore, nor of the struggle to save her, nor even of their present condition and distress. He wanted to know only one thing.

'Hanson, tell me or burn in Hell,' he demanded. 'Where is the prisoner?'

The *Beaver*'s captain sat opposite, shaking his head in distress. The poor fellow could not think straight.

'Leave him be,' I said, intervening. 'The man's ill. What prisoner, anyway?'

'He claims the prisoner was not aboard. That cannot be.' Puce-faced, McGruder shouted, 'You are lying! I say again, Hanson, was the bark making for or returning from Fort Rupert?'

'What does it matter?' I cut in. 'The bark's wrecked. There are no supplies left worth salvaging, if that's what's in your mind.'

Edward Hanson closed his eyes, trying to remember back to the distant days before his ordeal began.

'We were twenty days from home,' he said. 'Twenty days out from Saint John's.'

'What in damnation does such seaman's talk mean?' snapped McGruder. 'Was it twenty days till you got home, or twenty days since you left home?'

'He was on the outward leg,' I said. 'The *Beaver* was wrecked twenty days after leaving Newfoundland.'

McGruder's temper erupted like the heavy mortar on a bomb ketch.

'So she never reached Fort Rupert?' he said. 'Dam' and blast, blast and dam'!'

Hanson shrank away, cowed, his head drooping, a man on the point of collapse.

'How far is it – how far from here to the fort?' The Scotsman reached across the table, put his fist under Hanson's chin and jerked it up. 'Look at me, man! Answer my question!'

'Leave him, McGruder,' I said, and pulled his hand away. 'What are you thinking of?'

The landsman sat back, breathing hard.

'He shall answer for this most heinous crime,' he muttered, watching the captain so intently that plain fear showed in Hanson's eyes. 'Indeed, sir, you know very well what I mean. Your evil, unChristian behaviour.'

A stab of fear cut through me. The Scotsman had not gone ashore, I had made sure of that, but now he turned to me with a triumphant look.

'The Dutch fellow Rittel told me about your misguided attempt to hide the evidence. What happened is contemptible, the work of Satan.'

'Listen, McGruder,' I said quickly, 'I sent the

first mate ashore to give a proper burial to those seamen, according to the religions the captain here told me they held. What can be unChristian about that?'

He smiled. 'The six we rescued are criminals under God, let alone under the secular law. They were feasting on their brothers' corpses.'

Hanson let out an animal sound, a groan of anguish, and buried his head in his hands.

The Scotsman looked pleased. 'Well might you regret it now, captain. And you, Loftus, have tried to cover up the crime.'

I cursed myself for not having impressed upon Gaspar that he was in no circumstances to describe the state of those bodies. Even if Hanson and his men had made a gruesome transgression of the laws of nature, there was no benefit in plunging them into the jeopardy of the Ecclesiastickal Court and the Church's gibbet.

'It's unnecessary to add to their sufferings,' I insisted. 'And think of the wives and sons and daughters of the departed. It's best forgotten. I forbid it to be brought up again.'

'You are in no position to forbid anything,' said the landsman.

I leaned forward close to his face. 'This is my ship and I advise you to watch your step.'

Suddenly Captain Hanson was sitting bolt upright. 'Five days. You can get to the fort in five days' sailing.'

'There!' cried the Scotsman. 'I have got my answer.'

The effort was too much. Hanson collapsed,

180

slumping sideways off the chair. Against McGruder's protests I led him to a sleeping cabin and got Billy Jenks to administer a draught for the nerves. When I re-entered my dayroom, the landsman was standing by the sideboard holding up a brandy bottle.

'A drink, Loftus?' There was a horrible smirk on his face.

I knew the man well enough by now to fear that look. Full of misgivings, I took up my seat.

'Landsman, if you intend that we sail to Fort Rupert, think again. The mission's done.'

He sat down opposite, supping the spirit, beaming as if we were the best of friends.

'Spit it out, man,' I snapped, snatching the bottle and gulping down a generous swig. It did nothing to quell the sickening doubts rising within me.

He smiled. 'Do you know what orders I hold from the admiral?'

'You were to oversee the search. Now the *Beaver* is found, your reports count for nothing. The mission is successful.'

His head went slowly from side to side. 'The mission is not successful.'

I pulled open the table drawer, snatched up a folded paper and thrust it at him. 'Here, these are my terms. I thought you knew them in every detail.'

At the document's lower corner was a generous blob of sealing wax with the deeply impressed image of the admiral's official seal, the breeder bull standing placid under its Lincolnshire tree.

'Ah, the famous Tompion patriarch,' said McGruder.

He studied the paper with interest, caressing the waxen impress with his fingertip. Then he tore the document into several pieces and scattered them over the table. Stupidly, I found myself scrabbling on the sole, until I heard his soft laugh.

'Loftus, you do not know all the circumstances of this voyage.'

I straightened. I should have known he had something more up the frilled sleeve of his silk shirt.

He snickered. 'I have a secret commission.'

'From Tompion?'

'From the Sovereign, though the admiral knows of it. I am a diplomat on Her Majesty's service.'

'For Her Majesty? On what service, dam' you?'

'It's about the prisoner.'

In dread, I listened as McGruder described how delighted he had been to receive the Queen's own commission, imparted to him in London by her Minister for War. There was, he told me, the matter of a treaty vital to the Sovereign's aims. It was to be agreed between Great Britain and the Missacaibi Indians, a tribe of untamed savages occupying the lands east of James Bay, who had time and again attacked Fort Rupert. If the natives could be induced to sign, then the fur bark's voyages and the fort's resupply were assured, keeping alive Great Britain's claims over the High Kanada Lands. McGruder himself, he crowed, had been instrumental in getting the proposed terms approved at Court. Despite opposition from many quarters, he was determined to see it through. It would make his name as a diplomat, a broker of nations, and launch him into a career of celestial heights.

'And who then is this prisoner?' I asked quietly. 'Why is he so important?'

'It is Chief Chanatuk, leader of the Missacaibi tribe.' His eye gleamed. 'The *Beaver* was to bring him back to Boston to sign. If Hanson never reached the fort, then the chief is still held there.'

I reached for the brandy, swallowed the reviving spirit and stared him down, though in my guts I sensed everything slipping away.

'Over my dead bones, McGruder.' I spoke with as much conviction as I could muster. 'We're on our way home.'

He was not the least swayed. 'You have not completed the mission.'

'You can tear up my terms but you cannot undo the facts, dammit. I found the *Beaver*.'

'The mission is not complete until I say so. Are you prepared to risk it with Admiral Tompion?'

I felt hatred for McGruder and Tompion for their perfidy, but it was tempered with disgust at myself in being so easily fooled.

'If I had known about all this, I would never have agreed to the mission.'

'Precisely so. Both I and the admiral had calculated that,' said McGruder with malicious satisfaction. 'And it is not merely a matter of losing your little bark, Loftus. Is it?'

He meant the Intendancy. And everything that led from it.

'Five days there, five days back,' he was saying. 'What difference can ten days make?'

'Depending on the weather, it might be twelve or fourteen days,' I protested. 'It's September end now.

183

Do you want to fall into the fate Hanson and his men suffered – stranded ashore, frozen, starving?'

'O, I don't think they starved, Loftus. Not the last six, at any rate.'

He poured himself a slosh of spirit, then filled another mugful and held it out for me. I refused.

He settled himself in the chair, wearing that sly, mocking grin. 'You know what you must do, Captain Loftus, do you not?'

When I mounted the companionway steps and gazed out along the *Pursuant*'s decks, she was in fine sailing fettle, smashing her way briskly northwards across a choppy grey sea. She seemed eager to be on her way home. Gaspar smiled on seeing me, as if to say, look how well she goes under my guiding hand.

'Sailing master,' I said, 'wear ship.'

His face fell faster than a jibsail collapsing with a parted haulyard.

Then I bade him set course south for Fort Rupert.

10

Cold Harbour

McGruder took to strutting about the quarter as if he owned the bark, giving orders, eating freely of our diminishing vittles in my dayroom, caring nothing if the rest of us went on short rations. By contrast, Captain Hanson steadied himself at the rail despite his weakened condition and helped me guide the *Pursuant* through the dangerous, little known reaches of James Bay.

That great southern appendage was a lake rather than a sea, with breezes and swells determined by the surrounding land. Sometimes icy air breathed down from the north, but when it blew from the vast forest tracts lying to the west the wind was cool and wet. With rocks and low islands everywhere, my Navigation depended heavily on Edward Hanson. Reviving day by day on rations of hot broth and saltfish, he piloted us past endless stretches of barren flat coastlands and amongst shoaling waters beset by treacherous currents. The *Pursuant* would never have reached Fort Rupert without the *Beaver*'s captain.

Being a natural pilot rather than a taught Navigator, he had paid little heed to voyaging records beyond the sailing logs, but now he marvelled at my observations and assisted in taking angles and surveying landmarks, all of which would be added to my pilot book when I claimed the works back from Admiral Tompion.

McGruder showed no appreciation of the captain's efforts. He lolled in the dayroom drinking spirits and regaling me with tales of his exploits in the ambassadorial drawing rooms of London and Antwerp and Utrecht.

After five days, we sighted Caribou Island in the approaches to the Rupert River. Negotiating a bar at the entrance, we felt our way gingerly upriver sounding by the lead until we came into the anchoring pool and let go our main bower.

Fort Rupert stood on the only rising ground. Signals answering our own flew from the flagstaff, though it was plain the installation had never amounted to much. Indeed, its ruinous state was apparent from afar. The spying tube showed a crude wooden stockade of spruce trunks set vertical, cut to spikes at the top and braced all around by roughly sawn planks. It spoke of nothing so much as transience, lacking the permanent air of stone fortifications and proper walls. Yet it was the sole manifestation of English might for a thousand leagues, defending the Sovereign's claim upon a million square miles of territory.

The fort gates swung wide and a ragged band of soldiers led by a uniformed officer marched out and came down to a lopsided wooden jetty, its piles blackened with the brackish river water. They embarked a long-boat and pulled out. By the time we had let go a second anchor in the trading pool below the gun emplacements, they had closed to within hailing distance. A tired looking officer, unshaven and wearing a faded soldier's rig, stood in the bows.

'What ship are you?' he cried.

'The *Pursuant*,' I returned, 'out of Newfoundland.'

A minute later, the boat bumped alongside at the waterline. The soldier grasped the boarding ropes and gazed up.

'We have heard no news from outside for two years. Where is the *Beaver*?'

Then he caught sight of Captain Hanson, pale and drawn, unsteady on his legs, leaning over the rail.

'Hanson! Edward Hanson, you are alive!' he cried. 'Thank the good Lord – we had given you up for lost.'

When the soldier scrambled aboard, Hanson grasped his hand and said, 'I am alive, though the *Beaver* is wrecked and most of her crew dead.'

'Good Lord! How on Earth did you survive?'

'Saved by the timely arrival of Captain Loftus here.' Hanson gestured towards myself and McGruder. 'I introduce to you Lieutenant James Glaisterby, garrison commander.'

'Lieutenant, do you have the chief?' said the landsman, stepping forward. 'I demand to see him at once.' He had the appearance of a bilge rat which has gnawed its way into the breadroom, a-twitch at the scent of reward.

The lieutenant flinched at his abruptness. 'I trust you shall not think it impertinent, sir, if I beg your credentials?'

'You are addressing Finlay McGruder, envoy of the Royal Court and emissary of Admiral Tompion of the Newfoundland Fleet. Where is the prisoner?'

187

A troubled look passed across Glaisterby's face. 'Sir, there has been unrest with the savages. Chief Chanatuk escaped some time ago.'

'What – you let him go?' A look of fury suffused McGruder's face. 'Dam' and blast you, where is he now?'

'I beg you, sir – there have been great difficulties –'

'No excuses, lieutenant. I have come a long way to find this chief.'

'If you would let me explain, sir,' said Glaisterby. 'After much fighting and bloodshed, I captured his eldest son. He is the sole reason we are not attacked and overrun.'

'His son? It's the chief I want, not some dam' whippersnapper. Do you not understand there is a treaty at stake here?'

Lieutenant Glaisterby's desperation was plain. 'Praise God for a treaty. We cannot survive here without a peace of some sort.'

'The army shall have to answer for this failure,' replied McGruder. 'Lieutenant, assemble a force immediately. We shall go and flush out Chanatuk.'

'Sir, I no longer have men and muskets in numbers enough to enter hostile villages.' Turning to me, the lieutenant said, 'Captain Loftus, what resupply has the *Pursuant* brought? We are in dire short supply of munitions – muskets, ironshot, powder, wadding and the rest. I need men to replace those killed in the fighting. I must have dry stores such as rice and grain, potato and seedcorn.'

'The *Pursuant* did not come equipped to resupply you,' I said. 'We have little enough for ourselves.'

'You have an armoury, Loftus,' cut in McGruder. 'Furnish his soldiers with musket and ball so that I may go and deal the savages a salutary lesson. The Beothuks of Avalon were no opposition to a firm hand.' He shot me a look. 'I order you to provide the lieutenant with the necessary munitions.'

'If I may interject,' said Edward Hanson, coming forward tentatively, 'it may be as well to listen to Glaisterby, you know, and take the chief's son home as your prisoner. He counts as a prince –'

'Hold your peace,' said the Scotsman. 'Lieutenant, make ready to leave the fort tomorrow at first light.'

'Listen to him, McGruder,' I said. 'He knows this country well.'

'I have come to understand these people,' insisted Hanson. 'They shall resist fiercely. You are sending soldiers to their deaths.'

'It is no part of your business,' snapped the landsman.

'But Lieutenant Glaisterby is right,' said Hanson, reaching for his coat sleeve. 'The son can count for his father. I beg you to reconsider –'

'You are in no position to beg anything, given your disgusting crimes.'

The Scotsman dashed his arm away so violently the captain staggered and fell to the deck-boards. At once I extended a hand, helping him back to his feet.

'I'm taking this man below for rest,' I said, pushing the Scot aside and heading for the hatchway with Hanson on my arm.

McGruder called after me, 'Loftus, your priority

is to provide arms and men as required – forthwith. I shall go ashore with Lieutenant Glaisterby to make arrangements for the action.'

As the party descended to the waiting boat, I told Billy Jenks to see Hanson safe into my dayroom, then instructed Gaspar Rittel to set about arranging whatever resupply we could muster.

'Here, take the armoury keys,' I said, handing him the ring.

'Aye aye, captain.' Then the Dutchman hesitated. 'What's on your mind, Mister Rittel?'

'Sir, I fear we shall be too late to get home.'

I needed no reminding of that. 'Then the sooner you get your task done, the better. Carry on, sailing master.'

In my dayroom, the *Beaver*'s erstwhile master was sitting up, nursing a mug of small beer. His face was drawn.

'You should be resting in your bunk,' I said, ladling myself a draught from the bowl on the table and sitting opposite. When Hanson spoke, he voiced my own thoughts.

'That landsman's going to be the death of us all,' he said. 'It'll take days to find Chanatuk. Weeks, even. He'll have to burn their villages and torture the men before they give him up. We're running out of time.'

'Look, if it comes to the worst,' I said wearily, 'we could overwinter here at the fort. Surely that's better than being trapped in the ice in the far north.'

I could hardly believe I was hearing myself say it. The prospect of not getting back to Newfoundland till next summer was appalling. What might happen to Grace during that extended absence?

Edward looked gaunt. 'It would not be better at all. Look at the state of the men here – under siege and already starving. The *Pursuant*'s low on vittles. None of us would survive.'

Perhaps I was on edge, but somehow the captain's miserable countenance irritated me. Dammitall, who had told McGruder about the fort?

'If you hadn't blurted out how close the fort was, we should never have come here.'

A shadow passed across his face. 'I was distraught. I was ill – I did not know what I was saying.' He leaned over and clutched my sleeve. 'Listen, you must persuade McGruder to accept the chief's son. For God's sake, get him to sail home without delay.'

'He won't leave here without this Chanatuk fellow.'

'Then get Irocaibi to make a deal.'

'Irrokybee?'

'The son. Strike a bargain.'

'How in Hell's own name could I do that? I know nothing about these people, or the fort, or the country. Let alone this damm'd treaty that's suddenly so important.'

'But I do,' said Hanson. 'I believe Irocaibi can be persuaded to bring his father forward.'

'How? By torture, I suppose?'

'Torture would have no effect on such a man. You must let him go.'

I laughed out loud. Was Hanson's mind fevered?

'Let him go?' I said. 'We'd never see him again.'

'No, no, hear me out. Let the son go free on the understanding that he brings his father forward in his place. In return, you agree to stop the reprisals.'

'How can I do that?'

'Tell Irocaibi that you shall take McGruder away on the ship.' Hanson became desperate. 'Don't you understand? The ice is piling up at the Great Northern Cape. We cannot delay longer than a day or so.'

'I wish you had told Finlay McGruder this. Back at the *Beaver*.'

'But I did not realise what he would do here.'

'Well,' I said doubtfully, 'how could I get to see this prince, this Irocaibi?'

'James Glaisterby shall help you.' Edward Hanson leaned close. 'Think on this. McGruder's going to stir the Missacaibi up for no good purpose. They'll seek their bloody revenge after we have gone, and Glaisterby knows it. He'll grab at anything.'

I was calculating rapidly. Even with fair winds all the way, it was seven days to the cape. We were already desperately late. Hanson's plan sounded improbable – what did I know of Indian affairs? – yet surely it must be worth a try.

'Edward, if it goes wrong, McGruder can destroy us. We'd both hang, and you know it.'

'Unless we kill him.'

I was stunned into silence, appalled to realise that the same thought had struck me – and not for the first time.

'I shan't hear of it, Edward,' I said with finality.

'Then we are done for,' he said. 'Another winter on the ice. Sickness, lack of food, starving men. You have no idea.' His tired, frightened eyes held mine.

192

'Go ahead and give McGruder the arms, let him wreak his destruction. Why not go ashore and help him? A little butchery won't make any difference.' He gripped my arm. 'Dam' you. Dam' him. We're all going to die!'

'Control yourself, man,' I said, pushing him away.

I left the dayroom, deeply troubled. Understandably, Edward feared starvation and the risk of the bark becoming iced in. But the *Pursuant* had overwintered before, in Labrador, and survived by choosing a stable place free of dangerous, shifting pack ice. No, what concerned me most was delaying till next year. Being gone during a brief summertime was one thing, but disappearing for a twelvemonth was quite another. I could not leave Grace that long.

On deck, the crew were loading the harpooner launch with dozens of muskets, racks of ball, powder kegs and wadding rolls – the greater part of the armaments the *Pursuant* carried. The little shallop was laden to the gunnels with our last bags of rice and sacks of grain as Billy Jenks stood at the rail, shaking his head, watching his precious stores taken away. At that point, I heartily wished the Scotsman had gone overboard off Cape Chudleigh, taking his politickal ambitions with him.

'Look here, captain!' It was Gaspar, down in the launch, wielding a long pole. 'We shall be lucky to get the launches ashore through all this.'

I peered over the rail. It was ice. Grey-green chunks jostled busily at the *Pursuant*'s waterline like a crowd at the buttery hatch. Some were the size of kegs, others big as barrels. Many were

193

much larger, and encrusted with fresh growth on the outside as the late summer temperatures fell.

'Is that coming downriver, Mister Rittel?'

He drove his pole onto a large floe and struck off some shards. Bending, he scraped up the pieces and touched them to his tongue.

'No, captain – it's salt.'

I squinted seaward, beyond where the lower reaches of the Rupert River met the waters of James Bay. With the sun warming the land, an onshore breeze had picked up, driving little wavelets in from the offing. Right across the bay, from horizon to horizon, the sea's surface seemed alive, flickering and glinting with movement. I took up the spy-glass and saw thousands upon thousands of floes, great and small, floating at the sea's surface, their edges catching the weak northern sun, the rays reflecting off the restlessly shifting pieces. They were the half-melted remains of larger floes sent down from the north. So soon, I thought – the sea-ice is returning so soon.

The Dutchman had hauled himself back up the boarding rope and stood at the rail directing the bags and kegs being hoisted overside and into the launch.

'Sailing master,' I called.

He looked round expectantly.

'Halt the loading, Mister Rittel. Restow all the dry stores. Return the weapons to the armoury and bring me back the keys.'

This time he barely even raised an eyebrow.

In the light of the whale-oil lamp held by Captain Hanson, the half caste looked me up and down as if I were something caught in a gin.

Hubert Nitchequot was a fur trapper, half savage and half Frenchy. In the dead of night, four of us were assembled in Fort Rupert's tiny prison house – Hanson, the half-caste, myself, and the Indian prince, son of Chanatuk. The prison was a low cabin of axe-cut logs roofed over with cedar shingles, standing in a far corner of the compound. McGruder lay asleep some yards distant in the lieutenant's quarters, having readied himself for the morning's assault by consuming quantities of the fort's dwindling spirits store.

'Explain to the prince,' I whispered, 'that Chief Chanatuk must come forward. Ask him to hear our offer.'

Nitchequot translated my words into the Indian tongue. Glaisterby had insisted we use the half-caste, even though Hanson reckoned Irocaibi understood more English than he admitted.

I listened intently, acutely aware of how great a risk it was merely being here with the prisoner. At dusk, Hanson and I had slipped ashore unseen. On entering the palisades my despondency had deepened. The installation was a sketchy affair at best, thrown up hurriedly and poorly maintained. The outside walls and the low, crude huts inside were no more than cabins built of logs laid one atop the next. Altogether, an air of defeat hung over the fort and the isolated little community it supported. Musket-bearing soldiers made laggardly patrols around the walls and dragged themselves across the central area of beaten earth, going about their various duties. Native men and women moved listlessly in foot-shackles, enslaved as reluctant servants of the Crown. Dressed in worn buckskins and coloured blankets, they carried out the heavy or dirty tasks the military considered beneath them, hefting sacks, hewing wood and bearing slop buckets, followed everywhere by hollow-eyed, half-starved dogs.

When we met Glaisterby, well away from McGruder's gaze, the garrison's beleaguered commander railed against the Scotsman for misreading the circumstances. Far from flushing out Chanatuk, he said, a show of bloody force would drive the Missacaibi into further savagery. McGruder's view – that the only way to deal with the natives was by terror – was disastrous. Why, raged Glaisterby, banging his fist into his palm, did the wigs and buckles in London send out such a man?

When I suggested he close the garrison and ship his remaining men aboard the *Pursuant* for our return voyage, he was aghast. He would never abandon the fort, never fail his Queen, never submit to the enemy. He would die first, and sacrifice his men too.

Then Hanson revealed his plan to win over Irocaibi and persuade him to bring out Chanatuk. While Glaisterby was considering this, I told him that once home in Newfoundland I would urge Governor Spurgeon to reinforce and strengthen the garrison. So if Glaisterby let us see his prisoner, it meant he could fulfil his pledge to the Sovereign. If not, the consequences were dire. I had already halted the armaments delivery and was making the *Pursuant* ready for sea. By dawn, he and his fort would be abandoned without fresh supplies, without arms. In the end, he saw the advantages. But he in person could have nothing to do with it, and he left it to Hanson and myself to face the savage chief's son.

As Nitchequot spoke quietly to his master in their own tongue, Irocaibi listened intently. He was a native man of perhaps twenty or twenty two years, standing erect and about my height, wearing a buckskin jacket and briches, with soft boots on his chained feet. In the flickering lamplight, I saw the jet black hair scraped severely back and tied at the nape of his neck, the mahogany skin glossy and smooth. His penetrating eyes held me. It was almost as if our conditions were reversed – he the captor, we the submissive prisoners.

'Tell your master,' I instructed Hubert, 'that if he brings Chief Chanatuk to me, I shall stop the reprisals. I pledge to protect his father's safety while he goes to Boston. And Irocaibi himself may go free in return.'

The savage seemed to understand almost before the half-caste translated. Then Nitchequot said, 'Irocaibi must know how you can promise such a thing. What office do you hold?'

I held out my hand and showed the seal. 'I am Deputy Intendant of Esperantia. Owner and master of the bark, the *Pursuant*, commissioned by Admiral Tompion, commander of all English Naval forces in Newfoundland.'

Irocaibi bent forward to examine the ring and its design. Then he looked directly at me with an intense, questing gaze. This is my people's land, his high-boned features seemed to say, and we are the men who live enfolded within it and know its ways, while you are interlopers, bringers of war and contention. How can I trust you?

I held his eye. 'I shall keep my word, Irocaibi. And you must keep yours.'

The prince spoke in a husky voice.

'My master agrees to these terms,' said the half-caste.

Hanson looked mightily relieved. The four of us, Hubert Nitchequot included, clasped hands to seal the bargain. Making the least noise, we left the cabin and silently crossed the hard dry earth of the square towards the compound gates. We waited as Hubert padded silently over to the lieutenant's cabin to rouse him.

All at once I found myself staring upwards, transfixed. It was a clear and settled night, the deep canopy stretching above our heads with the scattered pricks of light I knew so well as the Navigator's guiding stars. There was no moon, yet half the blackness above was filled with an eerie glow, as if alight from no apparent source. Across the arch of sky rode a moving curtain of pale brightness, swirling and swooping like the skirts of women at a grand ball. These hanging walls of light seemed to step forward, grow in luminosity and then recede like dancers in a quadrille. From one end of the sky to the other, the luminescent drapes extended across a vast distance, covering all Hudson's Bay and the forest and bare plains that ran for hundreds of leagues to the north, even reaching as far as the Polar ice region itself, the Frigid Zone.

Hanson whispered, 'Have you never seen the Northern Lights?'

'The Aurora Borealis!' I exclaimed under my breath.

In a moment Glaisterby appeared, tiptoeing from his cabin, and Irocaibi raised his hands to show the shackles and chains.

'Is it agreed?' whispered the lieutenant.

'Aye,' I said, and he produced the key to release the native.

Irocaibi started for the gates, but I held his arm. Speaking low, I said, 'Hubert, ask your master what does the sky signify? Good or ill for our bargain?'

When the Indian answered, Nitchequot leaned close to my ear. 'Irocaibi says The Dancing Light in The Night Sky foretells neither the future nor the past, only the largeness of the land over which it suspends.' Hubert smiled. 'The chief's son says there is no sign nor god nor guide in the sky. Men must trust each other, for no truths exist beyond what is carried in the heart.'

So much for the sophistries of the white man's religions, I thought. A priest, admiring such pulchritude in the Heavens above, would have proffered the faith and beliefs of his creed, saying the wondrous display of light proved beyond doubt that God existed to oversee all his children's petty actions. Yet this native prince showed no such superstitious or artful tendency. He was as down-to-earth as a tundra fox.

Glaisterby had gone ahead to speak to the guards. They unbolted the gate and, with no more than a briefly raised hand, Irocaibi loped off across the cleared ground towards the forest. In a moment, he had disappeared into the night.

James Glaisterby came to my side. 'Well, Captain

Loftus, if Chief Chanatuk appears, you have broken the stalemate. If not, then you have freed a general to rally his troops.'

We waited through the long hours crouched a-top the fort's wall by the main gates, watching the approach path. In Glaisterby's cabin below, McGruder slumbered on, his snores thunderous in the still of the night. Overhead, the sky blazed with its magnificent auroral dance, bright enough to throw a cast over the Rupert Bay anchorage. Tucked into the silvery water behind Caribou Isle, the *Pursuant* sat quietly nodding to her fore-and-aft anchors as the river current tugged at her keel.

Hanson gazed out. 'She's a stout little ship, just like my *Beaver*. Good enough to make the voyage year in and year out.'

I grimaced. 'I shall stick to the Labrador and Gulf trade. The voyaging here is too fraught.'

'Even for fifty thousand marks a season?' Hanson saw me hesitate. 'You could buy a few barks with such profits.'

'If she made good profit, why was Governor Spurgeon obliged to subsidise her?' I said, more to prolong the conversation than anything. The time had passed too slowly. Irocaibi had sworn to be back before first light, and there was only an hour to go.

'He did not. He merely underwrote her hull.'

'Then he must be sorely disjointed at her loss.'

'Aye, I suppose so. But there were good years.' Hanson sounded wistful. 'When I first came here to load beaver pelts, bearskins, buckskin and the rest, I traded with all the trappers, both natives and mixed-bloods. Demand for fine furs soared and I shipped in a handful of English trappers.' He sighed. 'Then French trappers came, attracted by better prices than sending their wares all the way down the canoe portages to the Saint Laurent towns. The merchants there found supplies drying up, so the Quebec authorities recruited armed tribesmen to throw us out. England was obliged to reinforce Fort Rupert.'

'Now that the Hudson's Bay Company has abandoned its duty,' put in Glaisterby, showing a touch of pride, 'this fort and Edward's bark are all that keep the Sovereign's claims alive.'

'What about this treaty of McGruder's?' I asked.

'O aye, McGruder and his treaty,' said Hanson. 'He's an influential young cove in the diplomacy, he tells me. Connections in high places. Ambitious for greater things, which he believes he can achieve by pushing through this treaty. Yet I fear it cannot work, for it takes their lands and forces the Missacaibi to become subjects of England.'

'Subjects of Great Britain,' corrected Glaisterby self-importantly. He had been overjoyed to hear from me about the recent Union.

Hanson gave a wry chuckle. 'No matter. These savages are a self-respecting race, too proud-hearted to submit to McGruder and his bloody treaty.'

'What about Chief Chanatuk?' I put in. 'Won't he sign it?'

'I doubt it,' said Hanson. 'If anything, they'd be better off treating with the French. They would take their furs without enforcing a false allegiance upon them.'

'You think?' sniffed Glaisterby. 'My Indian informants tell of rumours about a French plan to bring a force by ship up the Saint Laurent. They would launch an assault from Trois Rivières to subdue the savages.'

Hanson snorted. 'Preposterous! No land army could reach here. Trois Rivières is a hundred and fifty leagues distant across impassable terrain. The troops would die in their thousands, lost in the forest.'

'Where is this place, Trois Rivières?' I asked.

'On the Upper Saint Laurent River, where the Saint Maurice joins it,' said the lieutenant. 'The river is Navigable that far by fair-sized ships, I understand. But the Indians say the French authorities there believe the invasion to be lunacy.'

'Just as lunatick as McGruder's treaty,' said Edward. 'I wish the Newfoundland Governor had listened to me instead.'

'No matter what armies or fleets the French send, England shall win the war,' said Glaisterby in a burst of patriotick hubris. 'Then after the peace bargaining, we shall rule the Hudson's Bay territory unchallenged.'

He misunderstood the realities of diplomacy. McGruder could tell him how settlements, ventures, colonies, trading concessions – certainly Naval or military emplacements like this fort – had their fates determined by whispered half-conversations in palace corridors in Paris and London. Glaisterby's life and those of his men were bagatelles of no consequence to the wigged and perfumed envoys and secretaries at Court.

'Treaties are worthless without force behind them,' I said. 'The French would need to sail in here with a fleet of ice-strengthened barks to threaten this fort.'

'Are you saying the fort has no future, no purpose?' Glaisterby sounded angry.

'Only pointing out, lieutenant,' I put in mildly, 'that your future here depends on the Admiralty making the necessary military and Naval commitment.'

At that moment the conversation terminated as McGruder's snoring abruptly ceased, to be replaced by muffled grunts. He had woken and was making his customary irascible demands.

'I put a soldier in there to wait on him,' said Glaisterby, by way of explanation.

'Dammit, he's up early,' I muttered. 'It's not dawn for half an hour.' Then, more to reassure myself, I added, 'Surely he cannot leave before it's light.'

Edward's thoughts were elsewhere. 'If only Governor Spurgeon had listened. I said we should let the savages accommodate with the French, but still maintain a limited garrison to validate the territorial claim. It was a subterfuge that would have allowed trade to continue. He refused to propose it to Boston or London. For her last voyage, the poor *Beaver* was laden down with arms and guns and shot and stores for James here. She was overloaded. That's partly why she was driven ashore.'

'May I remind you,' said Glaisterby a touch defensively, 'that she was supposed to resupply my garrison. And by the way, I would never accept the Missacaibi signing a treaty with the enemy.'

There was shouting from the cabin.

'Sounds as if someone's getting a scolding,' I said.

'Dam' the war,' said Hanson as if he had not noticed. 'Dam' King Louis and his claims on Kanada. What does the Catholick succession matter to a man like me? All I want is peaceful trade.'

'You need military protection for that,' said Glaisterby.

A soldier burst from the lieutenant's cabin and dashed across the compound in the direction of the barracks, calling for the men to rouse themselves. He was immediately followed by the Scotsman, bawling irascibly.

'Lieutenant! Glaisterby, where in Hell's name are you?'

A horn sounded across the compound. There were grunts and curses mingled with the clatter of arms and many boots clumping over wooden floors as the soldiers roused themselves.

'Delay, lieutenant,' I whispered, 'do whatever you can.'

McGruder's voice rang out again. 'Glaisterby, show yourself this minute.'

The lieutenant scrambled off the gate-top and descended the ladder. Our plan looked like going massively awry. In the next few minutes, the Scotsman would discover Irocaibi was gone.

'There you are,' we heard him growl. 'I want the men assembled at once.'

'It's not yet light,' replied the lieutenant. 'We cannot march until the sun's up.'

'Your persistent procrastination and cowardice shall be entered in my reports, Glaisterby. No more excuses – make ready to leave the gates in five minutes.'

The lieutenant accepted defeat and went off to see to his men.

Now I heartily regretted listening to Edward. And trusting an Indian, prince or not. Irocaibi had sworn to return before first light, but he had betrayed my trust. What a misconceived plan this had been. Putting my head above the stockade, I anxiously scanned the dark forest. It was deep and still and silent, and nothing seemed alive.

Then in the faint boreal glimmer there was a movement. A figure appeared at the edge of the clearing around the fort, then another. They came forward without haste, progressing up the track towards the gates. One walked slowly but with a lordly bearing. The younger man held out a steadying arm.

I slipped down the ladder and swung the gate aside as Hanson came to join me. The oncomers stopped a few yards off.

'It's Chief Chanatuk,' whispered Edward.

The old man took a pace forward. The lord of the tribe and the river lands called Missacaibi had delivered himself to save his people. With a hand raised in farewell, his son turned and loped back along the track. By the time the chief had stepped across the compound's threshold, all sight of the young savage was gone.

But Irocaibi had been as good as his word.

11

Stone Dead

The *Pursuant* scudded merrily along, heading out of James Bay and northwards for the Great Northern Cape. The ship's company had come alive at the prospect of being homeward bound, and the pressed men worked with a lusty will. I even heard the occasional glad chanty. We were on our way back to Esperantia at last.

Broad reaching before a light southwesterly on the larboard quarter, we carried a mizen staysail as well as topsails, courses and spritsail. To catch yet more of the breeze, I had two jibsails set wing and wing on the bowsprit. Still I wanted speed and bade Gaspar Rittel send men aloft to run out the studding yards. The sailing master grinned as he sharpened the seamen to their tasks, and soon the stunsails were set outboard of the fore and main. They drew well, the *Pursuant* rolled a little more, and her speed increased.

There had been, of course, the most earth-shaking detonation of McGruder's temper when he understood how I had interfered. Beside himself with righteous rage, he threatened me with charges of insurrection, disobedience, treachery and spying. The loss of my captaincy and my ship, he said, would be as nothing to the fate that awaited me in front of Admiral Tompion. I should be stripped of the Deputy Intendancy, then grated for a whipping. After that, he would despatch me to Saint John's to face the Governor's Court and his hanging powers.

Then the Scotsman came face to face with Chief Chanatuk and understood. The volte-face was astounding. At once, he congratulated me on my bargaining skills. He admired my good sense and judgement. His reports would be aglow with praise.

Declaring that Chief Chanatuk should be treated like the aristocrat he was amongst his own people, he requested me to oversee the chief's going aboard while he tidied up matters with Glaisterby – meaning, while he drank the last few of his brandy shots. Taking the landsman at his word, I had gone out to the *Pursuant* with the old Indian and installed him in the best cabin, formerly McGruder's own quarters.

Light-headed with anticipation for the voyage, I got busy making the bark ready for sea. By the time the Scotsman arrived back on board, the spirit had restored him to his former, marginally less disagreeable self. His mood was further lightened by the prospect of a small private venture, as he called it – some bales of furskins he had purchased from Glaisterby, hoping for a profit back in Saint John's. It was a paltry acquisition compared with what the *Pursuant* might have loaded if only we had had the time. I held my peace on that score and, leaving Gaspar to see the bales hoisted aboard and stowed in the hold, nipped smartly below with Edward to prepare my charts and instruments. Nothing else would do now but the quickest route to the cape.

Since breaking her anchor from the mud and

gravel of Rupert Bay, the little *Pursuant* had made good speed, trolling along at six and a half knots. With the Rupert River two days astern, Cape Jones Island came in view at the northeastern point of James Bay. The Navy's sea-charts showed it had also been named Pointe Louis XIV, although since the nearest French garrison was a hundred and fifty or two hundred leagues distant it seemed safe enough to ignore that. Whatever its name, this cape was our departure point not just from the waters of James Bay but from the land itself. The open sea stretched clear to the cape, four or perhaps five days' sailing away.

Dropping down the companionway to plot a position, I unlocked the door to the Indian nobleman's cabin. Chief Chanatuk rested on a bunk with a straw palliasse beneath him. He barely raised his head to survey me. The gleaming eyes flickered with alertness, but otherwise his body was stiff and aged, a desiccated old oaken cask which creaked with fatigue. Conversation was impossible, for he spoke no English nor any French, and McGruder had refused to embark the half-caste Hubert Nitchequot. When I enquired how the treaty negotiation was to be conducted, the Scotsman laughed and said it hardly mattered as long as they had the chief's person.

Quietly, I withdrew, leaving Chanatuk to his dignity. In the dim passageway, where only the faintest glow of grey northern light filtered from the open hatch, I saw a figure coming unsteadily down the companionway steps.

'Eli?' I said. 'What's on your mind?'

The old fellow had recovered enough to occupy

a hammock in the foc'sle, but nevertheless was feeling his age. He put a hand out to steady himself against the *Pursuant*'s rolling, cleared his throat and whispered, 'Is that landsman asleep, Captain Matthew?'

I nodded. In the next door cabin, McGruder slumbered on in his brandy dreams.

'And Captain Hanson?'

'Busy in the dayroom making up the work for my pilot book.'

'Then would you come to the forward hold, captain? You'll see what it's about when we get there.'

Though I preferred to stay and work the Navigation, I humoured the old fellow. The courage he had shown during the Ungava Bay tempest was an example that had shamed the reluctant crew into sharpening their look-alives all round. Yet the cold and hardship of this voyage had done Eli no good at all. His hands as he clawed at the companionway rail were bent into talons and he mounted the steps with a stiff gait.

We crossed the waist, climbed down the hatchway and entered the foc'sle. The off-watch lay resting, warmed from the dying galley fire nearby. We had fuel enough to light it only once a day, for the noontime meal. Heavily canvassed, the ship swayed as we ducked past the seamen in their swinging hammocks and went aft. Eli opened the bulkhead door and we crouched through into the hold. Apart from McGruder's private bales of prize buckskin, we were lightly loaded, having by now consumed much of our stores. Between the stacks of boxes and bundles and the hold's hatch cover, dogged tight in case of bad weather, spaces remained.

A hundred creaks and ticks resounded off the wooden walls as the bark heaved herself along, the deck knees and ribs working, the foremast step at the very foot of the bulkhead issuing intermittent groans. Outside, water slushed past the hull, hissing and foaming as we encroached on that seventh knot of speed. Eli had brought a candle but still my eyes took some moments to adjust to the gloom. I struggled to understand what possessed him to bring me here.

'Look, captain,' he said. 'A fellow from steerboard watch let slip something and I came down to see for myself.'

He gestured at what I took in the dim glow for a bale of buckskin lying a-top several others, sunk half hidden in the folds. When I peered closely, I saw the whole thing was strapped to ringbolts let into the wooden wall. The ship lurched and the bundle moved.

'Good God!' I cried, stepping back. 'Is it alive?'

Snatching the candle, I saw it was a man, not just trussed hand and foot but gagged too.

'O no – it can't be,' I muttered.

Pulling out my knife, I slashed the gag in a single movement. In the guttering candle flame, his eyes flashed.

'Traitor,' spat Irocaibi.

'It's not true!' I protested. 'I had no idea that –'

I rocked back on my haunches. He had spoken in English.

Suddenly I felt foolish, taken for a simpleton by everyone. Far worse, I understood what a great betrayal had been laid on the Missacaibi savages

– a betrayal of my word, and Glaisterby's too. Only McGruder could be behind this. At last I saw how dangerous the Scotsman was, and when Irocaibi struggled I hastened to put the gag back on. McGruder must not know I had discovered his secret cargo until I was ready. We were all too unprepared – unarmed and vulnerable.

'Keep him quiet, Eli,' I whispered. 'I'm going to get weapons.'

Handing him the candle, I turned towards the bulkhead. The gloomy light filtering through the square opening darkened as someone blocked the way. With my knife in my hand, I stepped forward and barged into a burly seaman. We tumbled through and ended up in the crowded foc'sle. The men were no longer asleep in their swinging hammocks but up and waiting. In the middle was Finlay McGruder, holding a brace of pistols.

'The prisoner's escaping!' he cried.

There was a movement behind me and I got a shove in the back so hard I went flat to the boards. McGruder's pistol jerked up.

'No!' I shouted.

It discharged with a deafening crack and a blast of heat and sparks from the pan. Momentarily the darkened, packed foc'sle was illuminated like midday in an orange-red glow. I remember a tableau of figures standing stock still, as if time had frozen in that instant when fortunes reversed.

There came another discharge, a shot from McGruder's second pistol. It went wide, crashing against the bulkhead timbers. From the sole, I lunged up and knocked him into a staggering backward

211

retreat. Striking an upward blow, I caught him under the chin and, with an exhalation of air, he crumpled.

I heard horrible groans. There was a seaman lying prostrate on the sole.

'Bring a light,' I snapped.

Someone lit a candle-lamp, and its yellow flame illuminated the confined space. I bent down, holding the lamp close. It was Eli. He lay doubled up, his cheek driven down onto the boards, his back arched as if in agony, a sticky pool of blood emerging from under his guts. His arms and legs were moving like a man swimming – yet Eli Savary, of all seaman, had never had truck in all his life with something so lubberly as swimming.

'Get Billy Jenks,' I rapped, and the foc'sle men parted to let someone go through to the galley.

McGruder got up with difficulty and came forward.

'Good God, Loftus,' he said, his voice shaking, 'what have I done?'

The Scotsman still held a brace of pistols, their muzzles smoking. They were my own, that I had stupidly left unlocked in the dayroom. He looked around at the assembled men and immediately began to defend himself.

'I thought it was the prisoner escaping. I saw the knife. I had to defend myself, did I not?'

Dumbly, I gazed down at the wounded Eli, whose hands clawed weakly at the boards. The bark gave a sudden roll, dipping her gunnels first one way, then the other. The wind had got up, and she was overcanvassed. When McGruder staggered, I caught him by the collar of his jacket and hauled his blinking face close to mine.

'I'll make you pay for this, you bastard.'

'It was an accident!'

I shook him so roughly his bones cracked. 'Not just for shooting Eli, dam' your eyes. Have a mind what's going to happen at Fort Rupert. Why did you take Irocaibi?'

'The treaty,' he muttered. Something like a nervous chuckle bubbled up and stopped halfway out of his throat. 'What if the old savage died on the voyage back?'

'You bloody fool,' I said.

Billy Jenks came scrambling down the steep steps, bearing his precious Physick bag. He bent over the bloodied, misshapen form lying in a sorry heap on the sole.

But Eli had stopped swimming.

Pacing the quarter-deck, I cursed the wind that had sped us on our way so well. From fair it had become foul, and we could make no headway back towards the Rupert River.

The *Pursuant* was at anchor, tucked behind a low spit of land with both bowers laid out on six shackles' length of cable. What had been a moderate southwesterly, the breeze for home, had risen to a screaming wail the moment I turned back for the fort. After three fatiguing days and nights beating into it, I had run the bark inshore for shelter till the weather abated. Still the gale blew, relentless, thwarting our return.

Finlay McGruder remained not the least contrite

about the mayhem that must follow at the fort when the savages discovered the white man's betrayal. Lieutenant Glaisterby and his entire complement faced slaughter. And after such a show of the white man's perfidy, I was convinced neither Chanatuk nor Irocaibi would sign a damm'd thing, let alone a treaty by which they abandoned any claim to their homelands. The Scotsman's stupidity had not only killed Eli, but fouled the Hudson's Bay strategy he so dearly promoted.

Edward Hanson put his head up from the companionway and sniffed the air. He carried a pistol, primed and charged, tucked conspicuously into his belt. I carried my own pair, and so did all three mates, Gaspar, Nat and Luke. The landsman was confined below, locked in my dayroom. I harboured no qualms about explaining to Admiral Tompion how he had jeopardised the entire undertaking.

'Edward, for what it's worth,' I said, 'what do you think of the weather?'

'Looks set in.' He grimaced. 'If we did get a northerly to take us back to Fort Rupert, that's the very wind to pack the ice onto the cape.'

'I am fully aware of that.'

In truth, since turning back we had discussed the matter many times. It was perilously late in the season to be this far from the cape. Though the afternoons could still be sticky and hot and the coastal air full of blackfly, the chill nights and shortening days told of rapidly approaching autumn.

Hanson was watching me. 'You must head north while we still can. Have him put ashore, Matthew, as I suggested. Let Irocaibi make his way overland.'

It was fifty leagues back to the Indian's territory. This tundra land was dangerous country, according to Hanson, a land without people, a trackless terrain. Yet a little further south, the trees and lakes began. The Indian could build a cedar-bark canoe and progress via the water leads. We could furnish him every assistance of weaponry and supplies. If anyone were capable of such a trek, it must surely be Irocaibi.

In my heart, I had already decided the delay must end. A return to Fort Rupert now was out of the question, whatever the fate of Glaisterby and his men.

'Very well, Edward,' I said. 'Have him brought up.'

The younger Indian had suffered the indignity of being confined below to stop him simply hurling himself overboard and swimming for the shore. He would be dead of cold and fatigue before he had gone half a cable. I called the sailing master over.

'Mister Rittel, lower the shallop and detail four men at the sweeps. The Indian is going ashore.'

He shot me a questioning look and I followed his gaze. My eye fell on the sombre parcel tucked under the taffrail, the downwind point of the ship. Swathed in black slops, tightly bound, Eli Savary's corpse was long past its due for burial. I had refused to let his remains go overside. Though he wanted to die at sea, his wish had always been to be buried on terra firma.

'Put a pair of picks in the boat, sailing master,' I said.

As Rittel got a party of men to carry the corpse and

lower it into the shallop, Captain Hanson reappeared on deck with Irocaibi, bound by the hands, held between a pair of seamen. Impassively, the Indian studied the bleak landscape.

'Irocaibi, I must take the ship north or be caught in the ice,' I told him. 'I am setting you ashore.'

His eyes ranged uneasily over the barren land and its grim rocky aspect.

'In the boat, you shall find an assortment of knives and tools, pistols and a musket with a dry horn and shot bag, clothing and food,' I said. 'Take whatever else you need. Anything we can spare is yours. Your bonds shall be cut when you reach dry land. May the Fates see you safe.'

His face remained impassive.

The jack-tars led him down to the waist and handed him into the shallop. Four fellows were down in the boat, standing with sweeps raised. Between their feet lay the sorry black bundle that had been Eli, who had surely known he would never see Esperantia again. Far better, I thought bitterly, that he had been thrown from the ratlines in a gale and died like a seaman instead of being shot by an arrogant fool. And even then the old salt's last act had been to intervene to save my life.

The Dutchman looked to me for a signal. 'Shall I let the boat go, captain?'

'One moment,' I said, going to the side and gazing over, thinking of Eli in times past.

For a moment, resting my head on the damp rail, I closed my eyes and listened to the sound of the wind rattling a block somewhere high above as it hunted through the shrouds. I heard the anchor cables straining as the bark shifted at every boxing gust. I caught the urgent, rhythmical lapping of wavelets at the waterline. These were the sounds Eli Savary had lived with every waking and sleeping moment of his long and well-tempered life. Now he would lie forever in an unknown place, with only the sound of waves coming ashore.

Footsteps thudded on the deck-boards behind. I broke from my reverie and lifted my head expecting to see Captain Hanson. All at once, there were powerful arms pinning me to the rail and hands groping at my belt. I grabbed for my pistols but they were whipped away. Startled, lashing out, I struck someone's face, but there were too many. I was overpowered.

'Gaspar! Edward! Nat!' I shouted.

My sailing master lay flat on the boards under two hulking fellows, his arms wrenched back as they tied his feet to his hands. Nathaniel Gunn and Luke Tatchell emerged from the foc'sle companion.

'Don't resist, lads!' I shouted, still pinned by the arms, helpless. 'They're all armed.'

But their hands were already tied. I saw they were captives of a band of pressed seamen, and it all fell into place. McGruder had got the crew behind him. When Edward Hanson approached, somehow it was no surprise to see his pistol directed at my belly.

'It's the only way, Matthew,' he said, sounding sick at heart.

Finlay McGruder's head appeared at the hatch-way. Edward must have freed him, and he was armed with pistols. Then the Scotsman began bellowing from the break.

'Where's the Indian, you idiots – is he back aboard? You fellows there, have you got Loftus tied up? Someone see that the deputy mates are in custody.'

But it was all in hand, for Hanson had quietly taken command. Oblivious to this, and quite as if he were a captain or a master, McGruder issued sailing orders – of a kind.

'Get that bower up, or whatever it's called,' he said. 'Raise the anchor, is what I mean. Shake out some sails and courses, or whatever they are. Get us moving.'

One party went forward to the beak, slotted poles into the windlass and started cranking home the cable. Other seamen moved uncertainly about in disorder. A few went aloft then stopped to see if anyone followed. Some tars stood by the belays, looking about. The oarsmen in the waiting boat craned up to see what was happening out of sight. Everyone looked confused.

A flash of anger passed across Hanson's face. 'Landsman, leave the sailing orders to me!'

He went over and told Nat and Luke they must oversee the men's work or be shot. Then he issued a series of sailing commands which everyone could understand. With whoops of delight and cries of 'Home, boys!' a dozen jack-tars leapt off to get the anchor and loosen out canvas.

Edward came back to the rail. 'You fellows down there, step up from the shallop with the Indian.'

Two of the oarsmen collected all the sweeps and clambered up. The others turned to deal with Irocaibi. He sat motionless in the stern, his hands bound, a frozen figure, waiting, Eli's shrouded body at his feet. Yet as soon as the seamen tried to haul him up the boarding rope, he kicked out with all his might. It took all their strength to bring him back on deck, where he continued to struggle. With an oath, he knocked one man down and went at the other like a wild animal.

Hanson stepped back in alarm. The two seamen holding me faltered. I wrenched free and brought my foot up to catch Edward at the crutch of his briches. He doubled forward and up came my knee onto his chin. There was a crunch and blood spattered from his mouth. With a gasp, he staggered back. I grabbed the pistol from his belt and swung round looking for McGruder.

The Scotsman stood transfixed at the break with his mouth hanging open. I might not get another chance. Bringing the pistol up, I levelled the barrel and squeezed the trigger. The lock clicked, the pan hissed and the piece bucked. McGruder's arm whipped backwards in a welter of ragged cloth.

But my resistance was short-lived, and Irocaibi's too. Seamen were clambering back aboard over the rail, and others on the weather-deck charged over. We were grossly outnumbered. They fell on the Indian, forcing him down. One fellow came at me with a sweep raised, and a two-handed grip on the loom. Before I could duck, the yellow pine blade swept viciously through ninety degrees of arc. It caught me full on the cheekbone and knocked the fight away. Stunned, my head ringing, I sank down on the boards.

Edward was shouting.

'Overboard!' he cried.

I was manhandled to the top of the rail and hurled bodily into the shallop. Landing in a heap, reeling from the fall, tasting blood in my mouth, I found myself on my knees staring at the boat's ribs and following the slop of bilgewater as it rocked to a standstill. Further blows struck my back and something clattered onto the thwarts alongside me. It was a pair of sweeps.

There were more shouts and the boarding rope snaked up the topsides out of reach and disappeared. Then the wavelets slopping at the bark's waterline began to foam and fall away sternwards. With a sickening lurch of the stomach, I realised the ship was moving. Far overhead, the white topsails strained full of wind. The braces and sheets creaked as they came home. The shallop, still tied on, bumped against the planking, shied away, then closed again. The *Pursuant* already had two knots of way on.

In desperation, I grasped the painter and held on. I heard the Scotsman shouting, so my shot must only have wounded him. High above the channels where the topsides curved home, Edward Hanson's face appeared at the rail. My mouth felt like wood as I tried to form words.

'Hanson – why, dam' your eyes?'

'McGruder made me do it!' he shouted. 'He's going to put charges against me. For the loss of the *Beaver*.' His face was suffused with horror. 'And the men ashore – the starvation.'

'But I told you I would bear witness on your behalf!'

'You can't fight him! He wields more power than you.'

He was fumbling to untie the painter from the small midships bitts under the rail. A jack-tar, one of the pressed men who had so gladly fallen in with McGruder, reached down with his knife and sliced the line clean in two. By instinct, I caught the loose bight as it snaked down. What a futile act. The shallop was free, falling away from the bark's bulky topsides.

Then a figure leapt lithely onto the rail. Next second, with a great crash, Irocaibi landed in the boat. It rocked violently and I lost balance, falling towards the freezing water. Somehow, even hampered by the wrist bonds, he caught me and gathered me in his arms as if I weighed no more than a bag of apples. With a grunt, he hauled me safe inside the gunnels.

There were shouts but the shallop had fallen too far clear of the *Pursuant* to recover it. The bark's topsides receded so fast I could soon see what was happening on deck. Hanson ran onto the quarter, remonstrating with the steersman, arguing with McGruder, who leaned heavily on the taffrail, his arm hanging limp. If only, I cursed, if only my shot had struck him mortally.

The bark was moving fast. With fore and main-topsails drawing, she caught the southwesterly – the wind for home. She heeled to the half gale, yards and bracelines creaking in protest, then smashed her way out to sea, leaving nothing behind but a broken wake. There was no catching her in a rowboat.

Out of the temporary shelter afforded by the bark, our little shallop sheered away downwind, heading for the anchorage's leeward shore. On the sudden lift of a wave, Eli Savary's corpse slumped to one side, and I lunged across to haul it back inboard. The shore was approaching fast. It wanted a hard row to keep us from being dashed on the rocks. Still half stunned, I took up a sweep and slotted it in the rowlock, gesturing at the Indian to do the same. He held up his wrists, so I got out my knife to slice the bonds through. Even then, he held the loom awkwardly, finding the oar difficult to wield. Indians paddle, not row, I thought dumbly, getting the second sweep in its lock and shoving him aside. Irocaibi obediently moved to the after thwart and steadied the corpse.

Pulling hard, each effort bringing a throb of agony to my bruised cheekbone where the oarsman's blow had landed, I brought the shallop round by sheer force of will. The blades dipped time and again until my breaths came short and hard. By degrees, the boat drew into the head of the inlet and found shelter from the wind. A narrow gravelly strand appeared between the rocks and I drove on until the stem grounded. Then I slumped forward, utterly exhausted.

After a minute, there came a hand on my shoulder. Looking up, I found Irocaibi, eyes narrowed into the sun, pointing out to sea.

With courses set and the offshore breeze full in her sails, the *Pursuant* rolled away, running off fast. Approaching the far headland, she dipped her yards as if to say farewell. I watched, unable to speak or think, until all but her stern quarters showed. Then quite suddenly there was no sign in the whole land nor the entire sea of the ship and her occupants and all her works. She had cleared behind the land and was gone.

There was nothing left in that vast and empty landscape save the little shallop with its cargo of two abandoned men and a poor old sailor's corpse.

12

Bare Escape

Irocaibi and I faced a simple truth. We had to reach Fort Rupert or die.

Before us was a sea passage of fifty leagues in an open boat along a coast strewn with rocks and shoals. The contrary wind kicked up a vile sea yet we were only two men to row, one of whom had never plied a sweep in his life. We had no compass nor cross-staff. Even my pilotage notes were aboard the *Pursuant*. There were rations for one man, some knives and tools, and a few arms, the equipment put in the shallop for Irocaibi's lonely trek.

But first things first. The picks were still in the boat. I took one and crossed the foreshore to the start of the land, where there was a low escarpment leading a few feet up to a flat plain. The tundra stretched baldly away in hues of grey and green till it met the bottom of the great dome of sky. I scraped at the rocky ground but after half a glass had gouged no more than a scoop an inch or two deep. Wearily, I gathered beachstones and carried them up the rise to lay them beside the hollow. At first, Irocaibi watched. After a while, he fell in to help.

An hour later, with a suitable pile built, we lugged Eli's mortal remains to the grave. When we had done, the old salt lay there under the smooth, rounded beachstones heaped into a cairn. Briefly, a sense of calm overtook me, despite the turmoil of my mind, as I stood over the grave and spoke a few plain words, though without priestliness in them. It might have been as desolate and lonely a spot to lie as anywhere on the globe, yet in its ocean-like serenity it seemed a fitting place for a seaman like Eli Savary.

Back at the boat, I hefted out all unnecessary items such as spare knives, the musket and shot, extra skins and clothing. For the sake of lightness I left only the food, the pistols and one knife a-piece, for this was going to be hard enough without carrying unnecessary weight. In landsmen's parlance, it was more than a hundred and fifty miles by sea to the fort and we had a heavy boat with just two men to row it into a stiff wind and sea. The sooner we made a start, the better. My first object was to scull to the inlet's windward side and judge the state of the sea.

'Irocaibi, you shall have to learn the white man's way of rowing,' I said, and indicated that he should bend his weight to give a shove off.

He stood immobile.

'Look alive there, man,' I said, 'I can't do it on my own.'

He glanced with distaste at the boat and its contents.

'We walk,' he said.

I gave a hollow laugh. Not only had I lost my ship, been deprived of my future at Esperantia and just buried my oldest friend, but I had been stranded ashore with only a fool for company.

'Get in, Irocaibi,' I said curtly, 'we can't waste time arguing.'

With some dignity, he bent to collect up all the discarded spare gear and clothing, stepped aboard and sat on the centre thwart. Between his legs he held the long-musket and its shotbag.

'That's just extra weight,' I protested.

He did not budge. With superhuman effort I managed to shove the boat back off the sand, splashed into the icy water and threw myself aboard.

'Irocaibi, move over.'

If he would not row, he could at least sit out of my way. Yet now he reached down and got an oar in the lock. I took up my own oar and laid back. He watched closely, then copied the action. At first, his blade skittered across the surface on one stroke, then dug too deep at the next, forcing me to backstroke lest we drove around in circles. Indians shall never make oarsmen, I thought, remembering the little canoes passing to and fro on the river by the fort, frail and lightweight as cockleshells, requiring no strength or skill to send them scudding along.

Yet after a few dozen strokes, Irocaibi got the method. Soon he was matching my own strokes, and we increased the rhythm. After some minutes more, we were pulling together as if he had been rowing white men's wooden boats since the day he left his mother's womb.

With Irocaibi's muscular efforts more than matching my own, we should have made easy work of the inlet. But the short chop battered at the boat's prow and the wind pressed against her freeboard. It was like rowing through a vat of molasses. By the time we had clawed over to the windward side, we had barely the strength to drag the boat onshore. Labouring up the rise for a vantage point, I studied the sea. The wind battered my face and spray stung my eyes. For as far as I could see, tossing waves rose high across the sea-scape.

'We shall wait a-while here, till the weather abates,' I said. 'It'll die away soon enough.'

Irocaibi was silent, his face inscrutable.

'Dammit, what else can we do?' I said. 'There's no going on foot. The land between here and Fort Rupert is either swamp or tundra. The shore's so cut through with indents and bays it's a week's walking to a day's rowing. The only way is by sea.'

Then I stopped short and sat down on the launch's gunnel. What was I saying? If anyone knew this country, it must be the native.

'Boat too heavy,' he said. 'Go by land.'

He unloaded the shallop and assembled a collection of artefacts quite the opposite of mine. Where I had rejected the long-musket in favour of the lighter pistols, now it rested at the top of the heap. Apart from two knives, he left all the precious tools and ropes. He dumped half the warm clothing. To my astonishment, he discarded all the food, barring a few breaks of ship's biscuit.

'And what do we live on?' I said. 'Is there anything to shoot with that old banger?'

Again, the solemn shake of the head. 'This land very bad land, not like Missacaibi lands. We move fast, eat little. Keep eyes sharp.'

He gestured at the landscape. It was a bare plain of moss and sedge with rocky outcrops and boggy pools interrupting the water-sodden ground. Without a tree in sight – not even a stunted spruce – it was altogether harsher and more hostile than the forest and deep cover of the Rupert River and Missacaibi lands.

The Indians, according to Edward Hanson, moved about by water, for the forest was shot through with a thousand rivers, tributaries and streams linked via navigable lakes and sluggish leads. The savages travelled light, taking what they needed as they went. Food grew in bush and tree and root, birds could be shot from the boughs with bow and arrow. If they had want of a canoe, they stripped a cedar's bark, cut down a sappy fir for ribs, took spruce roots and twisted them into lashings, then built the vessel on the spot. Going from a lake to the next stream, or from one river to the next, they carried their delicate, lightweight craft on their heads. If the distance were too far, they left the old one, walked on and fashioned another at the next water.

All at once, the shallop appeared an unwieldy object. Merely to hoist it aboard a vessel required tackles and blocks and lifting haulyards and booms. And it wanted many men to row against wind and sea.

'Very well, Irocaibi,' I said at last, 'we shall do it your way.'

He smiled. I had never seen him smile, and it was as though the sun had broken through after rain and cloud.

He shouldered the musket and we distributed the remainder of the load between us. At the last moment I gathered up the pair of pistols, shoving them inside my bundle. Irocaibi watched but said nothing.

We hefted our burdens and set off south from that windward shore, leaving behind the shallop I had sequestered in Esperantia, such a far off time, it now seemed. After a little, I paused, shoulders hunched against the freezing blasts, and peered across the deserted inlet's wave-torn waters towards the place of our first stranding. The icy wind cut my eyes but I ignored the streaks of cold wetness on my cheeks and squinted hard. Just discernible was the humble pile of stones we had built. I dipped my head in his honour, knowing no man would ever look again upon Eli Savary's last resting place.

Irocaibi had stopped a hundred paces ahead, waiting. I turned away and fell in behind him.

I woke with a start, shivering violently. A thin covering of snow had fallen in the night, and the dawn was hushed and frozen. The hunger in my belly was like an iron grip. By God's bones, it was cold on the tundra plain. This was not the biting chill of the Baltick Sea nor the damp creeping iciness of a Newfoundland winter. It was an oppressive, strength-sapping frigidity that enfolded a man's body and brought him to a standstill. On Irocaibi's insistence we had not stopped, until at last I had been unable to go further without respite.

All round was utter silence. Nothing moved across the whitened landscape. With a twinge of alarm, I realised there was no sign of the Indian.

Several hundred paces distant came the flash of a movement. Then there was another flicker of disturbance, as of someone creeping stealthily amongst the greystone boulders dotted about this uncompromising landscape. There it was again, almost as if the savage were hiding himself. Was he hunting? Doubt crept furtively up my spine. The figure was larger than a man's. I fumbled inside my fur jacket for my single pistol. Irocaibi was right – the pair had proved burdensome to carry and I had long since jettisoned its twin.

A pale shape appeared two hundred paces off. I blinked and looked again, heart thudding against my ribs. Unmistakeably, it was the form of a sizeable creature. Breaking cover, it padded across the boggy sedgemoor, a powerfully-built animal with a massive body supported on legs like tree trunks. The head was held forward and low, the dark nose pointing ahead of two cole-black eyes. Its thick, shaggy coat was yellowed and dirty at the feet. Elsewhere, its fur was perfectly white.

Irocaibi had told me the white bear was a beast whose hunger is never satisfied. Unlike the brown or the black or the grey-bearded bear, or even the great wolf from the timber lands, who are shy of mankind, he cannot be stopped. The white bear always comes on. The Missacaibi lived in fear of it above all other creatures, and moved in its country only if they had the pale-skinned man's musket. Nothing else could bring it down. Dam' for Irocaibi's long-musket now, with its good, solid, heavy ball. Where was it? And why had he left me alone?

I spun on my haunches to follow the bear's slanting progress. It loped so easily over the rough terrain, there was no point trying to run. Nor did jumping into the icy water of a nearby pool offer hope, for I knew the white bear was sometimes seen many miles offshore, swimming unconcernedly through the ice-strewn sea.

With the least movement, I cradled the pistol, trying not to make a sound that would give me away to this animal's wondrous hearing. Then I remembered too that the white bear could smell a seal, or a fox, or a beaver, from beyond the horizon. Even when there is no wind, or a contrary wind, the bear could scent an animal in his territory. Or a man. Dammit, was there not a flaw in the beast?

At a hundred paces off, it was plain that conceal-ment was futile. Every part of the bear was homed in on its quarry, its every rolling, padding step, driven by hunger, bringing it closer towards the scent. Its face showed the black snout pointed my way and two small eyes with their bead fixed pin-sharp. The bear had its prey under the minutest surveillance. The prey was me.

At fifty paces off, I stood up and began beating a boulder with a stick. When the flat sound fell across the dead, frozen plain, the bear stopped in its tracks, its gaze blank and uncomprehending. The flanks lifted and fell with its breathing. The snout glistened wetly, the nostrils flaring and twitching. Encouraged, I banged and slapped and shouted and raged at the thing to go away, to leave me be, to find another prey. The white bear lowered its head to show me its long and massively-muscled neck held on mighty shoulders. It took a pace forward, then another, and came on.

When it was no further off than the *Pursuant*'s length from her taffrail to stemhead – not even thirty paces – I raised the pistol. My hand trembled and I brought up the other to steady it. The sharp click was piercing as I sprang back the flintlock.

'Stop, dam' you!'

My voice sounded oddly unfamiliar in that great open space. The bear showed its teeth, revealing curved canines two inches long, and behind those, twin rows with opposing points like a saw's blade. Then it charged.

The head or the chest, I thought. When the creature reached the point of leaping on me, up came its front paws spread for the strike, the jaws agape. The chest opened to my aim and I squeezed the trigger. Had the desiccated northern air kept the flash powder dry? Had I loaded with care and made the wadding tight? A hand pistol, like a long-musket, is a chancy weapon at the best of times. This was not the best of times.

The lock sprang home, the flint sparked, the pan flared and the pistol bucked. I hardly registered the noisy, crashing discharge sounding so blank and heavy in the still air. My eye followed the ball's very path, and it was true. The shot struck the animal dead centre at the chest. There was a great thud and the yellow-white fur turned black as the hot ball passed into the folds of its skin.

The eyes flickered once and the bear came on. With a roar of agony or anger, the creature reared up and sideswiped with its paw. I tried to fall out of the way but the blow struck my ribcage with winding force. I crumpled. The white bear's head was within a handspan of my face. Its ripe and fish-stinking breath enveloped me. The fangs, held wide, revealed the red cavern of its gaping mouth. From this emanated a chilling roar as if all the beast's strength and spirit had been gathered into a single sound, all the power of its bodily muscle and lungs forced out through the throat. The noise burst into the world of the passive and silent tundra and dinned in my ears.

The bear threw its massive body forward and collapsed on my legs, crushing them hard against the ground. The roar faltered as it fell and its weight seemed lifeless. Not two feet from my own, the head lolled sideways with the mouth hanging open and the tongue licking and flicking at its flesh-ripping teeth. The huge arms were spread-eagled across my belly, twitching and flexing. Suddenly, horribly, a gallon of blood vomited from its gullet and spattered warmly over me. Its great chest heaved a sigh and a gale of rotten air rushed out, spraying a fine mist of blood-soaked vapour into the cool air. Then the beast lay still.

My shot must have got it in a main blood vein, or in the heart.

I lay rigid with fear, unwilling to believe what had happened, loth to risk rousing the creature. By degrees, the stench of putrid flesh from the last meal in the bear's belly evaporated, leaving only the lesser smell of wet fur and the warm metallic tang of fresh-spilled blood and a damp sedgey aroma from the earth on the undersides of its dinner-plate paws.

The enormous carcass pressed down, trapping me beneath. My legs were running, trying to put distance between me and the beast. Like poor Eli in his death agony, my limbs were beyond control. I bade my legs stop moving, but they continued to struggle, heavy as lead weights. Stabs of pain shot through my ribs. The mere act of breathing was a torture.

I whimpered quietly, limbs jerking, hands trembling, heaving and sobbing. The bear was dead. I had killed the white bear. I lay back, all but insensible, submitting to the sheer ecstasy of relief.

Irocaibi's face appeared above my head. Beside him, the barrel of his long-musket stood out darkly against the grey sky, a single lazy wisp of smoke curling from the muzzle.

'Only musket kill white bear,' he said.

Then he set to work to roll the carcass off me. All the while, pushing and shoving at the heavy folds of fur and flesh, Irocaibi spoke of the creature's strength and determination and how any man who survived an encounter with the white bear, musket or no musket, pistol or no pistol, came close enough to death to draw out for himself something of the beast's power and grow toughened in his own sinews, while nevertheless in the killing also losing some part of his spirit, which the dead bear took back with it to the earth.

His words made little sense. At last, working first one leg then the other free, I rolled clear. Kneeling, drawing air in agonised breaths, I stared wide-eyed at the vanquished animal, killed by musket, not pistol. Irocaibi's knife flashed as he delved into the bear's massive form, peeling back layers of blubbery skin and fat until he held something aloft in triumph. It was a dark ragged trophy the size of a large powder bag. Steaming in the frozen air, it dripped its warmth onto the snow. It was the bear's heart.

'Man must eat this part,' said Irocaibi.

In minutes, he had gathered dry moss by stripping it from boulders and begun furiously twirling one twig between his palms as it rested in the hollow of another. The moss smouldered, smoked and burst into flames. When the fire had built, he skewered the organ with his long knife and roasted it. He offered me a slice of the rubbery flesh, speared on his blade and sizzling. The taste was over-rich and made my throat gag, but I fought the urging of my stomach and chewed manfully. On the instant of swallowing the meat, I revived.

'Bear's heart gives courage,' said Irocaibi.

When we set off, I walked more warily than ever, following the native's loping footsteps, keeping pace with difficulty. He moved with unwasted effort, gliding ahead until I breathlessly caught up, then moving on again before I had properly collected myself. The Indian never spoke a word except to exhort me to walk on.

I did not complain. I had learnt my lesson. Without Irocaibi, I was a dead man.

Day after day, we trekked on. As we covered the leagues and closed Irocaibi's homelands, the Indian's need to know his people's fate intensified. We covered the ground relentlessly, both driven by the same grim determination to get home alive.

If we did stop briefly, it was at dusk and on high open ground, resting on our cloth and furskin bundles laid on the bare earth, huddling by a fire as the sun left the day and cold crept in all around. After our ship's biscuit was gone and we had consumed the last of the bear's innards, we lived on thin liquids boiled from bark and grasses gathered by Irocaibi. There was no sustenance in them and they did nothing to alleviate the clawing hunger in my belly yet, like a tea, they somehow refreshed my spirits. The flesh dropped away from my bones as if the Indian's brews speeded the body drawing on its own resources, giving temporary strength but depleting the corpus faster.

With southing, the landscape of bare flat plain with bouldered outcrops gave way to softer terrain where coverings of stunted spruce grew in the sheltered valleys. The vegetation increased until at last we entered the forest proper and were enclosed by stands of straight tall pines. Deeper in, the tree canopy rose higher above our heads, and woodpeckers and squirrels abounded. In the leafy gaps shone a blue sky and, glancing up, I saw a majestic eagle glide in lazy circles far, far above. As we toiled south, it grew markedly warmer. The sun's rays radiated from a piercingly blue sky. Day long, whirring blackfly infested the air.

On the morning of the seventh day, we stood high upon a greystone outcrop and for the first time gained a grand overview of the forest, stretching away over endless ridge and valley, valley and ridge. Breezes disturbed the tree-tops, passing through the foliage like great swells upon the sea's surface. To Irocaibi, this land was as familiar and natural as the ocean is to a seaman. It was not for him a place of incomprehensible fears and unknowable threats, as it was for me, but rather the land where he lived and prospered.

While to the south and east the forest undulated away forever, to the west the blue expanse of James Bay rested in the basin of the earth, flat and calm like a lake. The contrary wind, so unfortunate for our bid to regain Fort Rupert, so prosperous for the *Pursuant*'s course north, had spent itself.

Again, for the hundredth or the thousandth time, my agonised thoughts turned to the ship. For a week now she must have sailed before that strong southwesterly, making forty or fifty leagues in her noon to noon run. She would have rounded the Great Northern Cape before she lost that wind, and must surely be crossing the bight of Ungava Bay. In a few days more, she would turn south along the Labrador Coast to come within a week of reaching Newfoundland.

I thought of Hanson, the despicable turncoat, sailing the *Pursuant* home. In my mind's eye I saw Finlay McGruder with him on the quarter, crowing in triumph. And Factor van Schreik – what grim smile might he wear on learning of my demise in the frozen north? He would dismiss Matthew Loftus from his memory and turn to his future – marriage to Grace. Disgust and anger in equal measure welled up inside me.

As we sat resting and drinking bark tea, the Indian broke into my train of thought.

'The river,' he said, pointing.

Unmistakeably, there was the delta, with Caribou Isle at the river's mouth and the fort nearby.

'The Rupert River at last,' I breathed. For the first

time, I felt sure I would get home. Somehow, I would find the will to return.

Irocaibi shook his head. 'Soldier's name, not Missacaibi name. River is called Nasquinoba – Bright Water Running Towards Evening Sun.'

'Irocaibi,' I said, 'what do you think your warriors shall have done when they learnt of your kidnapping?'

'Make war on fort, kill all white men.'

I cast my eyes down, angry and ashamed at McGruder's betrayal.

'Fighting only stop when Irocaibi return,' he said. 'Men inside fort very afraid now. Shoot many Missacaibi – as before.' The Indian looked at me. 'You go to Glaisterby and tell story. Only you can make truce.'

If we pressed on, he said, we would gain the fort before dark. I scrambled about gathering up my bundle, kneeling to bind it tight with a leather thong. Then I stood up, kicked over the remains of our fire and was ready to walk.

'Irocaibi, as soon as things are settled at the fort,' I told him, 'I must set off south. How far is it overland to reach the river? The great river, I mean – the Saint Laurent.'

Again, the Indian noble shook his head. 'Winter comes. Matthew cannot survive in forest.'

I shrugged. 'I understand if you cannot help me. I shall go alone, carrying a musket. And Navigate by the stars.'

'Matthew not know how to travel.'

His calm intransigence was exasperating. 'Did you not hear me? I'm going back.'

'No, you follow Irocaibi's way. We must get treaty.'

What was he talking about? It was no longer any concern of mine. At this juncture, I gave not a fig for the damm'd treaty.

'We make treaty with French.' He looked into the distance. 'Better for Missacaibi people.'

'With the French?' I repeated, struggling to comprehend. The rigours of the last days had left me weak, unable to think straight. Then I remembered Hanson saying the Indians preferred to deal with France. But what was any of this to do with me?

'Matthew must help,' said Irocaibi, turning to me.

I almost burst out laughing. 'Do you expect me to participate in some treaty-making with the enemy?'

Seeing the native's face to be deadly serious, I determined to put him square.

'Look, face up to it, man – McGruder's going to get his terms through. There's nothing you can do. The Missacaibi are going to become subjects of Her Majesty as soon as Chanatuk signs.'

The Indian's head moved almost imperceptibly. 'Chanatuk not sign. Chanatuk die.'

'I'm sure he shall live,' I insisted. 'He may not be strong, but surely not near death.'

'Missacaibi chief never sign such treaty. Chanatuk make himself die.'

It took a moment to sink in. All along, had I been sending the old Indian to his death? It could not be.

'Then why did you bring him from the forest?'

'Gain time for Irocaibi to go to French. Try to make new treaty. As captain tried before.'

'Captain Hanson?' He had said something about going to Governor Spurgeon, suggesting that if the territorial claims and submission of the Missacaibi embodied in McGruder's treaty were dropped – or even merely suspended – then both sides, British and French, could withdraw without compromising their positions. The natives would leave the fort alone and quietly continue trading with all parties.

'Missacaibi only want to trade furs. But now we hear French make war, come to kill Missacaibi. Only because of English treaty.'

'But how can you be so sure the French are planning to invade?' I asked. Could it be that McGruder's treaty, by provoking France into retaliation, was going to lead to a massacre of Irocaibi's people?

'Word come from Trois Rivières, brought through forest. Soldiers come to Missacaibi lands, attack fort.' Suddenly Irocaibi's eyes were afire. 'White people fight over natives, kill us, starve us, bring death. Matthew owe Irocaibi.'

'I long to help you,' I said, 'but I cannot.'

'Yes, Matthew can. Go to French, make new treaty. Then English leave my people free. French not send soldiers.'

It was absurd. Here I was, in the middle of the greatest wilderness in all Americka, high-boned and half-starved, a sea-captain who had lost his bark and been stranded ashore, arguing with an Indian nobleman who wanted me to negotiate a treaty. And not just any treaty, but one with my country's enemy.

'I can do nothing for you, Irocaibi,' I said hefting my bundle. 'Let's get on to the fort.'

He moved to stand in my way. 'You come to Trois Rivières.'

'By all the sharks in the China Sea, Irocaibi,' I protested, 'what damm'd good would that do?'

'Matthew has ring and seal.'

'My seal?' This time I could not hold back a harsh laugh. 'My seal as Deputy Intendant of Esperantia? What do you think the Frenchy governors and diplomats are going to say to that? Out of my way, man. I'm going on.'

Irocaibi did not move. Slowly he turned his head to gaze out towards the Nasquinoba River, a distant, silvery strand in the morning light. There beside it stood that bastion of English rule, Fort Rupert, named after a warrior prince dead half a century ago. An air of defeat hung over its crude, dilapidated stockade walls.

Irocaibi's face was like a block of stone.

'Matthew come to make treaty,' he said, 'or he never see his home again.'

13

Indian Summer

'You're a damnable traitor, Loftus!'

The voice of Lieutenant James Glaisterby, sole representative of Her Britannic Majesty's might in a million square miles of wasteland, drifted faintly down from the palisades of his fort. A hundred yards off, I crouched hidden with Irocaibi and his men. Then I stood up, holding out a piece of white cloth.

'I'm coming in, Glaisterby.'

The reply was the dull crack of a musket shot. I dived back under cover as the ball whirred past and snapped into the undergrowth well wide of its intended mark.

'They're offering a truce, lieutenant!' I shouted.

The soldier was in no mood to listen. 'Do you know how many soldiers I lost when the Missacaibi attacked?'

He was drunk. A siege weariness infected his tone. While I might be deeply fatigued from a seven-day trek without proper sustenance, this soldier, after enduring years of hardship separated from society at the very ends of the survivable earth, had reached the limits of his reason.

'Thirteen men! Ten killed outright, three more dead of their wounds,' he called. 'Six in sick quarters who shan't survive. I am down to a quarter of my original complement. You shall pay, Loftus, when the story is told.'

'It was McGruder's stupidity,' I shouted back. 'He took Irocaibi aboard.'

There was a silence. Surely Glaisterby could reason it out – that as it was me who proposed the Chanatuk swap to save his fort, I would hardly be the one to foul it up. And it was the lieutenant who had allowed McGruder to acquire the furskin bales in which Irocaibi had been hidden.

His voice came back. 'There'll be peace when Chief Chanatuk is delivered into Boston. I shall stay at my post till then, defend the fort to the last man.'

'The chief will not sign!' I shouted. 'Irocaibi makes the treaties now – he's offering a truce. In return, you can send a vittling party into the forest for water, wood and whatever food you may find.'

'Never!' he cried. 'I shall never trust them again. They are worse than beasts. Heathens, ungodly, not worthy to be called men.'

'The Indians are offering to send you food and water. Medicines too.'

'Let them try! I shall kill every last one. Their women and children too!'

I put my hand upon Irocaibi's arm and said, 'He's deranged, that's all.'

The Indian remained impassive as Glaisterby's voice rang out once more against the mute forest.

'Loftus, do you hear?' I shall shoot any man who shows himself.'

'For the Lord's sake, if you carry on like this, you're all dead men,' I shouted. 'Listen – Irocaibi

243

says that if the Sovereign dropped the term binding the Indians to England, the fighting would end for good.'

There was a long pause. 'That is what the Frenchies want, so they can claim Kanada. Captain, you have been fooled!'

'No. Your fort would remain, the annual bark could still come in and the natives would quietly sell their furs. The French are hundreds of miles away – they could do nothing about it.'

My reasoning cut no ice with Glaisterby.

'You're going to deal with the enemy,' he called. 'That's treason.'

'Not when the diplomats do it,' I returned.

There was a thoughtful interval, but no reply.

'Glaisterby, the rumours were right – the French invasion is coming. If they get here, they'll take the fort.'

The lieutenant cried, 'They'd never reach us!'

'Perhaps not, but there'd be plenty of bloodshed along their way, think of that. And think of the Indians – they shall make you pay dearly for bringing that on their heads when you could have stopped it.'

He thought about it. 'You have no authority to make bargains with the enemy, Loftus. Be warned.'

'Don't forget I am Deputy Intendant at Esperantia. It makes me a representative of the Governor of Newfoundland.'

Another pause, then he cried, 'You mean that blasted little seal of yours? The one with the face engraved with a pile of stones?'

'Aye, that's Stack Beach – the symbol of Esperantia's prosperity.'

244

Over the intervening hundred paces, I heard an odd sound, something like the cry of the loon-duck calling to its mate across a lake. It was the soldier.

He was roaring with laughter.

The following day, our canoe party set out for Trois Rivières.

To my surprise, we did not head upstream into the interior, striking out for the forest wilderness, but instead paddled downstream and passed into the Rupert River delta, or the Nasquinoba, as I had learnt to call it, and headed west towards the sea.

Keeping to a series of minor channels and dragging our craft across a gravel bar, we avoided the unprotected waters of James Bay itself, where the chop might have turned our vessels turtle. Soon we entered the Missacaibi River, whose mouth lay a mere three leagues south of its sister, separated only by a hilly ridge. By following its twists and turns, and then by crossing from one waterway to another, Irocaibi said, we would find our way to the Saint Maurice, the fast-flowing river running south to meet the Upper Saint Laurent. Near this confluence stood Trois Rivières, the seat of French regional government.

As our party passed beneath the fort safely beyond musket shot, Lieutenant Glaisterby might have spied four Indian canoes progressing downriver at the edge of the current, a single white man amongst the buckskin-clad figures bent at their paddles. I was almost as bemused as he must be by the turn of events that was taking me to the enemy.

The French outpost was a hundred and fifty

leagues distant, but it stood beside a great river leading direct to the sea. The lower reaches of the Saint Laurent, ice-free as late as December, gave onto the Gulf and from there it was just a few days' passage to Newfoundland. How close I was! Yet the distance from Saint John's via the Great Northern Cape and Hudson's Bay – the *Pursuant*'s sea route – was more than a thousand leagues. The truth was that going to Trois Rivières brought me nearer than ever to Esperantia, for there Irocaibi would set me free.

As we left the lonely fort far behind, I sat in the prow of a two-man canoe, powering forward with deep strokes. The half-caste Hubert Nitchequot knelt right aft using his paddle to both drive and steer. It seemed a craft which the least of waves might push beneath the sea, though in flat water it went along merrily enough.

In the early afternoon, we pulled the four canoes onto a sandy spit at a curve in the Missacaibi River and unloaded them. I thought it too soon to halt for the night. Then, rather than make camp, everyone hefted their bundles and packs onto their backs, tipped the canoes over and hoisted them onto their heads. Hubert and I did likewise and our party set off inland, following a trail winding steeply up into the forest. So this was my first portage.

We entered a dense woodland of firs and spruce, the thickest tree cover I had seen since leaving the northern shore of Newfoundland, and moved along the path stepping now on rock, now on beaten ground, now on springy beds of needles and cones. The forest interior closed around us and the light of day dimmed, but the Indians never faltered.

At one point, a man took out his bow and arrow and crept off the trail, intent on a woodpecker sitting on a branch. When the bird flew off and he followed it into the woods, Irocaibi suggested I go after him. To my astonishment, I found that within a few dozen footsteps I lost sight of the party. Everyone but the hunting Indian had vanished, even though the trees were widely spaced and the ground cover far from thick. A bare few paces from the path the forest appeared the same in every direction, and I was lost. Trees, bushes, open spaces – all looked too much alike to identify the way I had come. I stuck close behind the Indian, who was now bearing a small feathered trophy, as he led the way back. I smiled sheepishly at Irocaibi, having learnt another lesson. In this country, off the path and without a compass, there was no means of finding the route. A white man in the forest alone was lost, and a lost man was a dead man.

After several hours the ascent ended and the track levelled. The woods cleared and before us lay an open view of a lake or perhaps a slow-flowing river. By the time we laid the canoes at the water's edge, it was near dusk, the end of the extended northern twilight. The darkening sky faded by degrees from deep blue to indigo and then black, with the sharp points of stars appearing here and there. Still we made no camp nor built a fire nor paused for rest, but reloaded the boats and embarked immediately. Our paddles dipped and the canoes filed swiftly out into the dark pool.

All night we progressed purposefully from lake to water lead to sluggish river and then into lake again, and after that yet another channel appeared out of nowhere. The terrain was nothing but a giant's maze of linked waterways, signless and trackless, yet the natives never once stopped to check the way. Neither did they pause to huddle in a parley as to the correct branch to take, nor did they glance above at the Pole-star or at Venus for a sign from the heavens. Better than a Navigator at sea, they knew their way through the ocean of the forest.

At dawn, we drew the little craft ashore at the edge of a broad waterway – whether lake or river or stream, I could no longer tell – and built a fire, the Indians heating teas and boiling grains. Sitting with Irocaibi, I scooped the food into my mouth.

'It's a mystery to me how you find the way,' I remarked.

His face was impassive. 'Matthew can sail across the empty sea where the Missacaibi sees no marks.'

I wished he had not spoken of the sea. It made me hope again that the Scotsman had died of flesh-rot getting into his wound. Or perhaps, I thought despondently, if she has beaten the ice the *Pursuant* could be home by now. In contrast, our progress was unbearably tedious and drawn out, the trail an endless, slow-paced journey of paddling and portering and paddling again. In the long, unbroken hours of travel, I was plagued by doubts. What might McGruder do at Esperantia? What destruction might he and Factor van Schreik wreak together? Above all, I thought bitterly, Grace Trepanney would hear that Matthew Loftus was dead and gone. What would she decide then?

Hardly resting, portering the canoes across narrow

land bridges between water leads, but always following a way the natives divined, we continued for ten days. At night, I raised my gaze to the heavens and looked for the Pole-star, or by day judged the sun's diurnal arc as it moved west, and saw that we travelled south and east. But when I enquired what distance we had come or how many leagues were still to go, the Indians only shrugged.

At last we reached a vast open expanse of flat water, a broad lake whose blue-black hue in the sunlight told of many fathoms' depth. It stretched ahead between forested hills that widened and fell back on each side, opening into a different territory altogether. The relentless evergreen tree cover of pine and spruce was joined now by sugar-maple and willow, showing autumnal signs of browning at the leaves' edges. On south-facing slopes, evergreen and deciduous trees flourished side by side, and this mixed forest was more alive with animals. Loon-birds laughed in their mad splashing dances on the water, and kingfishers flashed across the dappled surface. Far overhead soared eagles, rising above the bluffs as if ascending a spiral staircase.

'We call this Lac Toujours,' said Hubert behind me.

Then Irocaibi, nearby in his own canoe, said something in his own tongue.

'He admonishes me,' grumbled the half-caste good-naturedly. 'The lake is called Big Water Where Tribal Lands Meet.'

Since leaving Fort Rupert we had met only one party of Indians and a lone trapper. Now, crossing the lake's great width, we drew the canoes closer to the shore where many columns of woodsmoke rose thickly into the air. A considerable party of natives, both men and women, was gathered there. As we came within hailing distance, an elaborate exchange took place with Irocaibi calling out in a singsong fashion and being greeted with answering hails. Though the languages spoken were unintelligible to me, the conversation's ritual nature was apparent. Amongst these natives, a branch of the Iroquois, were many fur trappers, some of mainly French blood, others mixed with more than half of native in their veins.

At dusk, we gathered to eat, the talk a confusing melange of tongues and accents. The Frenchies had brandy, and soon the discourse grew ribald – so I guessed – and the women joined in the laughter. Everyone smoked acrid-smelling tobaccos, quite unlike the sweet Jamaickan or cool Virginian leaves. No one seemed in any hurry to continue our laboured progress.

I leaned across to my canoe partner. 'Why have we stopped?'

'For a tribal parley,' said Hubert Nitchequot. 'All the native peoples gather to make a big army.'

Shadowy groups moved about the shore as more canoes arrived in the dark, seemingly out of nowhere. Each man carried arms, either muskets or bow and arrow. More bands of natives joined the ever-growing throng. Men were assembling here in massive numbers.

'We hear stories about a fleet of big ships coming soon up to Quebec,' said Hubert. 'It is said they shall disembark many troops into river boats at

Trois Rivières. The native peoples must make ready to defend their lands.'

'How do you get news, Hubert?' I asked. 'We are so deep in the forest.'

'There is a quick way to the Gulf. Runners come in days.'

'In days?' I had come to think of the forest as an endless ocean in which I was sunk forever. 'How many days?'

He exhaled noxious fumes of baccy and brandy, and merrily dug my ribs where the white bear's paw had swiped me. I let out a yelp of pain, but it only served to encourage his mirth.

'You want the quickest way to the Saint Laurent, M'sieur Matthieu?' Giggling, he waved his pipe into the night. 'Ah, you are so close.'

'How close?' I said, too eagerly.

Glancing across at Irocaibi, I saw him engaged with a senior of another tribe. He had not heard. Now the half-caste's bristled, grinning face, lit by the campfire's flames, was close to mine, bearing a conspiratorial smile.

'From this point, m'sieur, one could reach the river in three days.' He puffed out a cloud of smoke. 'And you would be at Tadoussac, much further downstream than where we go.'

Tadoussac in three days! The *Pursuant* had been along the North Shore to within a dozen leagues of there. It lay at the mouth of the Saguenay River where the Saint Laurent was already the salty Gulf – virtually the open sea. From there it was only three or four days' sailing to Avalon.

Hubert watched me slyly. 'Do not think you

could make this journey.' He tapped my knee. 'The Saguenay is the fiercest river in all Quebec Sauvage. Even the Iroquois, who are born in their canoes and whose parents begat them in their canoes, drown on this river. It is the fastest way to the Saint Laurent, *mon brave*, and the quickest route to death.'

'Hubert, I would never dream of it,' I said, with a chuckle that sounded false even to me. 'Let's drink our brandy.'

I poured him a generous measure and took a draught myself. Hubert drank his off in one, then sat puffing happily. Irocaibi bent again to his low murmured talk with the other native leaders. After some minutes, I drained my wooden tumbler and stood up, stretching and yawning.

'This is a fine beverage,' I said, 'but the smoke is disagreeable. I shall take the air at the water's edge.'

Not far off along the shore, the lake narrowed and seemed to transform itself into a slow-moving river. I found another group of trappers and Indians, every one of them heavily armed and come to join the ragged army of defence. By drawing signs in the sandy beach and gesticulating at the stars, I made myself understood. They pointed east where the river disappeared into the forest, and told me of the waterways and rivers and streams leading to Tadoussac and the Saguenay.

I wandered on along the darkened strand to clear my head. As the murmur of conversation and laughter receded, the night grew still as a monastery and twice as quiet. The depths of this silence were broken only by the rustle of some small creature in the nearby undergrowth, or the plop of a rising fish, or the distant cry of a water-bird calling to its mate, the hoots echoing off the smooth metalled surface of the water and dying away in the forest looming all round.

The current seemed stronger here. So this was where the route to the Saguenay and the Gulf began. It was dangerous, they had said, chancy enough for a native or a trapper born into the forest waterways, an impossible madness for a stranger to attempt. Yet it was fast, and it was direct. In a matter of days, I could be home. Or a frozen corpse lying in an icy river.

Running off now would be cowardly and self-indulgent, I admonished myself. And was I not in some part indebted to Irocaibi for saving my life? I had listened too to the terms he planned to propose at Trois Rivières. The French must laugh us out of court, I had thought at first, but with consideration I became less certain. The reluctant French governors were having the land invasion foisted on them by generals and diplomats safe in their Ministries in Paris. The regional authorities were said to be keen to avert the disaster. Was there a chance they might seize upon Irocaibi's proposal?

But there was one single overriding factor that meant I had to go on. Both Irocaibi and Hubert had told me about the chief French post at Trois Rivières. The holder's title was Seigneur Inférieur, and a new man had recently taken up that office. He was a cultured and elegant fellow, said the half-caste – who, like all his countrymen, was impressed by any show of style or display.

And when they told me his name, I sensed the guiding hand of the Fates at work. Of course, I knew of a man who had been posted to the hinterland of the Quebec Region – had I not been told long ago by Captain Beaupré of the *Tourmaline*? It was D'Amati. My one-time accordant from Plaisance, Alphonse D'Amati, was at Trois Rivières.

Deep in thought, I turned back for the camp. A few hundred paces from the smokey fireside, from where faint strains of laughter and song drifted, I met Hubert. Perhaps Irocaibi had sent him to look for me.

'You like the fresh air, m'sieur?' He gazed off into the night for a moment, where the river began its long run southward.

'I prefer the salty sea breezes.' I laughed, though not with any heart, and we walked together back along the shore. 'This journey is so arduous and slow. I can't help thinking about Finlay McGruder sailing home. He'll say I am dead, and claim the *Pursuant* for his own.'

The half-caste grunted. '*Bien sur*, M'sieur McGruder was a difficult man. A zealot who hates any man or woman from a Catholick country. He was drunk with Glaisterby, shouting about Papists and Frenchy spies. It was insulting to me.'

I halted. 'You were there? When was this?'

'After McGruder recaptured Irocaibi,' Nitchequot explained. 'You had gone to the ship with Chief Chanatuk, to make ready for sea. Glaisterby begged me to be a go-between, to stop the Missacaibi attacking when they found Irocaibi kidnapped. What hope of that, *hein*?' He snorted in derision. 'O, but they argued, m'sieur, like cats. McGruder threatened many bad things for Glaisterby. What he was going to write in his reports! The soldier's career and reputation!'

So Glaisterby had known about Irocaibi's capture all along, I mused.

Hubert continued his story. 'At last, the lieutenant capitulated. He even stopped protesting about his brandy. McGruder drank the last of it, good French cognac too. Ha, you English! You hate the French but love our drink.'

I took the half-caste by the arm. 'Hubert, when Finlay McGruder spoke of Newfoundland, did he say anything about Esperantia?'

'Esperantia is the settlement, is it not? He said he had the future – how did he say? *Alors*, the future there was sealed. With the marriage.'

'What about the marriage?' I said sharply.

Hubert smiled. 'He talked about a widow woman.'

The blood pumped in my temples. 'What did he say? Did he speak of van Schreik too?'

'Who is that?'

'Josiah van Schreik, the Factor.' Frustratingly, Hubert had got half the story and missed the whole. 'He's the fellow with designs on the widow.'

'It means nothing to me,' said the half-caste with a shrug. He frowned. 'But now I remember something. He said the Intendancy and the marriage are one. Yes, that was it.'

'Aye, indeed,' I replied miserably, 'that was going to be my reward, Hubert. The Intendancy Proper.'

'*Bon*, the Intendancy Proper.' The half-caste seemed

to be trying to remember something. 'But if that is so, what about the seal?'

'The seal?' I stuck my right hand under his nose. 'Here's my seal.'

He peered at the heavy ring, embossed with reversed lettering and the beach engraving.

'*Oui*, I just can see in the starlight. Very interesting. But I referred to McGruder's seal. He had a like seal.'

'A like seal?' I repeated dumbly.

'Certainly. He brought it out from within his coat to show Glaisterby.'

'But not a seal like this,' I said, with something approaching panic rising inside.

He peered again. '*Absolument*. It bore this design. Yes, his seal was the same, but larger. And made all of gold!'

I had the sensation of falling into a deep pit.

Hubert did not notice. 'There was some writing, M'sieur Matthieu. An inscription, I think you say.'

'On McGruder's seal?' Again, I gripped his arm. 'Could you read it?'

'Ah, but the lettering was large. As clear as the Moon.'

My mouth was dry. 'What did it say?'

The half-caste's voice waxed and waned against a thrumming sound in my ears.

'*Alors*, M'sieur Matthieu, it said, "Intendant Proper of Esperantia".'

14

Rough Passage

Four hours before dawn, in the absolute dead of night under a moonless sky unlit even by an auroral glow, the whole encampment rested peacefully at its slumbers.

Creeping down to the foreshore, I selected one of the smaller vessels drawn up on the foreshore, took a brace of spare paddles from another canoe and lifted my bag into the centre thwarts. I had taken food and a weapon from my friends but I had no qualms about that. Nothing would stop me now. No treaty nor deal-making mattered any more. I was going home, come Hell or high water. And by the fastest route possible.

Why had I not seen through their blandishments and conniving? First, Admiral Tompion had fooled me over the mission's purpose. Then it turned out my promised reward had been another black lie. Tompion had usurped the Dowager's charter powers and removed the Deputy Intendancy from Josiah van Schreik, giving it to me as a sop. But all along he had planned to appoint his young cousin McGruder as Intendant Proper.

After the first shock, I had puzzled over why the ambitious Scottish diplomat would want Esperantia. Then I realised he saw it as a stepping stone. From running the settlement he had designs on Governor

Spurgeon's post. From there he might gain a greater goal, perhaps high office in the Colonial Government at Boston.

But this was more than a petty contest over careers. It was about Grace Trepanney. The Dowager was ready to give her away to whoever became Intendant Proper, to ensure the succession. Grace would be told I was dead. With me gone, she would feel pressed into it, obliged to consent for her son Oliver's sake. I shuddered at the thought. And how stupid and blind I had been! From the very beginning, Factor van Shreik had never been my rival. All along, it was Finlay McGruder.

With anger bubbling in my heart, I pushed the craft into the black river. Instantly a current caught the almost weightless cockleshell and swung it parallel with the shore. I cursed it for being a flimsier, more insubstantial thing even than the two-man design Hubert and I had shared. Shoving more mightily, I sent the bow out into the stream, then splashed a couple of paces and jumped in. By all the Saints, these were poorly balanced boats, featherweight compared to any launch or cutter I had known and twice as tippy as a coracle.

Kneeling in the sternparts, I took up a blade and began to work along the shoreline. My progress was faltering. With only the one paddle driving, the canoe turned aside with every stroke so that I could make only one sweep before swapping it over. Keeping to the edge of the river and out of the main current, I laboriously covered a cable or so with the boat turning wilfully now this way, now that, anything but straight ahead.

Water slopped about at my knees. Dammit, out of all those, had I taken the only leaky canoe? Then I realised that every time the paddle came from one side to the other, riverwater dripped with it. Pulling over to the river's edge, I grabbed a large root growing from the bank and held on to bail dry. How I wished for a well-built and even-keeled ship's boat, and thought longingly of the shallop left to rot not far from Eli's grave. Heavy though it might be, one good oarsman with a pair of stout sweeps could soon make it skip along in flat water, even though carrying it between rivers would be impossible.

I thought hard. With two men in the canoe, one would sit forward and paddle one side while the other sat aft and stroked on the opposite side, correcting the steering. So how did a man alone make straight progress? When a native paddled alone, he hardly ever brought his blade across, let alone stroke by stroke. Yet the vessel never slewed round. Puzzled, more determined than ever, I pushed off again into the black pitch of the river-lake.

Reaching forward, I dug the blade into the water and drew it back. The canoe's head instantly cranked towards the paddling side. Then I let the blade come aft and twisted it, holding it vertically in the current. It acted like a steering blade and swung the boat's prow straight again. At last, my progress became more generally forward, albeit nodding a little from side to side. Elated at cracking the secret, I pressed onwards leaving a fanning wake with turbid swirls from my strokes. Soon, the native canoe was as familiar to me as a ten-foot dory. Forcing its pace was fruitless, for the least breath of contrary wind stopped it, yet it readily passed over gravel banks with only an inch or two of water. Where the river-lake shoaled and divided into many small rushing streams, it was easy to steer a course through. Altogether, I came to appreciate the design's aptness for its territory.

As the night wore on and I ran off the leagues, no one chased me from the encampment. The regular plash and gurgle of the paddle were the only sounds to disturb the brooding forest either side. Easing the little vessel across the watery expanse, I passed an opening that led away into the trees on a southwesterly heading. From the trappers I knew this to be a stream that became a fast-flowing tributary of the Saint Maurice river. That was the way to Trois Rivières, but Hubert's revelation about the seal had led me to abandon that plan without hesitation.

I stroked onwards for mile after mile, seeing no one, hearing nothing bar the crash of a beast lumbering off into the undergrowth, disturbed from its drinking at the shoreline. At least there should be no white bears in these latitudes. Nor could there be any icing up of the waterways, for these more southern rivers did not freeze again till December.

Now the waterway did indeed turn southward, and became what seemed the head of a lake. Just when it appeared that no egress by boat were possible, a branching lead opened between two rounded greystone boulders, standing like sentinels. It was just as the trappers had described. I dug the blade to go between the heads and entered a calm, currentless stretch of water carrying away southeast – towards the Saguenay River and the seaway beyond.

A day or so to the Saguenay, three days to the

Saint Laurent. If I were lucky to find passage on a bark straightaway, four from there by sea to the Avalon Peninsula. Seven days to home.

At what might have been a conjoining of two rivers, I stopped paddling and listened hard. To my left, there was an added rushing sound and the faint glimmer of water coursing over rocks, its foam and spume catching the starlight. It must be a tributary draining from the badlands, from the high tundra plains that stretched uninterrupted all the way to the Great Northern Cape. I pressed on down the main, south-going, river channel.

Still I entertained many doubts. Mastering the awkward canoe and its crudities was no more than a momentary diversion. How was I to Navigate – hardly the right term for journeying across country – through riverways half a thousand land miles long, without map or chart or compass or cross-staff? To the European mind, this territory was as trackless a waste as any great sea. The terrain was riven through with water courses that ran together and parted again without design, lakes that led to blank dead ends, a million marshy leads that went nowhere. For centuries, men in ships had wandered about the world's oceans before finding the astronomickal means of getting a latitude. Here, finding the correct way was an even greater obscurity.

Bereft of native guidance, my only hope was to keep the sun on my face by day, and by night hold the Pole-star on my left shoulder. Glancing up at the Plough and Polaris, I plunged on, the canoe sliding from water leads to still lakes and then into slowly draining streams where the current ran slack and listless. I rested only once, on a small beach at the river's curve where I drew the craft ashore and dozed for a quarter hour. Before resuming, I checked my supplies of bread and grains, dried fish and salted meat stolen from the sleeping trappers at Lac Toujours. There were extra clothes and furskins for the northern nights, and the pistol I had retrieved from Hubert Nitchequot's coat, a well-made piece that he would sorely miss.

I passed several more tributaries, reckoning to put the greatest distance between myself and any chase. Then the channel narrowed. There seemed to be high ground rising either side, the rock walls of a deep-cut gorge. Abruptly the way ended in a pool, and not far ahead came the crash and roar of a thunderous waterfall. There was an immanent glow of threshing waters cascading from above. I sat, dumbstruck, as the canoe bobbled gently on ripples spreading from the turbulent foot. Stroking over to first one rock wall, then the other, I found that on all sides but one they rose vertical, worn smooth for many feet above by the timeless passage of risen flood waters. Somehow, a river running downstream had become the head of a lake. There was nothing for it but to turn back.

An hour later, I found the missing waterway leading south and directed the canoe towards it. It was shallow, and my blade struck small boulders, then underneath those the hard and rocky riverbed itself. Pulling the canoe to the side, I walked along the stream bed until at the sound of rushing water I came upon a steep little beck tumbling down rocks towards a break in the trees. Peering into the gloom,

I made out a great, grand flow of black water sliding by not two hundred paces distant. Craning up to see between the enclosing branches, I caught a gap and checked the Pole-star. The river ran south.

It took half a glass to return, raise up the craft onto my head and carry it over the ridge and down to the new river. Fatigued though I was, my spirits improved with this successful transfer between waterways, my first portage alone. I made a brief encampment to rest and eat before continuing through the night, just as the Indians would do.

By the first glimmer of dawn, the surrounding country had changed. The confusion of leads and waterways lessened and the river grew more defined. Furlong by furlong, mile by mile, my progress improved. The sun rose, confirming that my direction, though inconstant, was generally east, if not south.

To my delight, the current increased. When I paused from paddling, the canoe drifted along at a knot or so allowing me to simply steer for minutes on end. The land rose again to enfold the river – no longer a sluggish lead but a swift-flowing channel – and the enclosing forested slopes climbed away to sharp, high ridges either side. The rivercourse twisted back and forth in this valley, descending satisfyingly with each mile. Now, I merely dipped the paddle to correct my course. I passed the hours estimating and re-estimating the time to reach the Saint Laurent Gulf. By now, my reckoning was down to two and half days, and excitedly I urged the canoe onwards.

By full sun-up, the terrain was sliding quickly

past. My little coracle rode through an extenuated valley where fir trees grew down to the water's edge either side, thrusting upwards and outwards at absurd angles in their struggle for light and air. Soon the river shrank to less than a cable's width. It no longer shoaled in the middle but ran deep and fast, and I was sure that no following party could catch me now.

Weary, I kept an eye out for a place to draw up the canoe and take sustenance, but the river flowed purposefully along between heavily bouldered banks. Even at bends, there was little sign of a strand or a gravel bar. When I did spy one, it revealed itself too late. By the time I had dug the paddle to turn the canoe inshore, it had swept past astern. No matter, there would be another. The swift progress only lifted my heart higher.

We seemed to be entering another gorge. The flow accelerated. High cliffs obscured the morning sunlight, throwing the river into dark shadow. The banks again became sheer stone escarpments, so I conceded to the river's will. Rest could wait. Once or twice, a boulder reared up dead ahead, but a plunge of the paddle into the current soon swung the bow clear. By now the canoe was travelling at speed, and as the work increased so my arms tired.

Rounding a sharp bend, I was met by a roaring sound. Above the river's surface rose a mist of spray cut through with briefly living rainbows where the sun's rays struck down through the narrow cut. Rapids ahead, I thought, casting about with some agitation, but still there was nowhere to draw up. The canoe became awkward to steer. Hands seemed to reach up from the foaming current and toy with it. I dug the paddle to drive this way and that, seeking a way between the rocks. Some were hidden by a reassuringly smooth flow over their backs but I soon learnt the treachery of that, for on the downstream side was always a vicious patch of turbulence. Other boulders created a pillar wave as the water met the obstruction and stood vertical, sometimes two or three feet high.

With a jarring shock up my arm, the paddle struck an underwater stone and broke. Discarding the useless remnant of its handle, I stretched forward to grasp the spare. My weight shifted and the canoe broached sideways to the current. Losing balance, I gripped the gunnels and forced myself to lean the opposing way. The canoe bore upright but was now going stern first. Somehow I got the spare paddle, but when I dug the blade the craft refused to straighten. The canoe seemed a wilful thing, sometimes obeying my commands, otherwise wrenching violently against my bidding. The effort depleted my strength. By the Lord's breath, I thought harshly, when do the rapids end?

By the time we reached calmer waters, my arms ached just to straighten the craft until I could hardly lift the paddle. My head drooped and the canoe was borne along, less frenetically yet still fast enough, through a stretch of turbid flow like the spring ebb at a river entrance. But I had safely passed down a set of powerful rapids, and knew it could be done again. Rapids were my friends, I decided, for they speeded my progress. Now all I wanted was to haul over and rest.

Letting the canoe drift along, I must have dozed for a few moments. I awoke to an enormous swelling of noise, a rushing, tearing din that billowed from somewhere ahead. The river bore sharply away to the left and disappeared into a high narrow cleft opening between rocky abutments. It seemed to descend like a staircase. I looked round in panic for a landing place, any way of getting out of the strengthening flow. By dint of great effort, I drew the canoe close to the bank and made a lunge for a rare overhanging branch. No sooner did I get my grasp on the rough bark than it was snatched away. My palms were cut and bloodied and my arms all but wrenched from their sockets. With no one steering, the canoe struck rock after rock, borne helplessly towards an even more terrifying set of rapids than the last. There was only one way left: to force through them.

I took up the paddle. As the bend opened, I saw with a pounding heart that the river fell steeply between the gorge walls in a demented torrent, rushing across rounded worn rocks, throwing sheets of spray high into the air. The roar rose up and echoed off the high-sided cliffs. Entering the maelstrom, my canoe bucked and dived like an unbroken horse.

Then the second paddle smashed to pieces. Now I could only grip the gunnels and hang on. The rock walls swept by and we descended at a dizzying speed. Moments later, the vessel angled sideways to the current but I had lost the means to straighten it. Ahead, a standing wave arched its back, the curled-over top foaming like a fountain. The little cedar-bark craft lifted, broached again, lurched sickeningly, then rose up the wave and shot into the air.

I have no memory of the landing. I was underwater in an icy, swirling world of bubbles and foam, the dark shapes of boulders flashing past, pieces of shattered wood and torn bark twisting this way and that like flotsam in a tide rip. Breaking surface, I thrashed my arms but the current flung them aside. With each gasping breath, I swallowed gulps of icy liquid. The flow's sheer force butted me bruisingly against rocks, my knees and elbows taking blow after blow, my body spiralling and tumbling through the maelstrom. Time after time, when a numbing shock took away my senses, the freezing water brought me awake again.

At last, the roaring diminished, the violent blows ceased, my head stayed above the surface long enough to catch air and satisfy my demanding lungs. Dumbly I stroked with unfeeling arms, thrashing my senseless legs until I half swam and was half thrown onto a gravelly strand. With the end of my strength I crawled ashore and lay there shivering, frozen and exhausted, every bone of my body aching.

The canoe had been splintered and carried away downstream. My supplies were gone – food, pistol, spare knives. I had lost most of my clothing, stripped away in the current. No furskins remained to cover my nakedness. The river's wilful nature had quite overpowered me.

I lay shivering, passing from awareness into oblivion and back, my head whirling with half-formed thoughts and dreams. One moment I was speeding downriver with the current towards the Saguenay. Then I seemed to be stranded again in the high tundra, exposed in the endless, open expanses where the white bear ran. Another time, I was standing outside Providence House, with Grace on my arm, gazing out over the peaceful harbour of Esperantia.

After a while, as the cold invaded my bones, drifting in and out of uneasy, fear-wracked wakefulness, I fell into a deeper sleep, or something worse.

Rapid pulses of light flashed, their brilliance flickering through the shell of my eyelids. I blinked them open only to be blinded by powerful sunlight on my face. My ears roared, full of thick sound, the gush of water cascading from a height.

I was lying flat on the ground. Before me stood a great bulwark of sheer grey rock, bare and wet. Through a slanting fissure shone the blinding sun. Across the aperture flowed a dancing waterfall, causing the sun's strange, intermittent flashes. As the water struck the rocky table below, drops of ice-cold spray were thrown high and spattered into my face with shocks like tiny, sharp darts.

My eye caught sight of a smashed canoe nearby, the bark prow flattened as if by a paddleblade, the gunnels stove in amidships baring the slender spruce ribs. Dully I thought I must have been thrown further down the rapids and landed up here. Wearily, bruised all over, I tried to rouse myself.

'Be still,' said a voice.

A hand touched my shoulder and pushed me back onto a roughly-made bed of grasses and shrubbery. Next moment, blocking the sunlight flashing in the waterfall's trembling flow, appeared the deep brown features of the Indian prince.

'Irocaibi brings you here to get strong again.'

He put a bowl to my lips and I took a mouthful of hot spicy broth. It tasted of pine needles and forest plants, and I felt a strange sense of detachment creep over me. Everything became dreamlike, remote and apart. Perhaps it was a potion intended to make me malleable, for within a minute I could no longer lift my limbs.

'Matthew make mistake running away,' said Irocaibi.

He talked on, his murmur blending with that of the falling water and the bouncing droplets splashing to earth beside me. Either I dreamed it, or he did truly tell me that tribesmen – of whom he had sent many searching down all the river's branches – had at last found me lying beside the river bank and lifted me into their canoe.

'Look,' he said, gesturing at the broken remains of their vessel.

Irocaibi was angry, because the Indians had risked their lives to rescue me. They brought me back here, to the waiting Irocaibi, leagues from where I was found. The tribal name of this spiritual place, he told me, was Hollow Of Falling Water And Dancing Light In Summer Sun. Because of the natural rock formation and the few high days when the sun's rays angled through the fissure it was held to be a sacred site, the source of elemental forces. Many a wounded brave had been brought here and lived, he said. Old men and women came at their days' end to pass back to the earth. Ailing newborns were left here at night to either sicken and die or wake up next day calling strongly for their mother's teat, demanding a new chance at the battle of life.

How long I lay there with the soothing sound of rushing water and the flickering sunlight warming my bones, I cannot tell. Sometimes I slept without dreams, at other times my mind filled with strange sensations. I was borne along on a drifting current, a waterway leading through high rocky country, then into exitless gorges, now into fast-flowing torrents. Once I woke gasping, fighting for the next excruciating draw of cool air to fill my broken lungs, possessed by an urgent desire to run away from something malevolent, or towards something deeply longed for.

At last I sat up, breathing more easily. I saw three or four natives appear from upriver, pulling their canoes onto the strand, talking excitedly to their chief, gesturing my way. After a while, Irocaibi came over and bent again to administer his hot brew.

'Brothers come. Long way back to lake.'

With a trembling hand, I reached up to steady the wooden bowl. 'Back to Lac Toujours? I mean, to Big Water?'

He nodded. 'We go now.'

I gazed around that magical place of falling streams and sunlight.

'Irocaibi,' I stammered, 'don't you understand? I must reach the Saguenay. I must get back to Esperantia.'

'Matthew go Irocaibi's way. To Trois Rivières.'

'No, please – let me go on downriver.'

His eyes flickered with anger. 'Matthew not go

downriver – this stream go north, never to Saguenay. Matthew goes wrong way.'

The wrong way? Had I been going the wrong way? I lay back in despair, thinking how impossible it was to get out of the nightmare of this endless forest.

'Matthew too busy in rapids to see river turns back. Back same way he comes.'

All at once, I felt respect and gratitude for these proud natives. Irocaibi's fellows had imperilled their own lives for my sake. And the Indian prince himself had saved me from the white bear. Perhaps those potions affected a man's mind somehow, but my heart filled with something akin to brotherly love.

'Irocaibi, how can I thank you?' I smiled up at him. 'You are a true friend to save me this way.'

Roughly, he grabbed my arm, spilling the precious medicine. His features were savagely contorted.

'Irocaibi saves Matthew for this!'

He shook the bruised and grazed hand in my face. In the pulsing rays from the Hollow Of Falling Water And Dancing Light In Summer Sun, metal glinted and flashed on my middle finger. It was the silver and gold seal accrediting me Deputy Intendant of Esperantia.

15

Savage Terms

The Seigneur Inférieur of the Region de la Toute Quebec Sauvage bowed from the waist, displaying the very top of his tight-curled and richly perfumed short wig.

Irocaibi, prince of the deep forest, Hubert Nitchequot, a half-caste, and Matthew Loftus, dispossessed captain, stood ill at ease before this highly-groomed figure. We were gathered on the lofty poop deck of a French bark, and surrounded by fancy polished hardwood. The ship's rail was delicately cut with designs of leaf, horn and arms, the wheel a masterpiece of the carver's art with turned spokes and brass inlaid handle-grips. She was the *Roi Soleil*, a magnificent three-decker, once the pride of the French Navy but now decommissioned and dismantled, towed upriver and anchored in the fast-running Saint Maurice river hard by the frontier settlement of Trois Rivières.

She served as temporary quarters while the Seigneur Inférieur built himself a splendid palace on rising ground halfway between the landing jetties and the heights above. Up there stood an impressive array of gun emplacements, an investment of men and materials that left no doubt as to France's intentions for holding onto the Kanada Lands. It contrasted sharply with the dismal and half-hearted installation at Fort Rupert.

Alphonse D'Amati and I had of course never met. Back in Newfoundland, we conducted our negotiations over Plaisance and Esperantia covertly via men such as Captain Beaupré of the *Tourmaline*. But D'Amati knew enough to recognise the seal I carried. He took my hand in his delicate paw and drew it close for inspection. The assayer in him took less than a second to recognise the Deputy Intendant's ring as no fake, while the diplomat in him dallied not a moment longer in calculating its significance.

'Captain Loftus,' he said, 'how intriguing that our first encounter should be in the depths of New France.'

'Indeed, Seigneur D'Amati,' I said, with a glance at Irocaibi, 'and I trust that this new-found familiarity may breed respect.'

The Seigneur's command of English exceeded that of most of my own countrymen, so I bade Hubert wait on deck. Then, with a gracious sweep of the hand, D'Amati invited us to follow him below into his splendidly decorated quarters.

To suggest that Irocaibi or I felt out of place would have been an understatement of monumental proportions. Plucked straight from canoes and encampments and brought aboard this decorated splendour, I felt like a peasant in a palace. The leather slips on my feet were falling apart and my chin was raw from a botched attempt at razoring off ten days' growth of beard. When I glanced at Irocaibi, I almost laughed, for his buckskin dress was better fitted for fishing and the caribou hunt

273

than the niceties of ambassadorial small talk over roasting coffee beans brought up from Martinique. We smelt of cedar bark and woodsmoke and sweat and animal skins, and looked what we were – men of the forest and the river, cast amongst the prinked and foppish gentlemen of French court circles.

Though our dress and bearing and taints were sorely out of place in such circumstances, I clung to the hope that our aims might find accord with D'Amati. We were here because Irocaibi rejected the treaty on offer from the British – the Finlay McGruder treaty, as I thought of it – which entailed the Missacaibis' complete subjugation. By contrast, the French offered at least a degree of freedom and dignity. That was what I sought too, the freedom to go home and deal with McGruder. Yet ever since Irocaibi had explained his plan, I had wrestled with finding the best way of playing the few cards in my hand. My chief worry was the aces D'Amati might hold hidden up the sleeve of his lace-embroidered jacket.

We passed down a wide stairway with handrails either side, into what – despite its being on a ship – could only be called an ante-room, and thence into a high-ceilinged Great Cabin more like a withdrawing room. The entire stern wall consisted of steeply raked Venetian windows, tracered with leaded lights through which the sun entered to fill the space and highlight the shining cabinetry and bejewelled fitments.

Rising and bowing obsequiously as we entered was a note-taker or secretary. He could not prevent his elegant nose from taking wrinkled offence at the sight and probably the odour of D'Amati's extraordinary guests. He was dressed in a brocaded long-coat, silken hose and buckled shoes – the same garb as his master save for its colour and its ornamentation, which was deferentially pitched a scale lower. Neither did he wear a wig but went bare-headed, his black hair tied in a pigtail by a miniature bow of blue.

The Seigneur moved to a high-backed chair behind an ebony desk and smiled for us to be seated opposite. When I laid out Irocaibi's credentials, the Frenchman listened carefully, with the occasional encouraging nod or smile.

'So Prince Irocaibi speaks for his tribespeople? I see. Captain Loftus, do explain the story of your arrival here. I mean, since leaving Newfoundland.'

Diplomacy rested on trust. Thus I revealed the story of the rescue mission up to and including McGruder's treachery. D'Amati would learn it all soon enough anyway from his paid informers at Saint John's.

'I see you have reason to seek revenge on this Scottish man,' he said when I had finished. 'But I am intrigued. Surely your mission was more than mere salvage or rescue? At heart, its aim was diplomatick.'

'Aye, indeed – keeping open Queen Anne's claims.' I shifted forward in my chair. 'Seigneur D'Amati, let us get to the nub of the matter. France is sending troops into the Quebec interior to subdue the natives by force.'

He smiled uncertainly. 'What makes you think that is likely?'

'Rumours are everywhere. There is said to be a

275

fleet – a Grand Fleet, I understand – on its way from Europe. The natives are massing to meet the attack. A slaughter is bound to follow, a slaughter of the Missacaibi perhaps, but of your troops for sure.'

D'Amati spoke briefly to his secretary and the man left the room backwards, giving one too many bows as he went. Then the Seigneur Inférieur leaned close.

'Captain, we know Admiral Tompion is at Saint John's. I suggest to you that if a fleet were putting out from France, its objective would be to meet the British Navy at sea. The notion of a land invasion of the Quebec interior borders on the preposterous.'

'I agree. The question of the Kanada Lands shall be decided by sea power and –'

'New France,' he cut in, correcting my name for the territory. 'But we agree on this – at the ultimate, the question of which nation controls New France can only be decided by a sea battle for the Saint Laurent Gulf.'

'I beg your pardon – New France, of course.' I bowed. 'Yet your war ministers prefer to mount a bloody and pointless land assault which they cannot win. The noble Queen Anne is most amused by this.'

The faintest trace of doubt played on D'Amati's face. Perhaps my bluff was working. I banked on the Seigneur – the man on the ground, with local knowledge – being at odds with the war planners at home.

'I am certain, Seigneur, your despatches to the home country have reflected your concerns, just as Governor Spurgeon's argued against the Navy being sent to Newfoundland. He saw the consequences, and so do you.'

D'Amati made a polite, unnecessary cough. 'My dear captain, these are mere speculations.'

'That is not what the Algonkins, and the Iroquois and the Missacaibi believe. Tell him, Irocaibi, if you will.'

Sitting straight-backed in the unfamiliar chair, the Indian described the recent tribal parleys for war. He indicated the numbers of warriors massing even as we spoke. He left no doubt about the natives' superior knowledge of terrain, their ability to travel the intricate waterways, to resupply from forest sources and to move swiftly across great distances. They could fight a prolonged and bloody rearguard action, inflicting devastating harm on a European army lost in the wilderness.

When Irocaibi was done I said, 'I put it to you, Seigneur, it is in Irocaibi's power to deliver your Sovereign from a defeat. Not just that, but he can help you reinforce France's territorial claims.'

D'Amati's gaze was intense. What was he thinking? That if he could somehow confirm King Louis's claims, might it be regarded in Quebec and in Paris as a triumph? Surely his reward must be a rise from regional governor in the remote colonies to a more central post.

He studied me. 'Captain Loftus, are you saying Irocaibi shall sign with France? Did you not know that England is already advancing a treaty with this tribe?'

I nodded. 'Aye, but the Missacaibi reject it.'

'And their prince shall deliver his people to the King instead?

'Not my people,' interposed Irocaibi. 'Our trade.'

The Indian explained that the Missacaibi preferred no foreigners on the land they had known as theirs since time began. The British treaty would render them landless and humiliated, subjects in perpetuity to an alien power. By contrast, the French had treated with other tribes to take the fur trade while leaving the people free. If that could be done with the Missacaibi, said Irocaibi, then so be it – France would have his people's fidelity.

'You would have to agree to trade solely with us,' said the Seigneur.

Irocaibi grunted his assent. The pack canoes, he said, rather than travel to Fort Rupert to trade with the *Beaver*'s successor, would journey south by the portage routes to meet the Upper Saint Laurent merchants.

The Seigneur Inférieur looked thoughtful. A treaty with the Indians and sole command of the fur trade would be a feather in his cap. But he needed more. It was time to press forward.

'An agreement with the Missacaibi,' I put in quickly, 'does more than bolster King Louis's claim to the lands. It leads to Britain abandoning the Hudson's Bay assault.'

'What do you say?' D'Amati sat up like a courtier being told his hose was stained. 'An assault is planned on Hudson's Bay?'

'Aye,' I said gravely, though feeling as if I just hooked a kingfish. 'What do you suppose Tompion's true purpose is? And do you think I was sent to rescue the *Beaver*, or to reconnoitre the attack?'

He fell silent, perhaps imagining French soldiers not just fighting every inch of the way through the forest, but finding a British Naval force and an expeditionary army at James Bay, if ever they got there. Now was the time to offer him a way out.

'There is a path away from this catastrophe, Seigneur D'Amati. You and I, together with Prince Irocaibi, can prevent this clash of armies. We three can make an accord, here and now, that obviates the Grand Fleet's invasion and renders unnecessary the British assault.'

The Seigneur's pupils were large and black. 'Please state your proposal.'

'It hinges on us deciding that neither Hudson's Bay nor the Missacaibi need be fought over. All else flows from that.'

His eyes narrowed. 'Continue.'

'I propose that the English – the British, I mean – agree to send no trading bark into Hudson's Bay for five years from henceforth, or until the end of the war, whichever may come first. In effect, the Queen's territorial claims would be in suspension.'

D'Amati's eyebrows lifted half an inch. 'In return for what?'

'In return,' I went on, 'for the French abandoning Plaisance for good.'

'Plaisance!' he cried.

'Aye. You know as well as anyone it's finished,' I said. 'The Breton wet fishing is in terminal decline. The produce no longer commands a market – except in the Antilles, as slave fodder.'

The Seigneur Inférieur put his hands flat on the table and levered himself upright. He opened his mouth to speak and thought better of it. Instead, he got up and went to stand before the middle

279

one of three vast windows reaching almost from sole to deckhead, a run of glass and framing a good eight feet high by my eye. Hands clasped behind his back, he gazed out over the torrential Saint Maurice, down whose fierce passes and along whose ripping currents the Indian and I had recently steered our canoes.

D'Amati surveyed his domain. Was he thinking of the years he had devoted to Plaisance? Perhaps, though, he imagined his career suddenly thrust on an upward trajectory. He returned to the table, resumed his seat and fixed his eyes on mine.

'You make many a valid point, Captain Loftus,' he said, his voice low. 'The arrangement suits all sides, it seems.'

'Exactly. The Missacaibi win a reprieve, the British lose very little face, and France saves a costly defeat.' I paused. 'May I beg you to consider how the proposal might be received at Quebec? They must appreciate a man ready to risk such a winning move.'

His eyes flickered, the calculations rapid. Then he said, 'Let us reiterate. In return for France giving up a settlement devoted to a branch of the fishing industry that is to all intents and purposes dead, the British relinquish Hudson's Bay for five years, giving France free rights and control of the whole fur trade.' He frowned. 'It would go far towards fulfilling His Majesty's desires.'

I nodded. 'Aye, and it would be achieved by the diplomatick enterprise of his noble envoy at Trois Rivières.'

He tapped the table with an elegant finger. 'Such a

treaty might indeed be proposed.' Suddenly his features relaxed into a smile. 'May I call my *secrétaire* back in? He can scribe it for us.'

By all the Saints of the sea and sailors, I thought, I have made a diplomatick deal! Then I remembered something and held up my hand.

'One small point, Seigneur. I must have safe passage to Newfoundland, for my immediate return to Esperantia.'

D'Amati looked surprised. Then he laughed so hard it rattled the window panes. 'O no, *mon capitain*! You cannot expect to abandon so lightly what you have begun.'

'What do you mean?' I retorted.

'I am desolated, but there is more to treaty-making than you perceive. First, we three shall journey together to Quebec to obtain the Seigneur Supérieur's approval. Then you must voyage on to Boston in the Massachusetts Colony.'

'Boston! What for?' I cried.

Massachusetts lay better than two hundred and fifty leagues south of Newfoundland. I already faced a time-consuming journey just to reach Avalon, but Boston was yet another week's sailing distance from there.

D'Amati was unmoved. 'The proposal must be accepted at both regional governments, Boston and Quebec, before onward transmission to our nations' capitals. And there is little point in your going back to Esperantia in your present circumstances.'

'How so?' I demanded.

'This Scottish man is there, or so you assume, and you wish to revenge yourself. But how, may

I ask? You have nothing – no men, no arms, no ships.'

'No – McGruder's finished, don't you see? His so-called treaty falls with this accord of ours. I shall go to Governor Spurgeon. Make my case, demand his help.'

The Seigneur smiled sympathetically. 'I understand poor Spurgeon has little power left. My agents at Saint John's tell me his troops are disarmed and confined to quarters. The Governor cannot go against Admiral Tompion's superior forces.'

'Lord. What can I do?' I said, suddenly at a loss. D'Amati was right. I was impotent to deal with McGruder.

'Hear me, Captain Loftus. Go to Boston and ask for help. With this accord in your hand, you have status. Bargaining power.'

I slumped back in my seat, aware of Irocaibi gazing at me. How would I cope with the tricky courtiers and office-holders in Boston? How long would I be forced to delay there, dallying with the wigs and buckle-shoes who inhabited those halls of governance? And what guarantee was there I would get what I needed?

'I am no envoy or legatee,' I protested.

'You have shown yourself quite as astute as any in the diplomatick service. After Quebec, I shall see you en route for Boston aboard a Navy vessel of France, as a protected person.'

'The sea passage to New England is patrolled by English cruzers,' I pointed out. 'As a private citizen, I can tread on French soil, but being caught aboard an enemy military vessel in wartime –'

I trailed off, gazing round at the *Roi Soleil*. Even this decommissioned vessel might count, let alone being caught aboard a warship at sea. With our nations at war, my mere presence aboard the vessel might be deemed treasonable.

'That is a risk you shall have to bear,' said the Seigneur.

His shoulders lifted at the same time as his mouth turned down at the corners, a shrug of such dismissiveness as only a true Frenchman could muster.

Waiting impatiently for our boat at the Trois Rivières dock, I nonetheless made a point of observing the comings and goings along the busy Saint Maurice River.

Riverboats abounded, being rowed and sailed as the conditions demanded. Chiefly flat-bottomed, they were designed like the natives' canoes for ducking through shoal waters. Most were heavily laden with trading goods and stores of all kinds, while others carried troops and weapons, lightweight gunnery pieces and portable mortars. Some valiantly stemmed the current on their way upriver, vanishing from sight as the stream bent away between steep forest slopes. Yet others flashed past downriver, riding the fast current, high-piled with bales of furskins.

A keeled sloop, suited to the river's lower reaches, approached the jetty with a crew of Frenchy matelots working her upcurrent. She boasted a single slender mast half as high again as her length, a gaff mainsail on a long boom, a triangular topsail hoisted above the main, and a jutting bowsprit carrying a great spread of jibsail. She was rigged to take advantage of the light and fluking airs of deepwater riverwork, beating upriver or ghosting downstream. In open waters, with her delicate rig and lack of freeboard, she was as vulnerable as a butterfly in a squall. But she was at home here and, to my sailor's eye, a treat to behold. She was the *Travailleur*.

Midriver, they hauled down the sails, unshipped their oars and sculled her in at the downstream side. The canoes in which our party had travelled so far were loaded aboard and stowed upside down on deck.

I breathed deeply, looking forward to being back amongst barks with sails and rigging and tillers. Our long journey was downstream all the way – first to join the Saint Laurent River not far off, then fifty leagues to Quebec. After that, it was a hundred leagues to where the Gulf ended and the sea began, and another hundred leagues to clear past Acadia. Then I faced the agony of sailing right by Avalon and heading on for Boston.

A signal gun boomed out from the heights where Fort Louis stood overlooking the Saint Maurice. The French skipper gestured for us to board. I followed Irocaibi, Hubert and the three natives accompanying us along the wobbly boarding plank the French called a *passarelle*, and stepped on to the sloop's smooth deck. There, on the quarter, separated for once from the *Roi Soleil*'s opulent furnishings and tall Venetian sternlights, stood Seigneur Inférieur Alphonse D'Amati, wearing a good silk blouson and best cream-toned briches, regardless of the pitchy, fish-scaled deck-boards upon which his buckleshoed feet were now planted. While Irocaibi retained his native dress, I wore a new fur jacket underneath a beaverskin topcoat, both generously granted me by the Seigneur as befitting my new status as special envoy.

D'Amati bore two parchment copies of the draft treaty terms, wrapped in buckskin and sealed in a sewn leathern wallet that neither damp nor rain nor seawater could penetrate. Once the Seigneur Supérieur's seal was affixed on these papers, the D'Amati-Loftus terms would become the Quebec Accord.

Irocaibi had been right from the first. We had our treaty.

D'Amati greeted us warmly, then spoke to the master. The matelots cast off the lines and laid back on their long sweeps. The current gripped the sloop's undersides and away went the *Travailleur* into midstream. Moments later, the sailors shipped oars and hoisted the main, running the sheet out free to let the long low boom swing outboard, tilting and dipping a few feet above the river's eddying swirls. The broad canvas bulged full and a rippling wake fanned out astern of the vessel's sweet counter, and we sailed out into the river.

The Seigneur made an expansive gesture, taking in the whole view of all Trois Rivières and its grand emplacements and military might.

'A frontier garrison at present, but one day a great city like Quebec.' Turning to me, he smiled. 'And quite as impregnable.'

I smiled back, happy just to be on my way

downriver. The seemingly interminable forest and lakes, the barren tundra and the high plains, the boreal forest of maple and spruce – that never-ending sea of green undulating across the mountains and valleys of the great Kanada lands – was left behind forever. It was heartening to be under sail again.

All through the next day and night, I revelled in the sheer joy of having a proper sailing boat beneath my feet, the feel of her tilting along through the water, the shiver of her sails catching the puffs. In the wispy breezes, the *Travailleur* showed a turn of speed my stout-planked *Pursuant* could never muster. Though smaller, she compared with the English-built schooners of the Antilles trade, whose powerful lines and tall rigs made them weatherly and fast in the steep Tropick seas of inter-island passage-making, and which were handsome load carriers to boot. For a vessel built by a nation whose shipwrights valued a swooping sheerline above an extra tun of burthen, or a sweet run aft over a stiff gait in a seaway, this little French sloop was a fine craft. And how I relished her carrying us so swiftly on our way.

Downstream from Trois Rivières, the sloop bore off to larboard and entered the Saint Laurent itself, the mighty river draining the great lakes of the interior. Even the fearsome Saint Maurice gave way as we were disgorged into the mainstream of its altogether mightier brother. At the waters-meet where the swirling currents opposed, the sloop bucked and twisted until the flows combined.

Soon, the river's littorals broadened into rolling countryside. The banks were close-farmed in strips, like most English field plans before the dreaded enclosures began. The strips ran back from the banks in equal measures – *rangs*, Seigneur D'Amati called them. Hour after hour we sailed past a cultivated land where the hot sun beat on the bare browned backs and white-hatted heads of peasants bending to till the soil. D'Amati, as relaxed as a king surveying his realm, told me the *paysans* and their families were shipped in droves from Burgundy and Provence and Languedoc. Given their allotted land, they settled in to grow grains for export to the motherland, and to feed the foot-armies of Europe.

These, then, were the colonies France hoped would prosper far beyond the poor settlements of Carolina or Virginia or Massachusetts. While the English persisted in the futility – as the French saw it – of growing luxury commodities such as sugar or tobacco, whose markets were always limited, France intended to become strong on the wheatlands of Quebec. How important the Sovereign reckoned this land was confirmed by the boatloads of uniformed men patrolling the river, and the regular occurrence of wooden forts where troopers guarded both waterway and farmland alike.

D'Amati leaned back and closed his eyes to savour the sensation of journeying endlessly through his fiefdom, but I did not allow myself the luxury of rest. My eyes darted everywhere, studying the shoreline, taking in the numbers of people there and particularly any military figures. I looked towards the bankside forts and their soldier detachments. I examined the river traffic, the men they carried, the directions they took. Then too, I noted any tributaries or shoals or pools where vessels might anchor. I watched the sloop-master choose the deepwater channels, and I checked the run of the current. After all, who knew when such intelligence might prove valuable?

After a while, I moved over to join Irocaibi. He sat at the stern, aft of the tillerman, smoking a tooled willow-wood pipe drawn around the stem with intricate designs. As ever, he seemed composed, observing everything.

'Rich lands,' I said, gesturing, 'for the European to pursue his quest for bread.'

With a grave nod, he said, 'White men come and native people must leave, go into forest.' He swept his arm in a wide arc that took in all of the vast tracts rising in ranks from the river's flood plains. 'All lands once belonged to tribespeople.'

'So the French stole away your fellows' lands,' I said sympathetically.

'No. Iroquois peoples lose land because they do not fight. Argue brother against brother, cannot make treaty. Have no right to live here.'

Irocaibi, the proudest of fellows, brooked no opposition to his notions. So I turned to the Frenchy master and, with Hubert's aid, addressed him with a request. The fellow laughed, then ordered the steersman to relinquish his grip, which he did with much amusement. *Alors*, only an Englishman would demand to do such menial work!

With relish I took up the tiller-bar and, getting the feel of the sloop's ways, soon sent her slipping merrily along. When we rounded a river bend and the wind came dead aft, I bade the matelots hoist up their biggest jibsail and let it go wing and wing with the main. They went to it with such a will that the sloop-master, taken by the fun of it, smiled with pleasure as we sped along. Then he nipped below and returned bearing a small keg. From this he filled a flagonful of brandy to pass round from man to man, as though it were necessary to ease the onerous task of ticking along in pleasant sunshine with the wind at our backs.

I relaxed and let myself enjoy the company and the sailing. Confronting death in the white bear's jaws and then in the rapids, I had not expected to live. Sometimes I had despaired of breaking free of the forest. Now there loomed the prospect of dealing with Finlay McGruder at last. I was determined to become Intendant Proper – as was my right – but somehow it seemed less important than before. I wanted the *Pursuant* back. And I yearned for Grace Trepanney in my arms. That was all.

As the afternoon wore on, the farms and ranges gave way to hilly ground, steeper and uncultivable. By degrees, the river narrowed and ran faster till our speed past the banks reached eight or nine knots, three or four from sailing and the rest from current. Massive bluffs rose either side, closing in, forcing the river into a tighter course, our descent towards the far-off sea becoming ever more tortuous. For a moment, I feared rapids.

'*Regardez!*' cried the Frenchy master, gesticulating ahead. '*La cité de Quebec!*'

Half a league downriver, a sheer cliff of greystone rock loomed high over the northern bank. Ahead, the Saint Laurent split itself asunder to roar in twin torrents either side of a lofty, sharp-edged islet a mile or two in length and set in midstream. As we neared, gun batteries on bluffs to right and left showed themselves lit by the westering sun, standing out starkly against the sky, guarding the river's narrowest pass for a hundred leagues. Within the next half-glass, we rounded a vertical buttress and came under the crags and heights.

We had penetrated to the very heart of King Louis's northern power in the Americkas.

It was approaching dusk by the time we reached Quebec City's harbour. Jammed on the shore beneath the heights, it turned out to boast a far more extensive landing-place than Trois Rivières.

Long rough-planked jetties extended into the Saint Laurent, built on great timber baulks, the stripped trunks of giant pinewood trees piled deep into the gravelly river-bed. The dockside fairly teemed with life. All ranks and positions, from soldiers and sailors, marines and matelots, market women and quayside whores, wharfmen and shipmasters, bustled about their work.

Several sloops and a large sea-going vessel were tied alongside, the smaller vessels unloading sacks which were added to an enormous stack waiting to be loaded into the carrying bark. Teams of dockmen raised barrels from the big cargo ship's hold, swinging them on booms over to the jetty, and I caught the heady whiff of brandy on the evening's dying breeze. The stuff seemed to be the very fuel that fed and powered France's hungry colonies.

Without fuss or a raised shout, the master brought his little sloop to a jetty thrusting from the base of the great walls that were Quebec's natural defences. Though the city above was lost in the growing twilight, D'Amati had described the many castellated fortifications and lookout towers ringing the town, and within those bounds stood palaces and apartments of a grace and opulence for which an aristocratic fellow such as D'Amati himself would give up a Gascony chateau, a score of vineyards and several hundred *paysans* and their wives. It was clear to me that the reward he most craved was to set his calf-shod feet upon those embroidered carpets as holder of the great office of Seigneur Supérieur de la Toute Quebec. And our treaty brought that prospect a step or two closer.

We went ashore and prepared to make our way up to the city heights, embarking two dog-carts, each drawn by a single horse, with Alphonse D'Amati in the leading cart holding on to such dignity as the conveyance afforded, and Irocaibi and myself following in the second. Our party progressed uphill in fine fashion, or as fine as negotiating the narrow and winding pathway up the precipice allowed.

The Seigneur Inférieur proved the best of ambassadors. His sway over the doorkeepers of the Seigneurie, and the grand air he gave off as he swept into the palace, melted away all barriers. He was soon transported to the very seat of power and ushered into inner sanctums where I and my native friend were forbidden entry. He spent an hour with the Seigneur Supérieur himself, returning with a satisfied smile to announce the birth of the Quebec Accord. With astonishing speed, a flock of scribes produced new copies of the treaty, impressively crafted documents on rolls of expensive vellum leaf, enscribed in both French and English and prominently sealed with the Seigneur Supérieur's own true mark.

One of these D'Amati handed to Irocaibi, who acknowledged its receipt with an upward tilt of the nose, and the other to me, at which I bowed. Further, the Seigneur placed in my hands another parchment, recognisable to all officials of the French government as well as those of Boston. It proclaimed my legate status and gave me free passage from French into English territorial waters. D'Amati confirmed that in the morning, I would be joined on the sloop by an envoy of France, who would accompany me downriver into the Saint Laurent Gulf, through the Breton Channel and thence southward all the way to Boston. Irocaibi, along with Hubert and the three Indians in their party, would travel downriver with us only as far as the Louis River, where they would re-enter the interior and make their way home.

It was long past nightfall before all this business was done. When D'Amati announced his intention to stay for a diplomat's ball, it did not need to be said that the invitation was not extended to a rough sailor and a native from the forest. Thus, we bade each other a formal farewell. Relieved to be free of the confines of the palace with its fops and flunkies in abundance, Irocaibi and I eschewed the awkward horse-carts and all but ran the mile back downhill to the harbour.

16

Gulf of Delusion

As we approached the jetties, the glow of the harbour lights showed a knot of figures gathered by the sloop. On getting closer, I saw it was a band of French troopers.

The officer was engaged with the *Travailleur*'s master in what seemed a dispute of some rancour. The master shrugged, stamped his foot and struck his forehead in a range of dramatick gestures a stage actor might have envied. Seeing me, he pointed and waved excitely. Moving down the jetty, I reached inside my coat-jacket for a reassuring touch of the treaty documents and most particularly, if an officious soldier were offering any delay, the safe passage with D'Amati's seal and signature prominently upon it.

'What's the nuisance here?' I demanded.

The troop officer, edgy and mistrustful, glared back with obvious incomprehension at my words and considerable hostility directed at Irocaibi. I advised the Indian to board the sloop, saying I would join him as soon as the misunderstanding was dealt with. Hubert the half-caste stayed with me to translate. Nitchequot listened to the officer, then explained.

'He asks if you are the so-called envoy, the Englishman the sloop-master speaks of.'

I drew out my safe passage and held it up, bowing from the waist. The fellow snatched at the paper, giving it an insolent and casual glance before issuing another stream of French.

Hubert spoke again. 'He says that whatever he may or may not appreciate, M'sieur l'Anglais under-estimates the seriousness of the crime being committed.'

'What crime?' I said, nonplussed.

'He wonders how it has escaped your notice what this sloop is loaded with. The master is using your presence aboard as a cover for smuggling.'

'Tell him, Hubert. We have no knowledge of nor interest in the cargo.'

'*Cognac*,' said the officer, pointing at a keg by his feet, the self-same keg from which we had drunk away the afternoon trick.

Dismayed, I gestured towards the carrying ship further up the jetty and the stacks of reeking barrels recently disgorged from its holds. 'How can this master having a keg of brandy aboard count as smuggling? There must be a thousand barrels of it over there. The stuff comes upriver by the shipload.'

The Revenue officer smirked, striking his boot against the offending object, and adopted a triumphant air.

Hubert translated. 'Ah, he says, but this brandy is in small kegs. They are made at Toulon, and he has indicated the mark.'

I looked. Even under the weak lights, the impress of a small symbol was plain to see.

'It is Naval issue,' said Hubert, 'for the benefit of

His Majesty's deck officers aboard warships. There-fore anyone else carrying it must be smugglers.'

'Maybe so – but my documents take preced-ence over any small infringement of excise duties,' I protested. 'Hubert, request that he allow us on our way.'

Just then the officer spoke to a soldier and held out the parchment for him to take.

'Wait a minute, that's mine,' I said, stepping forward.

The officer shoved me hard in the chest. At his curt command, the other troopers lifted their muskets and held them out with menace.

'He orders us to stand aside,' said Nitchequot, 'or face arrest along with the master.'

To my dismay, the soldier set off at a pace along the jetty, bearing the safe passage.

'Hoy, there!' I shouted. 'Bring it back!'

But the running soldier disappeared into the night. The officer laughed, and spoke rapidly to Hubert.

'He says that when the sloop-master appears in court in a few days, or perhaps weeks, you may petition for the return of your papers. Until then the vessel, its crew, its contents and all its passengers are sequestered by the Quebec Revenue Guard.'

I determined to get back to D'Amati before this nonsense went any further. Just then there was a commotion along the jetty where some docksiders were advancing, gesticulating and shouting, appar-ently in defence of the sloop-master. It distracted the Revenue officer's attention and the master, who had been standing quietly all this time, seized his chance. He picked up the brandy keg and heaved it off the

jetty. No sooner had it hit the water than the fierce
Saint Laurent current bore it away like flotsam, and
in seconds it disappeared from sight. An expression
of black anger spread across the officer's face and he
lost control, shouting and ranting. Everyone joined
in and uproar ensued.

'What's happening, Hubert?' I said in alarm.

'He says that evidence has been destroyed. And he
curses the master's mother and all her offspring.'

The officer had his baton threateningly raised.
The guards seized the *Travailleur*'s master who,
protesting and struggling, received for his pains a
crack on the head with a musket stock. He called
to his mates for help and the response was instan-
taneous. His crew came bounding off the sloop
and the docksiders moved swiftly along the jetty
to join in. There was a great deal of shouting, not
least from the red-faced and enraged troop officer.
This misunderstanding was all too quickly getting
out of hand yet I was loth to intervene, fearing to
remonstrate with the hot-headed Frenchies in case
matters worsened.

A shot rang out. No one was sure where it
had come from, but seamen and dockmen and
traders alike dived flat to the boardwalk. One of the
musketmen collapsed groaning, his weapon falling
in a clatter. Then I saw that the sloop-master had
somehow produced a pistol from his belt. He had
shot his own countryman.

Hell broke out all around. Three or four troopers
fell upon the master, beating him to the ground. The
officer shouted an order and more shots echoed off
the bluffs. The sloop-master broke free, staggered a

few paces and fell. His crewmen, issuing fearsome whoops, charged the musketmen, some of whom had dropped to their knees and were tugging at their rammers in a hopeless bid to reload. Others, with more sense, drew swords. The two sides clashed, shouting and cursing.

Hubert and I ducked clear of the fracas, crouching low as another volley of musket balls whirred overhead. Reaching the sloop, we found Irocaibi and his native companions standing by the *Travailleur*'s rail, knives at the ready.

'No, no,' I urged, 'stay back!'

Irocaibi opened his mouth as if to speak. More musket shots discharged. A ball hit square on the Indian standing beside him, jerking his head backwards with sudden force. He staggered, then collapsed. Before anyone could reach him, he fell clean over the rail and into the dark waters swirling under the jetty. Irocaibi was overside in an instant, his head bobbing below the surface as he struck out after his friend.

'The stern, Irocaibi,' I shouted, 'make for the stern!'

Aft was where the riverboat's freeboard was least, the only place to get back aboard. There was an awful moment when he seemed not to grasp what I was saying. Then, grabbing hold of the dead brave by the shoulders, he struggled towards it. Leaping aboard the sloop, I raced aftward and threw a thick hempen line for him to grasp. He missed it and took my arm, all but jerking me into the water. His hand slipped and fumbled on mine, then he took my leg. The native's body, caught up in the current, was dragging both of us down, but Irocaibi would not relinquish his grip.

'He's dead, man,' I cried. 'Let go!'

With a look of disbelief, Irocaibi stared at the youth's face. There was a hole in the forehead, oozing darkly. Still he would not release him.

Desperately I tried to haul Irocaibi clear of the icy water but the current's pull was too strong. Hubert and the others had clambered aboard, and I opened my mouth to shout for help. Just then the troop officer gesticulated in our direction. His soldiers dropped to their knees and levelled their muskets.

A volley of shots echoed off the steep rock faces towering above the Saint Laurent and the balls whistled overhead or slammed into the wooden piles. Crouching, I could hold on no longer. The two men's weight together was beyond me, the current running too hard. My grip failed. Suddenly they were gone, swept off into the running black water.

'Irocaibi!' I screamed, but all I saw was the pale outline of his raised arm, disappearing at a rate of knots.

I stood up, aghast. A second later, I had my knife out and was sawing at the mooring lines, slashing like a man possessed. They parted, and the sloop fell away from the jetty.

'To the sweeps!' I urged. 'Pull out into midstream.'

Hubert took up one of the long oars cradled in hooks under the side rails, slotted it into a sturdy rowlock and dug in with all his might. The other two Indians scrambled to give a hand. The *Travailleur* lurched free and the current bore her rapidly downstream. Running back to the tiller, I steered along the shore, seeking a glimpse of Irocaibi.

The glow of the harbour lights silhouetted the troopers. They were on their knees again, reloading.

'Pull away, fellows! Lay back with all your might!' I cried hoarsely.

There were only seconds left before their volley. When the shots came, again we ducked low as the balls buzzed out over the water. A few struck the taffrail, splintering the wood and a dozen more sang harmlessly overhead. But by now the *Travailleur* was a good hundred and fifty paces off the jetty and at the edge of a musket's accuracy.

I headed in the direction Irocaibi had disappeared, with my crew hauling at the sweeps. Again and again I searched the waters, with growing panic, but saw nothing.

'Spy out for him, Hubert,' I urged. 'Get the others to look. He can't last long in the cold.'

The Quebec harbour receded as we were borne downstream, and the hue faded. Steering one-handed I searched back and forth. Suddenly there was a dim shape. When I threw the tiller-bar across, the sloop lurched sideways on to the current and a man's body bumped against the downstream side. I dashed for the gunnel, leaned over perilously and grabbed his arm. It was Irocaibi.

'Hubert!' I shouted.

He dropped his sweep and together we hauled the Indian sternwards, then hoisted his dripping form aboard and laid him on deck. When they saw their man, the natives stopped rowing and made to come over, leaving the sloop at the mercy of the current.

'Back to your sweeps,' I said. 'We've got to get clear. You too, Hubert.'

They got the meaning and hauled on, white-eyed, their stares never leaving their stricken prince, lying motionless on the deck-boards. I pointed the bows towards the middle of the great black river, then centred the tiller and lashed it. We had to put distance between us and the shoreside. Although the sounds of the fracas had diminished, astern of us the river was alive with shouts and the rattle of sails being hoisted and sweeps stroking. The troopers had taken to the water and were giving chase.

The half-caste and his native companions struck out in regular movements, the sweeps clunking in the locks, and the sloop moved swiftly downriver into the darkness. I had no idea of our direction, but I no longer cared a whit. Anywhere out here on the river in this pitch of night would do.

When I bent to him, Irocaibi's face was a rigid blank. His skin was freezing where I touched it. His eyes were closed, his chest did not rise and fall. His features were frozen into a grimace, as though enduring some great struggle. Lord above, he surely had not been in the river so very long. Come on, Irocaibi, wake up, I pleaded silently. I slapped his face and rubbed his arms and legs. I beat and pummelled on his chest to bring him back. There was no response. The life was ebbing from him. Numbed, I leaned close, barely able to think straight.

'Irocaibi, if you can hear me, listen. I shall see the treaty through.'

There never was any reply from my Indian friend. His chance to speak had gone forever. Sitting with his head cradled in my arms, I felt something evaporating inside my heart, leaving it shrunken, harder, full of bitterness.

After some minutes, the cries of pursuit from astern penetrated my stupor. If they catch us, I thought, they shall kill us all. I lifted my head and found the river's breeze brushing my cheek. Leaving Irocaibi, I went forward to hoist the mainsail, thinking that sailing must give better speed than rowing.

The two Indians' faces were white moons in the darkness. They had stilled their sweeps and were crouched, transfixed, disbelieving. Hubert caught my eye.

'Tell them to go aft,' I said, with a crack in my voice.

They dropped their sweeps and scrambled away. Instantly the night was filled with new sounds. The young native men were keening over their master's corpse.

I undid the boom ties, freed off the haulyard and dragged the sail up the wispy mast, the work diverting my mind from the immediate horror. The sail caught the wind and filled at once, and when I sheeted it in the *Travailleur* picked up speed, taking off into midriver, heading for the main current.

The mighty Saint Laurent caught hold of the sloop's shallow keel and catapulted us downstream at a rate of knots. There was no going back.

Nervously, I raked the fuzzy horizon with my naked eye. The *Travailleur* lacked a spy-glass, but – thank the Lord – it was plain enough that the flat, grey-blue waters of the Breton Channel remained empty of ships. The sloop was alone in the wide sea.

We had been on the run for five days, and the Gulf of Saint Laurent already lay many leagues astern. Now we were exposed and vulnerable, all too conspicuous, sailing through disputed waters.

The escape from Quebec had been touch and go. Every last trooper of the Revenue Guard was on the lookout for us, every river craft alerted to report a sighting. With my safe passage lost, we could not risk being caught. As an Englishman in a stolen sloop, and accused of the death of one or more troopers, I had no defence. Even with the Deputy Intendant's seal, trying to talk my way back into the Seigneurie would have been out of the question.

I still had the treaty documents, safe and whole. The Quebec Accord had to go ahead for the Missacaibi people's sake, for that was now a debt of honour I owed Irocaibi. Not only that, but the treaty was my only chance of salvaging a future from the mess, my sole means of winning help to return to Esperantia and claim what was mine. I had to go on. It was Boston or nothing.

Four nights earlier we had put Irocaibi's two surviving native friends ashore. Under cover of dark, we unshipped their canoes and respectfully laid their master's body in one. They gathered leaves and boiled bark for curing and binding up their prince's remains, determined to carry them home to the Rupert River – or to the Nasquinoba, I corrected myself, honouring Irocaibi's preferred name. Then they disappeared up an unknown river, heading north to find friendly tribes and seek the way back to their distant homelands.

Refusing to join them, Hubert Nitchequot remained with me on the Frenchy sloop. With Irocaibi gone, he explained, the forest held nothing for him. From henceforth, he would make his way in peaceful Newfoundland or perhaps Acadia, but never again in the Missacaibi lands.

Hiding by day and sailing by night, the two of us headed off downriver. Somehow we had to dodge French patrols and find our way through the Gulf, past Acadia and hundreds of miles southwards as far as the Nantucket Shoals – English waters at last. With ten hours of darkness, during which we made four knots by sailing and three by the current, we covered seventy or perhaps even eighty sea-miles before each new dawn. When the river broadened, its traffic lessened and I risked sailing by day. Along the Gulf's North Shore, we passed coastal features recognisable from my earlier ventures, and I knew us to be east of Tadoussac and the Saguenay River, the river I had tried to escape to in my canoe. The *Travailleur* pointed her bows seaward and the shore disappeared in the haze. Soon we were cutting along, deep in the Gulf and out amongst the schools of whales teeming there – rights and minkes and humpbacks.

Without compass or cross-staff, tools of no use to a riverboat, I steered by judging the sun and the stars. To estimate our speed, I stared for hours at the sea rushing past. I conjured up in my mind's eye the charts from my old pilot book. By these means, I estimated and deduced and reckoned, but above all I guessed. Clinging to the fragile belief that my dead reckoning was good, I calculated us to be passing Cap Aiguille, lying unseen below the horizon to larboard. This was Newfoundland's southwesternmost point and – cruelly – not a day's sail from Avalon. We had to pass it by, and turn our bows south.

Handing over the tiller to the half-caste for a spell, I lay on the sloop's decks, warmed by the sun, by turns dozing and thinking. I wanted nothing more than to return to Esperantia, to find Grace safe, to stalk down McGruder. Yet I had no means – neither weapons nor men nor barks. I must win help, but how? Would the Accord still hold in Boston? It was countersigned by the Seigneur Supérieur of all Quebec, but would the diplomats and governor's men there believe my story?

Hubert shook me awake, breaking my reverie.

'Look,' he whispered, pointing south and east beyond the bows.

In the lazy afternoon air, a worn haze smeared the sea's horizon. At first there was nothing more than a line of white smudges along the curve of the sea's edge. Then a row of topgallants appeared, pennants flying – first six, then eight, then a dozen. Minutes after, rising above the horizon, came the topsails and the yards and shrouds of many more vessels.

It was unmistakeably the canvas of a great fleet of warships. They were plying majestically through the Breton Channel and towards the Gulf. When I recognised the flags, the blood pounded in my veins. The pennants and standards were those of the Bourbon King's Navy.

There was no chance of the *Travailleur* going unseen. Without benefit of a spying tube, or a spare man to climb the mast and keep lookout, we had already let the great fleet come too close. By contrast, with many pairs of eyes at the foretops equipped with spy-glasses, the fleet must have long since spotted us. Altering precipitately and running off would arouse instant suspicion. I held my course, desperately seeking a way out.

Within a half glass, the hulls came up and Hubert emitted a low whistle. It was a massive flota of warships. There were two-deckers and three-deckers, frigates and galliards, attended by a flutter of sloops and sailing cutters scouting the way ahead or bearing messages and officers between the ships as they made their stately progress. They sailed free on the light southwesterly, rolling gently in the wafts, in ragged line astern, emerging like wraiths from the ghostly haze. Ineluctably, the *Travailleur*, fetching along with her main boom amidships and the jibsheets hauled home, bore down towards their midst. It could only be the rumoured Grand Fleet. It was already north of the Acadian ports, and must surely be bound for Quebec City.

Within a sea-mile, one of the advance guard of sailing cutters broke off and ran up to cross our course.

'Hubert, we shall have to pass off as fishermen. The talking's up to you. I shall play dumb.'

We looked unlikely codfishers, whether wet curers or salters. For a start, the *Travailleur* was plainly built more for river work than sea fishing. With her lack of freeboard at the bows and her sweet little counter stern, she was perfect for slipping along in flat water or a low chop, but hardly fit for hauling nets and longlines in a lumpy swell. What were we two doing out here, halfway between English Newfoundland and French Breton Isle?

The cutter closed rapidly, creaming along at a lick as she freed sheets and ran across the wind to cut us off. There were a dozen seamen aboard, mostly oarsmen idling with their sweeps shipped while the breeze did the work. In the sternsheets, the young Frenchy officer handed the tiller to his mate and stood for a better look at his quarry.

Our story sounded thinner than ever, even to me. There were only the two of us, and what fishing boat of thirty five foot would ship fewer than six or eight fellows aboard for all the work? Instead, I told Hubert to say we were traders off our usual river routes and plying down to Saint Jean Ville, the French port at Fundy Bay, a place where the tides ranged the height of a schooner's mainmast, fifty feet or more. The half-caste was to say his master had lost his tongue to the surgeon's knife after getting boils caused by eating bad meat.

'*Bon*, I understand.' He turned to hail the approaching cutter when a thought struck him. 'But if we are traders, what is our cargo?'

Below decks, the *Travailleur* carried nothing apart from her own dry stores, the usual lockers full of spare blocks and deadeyes, sewing palms, tubs of wax and pitch, coils of rope, along with bags of junk end and oakum for caulking seams. Otherwise her holds were full of nothing – nothing, that is, barring smuggled goods. The most cursory inspection below would reveal fifty small kegs of French Naval-issue brandy from Toulon.

Hails reached us across the twenty fathoms of intervening water. Two seamen stood at the gunnels, coiled lines at the ready. The officer spoke shortly to Hubert, who enthusiastically beckoned him to bring the cutter alongside. She was a sturdy boat, clinker-built of three-quarter inch planks, all varnished topsides, the oarlocks and rubbing strips made of bright brass – a treat for a Navy man to admire.

The cutter rounded up, dropped her jibsail, let the staysail sheets go free and jostled alongside with admirable precision, barely bumping the sloop's strakes. Two matelots stepped lightly aboard with the lines, made them off and stood awaiting orders.

My heart pounded noisily enough, it seemed to me, for everyone to hear. The half-caste and the officer engaged in a discourse, accompanied by the now familiar array of raised eyebrows, downturned mouths, lifted shoulders and heads cocked to one side. Its tone was civil enough, almost amicable, and I thanked the Fates for sending me such a natural diplomat as Hubert Nitchequot. He gestured my way with sympathetic shrugs and outstretched palms, as if to say, there is nothing worse for a Frenchman than to be denied the power of speech. I gave a wan smile, matching the shoulder movements and palm waving as best I could.

The cutter's crew appeared to be a hotch-potch bunch of matelots raked in from the back-streets and seedy *auberges* of Brest or Toulon or Bordeaux, like any job lot scooped into the English Navy from the inns and whorehouses of Portsmouth or Wapping. But if these were seamen, they were as yet untoughened, without the leather-skinned look of time-worn tars, lacking the horned feet and palms calloused through chafing on rough hempen or manila ropes as they hauled the storm-topsail sheets home in a gale. Neither did they sport the tattoos so favoured by the old voyaging hands, to impress not just the harbour girls but the land-bound farmhands left behind in their villages to gape open-mouthed at the returned travellers' wild tales.

Any sailor who passed across the Atlantick Ocean, or ventured below the Tropick Line of Cancer, or was carried south beyond the Equator, got ink tattooed on his skin to show for it. If he ran between the Pillars of Hercules to enter the Mediterranean Sea, or called at the Canary Isles for sweetwater, or sunned himself in the Spice Isles and Batavia, he paid for a design to be pricked into his ankle or needled on a forearm. Or he got a motto – which he could not read, whether in Latin, Greek, Creole or his own tongue – enscribed upon one nutty-brown buttock. He might acquire a spider's web across his shaven skull. He might choose to get two eyes drawn on his closed lids to gull an officer into thinking he was awake on watch. They were the trophies of travel and adventure and war and battles, or storms in the Forties and capes passed at sixty degrees south. Yet this cutter's sailors boasted none of these, not one. They were undecorated, soft-muscled raw men on their first trip from home.

The youthful officer stepped ceremoniously aboard,

seventeen or eighteen if he was a day, pale-skinned from serving in northern waters, a Bresterman, I reckoned, or a Dunquerquer. Like his matelots, he too was a first-timer.

Hubert was valiantly trying to keep him talking, but the fellow rapped on the deck-boards, giving me a direct and enquiring look. I met his eye and pointed to the hatch cover, then pressed a finger against my lips and hoisted my brows high, eyes bulging, head going from side to side.

The Frenchy frowned in annoyance and spoke sharply to Hubert, but I stepped over and gripped the officer's arm, motioning him to keep quiet as if we might be overheard. Gesturing again at the cover, I made the motions of raising a glass to my lips. Wearing what I hoped was an idiot's grin, I drank, swallowing the make-believe liquid, relishing it as though savouring the smoothest, most delicately flavoured brandy ever produced, a brandy from the regions where, as everyone knows, the best of Frenchy spirits are distilled.

'*Cognac?*' he said in astonishment.

I signed for him to lower his voice, my eyes darting to the fleet passing close by. When I pointed from the hatch cover to his uniformed chest and back, he grasped the point at once. I levered open the hatch and dropped inside. Cradling it slyly, as if it were a treasure beyond compare, I brought out a brandy keg. Hefting it over my head and rolling it onto the deck-boards by the young man's feet, which were shod in smart, unworn leather-slips, I presented it for examination.

The officer stared at the keg. Real French brandy!

Then I shook the pockets of my briches, as if making a few small coins rattle brassily.

'*Comment?*' he exclaimed, incredulous. He must pay for this?

I smiled, beckoning him to look inside the hold. He peered in and let out an agonised whistle. Hubert's head joined him and soon all three of us were muttering, arguing, moaning as befitted our various roles. It was a scene out of a Breton vegetable market or a Gascony wine auction. We were haggling over the deal, the half-caste play-acting with gusto, his expressions ranging from the rage of an affronted stallholder to the indignation of an innocent man stepping onto the scaffold. The officer matched these and more, first adopting looks of childlike wonder at the price Hubert proposed, then an air of sad bereavement when it was clear he would not be budged.

'*Je ne bouge plus!*' cried Nitchequot, and held up ten fingers.

But ten casks were not enough for this eager tyke. The boyish officer could clearly see, even in the below-decks gloom, at least four dozen stowed neatly on the sole or tucked into the spaces between the sloop's ribs and frames, lashed with ropes to prevent movement in a seaway. By now, I was sure, this youthful cove reckoned to have stumbled on a piece of luck all his fellow officers would envy and his superiors admire. What, coming upon a trading sloop carrying good French brandy, when the quarter-deck steward's supplies were low after crossing the ocean? And me here, a fresh young gentleman officer with coin in his pocket to buy it and serve it to his masters on the poop, compliments of a most courteous and attentive midshipman? An opportunity far too good to miss.

He swept his hand right round the hold, indicating he was going to buy the lot, dammit, and at a bargain price. Hubert buried his face in his hands and wailed. I acted mute distress and servile pleading in equal measures. Brushing aside all objections, including my half-articulated moans of protestation, the young man straightened and issued a stream of commands to his sailors.

So it was that, ten minutes later, the *Travailleur* rode an inch or two higher and the cutter dipped her gunnels low in the water, wallowing, overloaded with half-price brandy. Hubert and I stood at the quarter, feigning loss and ruin. His curses began to sound so dangerously inciting I squeezed his elbow to encourage him to temper their ripeness. The officer stepped haughtily aboard his boat, followed by the two matelots taking off the lines. The Frenchy tars had the Devil of a job in raising the staysail and sheeting home, let alone locking out the oars to row. Between their feet, piled high amidships, were all fifty brandy kegs.

Without undue haste, Hubert and I hoisted sail and bore off, heading straight for the approaching fleet. By now, the vanguard had passed ahead and the main body of ships had drawn within two or three cables. Triumphant in his cutter, the youthful officer raised signals up her flag haulyard for King Louis's officers. No doubt they examined them with their tooled spy-glasses from high on the towering quarter-decks of the galliards and frigates slouching

311

by on their way up to the Gulf. I prayed that those signals said we had been duly hauled over, examined and given free passage.

With luck, we could pass clear of the fleet and get upwind before the officer discovered his mistake. As a raw man newly abroad, he had not recognised the kegs, but as soon as they were boomed aboard his capital ship, some old hand would cry out, 'Look! Those are Navy issue – the kegs have the Toulon mark! Why, he's bought back the Navy's own smuggled brandy, and paid a handsome price for it too!' The poor Devil likely faced six days in a cell and a month's loss of privilege. There was to be no quaffing of brandy in the admiral's *Grande Cabine* for him.

Closehauled, we pointed up to the heart of the fleet. Soon, we passed under the golden beaks of warships festooned with decoration and gilded paintwork, three-deckers and four-deckers too, with forecastles thirty feet above the waterline and poops loftier still. Officers crowded the rails, dressed in fine white hose and briches and buckle shoes, powdered wigs beneath blue tricorn hats, gold-braided long-coats and the glint of mother-of-pearl buttons. The common matelots were uniformed in striped blue loose shirts and white pantalons, a far cry from the rough calico slops of English Navy issue, or the make-do clothes of a privateer crew.

But there were throngs of other uniformed men aboard. They stood around in the waist, smoking and idling. Below decks, their myriad faces appeared in the dark squares where the upper gun-deck ports were allowed open for fresh air. Some of the greater vessels carried what looked like many hundreds of these men, making thousands altogether. And every one of them was a soldier.

All the fleet had watched us being hauled over, so no one else would bother us now. Returning their regal waves, we sliced between the lumbering sea fortresses and bucked across their wakes, until at last we came clear and found only a few straggling cutters in their rearguard. Then suddenly we were free. The *Travailleur* was not chased. She rode prettily along, disburdened of her unlawful load and making a half knot the better for it.

The half-caste broke from staring at the fast-receding Grand Fleet and smiled wanly.

'Sometimes,' he said, jangling a weight of loose coin in his pocket, 'a man's silence can be golden.'

Savouring the sloop's extra speed, I let myself be momentarily overcome by a delicious relief. But it was all too shortlived. Those thousands of soldiers must be on their way to Quebec – and then Trois Rivières. Hubert, surely reaching the same conclusion, fell silent and brooding. The French invasion was going ahead, and the leaderless Missacaibi faced the slaughter Irocaibi had sought to prevent.

And where was Queen Anne's Navy squadron under Admiral Tompion, the force sent out to intercept this French fleet? We had just watched the enemy sail unperturbed through the Breton Channel and straight into the Gulf.

Grim-faced, I leant on the *Travailleur*'s tiller and sent her heading south – south for the waters of Nantucket and beyond. Boston still lay six or seven days' sailing away.

17

Broken Promise

The *Travailleur* slipped along in a light breeze. By my reckoning, we had passed in the night as close as twenty leagues from Esperantia. Now it lay far astern.

I sat at the tiller day-dreaming of Governor Spurgeon sentencing Finlay McGruder for ship-stealing. Then in my imaginings he granted me a warrant to hunt the man down. No longer a ragamuffin sailor on the run in a tatty French sloop, I became instead a vengeful warrior. The dream drifted slowly on towards a yet more fulfilling vision, one in which Grace Trepanney was sure to appear.

Just then Hubert's excited shouts cut short this idyllic fancy. The dream evaporated.

'A sail! A sail!'

I stood up and squinted. Fatigued beyond measure, we had once again let our watch-keeping slacken and the newcomer's hull was already well above the sea-horizon. She was a two-master with the red and white emblazon of the Cross of Saint George fluttering high at her truck. At last, I thought, the English Navy is in the right place for once.

I heaved on the mainsheet and shoved the tiller-bar across to bring the sloop close-hauled, then sent Hubert forward to sweat the headsail home. The

Travailleur heeled hard on steerboard tack, dug in her little gunnels and cantered off towards the warship. In response, the stranger came on a reach to cross our track and intercept us. She soon showed herself to be a small cruzer of the type commonly stationed on patrol in the Western Approaches to the English Channel. Such cruzers might be lightly armed, usually carrying four in the broadside, but were fast enough to outrun sluggish French fortress ships.

A cable or two off, her forward swivel blazed once and a shot fell ahead of our bows, dead on the line of our course. Dam' and blast, her gunners were all too accurate. Then she opened her gunports and the deck-pieces rumbled out, poking their snouts into the fresh sea air. For half a second it looked as though she had determined we were enemy and was going to blow us to splinters. And record a victory.

Hubert and I dashed to let fly the sheets and drop all sail. The *Travailleur* lay quiet and submissive as the cruzer approached. On the quarter-deck stood uniformed figures, spy-glasses raised, scrutinising our every move. A longboat was lowered, heavily manned with oarsmen – musketmen too, their barrels raised. The boat broke clear, stroking in a wide arc astern of the *Travailleur* so that she and the mother vessel covered our stern quarters but did not stand in the way of each other's fire. The muskets were trained on us. They were according us the respect of a powerful and dangerous enemy.

'Sloop ahoy,' came the officer's hail.

'We're English!' I shouted back.

There was a puzzled pause. Then the voice called,

'You are in disputed waters and arrested by Her Majesty's Navy. Prepare to be boarded.'

The longboat closed, a dozen muzzles pointing our way.

'Easy there, lads!' I called, but they paid no heed.

The twenty foot open boat crashed into the sloop's gunnels with an almighty crack. Armed men swarmed across with profane shouts. Hubert and I raised our hands but were thrown to the deck-boards and roughly bound at the wrists. Then we were shoved into the longboat and sculled without delay to the cruzer. Coming under the topsides, I saw her officers leaning over the quarter.

'I am English,' I shouted, 'with important news about the enemy!'

The longboat juddered alongside. We were man-handled up the boarding rope and pushed onto the quarter-deck to face a young man of about twenty years. He wore a Naval coat denoting him a lieutenant and was clearly the ship's master, though once again a freshman. He ordered a crew put aboard the sloop, then busied himself with getting his ship under way.

'Lieutenant,' I began, 'I am an envoy –'

'Be silent,' he said.

He seemed nervous, irritated by us and glancing at our rough clothing – Hubert still in a buckskin jacket and moccasin slippers, myself in a better coat but beneath that wearing loose and dirty briches.

'Your vessel is a Frenchy one, going by her look. I should think you must be a scout or spy.' Frowning, he nodded at the *Travailleur*. 'She is a prize, by the way, of the cruzer *Regard*.'

Another fellow on the quarter-deck stepped over, a landsman, going by his long-coat and heeled shoes.

'Lieutenant Balty, I heard mention of a spy,' he said. 'Perhaps then this might be an affair to concern me? What do you think?'

The younger man swivelled round. 'I think so very well, Second Deputy Assistant Sub-Commissioner. They are all yours. I am keen to get under way.'

The lieutenant went off to the break to oversee his sailing orders. The landsman lifted his head – with the high-heeled buckle-shoes he just reached my height – and looked along his nose. A pair of spectacles balanced on the bridge, and in their tiny lenses the doubled images of his eyes were the size of peas.

'English, is that so?' His tone was suspicious but not hostile. 'And you claim to be an envoy? For whom?'

Above the bustle as the Navy jack-tars sprang aloft and chantied out on the yardarm, or laboured at the sheets with grunts and shouts, I heard a cry go up from the *Travailleur*. A prize crew had been put aboard and now the boarding officer was stroking back in the longboat. Held high in his hand like a trophy was a sheaf of crumpled papers. My pilotage notes, dammit – the hastily scribbled notes I had made of my observations along the Upper Saint Laurent and parts of the Gulf. All of it was enemy territory.

Quickly I flashed my Deputy Intendant's seal. 'I am an envoy of Septimus Spurgeon, Governor of

317

Newfoundland. And I have vital news for Admiral Tompion of the Newfoundland Fleet. Are you part of his forces?'

'No, we have come direct from Plymouth,' said the landsman, 'sighting but not touching at – as the lieutenant says – Cape Race. Something about finding our fix. But if you are a spy, perhaps I should not have told you that.'

The longboat came alongside and the officer leapt aboard. After a brief word with the lieutenant, he stepped up to the landsman, saluted and handed him the papers.

'The lieutenant suggested you should see these, sir.'

'My word,' he said. 'What is all this?'

'Notes for my pilot book,' I put in hastily. 'I am a fur trader on the Labrador Coast.'

He leafed over a few pages and read the headings. 'Ah, I see – *Notes For A Pilot Of The Saint Laurent River – Trois Rivières To The Quebec Jetties*. And here, *The Saint Laurent Gulf – Point des Monts To The Saguenay Entrance at Tadoussac*. These are the titles of your chapters, one presumes? Most interesting.' He fixed his smiling face on mine. 'First, we find you in disputed waters, as the lieutenant describes them, and your vessel turns out to be French. You say you are an envoy, but next you claim to be on a mission for an English admiral. Then you declare yourself a fur trader from Labrador, yet I discover plans and charts covering parts deep within enemy territory. It does look most incriminating, does it not?'

'If you would give me a moment to explain –'

'I think you shall have as much time as you care for,' said my interrogator, though not unpleasantly.

The cruzer's canvas was being hauled home to a great deal of robust chantying at the belays. She bore round, came on a reach and settled on her course. Satisfied, Lieutenant Balty came over, gazing first aloft as the tars scrambled down from the yards then casting agitated glances at the sea-scape all around.

'Beg pardon for my distraction, Second Deputy Assistant Sub-Commissioner, but we are in hostile waters. The enemy could be anywhere.' He gestured at the *Travailleur* falling in astern of the *Regard*, her new crew quickly getting her under their feet. 'However, it seems I have collected a prize, even if a meagre one. Excellent, so soon out of Plymouth and on my first commission.' Then with a nod towards me he added, 'And you have caught your first spy.'

The Second Deputy Assistant Sub-Commissioner looked astonished.

'Have I? Do you really think so?'

The landsman glanced down at the papers, fingering them as if they were the finest silk. Then he gazed at me in wonder. Or was it awe?

'O yes, perhaps I have. How exciting!'

'It is plain as a pennant on a pinnace, Loftus, that you are an *espionageur*. A scout for the enemy.'

Second Deputy Assistant Sub-Commissioner Archibald Strutt smiled, stubbornly blind to what I had been trying to tell him about the treaty and the Grand Fleet.

Many days had passed since the *Regard*, under

Lieutenant Balty, had brought us into Back Bay, Boston Harbour, Massachusetts. The prisoners Hubert Nitchequot and Matthew Loftus had been taken off, put in irons and with some ceremony transferred to this prison ship, a broken-backed old three-decker called the *Promise*. Long and cruel since then had been the hours and days of my confinement, in which I heartily regretted not hauling the *Travailleur*'s sheets and standing in for Avalon the moment we had duped our way past the French Grand Fleet.

'Consider the case,' Strutt continued. 'An Englishman is caught by our patrol in enemy waters aboard a Frenchy sloop. His crew is a miscegenated cove, half Indian and – mark this – half Frog. Worse, he carries drawings and mappings showing harbour entrances, channels and passages, fortifications and batteries of enemy territory. What am I to do but take him for an agent of the King of France?'

The Second Deputy Assistant Sub-Commissioner was enjoying this interview, even though it was not our first. Far from hearing my case, he merely repeated his own against me, fastidiously ignoring its preposterous premise – namely, that I was a spy. He worried at it continually, like a pock scar on his cheek. A pen-pushing functionary of forty five years or so, he must have been frustrated at having risen no higher than the most minor of official posts in the remote colony of Massachusetts.

'Only a spy would carry sketches of enemy-held coastline,' he concluded.

I released a sigh. My hastily scribbled pilot notes of the Saint Laurent, the Gulf, the Tadoussac Shore and Anticosti Isle had led him to entirely the wrong conclusion.

'I have always surveyed and sounded on my voyages,' I told him for the umpteenth time. 'Those drawings are valuable intelligence for the war effort.'

Strutt was impervious. 'Valuable intelligence? You are an *amateur*, as your Froggy friends might say. You produced this cock-and-bull story about a treaty, the so-called Quebec Accord, yet your claim to be a diplomat in some fashion, a *soi-disant* envoy, only serves as further proof of your treachery. O, Captain Loftus,' he reproached, 'I beseech you, do credit Her Majesty's officers with more gumption. Why, I should be laughed out of court if I so much as mentioned your ridiculous – may I say fabulous – tale at Government House.'

The Second Deputy Assistant Sub-Commissioner had already regaled me with accounts of his all-too-rare, so he admitted, visits to the Colonial Governor's hallowed seat. By contrast with the splendour there, we sat at a worm-eaten captain's table in the ruined Great Cabin of a prison hulk.

Many years before, this old warship, sans masts and rigging, her guns and armoury stripped out, minus any shred of her former dignity, had been towed into Back Bay and set firm with rust-encrusted chains to stakes ashore. The *Promise* lay abandoned on the mudbanks, eviscerated, never to touch an ocean again. Only the galley furnace was kept working, boiling up a daily hundred gallons of gruel to feed the horrible legacy of war she carried in her crumbling belly. Teeming in filth and stench, chained below decks, languished four hundred French, Indian and half-caste men. Like us, they had been caught, accused and confined as prisoners of war, even though the conflict itself was a thousand leagues away.

In these black moments, I felt doomed to lie here as long as the war lasted, or while the various governors argued over the release and exchange of prisoners. Or while the short-sighted Archibald Strutt dissembled and procrastinated, while nevertheless collecting his clerk's pay of sixteen shillings a month, and four pound of boiling bacon every fortnight.

He dismissed my news about the French Grand Fleet as rubbish. He refused to recognise the Quebec Accord as a genuine document. He denied the relevance of my Deputy Intendant's seal. He refused even to send a letter to Governor Spurgeon in order to establish my bona fides.

I thought of Finlay McGruder. How long now since he had reached Esperantia? The torture of having been so close, and now being caught in these circumstances was unbearable. Still Archibald Strutt prated on. Unable to listen to his droning any longer, I let my head fall forward and emitted an agonised groan.

'It troubles you, does it,' said the Second Deputy Assistant Sub-Commissioner sympathetically, 'what I have been recounting of the European war's progress? Events are moving apace, you know. With the land victories, the war draws to its end. Or so it looks. In Flanders there has been another splendid engagement. After Ramillies, now Oudenaarde.

Such strange names, do you not agree? Nonetheless, a grand victory for the British Alliance under the great general Marlborough. Though the field took on the look of a slaughterhouse, as the reports had it. Loftus, do examine these journals.'

He pushed some well-thumbed printed papers across.

'You have not been in England in recent years, have you? The "news-prints", these are called. Published weekly in London and sold on the street at a penny a time. They carry true and accurate accounts of every contest, whether of battlefield gore or semantick fencing in palace corridors. Do you see it? Trials in blood, sparring in diplomacy.'

He seemed pleased with this connection but I did not respond.

'Look here,' he said, 'Massachusetts has its own "news-prints", though a somewhat provincial emulation, if I may say so. You yourself have appeared in *The Boston Gleaner*.'

He pointed a finger at the crudely impressed page. Across two columns, in large bold characters, it said:

FRENCH SPY HELD
IN BOSTON HARBOUR

An enemy spy and English traitor has been apprehended by a Navy patrol in the disputed waters of the Breton Channel. Disguised as a Frenchman, skulking aboard a fishing sloop with a half-breed accomplice, Matthew Loftus, a former Whitby man and notorious privateer of the Caribbee Sea, was taken

into custody by Her Majesty's cruzer,
the Chatham-built Regard, *master Lt*
Fred. Balty.

The cruzer, on her first foreign com-
mission, enjoyed the presence aboard
of Second Deputy Assistant Sub-Com-
missioner Archibald Strutt, journey-
ing out to take up a post under
Government House, his predecessor
having demised after a bout of Bay
Fever. The spy Loftus, refusing to
confess, is held aboard the prison
hulk, the Promise, *in Back Bay, await-*
ing trial and execution.

'Such excitement!' said Strutt, with a self-satisfied air. 'You are talked of everywhere.'

I glared back. 'These are lies. I suppose you were their source? Gaining a little glory for yourself?'

He put his fingertips together. 'As Second Deputy Assistant Sub-Commissioner, I considered that a refusal to divulge such important news to the public prints would be unnecessarily restrictive.' He eyed me cautiously. 'There is more to tell. You know Newfoundland, or so you claim. Well, of all places, that desolate island has become an element of the horse-trading, as we diplomats say – the bartering in Paris and Brussels and Antwerp. This comes to me second hand, of course. If only I were a little higher in rank! I've heard talk about the Grand Banks codfisheries. Something about the wet and dry divide? Is it not?'

I looked up, thinking how trivial and long ago

those disputes seemed, and said wearily, 'The wet-curers are the Breton Catholicks, while the dry-salters are the English fishers.'

'That's it. Now I remember. It's the schism, one might say, of the scales,' he said, with a shy smile at his own attempted joke.

'There is no reason why those settlements should not be open to all,' I said, wondering why I was wasting my breath, 'whether Catholick or Protestant, French or Spanish, Scottish or English.'

'Loftus, as an aside, may I remind you the Scotch are subsumed into our nationhood since an Act of last year? We of Great Britain' – he heavily emphasised the words – 'desire sole dominion over all Newfoundland, including any Frenchy fishing stations. There is an important one on – let me see – ah yes, the Avalon Peninsula. At a place called Plaisance. This is now claimed for Her Majesty.'

I sat bolt upright. 'Plaisance claimed? Has Tompion taken it?'

'You know of Admiral Tompion? How interesting.' His eyes narrowed. 'Or how incriminating.'

'I told you about Tompion from the first,' I protested.

'So you did. Well now, Plaisance is not sacked or attacked, O no indeed not. Plaisance shall be made British through diplomacy.'

Now I jumped up like a jack-tar at seven bells. 'What diplomacy?'

'Ah ha! Something the spy does not know! There is an accord by which France cedes the Avalon fisheries to England.'

'France cedes –? What accord is this?' I demanded.

'I am not privy to all the details,' he said with a self-deprecating look, 'but I gather it is to do with an annual visit by a trading bark somewhere or other.'

My face was hot. 'Not the bark that plies into Hudson's Bay and down to Fort Rupert?'

'Ah, that was it – Fort Rupert and the trading voyage. On behalf of the Hudson's Bay Company, though that charter seems to be in abeyance. I understand it was for the buying of animal skins from the natives. The beavers' fur trip.'

'The *Beaver*'s wrecked, dammit!'

'I'm not sure I follow –'

'What's the agreement for?' I interrupted.

'It's very far from an agreement,' he said, enjoying his moment. 'It is but a proposal which has only just been received by the Governor here in Massachusetts. Even to be considered, it must go to London by special envoy, then back here for signing before being forwarded on to Quebec. If it wins approval there it shall go on to Paris, where they may wish to consult with Quebec once again. Of course, each journey is rather lengthy, a month or more across the Atlantick Ocean and the same to return. Ah, but Loftus, you should know that, as a sailor.' He shuddered. 'Then it shall be sent back to us with amendments, no doubt, and then –'

'Where does this accord spring from?' I cut in.

'From the Governor at Saint John's in Newfoundland. One Septimus Spurgeon.'

I stared, trying to reckon what on Earth was going on. I supposed D'Amati must have learnt what happened at the jetty when his envoy came down in the morning and found us gone. Had he somehow sent word to Spurgeon suggesting he try to put forward the same accord? Alphonse D'Amati had never denied that Saint John's was stiff with agents on his payroll.

'What does the accord propose?' I asked, impatient for all the details.

'Did I not say? Why, it proposes to exchange the Plaisance station in return for a temporary suspension of the Sovereign's Hudson's Bay claims. The Boston Government is minded, I hear, to approve it. We concede nothing by it because the fur trading venture was in great difficulty. Conditions are said to be most inclement in the far north. Wild animals, and indeed untameable men. Storms and ice and so on.' He smiled. 'Part of it is called the Frigid Zone. Did you know that, Loftus?'

Strutt was discomfited by the dark glare I was giving him.

'Have you even bothered,' I said, my jaw clenched, 'to read the Quebec Accord?'

'The Quebec Accord?' He looked unsettled.

I sucked in air, trying to keep calm. 'The treaty document I handed over when the *Regard* apprehended us. It embodies exactly the proposal for the Plaisance exchange that you spoke of. And it's already signed and sealed with the Seigneur Supérieur. If you take it to the Colonial Government now, the diplomacy could be secured without delay – without months of to-ing and fro-ing back and forth.'

He looked confused, unable to grasp the significance.

'Quebec Accord?' he repeated. 'The treaty you talked of?'

327

'Aye! And listen, the triumph could be yours, Second Deputy Assistant Sub-Commissioner. Think of that.'

He was silent. Before him lay a mess of papers and documents, news-prints and poster-sheets. From amongst the pile, he withdrew a heavyweight parchment and examined it as if for the first time. It was the Accord.

'Read it, I beg you,' I said, with the sensation of treading on eggshells. One wrong word now and the fool would backtrack.

Scanning through it, he hummed and hawed and tutted. Then he laid it aside and gazed at me. His voice was a whisper.

'It appears to be as you say, at least at first sight. And I have had it in my hand all this time? O Lord.' He straightened as if a new thought had occurred to him. 'But are the seals true?' His voice rose. 'What if the document is a fake and you are not just a spy but a liar?'

'Go to the Colonial Government office here and check the document's marks against your impress of the Seigneur Supérieur's seal.' I leaned forward and said in measured syllables, 'Sub-Commissioner Strutt, I beg you to look again at the paper I wrote. If you remember, at my request you provided me with paper and ink –'

'Risking opprobrium, Loftus,' he put in. 'Such a risk, to give a prisoner those materials.'

I indicated the bundle of sheets lying on the worn table. 'Aye, but there's a wealth of intelligence on the Grand Fleet. And on the enemy's fortifications.'

With the luxury of time, I had written down the

details of the French Naval forces passing through the Breton Channel. I had enumerated the number of vessels, their size and type, and their rigging. I had described their armaments, the number of guns and the likely weight of their broadsides. I had set down my tally of the seamen and officers on each vessel, and assessed the numbers of soldiers they carried. From my estimate of its position and course, I stated that the fleet could not conceivably have been on its way to the Naval base at Acadia, as might be expected if a sea action were in train. It was going towards the Gulf, and Quebec City.

'I gave you as complete and accurate an account as any man could,' I said.

He peered myopically at the sheaf of papers. 'Yes, I suppose you did.'

'And this can hardly be the action of an enemy spy,' I pointed out, reminding him I had added detailed descriptions of the installations at Trois Rivières and the high fortifications at Quebec City, including the emplacements, the number of pieces in each battery and my guess at their weight of shot. I had even reckoned the batteries' heights and elevations and the angles and extent of their ranges. What an advantage such intelligence would be for the British Navy, if ever they attacked Quebec.

'Indeed,' he said doubtfully. 'Indeed, that is what you did.'

He was softening, so I quickly said, 'News of the Grand Fleet's presence in the Gulf might change the course of the war for England.'

'Great Britain,' said Strutt, wagging a finger.

'Aye, but will you act now? There is still time.'

Silence fell in the destroyed Great Cabin, disturbed only by a wind moaning through the gaps in the shattered deckhead. He was thinking. Or at least, he was stroking his chin in the manner of someone doing so.

'Supposing what you say is in fact the case. Just for the sake of debate, you understand. How can I go to my superiors and say I have had this intelligence in my hands so long?'

Of all the implications, he saw only the effect on his career. He might even decide it best to cover up his failure – tear up the parchment, shred my notes, toss them into Back Bay and deny all knowledge. Offering up a silent plea to the Fates, I leaned close to his ear and spoke in a low conspiratorial tone.

'Second Deputy Assistant Sub-Commissioner Strutt,' I whispered, 'a prisoner arrested some time ago on spying charges carried important news, yet that has only recently been brought to your attention.'

He sat back in amazement. 'O no! I have known all along.'

I shook my head. 'Incompetent subordinates aboard the *Promise* suppressed the fact. It has come to light by dint of your assiduous attention to duty.'

He closed his eyes in an agony of indecision. While the old prison hulk creaked in protest as the wind sought to drag her from her chains, I could only hold my breath. Everything hung now on this foolish man's ambition. I searched his worried face for a sign that my argument had hit home.

'Well?' I inquired.

'Well,' he replied, opening one eye to a suspicious

slit. The fingertips went back to his soft, rounded chin. He looked for all the world like a schoolboy puzzling over his arithmetickal lesson.

'Well,' he said again.

'Take these papers forward to Government House,' I urged. 'Gain the recognition you deserve.'

A deaf man could have heard the cogs of Strutt's mind ticking, the springs unwinding and tensing, the escapements flying back and forth.

'I could not put anything forward, Loftus,' he said at length, 'without thoroughly familiarising myself with the contents.'

'Aye, you must do that,' I confirmed.

He took on a sombre mien. 'I shall have to take the fullest note of every line before I present it.'

I inclined my head. 'A firm grasp is essential.'

'I shall have to rewrite certain portions of it in good, clear English.' His confidence grew. 'Words matter, Loftus. Complete command of the verbal niceties. A single infelicity, a mere nuance of meaning, might destroy all.'

I nodded like a condemned man reprieved on the gallows. 'Your assiduity shall be rewarded.'

'Assiduity rewarded,' he said, and seemed satisfied with the thought.

After rolling up the papers and carefully tying them with a frayed ribbon, he stood, fixing me with his stare over the pince-nez, one finger rhythmically tapping on the scroll.

'Advancement at last,' he said. 'From mere Second Deputy Assistant Sub-Commissioner to an altogether higher echelon.' He spoke as if it were a done deed. 'Ah, but can you not hear the ring of it? "First Deputy

Assistant Sub-Commissioner for Colonial Affairs (Prison Hulks) Archibald Strutt." I like the sound of it well.' He signalled for the guard. 'Loftus, when this is done, we shall enjoy a dinner together.'

He turned to go. In a few moments I would be returned to the below-decks Hell, to languish deep within the *Promise*'s rotting bowels in an agony of doubt, not knowing whether he would keep his word. Perhaps he would fail even to darken the threshold of the Boston Governor's ante-rooms, let alone gain an audience.

Just before the Great Cabin door closed, I called after him.

'Sub-Commissioner Strutt – are you sure there is still no word of Hanson and McGruder?'

He whirled round. 'Hanson? McGruder? Ah, yes, I remember! But no, not a thing.'

'You have not heard whether or when they reached Newfoundland?'

'No idea at all.'

'What about the *Pursuant*?'

'Pursuant to what?'

'That's my bark's name.'

'Your bark? O yes, so it is. No news about it . . . or rather, her.'

'Nor of Chanatuk?'

'Channel what?'

There was no sense to be had from the fellow, but still I asked, 'So you heard nothing of any slaughter?'

'Loftus, to what do you refer?'

I sighed. 'The slaughter of the Missacaibi.'

He shook his ass's head from side to side and turned for the door. Then he stopped, frowning.

'These Missacaibi creatures. Are they hunted for their fur?'

Strutt proved keen enough on his advancement, going ashore without delay. Soon, a boat arrived with messages for our gaolers. Hubert Nitchequot and I were released from the stinking Hades of the *Promise*'s tween-decks cells where we had lain chained to the deckheads. We were told to pick up our squalid palliasses and follow the guards up to the stern quarters. We found ourselves in the former officers' cabins, an improvement almost beyond belief, though a careful tread upon the sole boards was demanded since the yielding timbers were soft enough to send us flying twenty feet through three decks to rejoin the hapless Frogs below. Our new privileges included a ration of ship's biscuit to supplement the gruel, along with a mug of small beer, the same fare as our gaolers.

Best of all was licence to take the quarter-deck for a turn in the air. Waiting impatiently for Strutt's return, I stood near the taffrail – or rather, where the rail had been, for it had long since fallen crashing past the hulk's broken sternlights into the estuary waters – and contemplated Boston's Back Bay.

It gave an unpromising aspect of low-lying marshland and reed beds split asunder by numerous tidal reaches, with the sea lying miles to the east. On land, carts and carriages trundled to and fro in an endless procession on the drier ground, from where wooden causeways led across the boggy terrain down to jetties. Attendant fleets of small boats plied back and forth bearing passengers and light cargoes out to vessels riding in the deeper water. The anchorage formed a natural shelter, safe from surge and swell, and with room for a vast fleet to swing. In all, these crowded Roads showed Boston to be a trading port and Naval station of the first rank, a commercial and military centre that made Saint John's Harbour seem little more than a fishing village. Even the bustle of the Quebec City wharves paled by comparison.

I had always considered the New England colonies uncertain enterprises by comparison with Newfoundland, whose prosperity was so soundly rooted in fish and fur. At high season, our fishermen were said to walk across the very backs of the massed cod shoals. Whaling prospered too, providing tuns of high quality lamp-oil for export and blubber for our fires. The skins of seals and beavers and caribou traded at Newfoundland covered the heads and warmed the hands and shod the feet of the kings and queens and aristocrats and gentlefolk and merchants of all Europe, from the Tagus to the Volga, from the Baltick Sea to the Aegean.

In contrast, the Massachusetts Colony was an unproductive wasteland. The settlers were chiefly poor Protestants seeking enrichment through God's parable of the talents – that is, endless grinding labour. Or else they claimed to be fleeing the Devil's scourge upon the Earth – namely the Pope and all his works. Her Majesty's Government liberally granted them free monopolies for questionable ventures, while our fish and fur trades were mercilessly taxed to pay for the distant war. There seemed little justice in it. If ever I regained an ounce of say in Esperantian affairs, I would press our case for better conditions.

But first things first. I was still imprisoned aboard a hulk in Boston, waiting on a nincompoop.

Late in the forenoon, a cutter drew in under the *Promise*'s forlorn topsides. Archibald Strutt debarked, flustered and disarranged, waving papers at the half-caste and me as he approached across the quarter, breathless from clambering up the steps. The papers freed us forthwith.

Within half a glass, we were rowed across Back Bay to an anchored Navy warship, the *Fortitude*. Unlike the *Promise*, here new pitch gleamed at every deadeye and stay, while fresh caulking showed on her massive hull right from the Devil's seam to the waterline. We were brought from the well-holystoned weather-deck up to the high quarter before an assembled audience of officers and gentlemen. In our unwashed and ragged state, with dirty beards and altogether unkempt appearance, Hubert Nitchequot and I stood somewhat awkwardly, though unbowed, before this elevated company.

I barely listened as the freshly-advanced First Deputy Assistant Sub-Commissioner Strutt fussed over the courtesies, titles and ranks of the figures arrayed before us. I wanted only to know how soon I could embark some vessel, any vessel, for Newfoundland. After the formalities of the Naval officers' introductions, Strutt turned to the three or four lubberly persons whose fancy buckle-shoes and silk hose showed them up as gentlemen-landsmen – diplomats or government clerks, I presumed. He recited their titles and rank in turn.

The last of these was an angular man of forty years or so, tall, fair and pale-skinned. A narrow, bony body supported a head whose features were severe and bloodless, apart from fleshy lips beneath a protuberant nose. He wore an ostrich-feathered felt hat, unmistakeably Flemish in design, and throughout the formalities his eyes had remained fixed upon mine.

'And this gentleman,' said Archibald Strutt, 'is from Esperantia.'

Sweeping off his headgear with a flourish, the fellow flashed me a restrained smile and bowed low.

'Honoured to meet you, Captain Loftus,' he said in Dutch accents. 'My ship awaits your command.'

'Your ship?' I repeated like an idiot. 'Who are you?'

'I am Factor Josiah van Schreik.'

18

Hampered

'Crank, did you say, captain?' Josiah van Schreik gripped the rail and shot me a sharp look. 'As a landsman, I confess to being unfamiliar with the term.'

We were standing at the break, high on the quarterdeck of the old and somewhat leaky ten-gun bark, the *Forgiver*. Rolling sickeningly on the swells, she was on her way to Esperantia to restore the settlement to its former glory.

Factor van Schreik had recited all the story. Finlay McGruder, escaping the ice traps of the north, had brought the *Pursuant* home under Hanson's captaincy and taken over as Intendant Proper. Victorious, ambitious and intemperate, in the few weeks of his reign he had sorely abused his new-found powers. Under the protection of his cousin, Admiral Tompion, McGruder embarked on a bout of religious terror, sending away the Catholicks, disrupting the fishing and driving the settlement towards commercial ruin. Worse, he had illegally attacked and taken control of Plaisance. All Avalon was aflame with resentment and fear at his appalling deeds.

Governor Spurgeon, his powers suspended by Tompion, saw his profitable tax sources evaporating and, unwilling at such a critical juncture to leave Newfoundland himself, sent his only ally van

Schreik on a desperate assignment to Boston. The Factor was to plead for assistance, win the Colonial Government's reaffirmation of Spurgeon's authority and secure their backing for an armed force to restore order. If they refused, he was then to acquire a bark sufficient in arms and men to take on McGruder – the moment, of course, that the protector Tompion sailed his fleet away a safe distance.

As might have been expected, van Schreik's dismal nature and poor diplomacy did not help his cause. Furthermore, when the Factor had left Saint John's, Governor Spurgeon had known nothing of the Quebec Accord and its proposals, so – with little to offer – van Schreik was ejected from Government House with barely a hearing. With his pockets full of Spurgeon's gold, he went down to the shipyards, bought the *Forgiver* and gloomily prepared to sail home.

Then the Colonial Government got hold of the signed Accord through the newly-diligent Archibald Strutt. They at once recognised the vital necessity of the French holding Plaisance. Otherwise, how could it be bargained? And they remembered van Schreik's tale of the settlement having unfortunately fallen into the wrong hands. Re-summoning the Factor, they pressed him to oust McGruder from Plaisance and Esperantia – and released me to assist him.

So now we had what Governor Spurgeon desired, the means as well as the politickal backing to enforce his authority. My spirits were higher than ever. Revenge loomed closer, and my reward too. If only, I thought, the vessel beneath my feet was a fitter ship.

The *Forgiver* gave an unpleasant sway as she

rose to the top of a wave, slid down its face and wallowed in the trough. She was standing northeast on steerboard tack between Acadia and Sable Island, one hundred and seventy leagues out from Cape Cod. The southeastern tip of Newfoundland, Cape Race, lay not much more than ten leagues distant, but the weather was worsening. Despite my keeping her short-canvassed with topsails and a reefed forecourse, the vessel sailed like a hog in a mudbath. Every now and then she heeled far enough to dip her scuppers, ship a sea and send several tuns of water cascading across the waist.

'She's top heavy,' I said. 'It's the weight of the deck-pieces.'

'The Good Lord shall be my witness,' said the Factor, 'but I was poorly served by the Boston shipyard.'

In truth, what the Good Lord had borne witness to was nothing more than an extraordinary bout of pennypinching on van Schreik's part. He had saved his ha'pence of tar and ended up with an unseaworthy tub.

I called up my sailing master. 'Mister Partridge, wear ship and heave to on larboard.'

Thomas Partridge was a Boston-born fellow who had shrugged off his Norfolk ancestry to become the first fellow I ever heard call himself 'an Americkan'. Despite that, he was a reliable cove and at twenty five a proper seaman. By sheer good fortune – or, as van Schreik put it, thanks to the Lord at his side – the Factor had shipped aboard an able band of officers and men.

When Partridge roused up the off-watch, twenty

men came on deck to join the score already there. The steersman sent the wheel spinning and seamen briskly manned the belays or sprang aloft. When the sheets and bracelines flew off, the *Forgiver* – too damm'd unhandy to tack – began her slow, wearing turn downwind, then sluggishly settled herself, stopped in the water. The Factor snuggled further into the collar of his sealskin coat and drew the beaver's pelt hat down his brow, observing with attentive interest.

'I trust this does not delay us,' he said.

Delay was the least of it, I thought. With this bark, he would have done better to wager on an iceberg reaching the Tropicks than on us dealing with McGruder. I stamped off to the break.

'Mister Partridge, I want you to tackle eight of the guns below. Leave only the number three pieces, larboard and steerboard.'

'Aye, sir!' said the Americkan without any show of surprise.

We were in waters that France considered hers by right. Leaving a single piece up each side gave us a semblance of defence, but no more.

'If the *Forgiver*'s of a type,' I remarked to van Schreik, 'it's no wonder the French sink so many New England-built barks.'

He considered a moment. 'Captain Loftus, with the Lord's grace, I pray the ship's flaws do not jeopardise our mission.'

'Our mission is sorely in doubt without a stronger means than this vessel alone.'

'How can we assemble a greater force? After this purchase, I have no money left.'

Money was not what I had in mind. There were other ways of getting arms and men than buying them.

'Nor have I any money, sir,' I replied with a wan smile.

Finlay McGruder – confident, according to van Schreik, that I was dead and gone – had sold off my furskins, gaining twenty five thousand marks in cash. The sale of the salvaged Gillycuddy bark brought him ten thousand more. The tale he had told on the *Pursuant*'s voyage north, of van Schreik's designs on my assets, had been yet another lie. In truth the Factor had done his best to save them, though perhaps not so much for me as for his percentage. He guessed that I would pay my dues and that McGruder would not, and so far he had been proven right.

But then, in pocketing the trading and fishing imposts before they could be collected by van Schreik, McGruder made a gross miscalculation. These monies had habitually been transferred not to Her Majesty's Treasury's coffers but to Septimus Spurgeon's. And it was that which had finally spurred the Governor to act.

Mister Partridge stepped up to the break.

'Boom tackle rigged and ready, sir.'

'Very well, sailing master. Send them down one by one, larboard then steerboard, to keep her on an even keel.'

'Aye aye, sir.'

With courses and jibs furled, fore-topsail drawing and the main aback, the *Forgiver* rode on the slopping swells with a quick uneasy motion that betrayed her fatal imbalance. The boom tackle swung the four-tun guns one by one off the deck and into the hatch opening, the forward larboard piece first away, followed by its opposite number. There was an absence of fuss and chit-chat, for each man knew the consequences of error.

An awkward swell lifted the bark's stern and she tilted. The angle increased abruptly and I put a hand out for the rail. A look of alarm crossed van Schreik's face as he too grabbed for a handhold. The *Forgiver* rose up the wave's back careening ever more steeply. A yawning trough opened below us and for half a second it seemed she was going over. Cries of alarm rose from the waist. The massive second larboard gun, hoisted aloft, swung outboard above the sea. With the roll, the boom creaked under the strain and the deckhands ducked from under the tackle for fear of it giving way.

The sudden motion unfooted the Factor. He staggered and half fell over the rail.

'Lord save us!' he cried.

I grasped the collar of his coat-jacket and held on. The wave's peak passed, the roll ceased and the great gun swung inboard again. But the *Forgiver* did not come upright at once. She hung there, canted over, all her weight up too high. Reluctantly she began to right herself then, with a sudden unsettling lurch, came back upright. When I released his collar, the Factor sank gratefully to his knees, eyes tight shut in prayer. I wondered whether it might humour him to know that this was the second time a seaman's hand rather than the Lord's had saved a Protestant going overboard.

'The ship agents have a deal to answer for,' said

van Schreik when he had recovered. He well knew that in his pennypinching bargaining he had been seen off by the curmudgeons of Boston Harbour. 'She was said to be in every regard a vessel fit for a Navy. Fast and handy were the words I believe the owners used.'

'Never trust a guild of Massachusetts venturers,' I said.

These new Americkan barks were intended as lightly ballasted three-masters, ship-rigged with full topgallants for weatherliness and speed. All fine and well, I thought, until she took on her armour, loaded her munitions, fitted a galley furnace, then got vittled and stored for a voyage. By the time she shipped aboard forty seamen and eighty musketeers, the fifty tuns of stone and shingle tarped down in her bilges amounted to barely half the ballast she wanted.

With full-sized topgallant yards giving extra hamper so far aloft, it was too much. A common seaman can vouch that a pound of weight above the topmasts calls for twenty five pounds of ballast on the keelson. So I had sent down the upper topmasts and topgallant yards and sailed from Back Bay without them. Even so, at the first plunge of her stem to the Atlantick swells I knew she was flawed. A ship gives six motions at sea. Yaw, pitch and roll even landlubbers know. Surge, heave and sway are her movements forward and back, her lift and fall, her side-to-side character. All these together tell a sailor how a bark might go in bad weather. She was beyond remedy, a crank ship.

By the time the hourglass was spun twice, Thomas Partridge had all the deck-pieces safe below. The

Forgiver resumed her course and went along a mite easier, much to everyone's relief.

I summoned the sailing master back to the break. 'Hoist the guns up again when we reach inshore waters,' I told him. 'Meanwhile, double the lookouts aloft and halve their spells.'

It was a vain act. If a Frenchy patrol so much as spied us hull down, we could not escape. We should be mere target practice for her gunners. Our laggardly, partly dismantled and now largely disarmed bark could neither outrun the enemy nor turn and fight him.

'Are we not somewhat undefended?' said van Schreik. 'Apart from, I mean to say, the shield of the Good Lord around us?'

I smiled grimly. 'It's the admiral's shield of armour we lack. His squadrons should be patrolling these waters.'

Neither of us had any time for Admiral Sir Geoffrey Tompion. Van Schreik explained what had happened when the *Ascendant* hove into Esperantia that day. His reason for leaving the packet sloop and Grace Trepanney had been to go aboard and urge the admiral to afford the settlement better protection against the likes of the Gillycuddy brothers, which he saw as a Naval duty rather than a private Guardian's. But Tompion was interested only in lining his pockets through imposing levies, and was leery of risking damage to his ships in a fight. He would not challenge the Burin clan, let alone confront French warships. For his pains, the Factor had been illegally confined aboard the flagship as a punishment for insolence. And it came as no surprise to learn that the man behind that move was Finlay McGruder, the admiral's young cousin.

Yet Tompion's difficulties were manifold. His Newfoundland commission had been a disaster. It was enough that news of the annual fur bark's loss had reached London during his stewardship, but so far the admiral's trick at the Newfoundland helm had seen him take no enemy prizes of any worth. Worse for him, Finlay McGruder's treaty – the diplomatick triumph Tompion had hoped his cousin would gain – remained stalled through Chief Chanatuk's refusal to sign. He had not a single military or diplomatick achievement to crow about when he returned to Portsmouth.

On the other hand, if ever I encountered the bold Sir Geoffrey again I could point him in the direction of a potential Naval triumph. He had only to station his warships at the neck of the Gulf in order to achieve a complete blockade of the enemy's Grand Fleet for the duration of the war.

Desperate for a success, the admiral had encouraged McGruder into an unholy alliance with the Papist Gillycuddys to mount the attack on Plaisance, hoping to record a minor victory while carefully distancing himself if it failed. It did not, but the attack aggravated the French Acadian authorities into reprisals against English fishing settlements. Bloody skirmishes took place throughout Avalon, in which men died needlessly and the fishing trade was further reduced.

The ship's bell clanged.

'Eight bells of the afternoon watch, Factor,' I said.

As the dogwatch began, van Schreik and I repaired below with Thomas Partridge. Hubert Nitchequot, not enjoying the motion on a lumpy sea, joined us in the Great Cabin but fasted in miserable silence while the rest of us dined on meat pie with corn bread and fresh small beer to wash it down.

The Americkan colonists' vittling had proved first rate, even if their ship had not. Before departing Back Bay Roads, I told the cook to provide the officers' quarters with the very best fare. When roast beef and onions and dumplings appeared at our table, I bade him serve the same to the jack-tars and the soldiers alike, much to his astonishment. This met with Thomas Partridge's approval – he had Leveller leanings, as did many 'Americkans', but van Schreik was horrified at the expense. Yet this was no voyage of endurance, as was the *Pursuant*'s Hudson's Bay adventure where supplies were precious. If the wind held, we would spy Avalon before nightfall tomorrow. Whatever savings the Factor might have preferred, for what was to come it was best the fresh vittles filled my crew's bellies rather than rotted in the storeroom.

'It's a deal better than saltfish, sir,' remarked the stout-waisted Partridge, who never finished one mouthful of meat pie before embarking on the next.

'Aye, but we shall soon have all the codfish our bellies can hold,' I said.

'Indeed so,' said van Schreik, 'when we regain Esperantia.'

He raised a parsimonious forkful of meat to his mouth, but the *Forgiver* gave a flick roll. The morsel fell to the sole and he bent to retrieve it. Partridge, busy over his plate, avoided my eye. He was a fine seaman and knew what his captain was thinking, but was loth to abandon such good hot vittles.

'She's long on canvas again, sailing master,' I said, with a sympathetic smile. 'She's pigging, and you know it.'

Defeated, he laid down his eating irons, pulled his napkin from his collar and made for the door.

'I shall join you in a minute,' I called after his receding back.

As he stumped up the swaying companionway shouting for larboard watch to rouse up, I took out a brandy flagon and sloshed some into pewter mugs. The sight and smell was too much for Hubert, who promptly retired to his bunk.

'Only a little for me,' said van Schreik, one hand up.

'Which is it,' I inquired mildly, 'too sinful or too wasteful?'

He ignored the jibe. 'It is merely a shame to drink such good Cognac in metal. Are there no balloons?'

'It's a sure witness to a crank boat,' I said, sitting down opposite, 'finding no glass in the captain's cabinet.' I savoured the spirit a-while, then said, 'The last time I tasted brandy was not long before Irocaibi died.'

'Yours has been a remarkable adventure, captain, and the Good Lord has watched over you.'

Or Fortune and the Fates, I thought. 'And the last time I had a religious landsman aboard, it was Finlay McGruder.'

He put down his mug, affronted. 'Sir, you do not compare me with a ship-stealer?'

'Not in a thousand years.' I gave a sheepish grin. 'There was a time, though, when I feared you might steal Grace Trepanney.'

'Ah, the young widow,' he murmured, and sipped thoughtfully.

The truth was that I owed him a thanks. In taking Grace away on the packet sloop that day, his concern had been to remove her from the dangers, as he saw them, of remaining in Esperantia. Spiriting her away into marriage was far from his mind, even though it might have been uppermost in the Dowager's. But if the Factor was not to marry her, then who was? Had Lady Trepanney simply meant Grace's remarriage must be to whoever succeeded to the Intendancy? That was my great fear.

'Tell me again,' I encouraged, 'how she looked when you last laid eyes on her.'

'Serene, and as beautiful as ever. A remarkable woman, replete with God's fortitude. If she were a man, courageous would be an inadequate term.'

'You told me she returned from Saint John's, but when you left Esperantia, she was safe?'

'Incarcerated at Providence House, along with the Dowager Lady Trepanney. And the Intendant too.'

I gave an involuntary shudder. 'And though he assumed all the offices of Intendant Proper, you're sure there had been no marriage?'

'With the Lord upon my breast, not so far as I know.'

I closed my eyes. 'There is still time, then.'

The Factor put down his pewter and studied me. 'Captain Loftus, I understand your desire to avenge Finlay McGruder, but it must be secondary. First

348

and foremost, we are to restore the *status quo ante* at Esperantia. And do so at the least cost.'

'Cost in lives, or in money?' I said. 'Your carefulness with coin has already seen us poorly equipped.'

'Sir, that is somewhat unfair. McGruder spirited away so much of the Governor's funds. And by the by, it was rumoured he might spend a portion of it on new guns at Vantage Rise.'

I dearly hoped he had not done so. Mention of the batteries reminded me of the Gillycuddys' attack, when I had accused the Factor of interference. In truth, I now knew, he had sent Caswell Penn up to remind the gunners to keep the firing slow. He had sought to bolster my orders about the old guns, not countermand them.

'If there are new guns, Factor, all the more reason why we need a stronger force. With what we have, we simply cannot attack McGruder.'

'Retake Esperantia, you mean.' He was stern. 'Our commission is to restore both it and Plaisance.'

'I am fully cognisant of that.'

'Are you, Captain Loftus?'

He reached inside his coat-jacket and withdrew a small folded paper. It was covered in close black type. As he spread it on the table, I peered closer. It was clipped from a sheet of the Massachusetts news-prints, *The Boston Gleaner*. The extract was the very one I had cut out myself before we left Massachusetts. In large, smudgy print it declared:

TALKS ON QUEBEC ACCORD HALTED.

'Have you taken that from my private drawer?' I exclaimed, reaching for it.

He snatched it away, unsmiling. 'Indeed not, sir. It dropped by chance from your chart bundle and I found it on the cabin sole. Let me refresh your memory.'

He read: '"A proposed treaty between the warring nations has met with a further impediment. The Quebec Accord, designed to remove the stumbling block of the Hudson's Bay fur trade and Her Majesty's territorial claim upon the Upper Kanada Lands, was expected to be agreed by all parties. However, with the death of the representative of the Missacaibi peoples, those James Bay natives who occupy the territories surrounding Fort Rupert, progress has halted. The Colonial Government declares that the chief himself must now be brought forward to sign. Otherwise it is feared the Accord must fall."'

He cleared his throat. 'It goes on to discuss, at unseemly length, the import of all this for various functionaries' careers. I was informed by Archibald Strutt that you told him you were in some way linked with these Missacaibi people. He spoke of your owing a debt to the native who was killed.'

'And if I did, what difference does it make? If I find Chief Chanatuk, he can be brought back to sign the Accord. That shan't interfere with our purpose. After all, it's McGruder who has him. Assuming, that is, the old warrior remains alive.'

'The difference is this, captain. Your first mission is to regain Esperantia. That is what Governor Spurgeon is paying you to do, not to fulfil some vow of yours to these savages.'

I shifted uncomfortably.

'Nor is it to pursue a private vengeance against

350

McGruder for stealing your bark,' continued van Schreik. 'And neither for a rivalry over a woman. Apart from any Earthly considerations, may I remind you that revenge has no place in the Lord's canon? I pray that you understand.'

The Factor could pray for that, I thought, until his kneebones showed through his briches. Just then, the *Forgiver* gave another hogroll. Van Schreik's pewter slid across the table, hit the fiddle rail and tipped towards the edge. Anticipating a waste of good brandy, he grabbed at it and missed. The mug clattered to the sole and he followed it, scrabbling about on his hands and knees.

Pray on, Factor, I thought. I was hampered enough by a crank bark and a lop-sided mission without having to reckon with this cheeseparing, God-fearing, Dutch parsimonist forever reminding me of my obligations and duties. Without my knowledge of sailing and fighting at sea, there was no mission anyway.

I drained my brandy and stood. 'The wind's rising, Factor. I must see to our cranky ship.'

He was still on his knees when I left the Great Cabin and went on deck.

As far as Finlay McGruder knew, Matthew Loftus's corpse lay on the windswept tundra, his frozen remains preserved for a century or until the white bear scented them. If my luck held, I had a few days' grace before the Scotsman got word of my unexpected return to Avalonian waters, for the empty interior, cleared even of Beothuks, boasted no roadways over which messengers might pass. In

Newfoundland, tidings travelled by sea or not at all. Working fast, I might spring on him unawares.

Josiah van Schreik solemnly reminded me that the sword of justice must be swift and strong, and the hand that wields it firm in its Godly purpose. While thanking him for these comfortable words, I reassured him that Earthly ways and means were our surest stalwarts. I wanted firepower, strong deck-pieces, plenty of good powder and ball, and a handy ship. Above all, I wanted willing and able sailors, gunners and musketmen.

Nothing could be done about the crankiness of our bark, but men could be recruited in plenty. The Avalon dwellers would by now be sick of McGruder's regime, for the strife he brought had disrupted livelihoods and widowed the womenfolk. Those men who joined with me willingly would be welcomed, but those who did not would be sorely surprised. Though it was to be carried out by a private seaman, the exercise I intended was one to make the Navy envious. Like theirs, it was to be massive, sudden and inescapable. It was to be an impressment.

The *Forgiver* visited every harbour up and down the Avalon coast, missing no fishing station or fledgling settlement. Arriving before a village, the ten gunner – with the deck-pieces restored in place – hauled over and reached up and down to show off her firepower, discouraging any escape to sea. For all her faults, once she got inshore the Massachusetts bark was a powerful fighting ship. She boasted five main guns in the broadside, four swivels in the bows and another four swivels aft. And she carried a brace of twenty five foot cutters, heavily scantled attacking boats each of which could take ashore eight strong oarsmen and twelve musketmen.

The *Forgiver*'s fellows met little resistance in persuading the good settlers of Avalon. They rounded up every able man and commandeered their weapons. They bade the wives and girls bring out vittles wrapped in cloth, then embarked the men in their own boats and returned with the prizes. With an iron rule, I saw to it that plunder and rape were as far from my seamen's minds as harvesting a five-acre field of corn. Soon we had fifty new recruits, then a hundred. Our gathering of little boats towing astern grew to twenty, then thirty, until we had better than forty in our train.

At first, the pressed men showed themselves a touch resentful. Their fishing was interrupted, they said, and their families would starve. And were they to be sent into battle, or transported away, or hauled into the Navy? I told them that order and peace would soon be restored to Avalon. I explained that the old fishery regimes were to be reinstated and the lately-imposed taxes removed. When I declared my intent to oust Finlay McGruder from Newfoundland forever, to restore peace and order, to deal with the Gillycuddys and protect them from the French, their mood altered. They nodded and spoke to each other and said, well, that must be a good cause. And they joined with us.

Towards the end of the second afternoon, a flotilla of little boats sailed along the coast in ragged line astern with the *Forgiver* in their van. Barring

Esperantia itself, few populations remained unvisited. But rounding the head at Renowes Bay, the *Forgiver* met her first serious challenge. Anchored a few cables off the tiny haven and its low stone quays was an armed merchantman, a twelve-gunner, no less. She squatted in the middle of the bay like a spider in her web.

Being as it were in unfriendly waters, we were already cleared for action. At once I sent signals to the attendant fleet to prepare for rapid flight, then called the sailing master.

'Mister Partridge, hold on to your topsails. If she opens fire, take us back out to sea. We can't afford a pitched battle against this one.'

The Americkan went off singing out his orders. I swung the tube again towards the adversary. She was a trim and fresh vessel, almost new-built. On deck were no more than a few idle watchmen, quickly rousing themselves as if from sleep. The first they knew of our arrival was the hubbub of orders and acknowledgements ringing out from our decks. We fetched swiftly into the bay under fore- and main-topsails, gunports up and pieces run out, seamen massed in numbers at our rails, our tops packed with musketmen, and two score smaller boats trailing along behind.

Twisting the spy-glass tube, I raked the merchantman's decks and rigging. Tardily, jack-tars were scrambling aloft. Now her decks swarmed with sailors. Shouts rang out across the water as her officers tried to recover their wits. But they were unready as a seal caught napping on a floe in Kanada's brief summer sun.

'More speed, Mister Partridge,' I said. 'We shall close her.'

He sang out for the courses to be unbunted. The spreads of canvas dropped from the yards and chanties were chorused at the belays. I directed the steersman to bear up and run dead ahead for the enemy's under-protected stern. There was confusion aboard the other ship as the gap shortened to gunnery range then shrank to a couple of cables. Suddenly, three of the six gunports facing us were raised and the pieces run out. Thomas Partridge looked to me for the order to open fire.

I hesitated. The tube showed what looked like a dispute breaking out on the merchantman's quarter-deck. A handful of musketmen had climbed into her tops, but there they stood around in apparent disorder. Some of the jack-tars who had run aloft to loose out canvas and get under way were clambering back deckwards. Around the guns already run out, there was much hand-waving as argument raged. The other pieces stayed put, behind closed ports. They were in disarray. We had a chance to take her without a fight.

'Mister Partridge,' I called, 'prepare to run along-side.'

The sheets were flung off their belays, the courses bunted up and the bracelines made ready to send the main-topyard aback. Our steerboard pieces were run back and the gunports closed in readiness for going alongside. Men stood by at the rail with heaving lines and grapples.

The gap was ten fathoms.

'Musketmen aloft,' I cried, 'hold your fire!'

We crashed alongside, the irons bit into her meaty topsides and fifty armed men swarmed across with frightening cries and wild curses. There was no fight. Some fellows threw their hands in the air to show they were unarmed, the rest fell back quietly, unresisting. My men, bemused at the easy victory, shepherded the seamen into a huddle in the waist. On the quarter-deck, not fifteen feet from me, stood the master and his officers. With the two vessels jammed tight against each other, we could converse without even raising our voices.

'What bark are you?' I demanded.

'We are from Burin,' said the master. 'She is the *Griffin*.'

'One of the Gillycuddy barks?' I said in surprise. 'Why did you not put up a fight?'

'We know you who you are,' he said. 'Captain Loftus, we no longer give a fig for the Brothers Gillycuddy. There's been nothing but strife and disruption since you left Avalon and we've had our fill.' He bowed. 'Patrick Cluney, master, places his bark under your command.'

I felt mightily gratified. Circumstances had once made me deficient in ships and arms and men. First I had rectified the manning with an impressment of a hundred men in forty small cutters and shallops and the like. Now I had won this sleek, well-rigged and smartly trimmed bark with her powerful broadsides. She was as limber and weatherly a ship as ever a seaman's eye might rest upon. At a stroke, the Fates had put right my disadvantages.

Josiah van Schreik saw it differently.

'This is the Providence of the Lord,' he said sombrely.

Without further ado, I transferred from the crank and uncertain *Forgiver* to my new prize ship. With polite apologies, I put bonds on Captain Cluney and his mates and confined them to the quarter-deck under my sight. He had too readily changed sides for my taste and his new allegiance wanted a little testing. While Mister Partridge remained aboard the *Forgiver* to sail her as master under my flag, I exchanged second mates between the two vessels. But I left the crews intact, for no one knows their guns and rigging better than the jack-tars themselves.

Within the hour we were clearing Renowes Bay for Ferryland. I stood on the *Griffin*'s quarter-deck, revelling in her shipshape state, the well-tuned rigging all tarred and served, with not a spliced mainbraceline to be seen. Her guns were freshly blacked, her pine deck-boards well holystoned. Most of all, I relished her speedy gait through the water and plain weatherliness too. This one was no crank.

Ferryland Harbour was a settlement a league from Renowes Bay, and our final port of call. A small rowing boat might have made it past the rocky shore in less than an hour, so it was no rude shock to find that word had indeed gone ahead. This time they were all too ready for us.

Stretching right across in front of our approaching forces and blocking the bay were positioned fifty or more vessels, fishing boats of every kind to be found in Newfoundland, from cod-haulers to scallop draggers to mussel dredgers to offshore fishing sloops. Ferryland, the main east coast settlement on Avalon, had mustered every last working boat to resist my impressment. Well, I thought, gripping the rail and leaning forward, we are in for a fight this time. Ferryland was not going to stand in my way. If they fought, I had the stomach for it.

'Gunners, light your matches!' I called. 'Signal the same to the *Forgiver*.'

The *Griffin*'s former master was agitated. 'Captain, it looks to me as if –'

'Hold your peace, Cluney,' I told him brusquely, 'this is no business of yours.'

A commotion rose up ashore and I swung the tube. On a stone-built quay, folk had gathered in numbers. Shouts went up as argument raged amongst them. People ran about in confusion and a party scampered up the rise towards the signal staff. Dammit, they might bring out their rusty old muskets, even get the two small shore cannon on the hill loaded and fired. Why did they not capitulate? Why force me to bombard them?

I looked along the *Griffin*'s decks. Forty men stood by her twelve main guns, matches lit and at the ready. In close company was the *Forgiver*, with her own ten guns prepared. We had only to swing round and range them. We could reduce the village and the fleet to matchwood and bloody limbs in ten minutes of bombardment. That would be Finlay McGruder's way.

I raised my arm and ordered the fleet halted. Amidst a welter of gear clattering and lines running out, the yards came aback as we rounded up and stopped. For half a minute the only sounds were of

the ragged little flotilla bringing to astern of us –
parrels dropping, canvas collapsing in folds, lugsails
lowering. The *Griffin*'s stem gurgled softly through
the water until she lost way, stopped and lay easy.

If the good people of Ferryland, the last outpost
on Avalon, would not give up their craft and their
weapons, so be it. There was no need to press them.
I had enough men and boats and weapons.

A faint cry reached my ears from across the water.
I snatched up the spy-glass and saw a longboat
putting out from the main body of the force that
had massed in their village's defence. A light-haired
fellow stood in the bows, arms aloft.

'Ahoy, Captain Loftus! Hold off your fire there!'

My heart leapt on hearing the thick accent. Those
Dutch gutturals were unmistakeable. Frantically,
I waved back, shouting and smiling. It was the
Pursuant's sailing master, Gaspar Rittel.

But what was he doing turning his back on
me? Rittel appeared to be addressing the waiting
Ferryland craft. Seconds later, all the seamen and
fishers raised up their arms high over their heads.
They shouted, though with the distance I could not
distinguish the meaning. At last, from a ragged and
disparate chorus, the noise resolved into a single
unbroken note of harmony.

The men of Ferryland, all rising in their little craft,
were hollering and hailing fit to burst a gut. They
called out, stamping their feet, rocking the gunnels
of their fragile vessels nearly underwater. Time and
again, they cried out until it dinned in my ears.

'Loftus! Loftus!' they chorused.

When Gaspar looked my way, his face opened into

an almighty grin. These were not shouts of anger or rebellion. They were cheering.

This was no longer an impressment, but a rally.

19

Unforgiving

'No bottom found,' softly sang the leadsman.

It was the deep, dead hours of a still and moon-less night, the utter darkness of two hours before dawn. The *Griffin* led the way, fetching quietly along under topsails and jibsails, the least canvas for steerage way. Sailors stood at the belays and sheets, ready in case a windshift set her aback. We were close under the cliffs' lee, feeling rather than seeing the way. The lead went down time and again, seeking soundings and finding none. The sheer rocky walls of Avalon's coast, meeting the sea, fell steeply away underwater and the line at its fullest stretch – a hundred fathoms – stayed stubbornly taut.

Not a lamp showed, not a pipe-match was struck. Only the regular splash and haul of the leadline from the bow marked the fleet's progress along the shoreline. In the fluking breeze under the high land, every now and then a lugsail flapped or a staysail rustled, accompanied by a block's rattle or the crank and groan of sheets and haulyards. Once or twice came a murmured command or a muffled exchange from one craft to another. Otherwise, nearly three hundred men held their breaths and kept their peace as a brace of armed barks followed by a motley assemblage of sixty or seventy littler craft crept towards the bay.

I had a mighty force behind me, but was it enough? As attackers we had the advantage of prior knowledge, I reassured myself. We knew where the lookouts would be, precisely where the gun batteries lay, exactly where the beacon fires were piled. And we had the advantage of surprise.

Then the fog came down.

On the *Griffin*'s quarter-deck, I sensed the air grow moist. The rail became slippery to the touch and droplets of water formed in my hair. Even in the pitch of night, we had been able to distinguish the cliffs on our steerboard side because they loomed even blacker. Now in every direction the darkness was uniformly indistinct. A damp wraith enveloped the shoal of boats and the ghostly outlines of their little sails vanished. Even the stars overhead disappeared.

On the run down from Ferryland, breasting Cape Race and heading west around the tip of Avalon, we had been fortunate with the weather – blessed, said the Factor. Either way, it had shown uncommon forbearance. The wind was fair, ruffling the sea's surface into playful white-caps a foot or two in height, with nothing more than a barely perceptible southwesterly swell. The only flaw was this infernal Newfoundland fog. When the sea mist crept in, the flotilla was forced to close up, familiar landmarks disappeared, and the pilotage became a matter of conjecture alone.

Patrick Cluney was at my side, peering into the murk.

'It'd be a miracle if you found your way in tonight, captain,' he remarked. 'On the other hand, if you do, it's perfect cover.'

Cluney was now my sailing master aboard the *Griffin*, while the Americkan, Thomas Partridge, was in command of the fishing boat flotilla carrying a hundred men, half of whom had brought their muskets. Meanwhile, the Dutchman Gaspar Rittel was master *pro tem* aboard the *Forgiver*. For all that she was a crank bitch, he delighted in his command.

She was a dam' sight less crank now, though. Grappling the two barks alongside, we had tackled the *Forgiver*'s ten great guns off her decks and hoisted them one by one aboard the *Griffin*. As each one tun mass lifted off the *Forgiver*, she sat better in the water, but as the guns came overside to rest on the former Gillycuddy bark, her deck-boards had groaned in protest.

'She'll sail like a church on fire,' warned Cluney, 'when all the sinners have crowded into the spire at once.'

In truth, the *Griffin* bore her ten tuns of extra iron and brass well. It helped that I ordered fifteen tuns of stone ballast to be bagged, lugged up from the Americkan bark's bilges, hefted over the rails and laid on the new bark's keelson to compensate for the guns' extra weight. The only man who failed utterly to understand the point of all this work was Josiah van Schreik. I made my seamen swear to keep it secret, for if he learned of the *Forgiver*'s fate to be, he would surely forbid it on grounds of cost. I had advised him to remain in the cabin below while the action took place, and there he stayed.

When the *Forgiver* had been denuded of not only her deck-pieces but her stores and spares too, I sent the men about their work. Precision, I told them, was their watchword. They scratched their heads and chewed their plugs and spat yellow juice on the filthy deck-boards and rippled seams. By the end, the leaky old bark was unrecognisable but the work I wanted had been done – and done well.

Gaspar was distraught to see his first command treated so roughly.

'Ya, captain,' he complained, 'but is there no other way?'

'There must always be sacrifices,' I said, and reassured him that though she might be his first command, she should not be his last.

Now the fleet slid secretively under the high bluffs of the Avalon shore, the steersman keeping the *Griffin* less than a cable from the cliffs. Until the fog, we had kept our distance off by spying the white line of surf faintly glowing as it seethed at the foot. With the mist, we kept off by listening to the echoes of our calls on the rock walls, and by cocking our ears for the swish and sigh of the swell licking at their base. Soon, the compass showed we had borne off from a westerly heading and turned north. Then at last the lead, charged with sticky tallow, picked up the seabed.

'Bottom found, eighty fathom,' called the leadsman. 'Small shingle and slatey stones.'

By this I knew us to be less than half a league from rounding the heads at Barrier Heights. I called to Thomas Partridge, following close astern in the leading fishing shallop.

'Have that rowboat brought alongside,' I said, 'the one I chose this afternoon. Does she have a name?'

'Aye, captain, she's the *Lively*, I believe,' said the Americkan.

In half a glass we would come within range of the batteries. In a battle once before, seeing off attackers had cost four men's lives. Apart from Sam Lightfoot, a sailor, they were simple fishermen who wanted only to haul cod, salt down their catch, and cure it – one way or another, wet or dry, it mattered so little. Then they would sail across the sea back to their wives and daughters in Brest or Brixham, Dartmouth or Douarnenez. Those fellows, volunteers all, had never returned home. It would not happen that way again. This time I alone must take the risk.

A cluster of boats approached under the stern, oars dipping quietly. They were crowded to the gunnels with men. In the eerie gloom of the night-mist, I made out a forest of raised musket barrels.

Thomas Partridge's voice called softly. 'All's ready for your transfer, Captain Loftus.'

I hoisted up my briches. The belt was weighted down with a brace of pistols, ready primed and charged, and a handy short-bladed cutlass. I carried two seaman's knives. One was a narrow two-inch blade on a stubby handle, tucked into the belt's loop made for it. The other was a six-inch beauty from the *Griffin*'s captain's locker, with a pearl handle and an edge so whetted it had cut through a three-stranded painter drawn across the steel under

365

its own weight. The pockets of my short weskit and my briches were stuffed with match, flints and strikers.

Bidding Patrick Cluney keep his course and mind his canvas, I went to the break and stepped down to the waist. The musketmen were clambering up boarding ropes and assembling on the weather-deck when a figure emerged from the gloom to hold a free boarding rope for me to descend.

'Musketmen all ready, sir,' said the fellow.

The accent was familiar. Suddenly I gripped him by the elbows.

'Guy!' I cried. 'By the Lord's own blood, it's Guy de Chenalles. Where have you come from?'

'I was at Ferryland.' He gestured into the waist. 'See, Captain Loftus, I am taking charge of the musketry. I trust that is to your satisfaction?'

By now there were more than a hundred men aboard, standing about in the dark, shuffling their feet and shifting their weapons.

'Nothing could be more so,' I said, giving his arm an encouraging squeeze.

When I clambered over the rail and down the rope, the *Lively* rocked under my step but she felt sound and solid-built. An oarsman sat on the midships thwart. When I cast off the line, he stroked away.

I leaned across. 'Is she your boat, sir?'

'Aye, and brought all across the Atlantick on the deck of my bark.' He spoke with the burr of a Devon man.

'She might not see this night through,' I warned.

'Then I shall build her sister. Not of English ash

and elm but of good spruce and pine from here-abouts. She'll not be a Westcountry boat, captain, but a Newfoundland one.'

'And are you a Newfoundlander now?' I said.

'I am that, captain,' he said, 'and come to reclaim Stack Beach.'

'Good man,' I said, and touched his arm. 'Come to me after this and I shall give you twenty marks for your *Lively*.'

Not far off, the *Forgiver* moved through the night at a knot and a half or two knots, wearing topsails and jibsails alone. I caught the thrown line and we bumped alongside. At her waterline was a band of barnacles and trailing green weed, freshly exposed, for with her guns away she rode six inches higher in the water.

The skeleton crew bustled about, readying for departure. One after the other, I bade them good fortune as each man dropped down the boarding rope into the six or seven cutters tied off and waiting. Last to disembark was Gaspar Rittel.

'She's yours again, captain,' he said miserably. His command had been all too short.

'Mister Rittel,' I said, 'when you go aboard the *Griffin*, you are to take command on the quarter-deck. Patrick Cluney knows, and shall step aside.'

Even in the gloom, I saw his face light up. 'Ya? Captain – thank you!'

He descended into the last cutter. When it stroked off, I saw, pale in the blackness, a hand raised in salute. Then all the men and boats were gone, bar the *Lively* bobbing alongside the cranky Americkan bark like a faithful dog on its leash.

Alone aboard the *Forgiver*, I stood with one hand upon the wheel's spokes. The bark's decks were deserted and silent as a tomb. No men swayed high aloft on the yards, or sang out a chanty to heave home the lines. Not a sound of life nor a sailor's spirit reached my ears. Yet still she rustled along, sheeted in, courses and topsails drawing, passing under the invisible high ground, moving through the dank mist like a ghost ship, unseen.

Then, for both her first and her last time, she entered Esperantia Bay.

Hardly another ten minutes' worth of sand grains had filtered their way through the hourglass before I determined it was time. I stuffed fingers of gun wadding into my ears and lashed the wheel amidships. The *Forgiver* sailed obediently on.

Brushing the damp mist-drops from my eyes, I squinted round for a sight of the land I knew was there but could not see. How strange it seemed to have entered deep into Esperantia Bay again, to the place I had sometime called my home, yet find there was nothing of it to be seen. By now I was under the hill-top batteries, but they remained fog-bound and hidden. Not a thing stirred and no light showed through the dense mist.

Ahead, perhaps two cables off, must be Stack Beach. Beyond it, the village. The fog hid any glow of oil-lamps and candles gleaming from the windows where once drunks and sinners alike had gathered, meeting at the Salt Pillar Inn after a day's work done. No differences between the religions or nations had come between the people then, barring the language of their song or the hue of their tipple. I remembered the *Pursuant*'s earlier returns from Labrador, when Malachy and Lucy Skentles had so freely dispensed their mix of spirit and song and Old Testament proverb. Those carefree assemblies belonged to a past world.

Striking a flint spark, I fired a short piece of matchfuse. In this thick night, no one ashore would spy the flickering light – not that it mattered now. The *Forgiver*, a crank and tophampered bark out of the Boston yards, was to be no mere fire-ship tonight. In truth, she was well suited to that purpose, being built of pitchy pine and springy spruce and fir, sappy timbers that burned more fiercely than English oak or larch. But she must not burn yet. She had too much to do first.

I bent and touched the smouldering matchfuse end to a trail of firing-fuse laid across the deck-boards. The fast fuse glowed instantly, running away to the larboard side like a rat across the sole. Half a second later, there came an almighty roar as if Hades itself had opened its maw and disgorged fire.

By this time, I had touched off the next fuse. A second explosion followed instantly. Then I fired another fuse, and the next beside it, and then the one after. They ran away in zig and zag across the boards to the larboard side. The blasts went off in rapid succession.

Each fuse ran to an open half-keg, about the size of a Toulon brandy issue. The kegs were filled with powder and wadding, packed in tighter than jack-tars at the only whorehouse in town. Dozens upon dozens of kegs were lined along the rails both sides, jaws pointing outboard and upward. The gunners had worked hard and this was the pay-off.

Explosion after explosion sent deafening reports echoing round Esperantia Bay. A stream of hot sparks and flames vomited from each little barrel, spraying ten feet out into the night, the red drops of flame hissing and spitting into the black water below. The next half-keg went off, and the next, the next again, and half a dozen more. Then I stepped across the waist and touched off ten more fuses on the steerboard side.

To a sailor used to the engagements of battle, familiar with the roar of big guns going off nearby, these reports might sound a trifle dull, lacking the sharpness of a hard-tamped charge exploding in a brass gun and sending a six-pound roundshot half a mile. Yet to a sleepy watchman high on the bluffs above, or to drink-sotted revellers inside a tavern, I reckoned they sounded well enough. They sounded like deck cannon. Many deck cannon.

I went to the wheel, unlashed it and spun it hard over. The ship began a stately turn, wearing herself onto the opposite tack, passing the eye of the wind across her stern. Moments later, with no one at the belays to see to the sheets, she went into stays. Now she lay broadside on across the middle of the bay, and not half a cable off Stack Beach.

Matchfuse in hand, I ran about the waist touching off fast fuse after fast fuse. Then I was up at the foc'sle to touch off a dozen more, before running back the length of the ship and criss-crossing the quarter-deck, bending and touching, setting off gun following make-believe gun, until from end to end the *Forgiver*'s decks were lit with sparks and flames. The fuses had been laid parallel, leading to the rails where the barrels and old chain-pump tubes – anything we could lay a hand on – were aligned. From stem to stern, the ship reverberated with reports and explosions. With luck, it would look and sound like a broadside fired sequentially. It was the best we could do. I prayed it would be enough.

A thunderous boom shattered the night sky high above my head. There, three hundred feet up at Vantage Rise, was the reply I had hoped for. The first crack of the big guns was followed an instant later by a second and a third as the gunners at Beacon Top answered with their own voice, sending balls whistling from the twelve-pounders' mouths.

Twelve pound balls, I thought grimly. Those shots had to land somewhere. How good was the gunners' aim? But there was no getting off the bark now. I ran about the decks, touching and touching with my matchfuse. We had laid a hundred and fifty false gunshots and there must have been still a hundred to go.

Whump! A pillar of water, showing white in the darkness, erupted ten fathoms off my steerboard bow. Then a second huge column of water rose up beside it. The surface churned as more heavy shots fell, sending water high in the air and waves surging outward in circles.

Suddenly I realised I could see the guns. High above, on the hill-tops, gouts of flame and fire spouted out either side of the bay. Then I saw stars, and the planets even brighter. So the fog was lying in a low bank, close to the water, not rising far. Above and beyond the *Forgiver*'s mast-trucks, the night was clear and crisp. The blanket of mist was only fifty or sixty feet deep, yet the shore remained invisible only a cable or so distant. From on high, those gunners could not just hear but see my half-kegs going off. They could see where the ship was. And they were getting their aim.

Nearer and nearer fell the shots. Seconds later as I crouched low on the beak hard by the anchor windlass, a marker struck all too close. A pillar of water rose up and collapsed aboard, drenching me. My matchfuse was doused. Shivering, I drew another length from my pocket and flicked the sparker. After six or seven goes, the sparks flew but the fuse was wet and would not catch. I tried another piece, with similar result.

The *Forgiver*'s shot-less guns fell silent. No longer did she fire off a running broadside nearly every minute, nor loose off her mock swivels at the same rate or better. Blast and Hell, I thought, it's too soon. I want those hill-top gunners panicked into keeping up their firing rate.

My spare dry matchfuse was by the wheel. I abandoned the shelter afforded by the low beak and crossed the foc's'le heading for the waist. The quarter-deck seemed a mighty long way off. The *Forgiver* was only a hundred and forty foot on deck but with balls falling nearby every few seconds the distance stretched to an infinity. I ran in a half crouch along the rail past the boarding rope where the little *Lively* jigged and tugged her painter in the stirred up waters. Then it happened.

A shot struck the foc's'le steps. Ten seconds earlier, I had stood there futilely flicking my sparker. The hit created such an impact that I was instantly laid flat on the boards. The breath went from my chest. Heat passed over my skin, the blast ripping at my briches, tearing the weskit and shirt off my back. Numerous smaller blows and whip-like stings battered my body like a shower of stones and thorns. As this tempest from the Devil raged, my face remained pressed hard against the deck-boards. Then something struck a vicious blow to my head and all went black.

I smelt a pleasant woody aroma rising under my nose. It came from the deck-boards, but in my stunned condition it brought to mind resting on the warm, sedgey summer earth deep in the Kanada forest, as if I was stretched out on a blanket of pine-needles by the banks of a swift-flowing river. A comfortable, lazy sensation came over me and I felt safe, knowing Irocaibi was there. My eyelids refused to open, but light flickered through the veiny skin. I remembered lying somewhere by a waterfall. But where were the icy splashes of freezing meltwater? Where was the forest? And the river?

I began shouting a name.

'Irocaibi! Irocaibi!'

A dull boom reverberated against my cheek and all at once I came to. My face was jammed against the pitchy-pine planks of the deck-boards. There was no forest, no river, no waterfall, no sunlight – only noise and heat and choking smoke and explosive flashes. Blast after hot blast shattered the night. Falteringly, I levered onto my hands and knees, finding myself hard by the quarter-deck steps. I mounted them unsteadily and went to the wheel. There were my spare dry pieces of matchfuse. Then I was moving about again, sending off one fast fuse after another, letting off another steerboard broadside, then a rippling row of shot-less blasts from larboard.

Both high batteries stepped up their rain of destructive forces onto the *Forgiver*. Having found their marks, and with the bark making no attempt to manoeuvre clear, they were bent on destroying her. Before I had got through perhaps fifty shots more, a second heavy ball crashed aboard. This time it landed square upon the quarter-deck. A second angry buzzing swarm savaged the air, landing stings again. Hornets, I thought, dazed, going down a second time. Then it seemed a river burst its banks and drowned me in icy fresh water. But the stings were only wood splinters and the river just another pillar of seawater.

Rising, shaky on my feet, I fumbled with the sparker. Nothing. No light, no fizzing fire. My matchfuses were again useless. It was hard to think. Fuses. Matchfuses on the quarter-deck. Get on your feet, my own voice, distant in my ringing head, instructed. Go to the quarter-deck for dry fuses.

There came a further rib-crushing explosion. Moments after, breathless and shocked, I blinked at the quarter-deck. There were no fuses to be found up there. There was no wheel. The compass binnacle had gone. All I saw was a yawning hole in the deck-boards, with wisps of smoke rising from it. A jagged opening ten feet across lay where the matchfuses had been.

My hands shook, my mouth was dry. I was no longer running about the decks of a decoy attacker, swiftly and accurately firing off my fuses to show now her steerboard broadside, now her larboard, now the swivel guns. Instead, I was half kneeling, crouched like an animal on the deck of a ship that was nothing more than a death trap. I had no stomach for being blown into quartered meat. It was time to get off.

I reeled over to the rail. More shots landed on the forward bulwarks. Too close, I muttered, too damm'd close. I fumbled for the *Lively*'s painter, but could not unlash it. Dam' and dam' again, a simple clove hitch and yet my fingers refused to obey. I groped for a knife. The long-blade was gone, but my grip closed around the handle of the two-inch dagger sheathed in the pouch at my briches belt. With a single stroke, the line parted, and I thanked the Lord for the little seaman's saviour. Tumbling overboard, I crashed down the topsides, grabbing at the boarding rope to slow my descent. When I hit the bottom ribs of the rowboat, it all but broke the oars in two.

The *Lively* leapt about as falling shots churned the water. I locked in the sweeps and pulled for my life. As her bulk receded, the *Forgiver*'s outline was lit up in flames. Lord, I thought, have I done it? Have I let off enough half-barrels? I stopped rowing and stared at the ship, thinking of going back, just for one more broadside, a few more swivel shots, to show she was still in action, anything to keep those batteries going a little longer.

Another twelve-pound ball struck the *Forgiver*.

This time it sounded more like the beat of an immense bass drum than the rap of a giant hammer blow. The shot punctured her decks amidships and sent planks and splinters flying into the air. Pieces of sharpened timber zinged by as I ducked low in the boat. But there was nothing left in the magazine to blow up, for it was all transferred to the *Griffin*. No matter, for the flames were taking hold and she was nearing her end.

I pulled on the oars like a demented man, but my strokes were ragged. I had gained only a few fathoms when a shot struck her mainmast. I recognised the sharp, deathly crack that followed. The mast was coming down. I dug the blades and tried to open the distance. There came a singing sound, as though a child were whipping a sapling switch through the air, or rather twenty children doing the same with twenty saplings. It was the whistle of ratlines and shrouds on their way down to the sea. The *Forgiver*'s mainmast and the topmast together reached the height of a hundred feet above her decks. The *Lively* was still too close. I pulled harder.

A gale of wind passed over my face. There was a mighty splash and the *Lively* rocked so hard she tipped her gunnels under and took on water. The truck of the topmast bobbed in front of my eyes, then dipped below the black surface and was gone, leaving debris and broken ropes and blocks tossing on the sea. An enormous tangle of gear floated barely ten feet off.

Only ten feet off. At Boston, I had sent down the *Forgiver*'s topgallant spars to reduce the tophamper.

Still in place, they would have added twenty feet of height – and hit the *Lively* square.

I looked up, struck rigid by the narrow escape. From the *Forgiver*'s waist, flames burgeoned. She was dismasted by the main. What was left of her gear and rigging was ablaze. The stern quarters were broken open, the windows shattered, the planking split and torn apart. Her bowsprit drooped, the jibboom and its furled jibsail dipping into the water. I pulled away. Heavy shots rang out still, so the batteries remained in action. My reeling mind was even then thinking, if only more of my broadsides had gone off. My plan had failed.

But wait. I was confused, surely. The shots were not coming from Beacon Top and Vantage Rise. They came from the *Forgiver*. The last of the half-barrels, the decoy shots, the pretended broadsides, were firing off one by one as the flames reached them. The cantankerous thing was fighting to the last, before her inevitable plunge into fifty fathoms of freezing black water.

Then I understood what was happening. The hill-top gun batteries had indeed fallen silent. In panic, they had fired shot after shot without respite. First they had seen the bark through the thin fog layer and marked down their range. Then they had reloaded and dropped their shots closer. Scoring a hit, excitement overtook them and they loaded again, and fired again, and tried to pound the insolent attacker into matchwood. So eager had they been on this work, they had fired too fast.

McGruder had not used his stolen money – my money – to buy new guns. As I hoped, he had left the worn, cracked old pieces in place. And, just as once before, the Esperantia batteries had jammed.

Shouts and hails rang out nearby. The *Griffin* was coming to my rescue.

20

Honour Bound

Like a parent swan leading her cygnets, the *Griffin* advanced under short canvas past the stricken, half-sunk *Forgiver*. The small boat flotilla followed in formation astern under Thomas Partridge. Gaspar Rittel had charge of the *Griffin*'s quarter-deck, issuing orders by the bagful, while Patrick Cluney in the waist oversaw the gunnery.

When he was helped from the *Lively* and brought back aboard, their captain was found to be suffering from a minor but disabling incapacity. He simply could not remember which way up the world was. When Factor van Schreik appeared out of the dark and began speaking, I swore it was an apparition from Hell.

'Captain Loftus, what plans have you made,' he said, 'to save the *Forgiver*? There was no indemnity paid. What can I tell Governor Spurgeon if she goes down?'

I wanted to offer that surely the Governor would be pleased to learn his bark was safe in the hands of the Lord, who dwelt even at the bottom of Esperantia Bay, but my mouth seemed to be made of dry sand. Ignoring the Factor, waving away his persistent enquiries, I leant groggily at the break, watching, letting my head clear.

I noticed a gap in the fog. Whether the blazing *Forgiver* had heated the air, or perhaps just because dawn was coming, the mist cleared. Stack Beach was revealed half a cable dead ahead. In seconds, the swirling damp clouds had closed in again and all was shrouded, but it was enough for them to have seen us coming. A hail of vicious musket shots was loosed off from behind the beach defences.

'Down!' someone cried.

The balls seared out through the fog and spattered against the *Griffin*'s rails and topsides and into her rigging. Some hit softer targets and there were groans and cries as men went down.

With her six forward swivels – four of them a gift from the old *Forgiver* – blazing away at the beach, the *Griffin* criss-crossed her own course as she ventured into the head of the bay. Gaspar Rittel rounded up and brought the bark broadside on. Twenty jack-tars sprang aloft to bunt up her topsails, while two launches took towlines out bow and stern to keep her on station. When the *Griffin*'s own twelve deck-pieces had been supplemented by the ten donated from the plucky Americkan bark the carpenter, to Patrick Cluney's dismay, had been obliged to braddle and adze and saw openings along his ship's beautiful bulwarks. Now, through these rough gunports poked out the awful black snouts of her new guns. With the *Griffin* ranging an eleven-gun broadside on Stack Beach, it was time for Patrick Cluney to show off his gunnery skills.

'Gunners, are you ready?' he called.

There came a chorus of answering 'ayes' from eleven men standing by with raised linstocks. But when Cluney looked my way, I could not speak. I was struggling with the enormity, the sheer outlandishness, of what was coming. Was I truly about to give the order to pound Esperantia into submission?

Rittel glanced over enquiringly. 'Captain, the broadside is ready.'

The answer must be aye, I knew. In the light of my promise to the Avalon men, having come so far, retreat would be contemptible. The order must be given.

I nodded. 'Aye aye, Mister Cluney.'

'Larboard guns, fire!' he cried.

In the night, the lighted linstocks swept in bright curves down to the touch-holes. A welter of flame and sparks burst forth from all along the rail. The noise dinned in my ears, clouds of smoke followed the discharges and the smell of burnt powder filled my nostrils.

'Reload with roundshot,' came Cluney's command.

With mighty rumbles, the pieces ran back on their tackles and seamen swarmed about the mouths, barrels hissing as they sponged out the remains of the old charge, then threw in a fresh shot bag, tamped down the wadding and loaded the ball. A second wad was rammed home to keep it in place and again the pieces trundled forward until their barrel-ends pushed out through the gunports. The gunners stood back, linstocks held high.

'Ready larboard side?' cried Cluney.

I nodded, and closed my eyes.

'Fire!' shouted the former Gillycuddy man.

Again came the roar and noise and smoke of eleven

guns. The ship's deck-boards trembled beneath our soles. With the recoil, each gun snapped viciously back on its tackle and the *Griffin* heeled. After half a dozen firings, the pieces were well heated and the gun crews held back with their sponges and shot bags, afraid of cracking the barrels by cooling them too fast – or worse, ramming a live shot bag into a tube of red-hot metal.

But even as the sixth broadside was loosed off, Gaspar had called to the towing launches. The oarsmen, twelve sweeps to each boat, lay back to the work. The bark wheeled and in less than a minute had spun a full circle. With her larboard guns still smoking, her steerboard broadside now faced the shore, ranging eleven fresh, cold guns.

'Ready steerboard gunners?' called Cluney.

The touch-holes were lighted and another broadside sent in the direction of Stack Beach. The ship lurched under the shock, the balls whirred and groaned away. I listened for the heavy thuds of their impact. Our aim was good. We pounded the musketry emplacements time and again until their fire grew ever more sporadic.

High in the southeastern quarter there showed a tentative lightening of the sky, dawn's first glimmer. Vantage Rise loomed dark and massive, a dim glow indicating the overheated battery. My gaze followed the line of the hillside halfway down, where Providence House stood in the hollow. There was a faint square of light, as if someone were watching from a window. Was it the old Dowager, watching in silence from her stoney fastness? Or was it Grace Trepanney, wondering who came down upon Esperantia with such sudden retribution?

The launches towed the *Griffin* up and down across the bay to keep the hilltop gunners guessing. Their jammed pieces revived once, twice, then fell silent. Gaspar spun us round every few broadsides to bring the cooler guns to bear. Between firings, there still came the intermittent buzz and whirr of musket balls passing, so for minutes more we pounded the shoreline where Guy de Chenalles' old defences lay, the berms and ditches he had so carefully constructed, hiding McGruder's musketmen positioned there to meet a beach assault.

At last, the musketry ceased. The bombardment had done its work.

'Mister Cluney, hold your fire,' I managed to croak.

The crews, grateful for a break in the frantic rate of loading and reloading, fell back from their guns and all eyes gazed out over the scene. I cocked an ear for musket balls. There was nothing.

'Mister Partridge, send in the advance guard,' I called.

The Americkan's commands rang out from below the taffrail. At once, two longboats moved off and sculled determinedly forward. The forty armed men in them, led by a grim-faced Guy de Chenalles, bore rapidly shorewards. They landed unopposed, swarming up the beach to overwhelm the half-destroyed defences.

Suddenly a volley of musket shots loosed off from the village. The lead balls whistled and sang overhead, ripping canvas or thudding into the bulwarks.

As one, we flattened ourselves to the deck-boards, waiting for the storm to pass. The dawn showed a pall of gunsmoke rising above the misty curtain of fog. It came from the very centre of Esperantia village, where the musketmen must have made a stronghold. We had sent a hundred men ashore, exposed, defenceless. With a pit of hatred for McGruder burning in my belly, I decided there was nothing for it.

'Raise your levels by degrees,' I called down to Patrick Cluney, 'until you range the village centre.'

'Aye aye, captain,' came the answer, and the gunnery began anew.

Heavy balls crashed time and again, landing ahead of a hundred musketmen and yards behind Stack Beach. For a quarter hour more, the *Griffin* sent eleven heavy balls ashore every minute.

Finally I said, 'Make that your last broadside, Mister Cluney.'

In the growing morning light, at long last the mist cleared. It revealed a scene of devastation. A cloud of dust rose over the land behind the beach. Raking the shore and the village with the spy-glass, I saw only ruins. Nothing and no one moved. Esperantia village was destroyed.

Amongst the cottages and storehouses lay the smoke-blackened ruins of the larger building where the musketry had been. There was no firing from it now. Something flashed whitely in the dawn glow and I focused the tube. From the broken doorway emerged a ragged figure, holding aloft a yard of white cloth in surrender. Then as the morning light strengthened it revealed, in all its sorrow and destruction, the burnt remains of the Salt Pillar Inn.

The blood pulsed in my temples. I thought of Malachy and Lucy. What about the messenger boys? Lizzie Penn and the others? Where were they?

'Send in your flotilla, Mister Partridge,' I said thickly.

Sixty little boats moved out from the *Griffin*'s shelter. The gunners, their work done, gathered at the rail to clamber down into them. Suddenly I spied a familiar figure amongst them, a beaver-hatted fellow carrying a long-musket.

'M'sieur Hubert!' I called. 'Not you, my friend.'

He shrugged, hung back, and showed his disappointment. But I needed Hubert Nitchequot alive and speaking the Missacaibi tongue. He would be little use with a stray ball lodged in his skull.

The Americkan bellowed orders and the waiting boats struck out. Passing clear of the *Griffin*'s high bulk, they stroked to the shore ignoring the broken shallops scattered in the anchorage, smashed and sinking, their hulls splintered. When the flotilla grazed their stems ashore, dozens of men leapt across the bows and splashed to the beach, swarming up the rise. Following Guy de Chenalles' advance party, they stormed into the village and took it without further resistance. Moments after, other little vessels drove ashore at the foot of the heights and armed detachments rushed uphill to take control of the batteries. Esperantia was ours.

Gaspar Rittel joined me, breathless and triumphant, on the quarter.

'Ya, captain,' he began, 'the gunnery was pretty good and –'

'Where is she, Mister Rittel?' I said.

I had closely observed McGruder's defences in action. A hundred musketmen had sent a thousand balls out from the beach defences and the inn. The hill-top batteries had rained their heavy shots down at the *Forgiver*. But there had been no lighter roundshot, no fire from anything like the deck-pieces of a bark.

'Where has she gone?' I repeated.

He followed my gaze towards the beach and the village. Apart from broken fishing boats and shallops, and our own longboats too, there was no larger vessel in sight. The bay was empty except for the *Griffin* and a mess of floating wreckage and barrels and spars where the *Forgiver* had once been. I brought the tube onto the wharfside beyond the gap to the inner harbour. There was nothing. The *Pursuant* was nowhere to be seen.

'Ya, I think maybe she slipped out under the fogbanks while we laid down the bombardment,' Gaspar said.

That was what I was thinking too.

'Shall I make ready for sea?' said Rittel. 'Give chase before she gets away?'

His eager face was alight. He wanted Finlay McGruder's neck almost as much as I did. But ought I not go ashore and deal with any last resistance? See to the wounded? Find out who had suffered and who had lived? Or just go and get McGruder.

I cast my eye up the hill. Even in the early grey dawn, the squat bulk of Providence House stood out. At one window glowed a yellow light and I caught a movement behind the panes.

Patrick Cluney came up.

'Short on powder and shot, sir,' he reported. 'We're bringing up new stock from below.'

'Very well,' I said, 'and what condition are the pieces in?'

'Hot and tired, captain. We're cleaning them as fast we can.'

'Aye, then. You can have half a glass for the task.'

Poor Rittel was agitated. 'Captain – what about the *Pursuant*?'

I faced him calmly. 'The *Griffin* can better her speed by two clear knots on any point. Do you agree?'

'Ya, it's so. But –'

'Then she cannot escape in that time,' I said. 'Drop anchor, Mister Rittel, and muster a boat to take me to the beach.'

Eight oarsmen sat facing me, and behind them ten musketmen and their loaded weapons, when I descended into the boat. Carefully, I checked my arms: two pistols, a long cutlass, a new six-inch dagger.

'Take her ashore, fellows,' I said.

The stem crunched on the beachstones. Leaping over her bows, I planted my feet on the shingles of Stack Beach. Smoke drifted across, groans rose up from the wounded, the shattered remains of the cod-drying industry smouldered nearby. What a gruesome return this was for Esperantia's one-time Guardian.

Walking up the steep stone mounds towards the firing positions, I encountered a corpse thrown backwards into a grossly inhuman posture. Shreds of clothing clinging to the skin were wet through with blood and stinking effluents. The poor wight must have been hit directly by the *Griffin*'s well-aimed shots. There were more remains in the next ditch, and half a torso tossed high onto the rampart above. The torn limbs and bonework of former humanity were strewn everywhere.

After the first few, I hardened to the sight. Behind me followed the stumbling, shingle-crunching footsteps of my comrades. Some gasped in shock, others spoke in low tones, but all wondered at the grisly spectacle. My pressed men of Avalon were no battle-worn seamen or fighting marines, but ordinary fishermen and traders seeing for the first time what fearsome destruction can be wrought by a powerfully armed vessel bent on her purpose.

My face set, I entered the village. Cottage by cottage, storeroom by storeroom, the settlement had been laid flat. Many buildings were half-ruined or showed gaping black holes where balls had penetrated. One or two were rubble, such as the storehouses built simply of courses of unhewn stone carted up from the beach and crudely roofed over. Parts of the Salt Pillar Inn still stood, forlorn, broken and crumbling. The roof had caved in and only the inn's heavy, dressed stone foundations were untouched. The main door was blown in. Fearfully, I approached the gaping architrave, pistols cocked and ready, and peered inside.

'Ahoy, is anyone alive here?' I demanded.

Silence. Then a whimper, or a sob.

I stepped across the threshold. The place was a shambles, a shell of the old alehouse of so many good times in the past. But still it was recognisable. There was the hatch where ale was sold. Over there, we had sat and sung our drunken sea songs. There I had rallied the fisherfolk against the Gillycuddys of Burin.

Under an overturned table came a movement.

'Show yourself,' I demanded, 'with your hands in the air.'

The tabletop shifted, crunching on the gritty floor. A slight figure emerged, his clothes torn and dust-covered, brushing grit from his eyes and hair. He trembled uncontrollably and could barely stand. It was a boy.

With a pang, I belted my pistol and stepped over.

'Caswell Penn – are you whole?' My voice choked. Dam' for this smoke and dust. Resisting the desire to grasp him and hug him to me, I knelt down to test him first for broken or damaged limbs.

'You are not struck anywhere? Nor cut?'

He shook his head, tears running freely down his grimy face. He quivered in my arms as I scooped him up and bore him outside. The sun had risen over the eastern hinterland and in the brightening day Caswell blinked, wiping his eyes, and wailed loudly. Reckoning it a good indication he was not badly injured, I set him gently down.

A woman came stumbling up the rubble strewn pathway.

'Matthew, Matthew!'

Lucy Skentles threw herself against me and squeezed so hard my rib-bones cracked. Her muffled voice came sobbing through the tears.

'You are home, you are home,' she said. 'Don't go away again. I can't bear it.'

Malachy came up and took his wife by the arm. 'She's seen enough fighting. After the last time, we had to clear the corpses left rotting in the walkways and cottages. Now we shall have to do it again.'

'What fighting, Malachy?' My voice sounded hard.

'When McGruder forced out the Papists. He killed those who resisted, men, women and children alike. Then he transported the rest away.'

The innkeeper described the Catholicks enduring McGruder's harsh regime of mock trials, arbitrary penalties and salutary punishments for the merest infrigement. Dozens of Papists were driven from the curing beach by extortionate and discriminatory tax impositions, or subjected to open violence from the mob whipped up by the Scotsman's Protestant oratory. After a bloody episode, he forcibly transported every last Catholick away on a sloop bound for Acadia. The Skentles were driven from their alehouse for serving Guy and Catherine de Chenalles. They too were deported but Guy found his way back to Avalon hoping to rally folk against the Scotsman. He had been in hiding with Gaspar when the *Forgiver* hove in to Ferryland.

'And McGruder and the *Pursuant*?' I asked Malachy.

He jerked his head seawards. 'Got out just as the bombardment began.'

Lucy's eyes were pleading. 'Dearest Matthew, tell me there's to be no more bloodshed and sorrow.'

'I cannot promise that,' I told her truthfully. Then

390

I drew her aside, saying quietly, 'Tell me about the widow.'

'O,' she said, eyes cast down. 'Do you know nothing?'

All around us, Esperantia village amounted to no more than piles of charred timbers, heaps of rubble, and forlorn lost figures moving about. In the near distance came shouts from Guy and Partridge and the others assembling prisoners, arranging help for the wounded, marshalling transport to take them away. Sick at heart, I remembered the hopes I had harboured for this once proud and independent place.

'Nothing, Lucy,' I said. 'I know nothing. Tell me.'

Between sobs, she unfolded the tale. The Dowager had welcomed Finlay McGruder as a hero upon his triumphant return from the north. Everyone believed his tale that Matthew Loftus was dead. The Scotsman installed himself as lord not just of the settlement but as ruler of the household, which indignity the old lady had suffered stoically in the name of the greater cause, Esperantia's continuation as a free settlement. She had even sealed his Intendancy Proper in a ludicrous ceremony held on the lawns of Providence House.

As Lucy spoke, I imagined Lady Trepanney, in an ecstasy of self-righteousness, fawning to the man she thought of as torch-bearer for her supposed ideals. McGruder repaid this faith by setting about the destruction of every principle she held dear and violating the memory of her husband's life, a life founded upon a spirit of ideal hope. As the news worsened, the Dowager ailed, but Lucy doubted there was a physickal sickness. Rather it was a deliberate act of will designed to force her daughter-in-law to succumb, for she saw that her sole remaining hope of swaying the Scotsman was the prospect of the widow's hand.

By Grace's own account to Lucy, she had refused point blank to contemplate it. Lady Trepanney then set about enforcing the marriage bonds, locking her daughter-in-law in the house, confining the children to a cottage in the village. McGruder's stance hardened too. He took to relating with relish the fate of friends and servants whom Grace loved, and told her it was in her gift to ameliorate their condition. He could be generous in his mercy, but must have some pickings in return. She resisted still.

Not long after, the Dowager died – wrapped, as Grace had put it at the time, in a veil of invincibility. Esperantia, once in her thrall, had not mourned her passing. Indeed, under McGruder's excesses the villagers barely noticed it and the corpse was unceremoniously laid in the gardens of Providence House, the shrunken cadaver put to rest under a mausoleum of heaped beach stones. And if she was alone before, now Grace was left utterly exposed and defenceless.

After a few days she escaped from the house seeking her children Sophie and Oliver, but McGruder caught her, said Lucy, and took her back. Though she begged to see them, he refused until she gave him what he called his prize. Again, Grace spurned him, but when the maid came up next day with tales of his beating little Oliver with a stick, she felt herself cracking. Then he brought the poor boy to the house, bruised and cowed, eyes reddened from crying. Her resistance, Lucy said between her tears, crumbled at the sight. Though still she refused the marriage, McGruder got his way at last. He had taken his spoils in the bedchamber.

I was silent. Nothing came to mind save that I had been too late to save her from the horror of my most evil nightmares.

'Matthew, try not to judge her too harshly,' said Lucy, perhaps mistaking my mood.

'A woman must think of her children,' I said stonily.

In truth, I no longer knew what I thought or felt. I looked at Lucy Skentles. She was red-eyed, wiping the tears away, sniffling.

'I must see her,' I said, my voice sounding strange even to me.

She fell into my arms and hugged me. After a minute, I gently pushed her away. Lizzie Penn's little brother stood not far off, waiting.

'Caswell, you must know,' I said, 'where Mistress Trepanney is now.'

His voice was low. 'Yes sir, she's up at the house.'

Summer or winter, Providence House had always been a cold place. The Dowager's gloomy presence pervaded its very stonework, hanging over every room, every encounter, every exchange that took place there. Now even the very act of love itself would be tainted here, and not just because the old lady's unsettled spirit lingered on. A new malevolence had invaded the mortar and stonework. And its evil was ineradicable.

Grace Trepanney was sitting bolt upright on the window seat, watching my approach. At once I saw she was still the most elegant woman I had ever laid eyes on. This time I would not bend to one knee and take up her hand as before, brushing my lips across the smooth warm skin, prolonging the greeting's caress. Not this time. Lord, how I had longed for the moment of our meeting. Now here it was, and I almost could not bear it.

Quietly, looking drawn and tired in the aftermath of her extended ordeal, she greeted me with great dignity and complete apartness. Nor did the widow cry or give way to emotion in any visible degree. Suddenly I found this restraint, far from mollifying, quite the hardest thing of all. It stung me to the core that she withheld so much of herself. It left me unable to offer condolence, bereft of the chance to comfort her. I sat with her quietly, my senses dulled, longing to reach for her and take her in my arms, yet cruelly aware that the very last thing she could accept now was intimacy.

When I said Lucy had told me about McGruder and the Dowager, she stiffened.

'Then you know it all,' she said in half a whisper. 'Or almost all.'

I was stunned to find Grace had another chapter to add to the pitiable story, something that cut her more deeply – if that were possible – than even the constant, brutal violations that followed her submission to McGruder. As I listened, my heart turned adamantine, as grey and unyielding as Stack Beach itself.

At twelve years, Oliver was a slight child, the kind

of boy who would never grow into a strong and beefy fellow able to hoist barrels on his shoulder or throw another man to the ground in a wrestling contest. But he was a quick-witted young cove, and could be as intent on getting what he desired as an otter catching fish. One night, she told me, he slipped out of a back window while McGruder snored in his mother's bed, and went down to the quay. There, he got into a little rowboat, the biggest he could handle alone. He sculled unseen past the harbour entrance and headed determinedly out into the black and empty reaches of Esperantia Bay.

In his brave, innocent fury, he was bent, said Grace, her face at last becoming streaked and wet, on getting help from somewhere, anywhere – Ferryland, or Plaisance, Saint John's, who knows? But the next nearest landing-place of any kind was several leagues off, an impossible distance. The steep-to shores of western Avalon offer no refuge, no sanctuary from the sudden storms and southeasterlies. It needed no gale or tempest to overturn his fragile rowing boat, just a breath of rough weather, a slopping sea, a stiff headland breeze against a running tide. Oliver had likely got no further than a league from home before the sea took him.

The widow could hold back no longer. She flung herself face down on the sofa, her head buried in its cushions, intermittent sobs invading the room.

'Grace,' I said, moving to take her hand in mine.

She waved me away and stood up, trembling with the ordeal of recounting her agony.

'I must go,' she said, moving to the door. 'I left Sophie at the maid's cottage when I saw you coming up the hill. Is Caswell safe? He helps me look after her.'

'Caswell is safe,' I muttered. 'But why do the women not help you? Where are Lizzie Penn, and Mitty the maid?'

She blushed, embarrassed and confused.

'He kept them confined in the village,' she whispered.

She left unspoken what must have been, but I took her meaning. He had used them too as he wished.

She opened the door and let me into the passageway. At the last moment, she managed the semblance of a smile – a brave attempt though a remnant of her former self.

'Perhaps with time it shall become less raw.' Her voice was soft. 'For us all. For me. And for you, Matthew.'

I left Providence House without another word, walking away like a ghost. Numbed, making my way back down the hill, I cursed and cursed.

I cursed that evil, manipulative old soul, the Lady Trepanney. As if the memory were only yesterday, I saw myself poised awkwardly in the grand sitting room with its pictures painted in oils, the portraits of Trepanneys past, the Dowager's husband's imposing figure taking centre stage. Yet in the once rich and glowing fireplace of my memory, there lay nothing but grey cold dead ashes.

I cursed Esperantia too, for its divisions and conflict, for the way it drew me back, for holding me in its stifling grip.

But most of all I heaped profane curses upon the head of one man. Again and again I pictured what had happened to the young widow. I blamed myself for leaving her, for going on the *Beaver* mission, for not turning the bark for home when the chance had been there. Above all, I blamed myself for failing to see through that blandishing, predatory monster.

I cursed the soul of Finlay McGruder. I cursed him to Hell and back again.

Down on the beach, Lucy Skentles fussed over the wounded, arranging food and water for the tired warriors. When she came to me I brushed aside her ministrations, for no vittles nor any comforts mattered. Guy de Chenalles wanted to discuss the torn-down defences but I strode past with the briefest of words.

At the foreshore, a waiting seaman jumped at my sharp command. Eyes darting side to side not daring to meet mine, he rowed me swiftly out to the *Griffin*. In the waist stood Patrick Cluney, overseeing the repair work after the first action his neat little bark – or rather, my neat little bark – had seen. But I was not interested in that either.

'A word, Mister Cluney,' I said.

He fell in step with me, heading for the quarter-deck. At the break, Gaspar Rittel and Thomas Partridge, heads bent together in discussion, did not notice my arrival. Doubtless they were counting up the misfiring guns, the shot bags spent, the spare wads and rammers and roundshot left.

'Misters Rittel and Partridge,' I called, 'up to the quarter – sharply now.'

Startled, they jumped and both began talking at once.

'Be silent, fellows,' I said.

They closed up their traps and waited like rabbits at their burrows.

'How long before you can put this bark to sea?'

The Dutchman was first to protest. 'Why, captain, there are many breakages to repair.'

I turned to Cluney. 'Can she get under way in this state?'

'Aye, she can that,' he said, a touch proudly.

Then I addressed the Americkan. 'Mister Partridge, I want no crank ship. Take the spare guns from the *Forgiver* out of their firing tackles. Hoist them one by one on a boom, and release them into the water.'

He and Gasper let out a simultaneous gasp.

'Captain, those guns are valuable,' they chorused.

'I've no time for metal values,' I said. 'She'll have another knot of speed without them. Into the sea with them or you go over too, tied to their barrels. Dismissed.'

They all went off without another word. Soon, the weather-deck and the rigging were alive with jack-tars running about to set sail, soldiers and musketmen cleaning and charging their weapons, gunners hoisting the unwanted pieces into the boom tackle, youngsters nipping about with powder bags and wadding.

A boat bumped alongside. Before I could give the order to reel in the boarding rope, Josiah van Schreik hauled himself inelegantly over the rail. He held a paper in his hand, showing columns of figures in neat rows. He had been ashore assessing the damages, the cost of battle. I wondered what price he put on a man's life. Or a woman's honour.

He stood, affronted, staring at the first one tun piece as it swung outboard in the tackle. At my nod, Partridge gave an order and the straps were let go. The gun hit the water with a violent hissing eruption and descended into forty fathoms.

The Factor marched across the weather-deck and mounted the steps.

'Captain Loftus, what is this?' he cried. 'Those guns are of immense value. You cannot do this.'

I gave another nod and a second giant eruption of water announced another gun sent overside.

'Factor, have you been up to the batteries?'

'Indeed so. Everyone is arrested and the soldiers are in control,' he said testily. 'But why are you making the ship ready for –?'

'Has Guy de Chenalles remounted the defence positions?' I said.

More guns splashed into the deep.

'He has, and I have counted the broken muskets. But as Factor here I insist that –'

'As Factor nothing,' I said, rounding on him. 'As Deputy Intendant, I am bent on recovering certain stolen property of mine. Namely, the trading bark, the *Pursuant*.'

The guns were all gone. The *Griffin*'s bower cable was up and down, the anchor resting on the seabed. She shifted as the breeze caught her topsides. Men were out on the yards, busily loosing canvas. The anchor clanged home at the beak and was set in its catheads. I craned up to look under the mizen gear and saw the topsails set and drawing. The bark was under way.

'Steersman, take her out towards the heads,' I ordered, and glanced over the taffrail. The *Griffin* began to leave a froth of bubbles astern. Two knots already, I reckoned. She had speed all right.

Van Schreik was still not done. 'Captain, all I shall say,' he continued, 'is that you have stretched your remit as far as it may go.'

'I thank you for the advice,' I said, then called, 'Mister Rittel, what's the delay? Set courses at once.'

Bending under the mizen course as it fell loose, I watched the canvas spread out on the fore and main, billowing in the wind. The braces were brought round for a beam reach, and with her sheets hauled home the *Griffin* heeled gently, picked up her skirts and headed for sea.

Van Schreik looked at me, searching for something to say, but I spoke first.

'Mister Cluney, see the Factor into his boat.'

He spun on his heel and stalked off. At the break, he paused on the top step.

'You might care nothing for the cost, captain. Yet I ask, have you weighed the consequences for your soul?'

'I have,' I said with all the restraint I could muster. 'Your boat is waiting.'

Minutes later, van Schreik's cutter was little more than a distant speck on the water. I turned my attention to seaward.

We cleared the harbour cruising out past Barrier Heights towards the open sea. The breeze filled in a touch stronger and the bark put her shoulder to the waves, creaming along in good order. The decks were busy with seamen settling her lines, boys running about seeing to the shot garlands and powder bags, men bowsing the anchors into the catheads for sea passage.

The *Pursuant* had been gone barely an hour. With the small gale of southerly wind prevailing, she might be making six knots, but, relieved of her extra guns, the freshly-lightened and limber *Griffin* could manage seven or better. We would soon overhaul our quarry.

Then I decided it must surely be Edward Hanson giving the sailing orders, not McGruder, who would more likely be skulking below, out of gunshot, supping his brandy for courage. And what might the good Captain Hanson think? Would he see the lost cause in trying to run? It was better to hide.

I shouted for the Dutchman to bring his clogged feet back to the quarter-deck as fast as they would carry him. He was expecting a new course, or orders for more canvas. Instead, when I spoke, his eager face fell like a brass cannon dropped overside.

'Mister Rittel,' I said, 'when you were aboard the *Pursuant* with McGruder and Hanson, what role did you have?'

He turned down the corners of his mouth and shrugged, as if wondering where this might be leading.

'No doubt they forced you,' I suggested, 'to continue in your established capacity?'

He took on a shifty look.

'You were not her sailing master, as before, under me?'

He gave an uncertain shake of the head.

'I see. On pain of punishment, perhaps, they made you accept the role of first mate?'

He nodded guiltily.

'And in that capacity, did you discuss with Captain Hanson the nature of the Avalon coast?'

He answered quickly. 'Ya, captain, of course, because we had to bring the bark home here and so –'

He trailed off.

'Aye, of course. And did you mention any nooks and crannies? Hiding places for a bark, somewhere she could turn and make a stand?'

He opened and closed his mouth. No words came.

'Very well, Mister Rittel, I think you know what I am talking about. Now, I suggest you take the *Griffin* there.'

He gaped. 'Captain, I –'

'Jump to it, man!' I shouted, and he leapt away like a demented hare, babbling orders to his astonished seamen.

Patrick Cluney, having listened in silence to this exchange, now came over.

'Captain Loftus, would it be out of place to ask where we are going that exercises the Dutchman so much?'

'Mister Cluney,' I said, 'we are going to where Finlay McGruder is hiding my stolen bark.'

He looked puzzled.

'The *Griffin* is bound,' I told him, 'for Skull Cove.'

21

Stern Chase

'The lookouts spy nothing, captain,' reported Gaspar.

That was unsurprising. The bluffs were tall enough to hide any masts. We were two cables off the rocky, steep-to shore of northern Avalon, a mile or so from Esperantia. Before us was a blank sheer cliff into which was cut a cleft like an axe-mark in a soft log. There was little breeze, but a lazy surge at the entrance fringed the cliff base with a white, foaming collar. The slight swell was southwesterly, its scend passing straight inside.

Patrick Cluney stood patiently at the break while the flustered young Dutchman sailed his bark, the *Griffin*. With Thomas Partridge there too, my quarter-deck was well over-officered. But what a fine chance for Gaspar to show off his mettle.

'Mister Rittel,' I said, 'will you take us in through the gap?'

He looked dubiously at the entrance.

'I suggest topsails alone,' I said. 'And put down two launches, one ahead and one astern, ready with their towing lines.'

'Ya, captain, good idea.' He spoke so quietly it was almost lost in the wind.

'Mister Cluney,' I called, 'gunners to load doubled roundshot.'

He moved off to the waist. Gaspar, horrified, was about to speak, but I cut him off.

'Doubled roundshot, Mister Cluney,' I repeated.

No one was left in any doubt about my intentions. Patrick Cluney barked out the orders and at once a form of mayhem broke out all across the weather-deck – mayhem to a lubberly eye, but these fellows knew their business and went about it well.

There was only one way to get the bark inside – with a firm hand on the wheel, no hesitation and a direct approach. Rittel knew it. He collected up all his sailing skills and let the bark drive ahead. She came round as the seamen sweated home the sheets and braced up for a reach. Then he let her stand in with good speed and steerage way. The gap was so narrow its width matched the *Griffin*'s length. She slushed through with the stone portals only a few fathoms either side. When she rounded the narrow entrance and negotiated the dog-leg, we had a clear sight into the head of the cove.

I stared, unable to speak, my heart weighing like a stone. Before us was a solidly built vessel of perhaps a hundred foot length on deck, with a fifteen foot bowsprit. She boasted a short three-masted square rig with topsails. She wore a distinctly blunt look about the beak, as if she were made to push stub-bornly against a sea, or against ice, such a stout and motherly little vessel. She was the *Pursuant*, and it stung me to the core to see her.

The bark lay at the far end where rock buttresses closed in on three sides. Mooring lines snaked out from every quarter, made off to stakes driven into rock wedges or tied round boulders. She held herself no more than five or ten fathom from the walls, tethered like a nervous mare in a stall. She rocked on the sluggish, threatening swell creeping sibilantly in through the gap.

I had not clapped eyes on her since Irocaibi and I were stranded with Eli Savary's corpse. I did not want to see her like this. She was like an animal awaiting slaughter, trussed in her mooring lines, restive and fearful.

If any doubts had lingered about McGruder's presence, they were dispelled the instant I brought the spy-glass to bear on the quarter-deck. There was the cocky figure in his dress of a gentleman's coat and briches, with a tricorn hat added as if he were some variety of a seaman, standing out from the plainer garb of the men around him. Seeing us, he dived below. Squinting closer, I watched a storm of argument amongst his crew, their arms waving in angry gestures. How long would the Scotsman's fellows stick by him? Long enough to cause us trouble, was the answer. Spying the *Griffin,* they ran aloft with muskets and sent down a spasmodic fire.

I called to Thomas Partridge, 'Musketmen to the tops.'

Some of McGruder's men aboard the *Pursuant* went to the guns and loosed off a ragged attempt at a broadside, amounting to a volley of no more than two or three roundshot. The balls fell short or veered either side, crashing into the cliffsides amidst a welter of rock shards. Patrick Cluney threw me a questioning look as his men held lighted linstocks over the touch-holes. The enemy has fired first, his face said.

Gaspar Rittel was beside himself. 'Captain, I beg you –'

'Gunners!' I said. 'Wait for my order.'

Deep inside the cut, there was no breeze. The *Griffin* lost way and stopped.

'Bunt up your topsails, Mister Rittel, they're no longer drawing. Send the tows ahead.'

The launches went out, lurching and heaving across the swell. Was the surge simply working against the confining walls, or had it risen in the last few minutes?

Intermittent musket fire gave out from the *Pursuant*. One unlucky oarsman caught a ball and slumped over his sweep.

'Return musket fire,' I called.

A cry went up from the Americkan and instantly the discharges cracked forty feet above our heads. The balls sang across and spattered like flung gritstones on the *Pursuant*'s deck. Every man aboard threw himself flat.

The *Griffin* towed slowly onwards until I told Rittel to have her pulled round.

'Mister Cluney,' I called down into the waist, 'ready with your broadside?'

Gaspar hopped from one foot to the other like a little boy. The *Pursuant* lay before us, a duck on a pond, right under our guns. And she was, after all, the bark he had always longed to command.

'Captain Loftus,' he wailed, 'please don't –'

'Give fire,' I said.

Down came Cluney's arm and the *Griffin*'s broadside went off like a sprung mechanism, all six pieces roaring in unison. Blasts of smoke and heat burst around the weather-deck and a low growl rumbled off the sheer cliff walls. The aim was good, the gunners' eyes sharp, but they could hardly have missed. The doubleshots – twelve six-pound balls in all – smashed into the bark at point blank range. Some thudded into the topsides and opened dark holes. Others ripped clean through the rails and tore across the decks, splintering her boards with their destructive force.

I had sent down a broadside on my own little bark.

No answering shots came. Cluney's gunners reloaded without ado. Two minutes later they stood, linstocks at the ready, awaiting the word.

'Hold your fire,' I said. Lifting up the hailing piece, I bellowed into its iron mouth. 'McGruder, surrender now – let your fellows live!'

'We surrender!' came a ragged cry.

Most of the fifteen or twenty fellows left aboard simply abandoned ship, throwing themselves over the side and striking out for the nearby shore. Some failed to reach it, though not through freezing in the ice-cold water. The swell, gaining now in strength, dashed them bone-breakingly against boulders, hurling them again and again onto the unyielding walls until they floated face down like rag-dolls.

One or two of the *Griffin*'s musketmen aloft swung their weapons and started firing on those still swimming. I glanced up angrily, until I saw they were Avalon fishermen, the fellows I had pressed. McGruder and his men had killed their friends, raped their womenfolk, destroyed their livelihoods. If anyone did, then I shared their need for a vengeance. But it was not to be yet, not this way.

'Aloft – hold your fire!' I bellowed.

The shooting died away, but the first balls had found their marks. The waters of Skull Cove, already churned and frothing from the rising surge, reddened. Bodies floated everywhere, flung this way and that on each succeeding wave. A few of McGruder's surviving crew reached a tiny strand, no more than a steep shingle ledge, where they moped dispirit-edly on the barren rocks, awaiting the outcome of the confrontation. On all sides, the cove ended in blank walls of sheer stone rearing up. There was no escape for them from the death's head trap that was Skull Cove.

The building swell made the *Pursuant* tug ever more desperately at her mooring lines. Even our tows found difficulty in holding the *Griffin* on sta-tion. There was not much time to save my bark now.

'McGruder,' I shouted, 'give yourself up.'

'You shall have to fight me first, Loftus!' came a far-off cry. It was the Scotsman's accents, though he had not showed himself.

'Don't delude yourself,' I cried, 'that you are worth it.'

'I've had everything of yours,' he called, 'that was worth having.'

I was stunned into a momentary silence.

Then a pair of figures appeared on the *Pursuant*'s quarter-deck – the last men left aboard. Each time the bark heaved on a swell and snatched at her lines, they staggered. Then they fell together and struggled. There came the crack of a light shot, echoing off the high walls. One of the two fell and lay still. The spy-glass showed the fellow standing to be Finlay McGruder, a smoking pistol in one hand.

'There's been enough killing, McGruder!' I shouted into the speaking cone. 'You can't escape.'

He looked around, then disappeared down the stern hatchway. Seconds after, at the dayroom's sidelights, a face showed, mouthing words. Faint though it was, all of us on the *Griffin*'s quarter caught enough to understand.

'Come and get me, Loftus, if you dare.'

I raised the cone again. 'McGruder, where's the Indian chief?'

The face appeared again at the sidelight and the words drifted over.

'Train your spy-glass at the hatchway!'

Seconds later, the head and shoulders of a man rose above the stout coamings of the hatch opening. Bareheaded and gaunt-faced, restrained by some manner of bonds or chains, he nevertheless wore a proud and haughty bearing. It was unmistakeably Chanatuk, chief of the Missacaibi peoples. Then the figure vanished from sight as though yanked from below.

'Come aboard, Loftus,' came the cry again, 'or the savage dies.'

Gaspar Rittel gripped my arm. 'Captain, you must not go.'

The cornered McGruder had nothing left to lose. Chanatuk was his last card, and he gambled that I wanted the chief alive. He was right. Little could be salvaged now from his depredations, save for one thing – my vow to the dying Irocaibi.

'Bring up from my cabin the two small pistols,

first mate,' I said, 'primed and charged. Collect me a couple of spare knives too. Have the cutter lowered.'

At the boarding rope, Gaspar fussed around like a mother hen. All I wanted was to get to McGruder before the bark cracked herself open on the rocks. The swells had grown, and were fairly raging in.

'Is there something on your mind, Mister Rittel,' I said, hoisting myself on to the rail, 'such as saving the *Pursuant* from being dashed to pieces? I forebore to pound her into smithereens, as you feared. Now, as you see, I am doing my very best to get to her before she breaks up.'

'Ya captain, but –'

'Aye, I know. If I die, you shall have command.'

He should have been pleased, but his face fell.

'Captain,' said Gaspar, his voice sounding forced, 'you remember the whales' heads? All those little carvings.'

'In my dayroom, on the seatback? What about them, man?'

With sudden fierceness, he caught my sleeve. Tears sprang from his eyes.

'When you were gone, I – I did not want anyone else to have her. Not McGruder, not anyone.'

Half over the rail, I stopped. 'What have you done, Gaspar?'

His accent became thicker than ever.

'*O Gott in hebben*,' he muttered. 'I found the channels leading from the whale's tongue.'

I closed my eyes in despair. 'The right-whale's tongue?'

'Ya, captain,' he said in a misery of remorse. 'I ran a matchfuse down to the magazine.'

Alone, facing astern, I stroked across to the *Pursuant*. As the little boat rose high on each passing surge, my gaze was fixed back at the *Griffin*'s lofty rigging crowded with silent ranks of seamen and musketmen, waiting.

Behind me, the Scotsman called out, 'Loftus, you come unarmed or not at all!'

I rowed on under the bulging topsides. They lifted five and six feet, then lurched back down in a welter of foam. The shore lines snapped taut, her bitts creaking with strain, then fell slack. Ceaselessly, the bark tugged this way and that, trying to break free.

McGruder shouted from the sidelight, 'Strip off your jacket and throw it in the water.'

I hesitated.

'My pistol's at the savage's temple, Loftus, and the lock's sprung back.'

I divested myself and threw the jacket into the water, along with the pistols. It sank so fast that McGruder let out a triumphant laugh.

'Your boots too – into the water with them.'

As I tugged the heavy sea boots free, both spare knives clattered from their hiding places into the cutter's bottom ribs, and the Scotsman chuckled again. The boots went over the side and I lifted the knives for him to see, then let them splash into the depths.

'Stand up,' commanded the Scot.

Cautiously, I rose, balancing in the tossing boat, and raised my arms.

'Shirt as well, captain, then turn right round once.'

I took off the chemise, spun once in the boat, then stood there in the cool autumnal air, bare-chested and unshod.

'You may keep your briches on for modesty, my friend,' he laughed, 'and that fine-tooled belt of yours to hold them. Step up to the quarter with your arms held up.'

I went hand over hand up the heavy, knotted boarding rope, crossed the waist and took the steps in two strides. Reaching the quarter-deck, I stopped short. A man lay quite still in the spreading pool of his own life-blood. He seemed asleep, his body untensed, but he must have heard my approaching tread on the boards.

'Help me,' croaked Captain Hanson.

'Leave him be, Loftus,' called the Scot, 'or I'll blow out the savage's brains. Come down to my dayroom.'

His dayroom, I thought. Had he left me nothing?

'I'm sorry, Edward,' I said, and stepped away.

Lowering myself into the hatchway, expecting at any moment to meet the blast of a pistol at close range, I went guardedly down the steps and passed through the doorway. Light flooded from the cabin as I reached the threshold, palms raised.

'Stop there, Loftus.'

Finlay McGruder sat opposite, grinning. He had a pistol in his right hand. The other was covered in a filthy, ragged bandage, I supposed from my shot during his and Hanson's mutiny. From the doorway, I could see no sign of Chanatuk.

Spread across the captain's table in front of the

Scotsman was an array of weaponry that an army soldier might have envied – straight swords and cutlasses, knives long and short, more pistols including a heavy long-barrelled example and a pair of old-fashioned lightweight matchlock pieces. With each surging wave, the collection slid first one way across the polished surface, hit the fiddle rail, then slid the other way, clinking rhythmically back and forth as the ship struggled in her bonds.

'Lock these on and hand me back the key.'

McGruder threw a pair of manacles over. I caught them instinctively and put my hands in the iron rings, which were joined by a six-inch length of chain. With some difficulty, I closed the hasp and turned the key. Two-handed, I tossed it back. He slipped it into his weskit pocket and nodded me towards a chair set apart from the table.

As I stepped forward warily, the Indian came into view from behind the door, which was flung back wide on its locking catch. He was manacled and shackled, bound to a floor-fixed chair some six feet from me.

'Chief Chanatuk,' I said, and bowed my head. Not a flicker of recognition or acknowledgement crossed his countenance.

'He's my King, Loftus, but you are my Ace.' McGruder gave a derisive snort. 'Won't Cousin Tompion be thrilled when he sees my catch? I have the native leader and at the Royal Court I shall deliver the Missacaibi people's acquiescence to the Sovereign in some certain style. Now to boot I have Loftus the traitor. The savage and the spy!'

He laughed.

'Chanatuk won't sign away his people, McGruder.'

'O, he will. Wait till the Navy tries him with the surgeon's tools. Then there's the prospect of an entertaining court case to follow. At long last, the spying and double-dealing Matthew Loftus brought to justice, facing the scaffold. Some compensation for that fool Hanson depriving us of his corpus for a cannibalism trial. An inconsiderate act, to die like that.'

I stared coldly back. 'He's not quite dead. Why did you shoot him?'

'He wanted to surrender the bark.'

The *Pursuant* tugged sharply at her mooring lines so that I staggered. I heard the hempen ropes creaking with protest at the fairleads.

McGruder barely paid attention. 'I quite lost my temper with the man,' he said. 'He was a damm'd nuisance from the first. He's got his comeuppance.'

There was an open brandy bottle on the table. The Scotsman had let the drink take hold.

'The Admiral shan't be well pleased at this outcome,' I said quietly.

'Quite the contrary. Tompion shall be most tickled with my capture of a celebrated spy.'

The room reeked of spirits, but there was something else too, a strong odour quite unfamiliar within the *Pursuant*'s dayroom, or anywhere aboard ship. I realised that the scent of oil-lamps pervaded the cabin, the aromatick tang giving no doubt that they were fuelled by hot-burning whale-oil. One hung suspended from a hook in the deckhead, swinging ever more crazily by the minute. A second stood on the sideboard at McGruder's elbow, slithering back and forth each time the bark rocked. Though they gave out a superior, inflaming glow, no one but a landlubber would allow oil-burning wick-lamps below decks. For a seaman, it was candle-lanterns or nothing, for they doused themselves. Then I remembered McGruder complaining my candle-light was too dim for close work.

The Avalon fog of the dawning hours had altogether cleared away, and the day held fine, with a bright morning sun streaming through the sternlights.

'You have forgotten to extinguish your night-lamps,' I said.

He seemed not to hear. 'My cousin the admiral has been busy patrolling the Breton Channel.'

'The John Cabot Strait,' I said, 'is the more patriotickal name.'

'What? Well, I am expecting him to show himself back in Avalon any day.'

'Don't count on it, McGruder.'

He swallowed a draught and smiled. 'Surely we can be on better terms of intimacy. First names, Matthew, a drink and a yarn?'

I ignored this. 'The Grand Fleet passed through the Breton Channel and into the Gulf. Tompion was nowhere to be seen.'

Just then the *Pursuant* gave a sickening lurch sideways and parted a stern line. She slewed nearer the unforgiving shore. Through the dayroom lights, I saw the wet, grey rock walls a few fathoms away, rising and falling. Wrapped in his delusions, the Scotsman took no notice.

'The French Grand Fleet? Good news! That plays into our hands. If the fleet's in the Gulf, the Frenchies have reneged on the Chessapeak Bay Accord. And if it's in the Gulf, then it surely means the admiral could declare the waters of Newfoundland clear of the enemy.'

I could not hold back my derision. 'He should be Court-martialled!'

Again, it passed the Scotsman by. 'The admiral shall take custody of his prisoners and install his cousin in a splendid cabin for the Atlantick journey home. Why Matthew, I shall be at Deptford in a month.'

As he spoke, I sensed a huge surge lifting the stern. It raised the bark higher than ever then dropped her back down. Under the impossible strain, she snapped another line and lurched violently. The sideboard lamp shot downhill and tipped itself onto the table. The oil spilled across McGruder's knees. Next instant, it flared into a sheet of flame.

'Dammit!' he cried, jerking backwards.

Yellow flickering tongues of fire ran across the table. Stray splashes of hot oil instantly set the charts and volumes on the sideboard to smouldering. The burning liquid ran on the cabin sole and licked at my bare feet.

As the Scotsman beat ineffectually at the flames, I lunged. McGruder's pistol swung towards me. Before his finger closed the trigger, there was a double explosion. A blast of heat hit me in the face and something sharp bit into the flesh on my forearms. The Scotsman flung himself into a crouch as metal and splinters flew about the confines, clanging on the deckhead, thudding into the bulkhead panels. The oil fire had set off a weapon on the table. Two or three others had detonated in sympathy and blown themselves apart.

Chanatuk let out a cry and tried to sheer out of his seat, but the bindings caught him. Still manacled, I awkwardly snatched a long-bladed cutlass from the flaming wreckage on the table. The Scotsman fell back and tried again to aim a pistol. The poor *Pursuant* struck the rock walls a second time, throwing him sideways. Jabbing with his bandaged hand to save himself, he let out a tortured scream.

With the cutlass blade held out, gripping it two-handedly, I launched myself at him. Heat and smoke seared my face as I flung myself across the table with my whole body behind the cutlass. The blade touched his jacket front and McGruder's eyes opened wide. The pistol bucked in his hands as the pan flashed and the charge fired, sending golden sparks in all directions. Where the ball went only the Lord knows or cares.

My forward motion was unstoppable. The *Pursuant* tried to give a hand by crashing her afterparts against the rocks. Rather than unfooting me, it added to my momentum and threw me forward. The cutlass blade struck bone, then slid off and penetrated the barrier of the Scotsman's ribcage. With all my strength and will behind it, the steel drove into the yielding organs, slicing the innards as it went, progressing through his body from front to back. There was a jarring shock as the blade's tip struck the bench behind.

The seatbacks were made of good Newfoundland maplewood, fine-grained and hard. The carpenter had built them with the grain perpendicular, for it pleased the eye that way. Now the cutlass blade, after tasting flesh and bone and lung and muscle, its work almost done, entered the wood going with the grain. Splitting the half-inch panel, the steel plunged itself into the space behind and jammed. At the other end, where I was, its hilt pressed hard against the cloth of McGruder's fur jacket. The handle was buried in its folds. We were face to face, an inch apart.

'God's mercy,' said the Scot, writhing under me like a stuck pig.

He put his hands on mine, clutching like a brother or a lover. The naked skin of my back was hot, agonisingly hot, for it was covered in flaming oil. Smoke, black and choking, filled the dayroom.

Flinging myself free, I dived across the room into the thickening fog, seeking Chanatuk. Fumbling at my leather belt, I drew out from its hiding-place in my belt my little model knife with its two inch-long blade, the life-saving knife every seaman carries lest he is caught in a rope's bight and swept overboard or tangled aloft like a rabbit in a snare. The billowing oilsmoke parted and Chanatuk appeared before me, bound to the chair, writhing. Under my slashing strokes, the bonds fell apart and I all but threw him at the doorway. He fell through it and stumbled up the steps.

The ship, her shorelines parting one by one, hurled herself against the rock walls with teeth-jarring force. There was going to be little of her left to save, but I had to try.

'Help me!' cried McGruder, pinioned in the searing heat of the fire.

I turned back towards the voice, but the smoke

was too thick to see. Going at the flames with anything that came to hand – old charts and volumes, a broken cross-staff, even the loose ropes of Chanatuk's bindings – I fought my way over to him. The blaze was strong. It already had hold of the deckhead. When I reached McGruder, he looked exhausted, his horror-struck face streaked with sweat and tears.

'I'm caught, Loftus,' he wailed.

I beat at the flames about his head, trying to extinguish them. Pathetically, he looked grateful. But I was not intent on saving him. He was dead meat anyway, run through the guts, skewered to the bark he stole from me.

'Help me, for God's sake,' he said.

Suddenly, I had my face right next to his.

'I'd burn in Hell before lifting a finger for you,' I hissed.

Savagely, I knocked his head aside as he twisted and banged it against the wood. His was a doomed, hopeless struggle, but perhaps mine was not. I was trying to save my bark.

For half a second, the smoke cleared from the panelling at the seat where the *Pursuant*'s captain habitually poised at his work. Behind was revealed the miniature carved wooden crest of the right-whale's head. Its cavernous mouth was open. I put my hand inside, feeling for the tongue, but my fingers touched only specks of gritty, burnt dust. The whale's tongue was gone, and so was the fuse.

The flames from the lamp fire had lit Gaspar's fuseline and sent it on its way. Its business end, long disappeared beyond reach and leaving only a charred trail, would be sparking briskly through the hidden channels, ever further into the deep spaces below. It was too late.

Struggling in the blackness, I pushed myself clear of the Scotsman's threshing limbs and groped for the doorway. The last thing I heard as I fought my way to the companionway steps was Finlay McGruder's strangulated cry, an unashamed appeal to all the gods and spirits and humours and graces of the Earth and the Heavens. He was a man about to die with self-abasement upon his lips.

When my head broke above the hatchway, Chanatuk was at the taffrail, stunned, retching and coughing. There was no time to get him down a boarding rope and into the boat. I shouted for him to run forward, but of course he could not comprehend. Only Hubert Nitchequot could talk to him, and the half-caste was waiting aboard the *Griffin*. With my two chained hands together, I hefted up the old chief, lifting his feet from the deck-boards. Half starved after months of captivity he was all but weightless, too weak to resist. Barely breaking my stride, I slung him across my shoulder and bore him the length of the weather-deck, bent only on reaching the foc'sle in time. I bounded up the steps and threw us both flat to the boards behind the raised scantlings between the hatchway and the beak. Chanatuk struggled, but I held him down.

'Help here!' came a faint cry from far aft.

Peering out from cover, expecting to see McGruder somehow having dragged the cutlass blade from his belly, my eye fell instead on Edward Hanson. Wreathed in choking smoke, he had got to his feet and staggered to the break. Sixty feet from me, he leant on the rail like a drunk, the eyes unfocused. His head drooped, his legs wobbled unsteadily. I opened my mouth to shout at him to get clear. The words died on my lips. At that moment, Hell on Earth broke loose.

If the sound and the rage of the *Griffin*'s guns going at full stretch had been like the roar of the Devil himself, what happened next was more akin to the boom heralding the world's very end. As I went down, I glimpsed Hanson's body blasted forward and upward from the quarter-deck like a child's plaything, hands and arms outstretched, head lolling. Eyes tight shut, I held Chanatuk's old body as if in an eternal embrace.

The *Pursuant*'s sternparts disappeared altogether, converted in a single instant to matchwood, kindling sticks and splinters. Thunder rolled around Skull Cove, echoing off the walls. A clattering rain followed as the debris, lofted into the air for a hundred feet or more, fell back across the waist and foreparts. When I looked again, all that was left of the bark's stout timbers from the break of the quarter right aftwards was a mass of broken, blazing shards amidst a dense thundercloud of seething smoke. The mizen mast, its yards and rigging, the quarter-deck, the wheel, the compass binnacle, the companion hatchway, the stern chases, taffrail, jackstaff – all gone, reduced to mere smoking ruins. A few desultory fires burned here and there. All around, blackened and split timbers fell into the water, raising plumes.

The magazine had been immediately below the captain's dayroom. The fuse's spark had entered the tightly packed powder store via the secret channelling that Carpenter Sedgewick had not had the time to destroy, and behind which Eli Savary had stowed away. But Gaspar had found those channels and ways. If the Dutchman followed gunners' practice, his fuse-line would have run like a dart to a carefully placed central keg in the powder room, holding fifteen pounds or so of hard-tamped saltpetre, the lid dogged down tight against a top-wadding. The force of its ignition in the enclosed, dry space was enough. It had set off the magazine in its entirety, in a single explosion.

Of Hanson, the only sign was a ragged arm, still cloth-clad, falling back to the blackened, smouldering deck-boards. Finlay McGruder must have gone to his Maker in a thousand torn pieces, only a few of them contrite.

The *Pursuant* lurched like a drunk. With her afterparts blown open to the sea, she faced a rapid end. The weather-deck tilted crazily, listing by the stern as water rushed into the ship's gaping hull, forcing the bow upwards. My feet scrabbled for grip on the quickening slope as the foc'sle canted abruptly. I raised myself off Chanatuk. Black smuts and charcoal streaked his face. He wiped his eyes, blinking, his gaze wandering. He seemed stunned by the force of the blast.

'We must get off, Chanatuk,' I gasped, my mouth dry as a desert.

I lifted his arm, hoping he would understand and follow. Suddenly, his hands were snatching at my belt. In irritation, I pulled him again, urging him up as the bow tilted ever more steeply. Then I looked down, non-plussed. The Indian had my little short-bladed knife daggered at my belly. I threw off his arm and stepped back.

'No, Chanatuk,' I cried. 'I am a friend! Friend!'

He did not understand.

'Irocaibi, Irocaibi!' I shouted, all but losing my footing as the deck steepened.

A look of puzzlement came over his face.

'Your son – Irocaibi was my friend,' I said in desperation, grabbing at the rail to stop myself sliding away.

Irocaibi. The name registered and a shadow passed across his face, a black look of deadly vengeance. He was going to kill me.

But instead of lunging, Chanatuk did something I cannot rid from my mind. He swapped the seamen's knife end for end and held it out at arm's length. Gripping the handle so hard that his knuckles whitened, he pointed the tip at his own throat. Then he let go a tortured cry and brought the blade in an arcing sweep across his neck. The short steel, so keenly whetted, sliced the collar of his buckskin jacket and opened the flesh behind. Red liquid sprayed out fully three feet, spattering the deck, running down the caulking lines of the sloping boards. Rooted, I watched in horror as he drew back the blade and held it ready. His gaze fell on me, unseeing and vacant, as he slashed and stabbed again and again.

The bark's forepeak reared up like a bucking horse. She was going down. I threw myself on top of the Indian and wrested the blade away. Raising him up, with a single thrust I flung him clean over the rail and plunged overside after him. The icy shock of the sea-water stunned me, but I saw Chanatuk's limbs thrashing only a fathom off. With the Indian chief wrapped in my arms, struggling still but ever more weakly, I struck out, hampered by the manacles, making a desperate bid to clear the *Pursuant*. Her bows stood high, the sprit pointing at forty five degrees into the air. The hull was under water as far as the waist, where boarding ropes and other detritus now floated freely about her rails.

She was dying. With something like the sigh of a slaughtered animal, she slid backwards and went gurgling and foaming beneath the surface, descending fifty fathoms to the bottom of Skull Cove.

Chanatuk groaned. We were swimming in a widening circle of red-hued water. The surface boiled with gasps of stale air bursting upwards from the sinking bark. The Indian chief frothed scarlet at the lips and, like the ship itself, issued gurgles from somewhere deep inside. Then he doubled up in agony, the muscles tensing, and was suddenly still. Like his son before, he too died in my arms.

A shadow cut the morning sun in half, and the stem of the *Griffin*'s longboat appeared above my head. Many hands reached down and hauled me dripping over the gunnels. The dead native chief was brought aboard, a shrunken crumpled thing like a half empty sack of barrel-corks.

Slumped across the thwarts, staring dumbly into the bottom ribs, unable to look up and take in the devastation that was Skull Cove, I struggled to understand how it had happened this way. The

424

Pursuant was gone. The Indian was dead. Grace violated.

I had got my revenge on McGruder, yet lost everything that mattered.

22

Settled Terms

July 1709: the Sovereign Settlement of Esperantia

Standing at the end of the garden contemplating the view over the bay, I heard footsteps skittering along the roadway towards me. At once I hid Sir Oliver Trepanney's magnificent long spy-glass behind my back. Seconds later, a little boy came bounding round the hedge and dashed up the pathway, red-faced and breathless as if he had run full pelt all the way from the wharfside without stopping. Under his arm he carried a bundle of packets.

Catching sight of me, he pattered to a halt.

'Here they are, sir,' he panted, handing me the ribbon-tied bundle.

The sloop had arrived from Saint John's. The despatches were weighty, being the first brought down from the capital since the winter ice broke. News of the war at last, I thought, and all the Governor's business too, sent down to his servant in the Avalon Peninsula.

'May we go in, sir,' said the boy, hopping excitedly, 'to see the new house and then –?'

He stopped short, having caught hold of the fact that I was hiding something.

'Sir, is it the long tube you have there? May I look, sir? O please, may I!'

I held up the spy-glass and said, 'Master Penn, this is the finest instrument in all Newfoundland, a prize piece if ever there was one. Can you remember how you're to handle it?'

'Aye, sir, I can that,' said Caswell. Planting his legs squarely apart, he raised his empty arms as if holding a musket. One eye closed, he squinted down the imaginary sights and said, 'A ship! Captain, sir – I spy a ship!'

'Very good, first mate,' I said briskly, 'and now for the real thing.'

When the tube was opened to its fullest extent it was almost as tall as the boy, yet he took it with a firm grasp and braced himself to lift it into position.

'A steady sweep right across the sea horizon,' I reminded him. 'Squint close along the line. And remember to skip where the sunlight's bright on the water or for ten minutes you shan't see anything in that eye but green spots.'

After scanning the empty bay and the desert seascape beyond, he said, disappointed, 'Nothing there, sir. Not a bark in sight.'

I took the tube back. 'Aye, but any day now. It's a fast thaw this year, and they'll come south with the bergs.'

'Icebergs,' he repeated, his eyes widening. 'I want to go to sea, sir. To sail north to the ice lands and see the seals and the white bears.'

'Well now, some boys go to sea at thirteen,' I said. He was two years shy of that, and his chagrin was plain. Then I added, 'But some go to sea at twelve.'

He brightened a touch. 'Next year for me, then, sir?'

I shook my head. 'Perhaps not. After all, your captain here did not go to sea at that age. He went to sea before he'd reached eleven years.'

It took a second to dawn. He opened his mouth to speak, but faltered. I could not keep him in misery any longer.

'Aye, Caswell, I think you shall go aboard one of my barks this summer. Learn something of the sea's ways and see your first winter here in Newfoundland waters. Then next year you may venture north to Labrador.'

His face shone with excitement.

'Labrador,' he whispered.

'Shall I take that as an aye, Caswell?'

'Aye, sir,' he said, still doubtful about my teasing.

'A little more conviction, Master Penn?'

'Aye aye, captain!' he said smartly.

'Very well. Dismissed into the garden to see the little miss.'

As he ran off calling for Sophie, I walked meditatively back up the path past the remains of old Providence House, which had been torn down to make way for something less forbidding, less sullied. The building works were finished and many of our things had already been removed from the maid's cottage, which we had been staying in meantime. Now – this very night – we would take ourselves into the new house.

I stopped to admire its handsome front elevation. It was done in the Queen Anne style, as some called it – though with rough-hewn Newfoundland stone quoins and a lack of stucco for the walls it would hardly pass muster in the grander parts of Gray's Inn or Bow or Bermondsey. But it was a fine, well-lit dwelling with tall windows, and it lifted my spirits that the old Dowager's gloomy interiors were gone forever. And it was fitting that Providence House's tomb-like walls, raised up halfway through the last century, should provide the founds for its successor to sit upon.

On the upper storey, sited centrally above the porticoed doorway, I had incorporated a particular feature, a tall arched window stretching almost from floor to eaves. At that window soon would stand the advanced Newton telescope I had ordered from England. In the great room behind, stretched around the walls, were shelves of charts and log-books, and my instrument racks. That was the room Caswell was so eager to visit. For him, it represented a treasure house of the sea and sailing.

New Beginning Manor, I thought – how the name grows on me. I had once considered calling it Pursuant House, but it was turning out a far more graceful form than my poor, stout old trading bark. The past is the past, I told myself, and this house and its name are unquestionably well suited to its intended occupants.

I took a last glance at the waters stretching from Stack Beach past Vantage Rise and out to Barrier Heights, and beyond to where the open reaches became an endless expanse of blue-grey sea. The early summer sun, still shy and low in the sky, had the colour of weak small beer. But the horizon remained blank and empty of ships, my own ships, the ships I knew must be making their way south from fur trading in Labrador.

This had been my first winter spent so far south for six years, and come to that my first sojourn ashore since I was a child. Shorebound, I had thrown myself into the responsibilities of my new position. Yet from time to time, ridding myself of the confinement of Esperantia, I had sailed out for a few days' fishing in a shallop. In December I had voyaged briefly to Saint John's and back in the small sloop the Navy sent for me just before the ice made the trip dangerous. Such sallies to sea were small compensation, and I sorely missed the venturesome nature of my old fur trips.

The expected barks should heave into view soon. Then, after greetings and songs and ale in the Skentles' rebuilt publick house, the Open Arms Tavern, the bargaining would begin and Factor van Schreik's every word on price and value would be weighed and sorted and interpreted. There would be joy in the homecoming, but I would not share it quite as before. In gaining wealth and position, something I loved had been lost: a long sojourn at sea, a voyage of unknowns.

When I ducked low to enter the modest cottage rooms we had occupied while the house was built, I found Grace in her customary situation at a table near the open window. She was busy gathering and sorting the numerous papers and rolls and bundles of parchments stationed in neat piles on the polished pine-top.

She looked up and smiled. 'I am almost ready. O, have you the packets there?'

'Aye, all the news from London and Saint John's.'

A glance had told me they contained the expected stack of printed London journals the new Governor sent regularly for my edification. There would be reports of the war's progress, the treaties and accommodations under discussion, the Sovereign's financial rectitude or otherwise, the Treasury's latest imposts, and all the other crucial tidings from Europe. And there would be lists of the prices and quantities of cod, both wet- and dry-cured, landed at Toulon, Bordeaux, Brest, Calais, Portsmouth, Bristol and London.

As usual, there were letters too, mostly addressed to me, though one or two had the name of Mistress Trepanney on their fronts. This time I noticed a letter, from a more recent correspondent perhaps, addressed to Grace Loftus.

I contemplated her a moment, the womanly figure plainly visible now that she wore a lady's bodice and elegant skirts, a welcome alteration from the Dowager's anti-sumptuary rules, aimed at a ludicrously unattainable equality of appearance. Her dress was wide on the shoulders, revealing a few inches of smooth skin either side of her slender neck, the delicate breast bones apparent above curves accentuated by the flimsy lace handkerchief at the embonpoint, so in fashion according to the London journals' engravings. At twenty seven, she was the very flower of womanhood.

I let my gaze stray around the room. Many of the fine furnishings from the Dowager's days were still crammed into what had been Mitty's little house. The old long-case pendulum clock tocked loudly in the corner, the sideboard held its crocks and crystals still, waiting to be taken to the big house. The Dowager's splendid grate was refixed in New Beginning Manor, its ironwork freshly blackened in the brief pause until the first fires of autumn evenings. Even the portrait of Esperantia's grand founding father would be hung there, for Sir Oliver Trepanney had been an honourable man whose judgement I had respected.

Yet all this worldly comfort, even the prospect of our handsome new dwelling, amounted to so little. At night, I would climb the stairs and, as ever, pass by Grace's bedchamber to gain my own quarters next door, to lie alone.

Breaking into my thoughts came screams of joy and laughter from Sophie and Caswell as they ran around the garden, the boy no doubt chasing her with some gross insect he had caught.

I went over and bent towards Grace. All but imperceptibly, her head tilted away and her shoulders stiffened. Nevertheless, I briefly kissed her neck.

'Is it truly a year this November since we were married?' I said, taking her hands, cradling them in my own. I had rehearsed this little speech many times. 'There's been so much to do since then – the new charter, fettling the trading barks, the fishing rights, arranging the transports, the building works. All the matters I had to settle with the Navy, and the Governor too. So much busyness, that it's only in these last few weeks there's been time to think. And now the house is done, I've been considering our – well, our life together.'

Suddenly embarrassed, I wrenched my gaze away and directed it through the window, far out to the sea's blank horizon. My mind's eye reached leagues and leagues beyond, to the most distant reaches of Labrador, Ungava Bay and the Great Northern Cape, the tundra plains of Hudson's Bay and the forests of the Rupert River, or Nasquinoba. Since that voyage, my life had altered for the better in every respect, bar one. We had married within weeks of McGruder's death, an act which did much to preserve her reputation. But she had suffered too grossly, not just from the Scotsman's violations but from Oliver's drowning. Our marriage remained an empty union, unconsummated.

'Everything I did was for you, Grace,' I said, speaking my thoughts aloud.

She seemed to understand what was in my mind. 'Dearest, there's nothing more I could ask of you. All it wants is time.'

'Aye, and time you shall have,' I said firmly, patting her hand. 'I shan't make demands, you know that.'

She got up and busied herself collecting her bundles of papers, covering the moment of awkwardness between us. With a quiet sigh, I returned to contemplating the sea view while she made ready to go.

In the end, the Quebec Accord had been overtaken by events. The European war, though to many minds appearing far from having run its course, had nevertheless gone well enough for the Sovereign to tear up any and every proposal or bargain tabled, either by enemies or allies. Admiral Tompion had been ordered home to Portsmouth, and news from Boston confirmed the Grand Fleet had likewise been despatched back to Europe the moment it reached Quebec City. Tompion and his counterpart *amiral* had both been denied a chance to decide the issues by sea power – not much, I suspected, to either's chagrin.

Before the autumn of 1708 had turned to winter, Septimus Spurgeon was posted halfway round the globe and a new Governor, Courtenay Arnold, installed at Saint John's. He refused to underwrite any expeditions to Hudson's Bay and so Glaisterby's fort was never resupplied. What became of the lieutenant and his garrison I could not discover, but at least when the French land invasion was called off the Missacaibi peoples were freed from the threat of massacre. With Irocaibi and Chanatuk gone, they might be leaderless but I was greatly relieved to think that they were no longer in the war's eye.

Governor Arnold had granted me a charter in perpetuity for both Esperantia and Plaisance. I was handed the golden seal and announced Intendant Proper, and the vellums were in London now for the Sovereign Queen's assent. With peace and security the two settlements prospered abundantly. Material wealth began to come my way in some measure.

Plaisance came under the English Crown – or Great Britain's – from the day I took the *Griffin* there to declare my authority over it. The French had to all intents and purposes abandoned its citizens to their fate after Finlay McGruder's illegal seizure. The Catholicks he had transported chose to stay on at French Acadia rather than return to the dying wet-fish trade and I re-populated the settlement with Westcountry fishers. There were few Papists left in Esperantia either, due to the slump in price of their brine-cured cod. There was little profit in transporting such disfavoured produce to Europe, and mostly it went to the Carolinas and Caribbee as slave fodder. The dry-cured saltcod trade, meanwhile, flourished.

As for Josiah van Schreik, our Factor had proved himself all that the Dowager might ever have wished for in an agent – a shrewd bargainer with an unerring knack of setting the season's prices. As a result, Esperantia's markets for fish and furs got all the trade they could handle. I collected the imposts for Governor Arnold and took my ten per cent, which was enough to assure me of a regular income amounting by itself to fifteen thousand marks in a year. On the strength of that, I had bought two stout traders at five per cent credit and sent them north for the winter. With the price of furs landed at Amsterdam higher than ever, a single season's profits should pay them off. Unlike the *Griffin*, the barks would be mine by right.

Rather to my surprise, I found my new responsibilities quite diverting. Clearing Stack Beach, rebuilding the destroyed settlement, enlarging the wharf and throwing up my own marital quarters had left me less time to fret about not going to sea. Though the demands of being Intendant Proper helped alleviate the landbound nature of my life, Grace – bless her – had seen how I chafed. She knew I would go back to sea, sooner or later.

She came over with a bright face. 'Matthew, I am ready. Shall we go?'

I put the long-tube under my arm and, with

a last look round, we left the maid's cottage. A minute later we entered New Beginning Manor, going straight upstairs to the first floor viewing room where we stood side by side gazing out of my grand, glazed window. Its broad aspect took in the entirety of Esperantia Bay, giving line of sight to both Beacon Top and Vantage Rise. When it arrived, my new telescope would look well standing at this magnificent light.

The shelves of books and almanacks comforted me too, though there was one I treasured above all. When Tompion had sailed for England, he did not even bother to take my precious, confiscated pilot book, a repository of firsthand knowledge of the coasts and harbours and currents and shoals of Labrador and the North Shore, Newfoundland and Acadia. He left it at Providence House where I found it lying unread under the Dowager's old high-back chair. Thus he had discarded in the remote colony of Newfoundland the most worthwhile and practickal help for seamen in all British Americka, while he went to debate and bicker over the greatest fallacy of our time. The admiral was to come off sea service and take up a post at the Navy Board overseeing a newly established Prize for that deluding myth, the solving of the Longitude.

Smiling at the irony of this, I poured brandy into two crystals and handed one to my wife. We raised them up and toasted our new beginning.

'Will you examine the packets this evening?' she said. 'Tell me all the news from London?' She enjoyed my reading them aloud to her.

'I shall indeed. I know how they please you.'

'You have good reason to feel pleased too, Matthew. You have progressed a long way.'

The brandy tasted smooth and warm – cognac, of course, from the Petit Seigneur's abandoned mansion at Plaisance. Perhaps it was the drink that made me feel a touch hot.

'You know, Grace, I might as well be at sea again for all the good it's done my spirits,' I said. 'I never was made to run a settlement, dispense justice in my little Town Court, oversee the book-keeping and taxes. Perhaps I should sail with the barks come year end and overwinter at Labrador.'

She caught my hand and drew me near so that we stood with our bodies touching. Her face was close, her warm hands caressed mine. I wondered if she knew how it tortured me.

Through the open window, the children's carolling voices reached us from the garden.

'Sophie and Caswell seem so well together,' she said, smiling.

'Aye, and I thought –' I faltered. 'I hoped one day for – well, nothing could take Oliver's place, for sure. I mean, no new child could become –'

I trailed off, my eyes pleading. Somehow, I thought, she must say or do something to keep my hopes alive. Her eyes were shining and she was about to speak. I held my breath.

Footsteps thudded on the stairs and someone knocked urgently. When the door opened, we parted as the maid's face appeared, creased with anxiety. It was immediately followed by a burst of noisy shouting and the sound of feet scampering into the hallway below.

'Sir, madam, beg pardon,' said the flustered Mitty. 'I can hardly stop them, you see.'

'Aye, send them in,' I said, hiding a sigh.

She stood aside to let the impatient Caswell enter, tugging Sophie along in his wake.

'Sir, sir – Captain Loftus, I spy a ship!' he cried.

'Are you sure, young fellow?'

'Yes, sir! I mean, aye, sir!'

I turned to the tall window and examined the far horizon. There was an unmistakeable smudge there, no more than a speck. As I watched, another shape appeared alongside the first.

'Caswell, fetch me the long tube,' I said, letting Grace catch my grin.

The boy went to the desk, gingerly took up the instrument and brought it over. I slotted it into Sir Oliver's great tripod and squinted into the eyepiece.

'Two vessels, both three-masted trading barks,' I announced, 'and bearing this way.'

Caswell jumped up and down as if he was barefoot on hot embers, while Sophie giggled, blushing and clutching her mother's skirts.

'They're broad reaching under all plain sail,' I went on, 'and by the looks, keen as beavers to get into harbour. What do you say, Master Penn – are they the Loftus barks come down from the north?'

'O sir, are they truly? If only I could see.' He looked up at me, his eye darting to the tube and back.

I pulled over a little boxwood case, one that used to hold an old almanack, and he stood on it to reach the eyepiece. Carefully he raked the horizon with a steady, even-handed motion.

438

'I see them, sir!'

Sophie dashed over and jumped onto the window seat, bouncing around blocking Caswell's view, much to his annoyance. A hand took mine, and I found Grace standing close, her hip warm against my body. Then she wound her arm around my waist. Perhaps, I thought, with a quickening of the heart, this new house – our house, our new beginning – might change things.

I cleared my throat. 'Can you say, Caswell, which barks those might be? Perhaps they've had a long hard winter in Labrador, and are loaded with fine skins for market.'

The boy turned from the long tube and spoke in deadly serious tones.

'Well, sir, I shan't be able to see any names yet a-while, but I'd say, going by the look of her rig, there's good chance the one in front's the *Provident*.'

'That's sharp-eyed of you. And if she's the *Provident*, what might be her sister bark?'

Caswell's face shone. 'Why sir, she's got to be the *New Beginning*.'

'The *New Beginning* indeed. And who is captain aboard that bark?'

'Captain Rittel, sir!'

'Aye, indeed. And could that be the very bark that a certain Mister Penn is to sail aboard?'

His mouth fell open. '*Mister* Penn, sir?'

'Aye, not Master Penn, that's for small boys. Nor Midshipman Penn either, that's for the Queen's Navy. When you go aboard my best bark, you shall be Mister Penn, and a proper seaman.'

Unable to contain himself, he took up the tube again and stared out to sea, while next to him Sophie clenched her fists in frustration.

Grace squeezed my hand and we laughed quietly together, knowing their antics hid an abiding enjoyment in each other's companionship. Then, while the children's attention was elsewhere, she raised herself on tiptoe and kissed me. This time there was no hesitancy. She gave me a full-blooded kiss on the lips.

It was the kiss I longed for. And it filled me with new hope.

THE END